STAR WARS®
THE NEW ESSENTIAL GUIDE TO
CHARACTERS

STAR WARS®

THE NEW ESSENTIAL GUIDE TO

CHARA

CTERS

Revised Edition
by Daniel Wallace
Illustrations by Mike Sutfin

 Ballantine Books
New York

A Del Rey® Book
Published by The Ballantine Publishing Group

www.starwars.com
www.starwarskids.com
www.delreydigital.com

A Library of Congress Catalog Card Number for this title is available from the publisher.
ISBN 0-345-44900-2

Interior illustrations by Michael Sutfin
Interior design by Michaelis/Carpelis Design Assoc. Inc.

Manufactured in the United States of America

Revised Edition: April 2002

Author's Dedication
To Andrew

Artist's Dedication
In loving memory of Nancy Fedou Getzelman and Vernon Sutfin

CONTENTS

Acknowledgments	9	IG-88	81	Sebulba	145
Pronunciation Guide	10	Ysanne Isard	83	Executor Sedriss	147
Introduction	11	Prince Isolder	86	Senator Viqi Shesh	148
A General Time Line		Jabba the Hutt	88	Darth Sidious	150
of Galactic History	12	Jedi Council Members	91	Raith Sienar	151
Admiral Ackbar	16	Jedi from the		Aurra Sing	153
Padmé Naberrie Amidala	18	Battle of Geonosis	94	Anakin Skywalker/	
Nom Anor	20	Jerec	95	Darth Vader	155
Wedge Antillies	22	Qui-Gon Jinn	97	Luke Skywalker	158
Darth Bane	25	Kir Kanos	99	Mara Jade Skywalker	161
Jar Jar Binks	26	Talon Karrde	100	Anakin Solo	164
Bossk	28	Kyle Katarn	102	Han Solo	165
Brakiss	31	Obi-Wan Kenobi	104	Jacen Solo	170
Shira Brie	33	Kueller	107	Jaina Solo	172
C-3PO	34	Exar Kun	108	Leia Organa Solo	174
Callista	37	Warmaster Tsavong Lah	109	Kam Solusar	177
Lando Calrissian	39	Owen Lars and		Nil Spaar	178
Gaeriel Captison	42	Beru Whitesun Lars	111	Grand Moff Wilhuff Tarkin	179
Tycho Celchu	44	Bevel Lemelsk	112	Booster Terrik	180
Chewbacca	45	Lobot	113	Bria Tharen	182
Admiral Daala	48	Garik "Face" Loran	114	Grand Admiral Thrawn	185
Jori and Gav Daragon	50	General Crix Madine	115	Supreme Chancellor Finis	
Gavin Darklighter	51	Darth Maul	117	Valorum	188
Dengar	53	Mon Mothma	119	General Maximilian Veers	190
General Jan Dodonna	55	Boss Nass	121	Vergere	192
Count Dooku	57	Nien Nunb	122	Quinlan Vos	193
Droma	58	Nym	123	Watto	194
Durga the Hutt	59	Ric Olié	124	Zam Wesell	196
Kyp Durron	61	Emperor Palpatine	125	Mace Windu	197
4-Lom	63	Captain Panaka	128	Prince Xizor	199
Baron Fel	64	Admiral Gilad Pellaeon	130	Yoda	201
Boba Fett	66	Sate Pestage	132	Warlord Zsinj	204
Jango Fett	69	Admiral Firmus Piett	133	Zuckuss	206
Borsk Fey'lya	70	Podracer Pilots	134	Appendix: Other	
Bib Fortuna	72	Ulic Qel-Droma	137	Personages of Note	208
Rokur Gepta	74	R2-D2	138	Bibliography	213
Greedo	75	Dash Rendar	141		
Nute Gunray	76	Naga Sadow	142		
Corran Horn	78	Thrackan Sal-Solo	143		

Author's Acknowledgments

This book would not have been possible without the help, support, and inspiration of others. Thanks go out to: George Lucas for creating this world and its core cast of characters; my editor Steve Saffel and Sylvain Michaelis and Fred Dodnick at Del Rey, who provided patient professionalism and a wealth of great ideas; Lucy Autrey Wilson, Chris Cerasi, and Sue Rostoni at Lucasfilm, who shepherded this book through a tricky incubation; Mike Sutfin for his dynamic illustrations; Aaron Allston, Jim Luceno, Mike Stackpole, and Kathy Tyers for advice on their characters; Ann Lewis for consulting on the timeline; Haden Blackman, who collaborated with me on an earlier, unpublished project, from which he developed the backstories for Raith Sienar and Nym; Jason Fry, Christopher McElroy, Michael Potts, Nathan Butler, Chaz LiBretto, and Bob Vitas for the *Star Wars* resources they have written; and Abel Peña, Enrique Guerro, and Mike Kogge for their valuable suggestions.

Illustrator's Acknowledgments

While this has been one of the most fulfilling and exciting projects I've ever been involved in, make no mistake . . . it wasn't easy. I want to thank the many people who were kind, helpful, and inspirational during the creative process. George Lucas for creating a myth that has kept my head in the clouds for all these years. The many talented artists and writers who brought life and color to the *Star Wars* universe. My friends at Del Rey: Sylvain Michaelis, Fred Dodnick, and Steve Saffel, for initially giving me the chance to work on my dream project and helping out along the way. Daniel Wallace for his extensive *Star Wars* knowledge and patient assistance referencing characters. Chris Cerasi and Sue Rostoni at Lucasfilm for being supportive and kind when my many questions infested their e-mail accounts. Mark A. Nelson, for I know I wouldn't be where I am now without his immense love of art and thoughtful guidance while I was at Northern Illinois University. My wonderful family: parents Bill and Gwen and brother Pete. And finally, the mighty K-crew: James DeJesus, Steve Parkes, Adam Sharani, and Garrett Splain. I'll never forget these days.

PRONUNCIATION GUIDE

Below are key pronunciation symbols to guide you in articulating character names.
Note: an apostrophe (') is used after the emphasized syllable in each name.

Vowels

ă: short *a* sound as in the words *bat* and *act.*

ā: long *a* sound as in the word *age* or *rate.*

ä: open *a* sound used for words like *part, calm,* and *father.* It duplicates the short *o* sound of the word *hot.*

ĕ: short *e* sound used in *edge* or *set.*

ē: long *e* sound used in *equal* or *seat.*

ēr: This vowel sound before *r* may range from ē through ĭ in different dialects.

ĭ: short *i* sound used in *hit* or *pit.*

ī: long *i* sound used in *bite* or *whine.*

ŏ: short *o* sound used in *hot* and *pot.*

oi: a diphthong vowel sound that is a combination of an ō and an ē, such as in the words *boy* and *toy.*

ō: long *o* sound used in *moan* and *tone.*

ōō: long *o* sound used in *toot* and *hoot.*

ô: relatively long *o* used in *order* and *border.*

ŏŏ: short double *o* sound used in *book* and *tour.*

ŭ: the short *u* sound used in *up* and *sum.*

ûr: the *u* sound used in *turn* and *urge.*

Consonants

kh: a hard *k* pronounced at the back of the throat, such as in *loch* or *ach.*

hw: a soft *w* sound used in the words *who* and *what.*

INTRODUCTION

I n 1995 I picked up the first edition of *Star Wars: The Essential Guide to Characters*, absorbed it with relish over several sessions, and began trading online postings with writer Andy Mangels. Patient and wry, Andy exhibited a love for *Star Wars* and a respect for the source material in all its forms. But above all else he communicated an understanding that everyone, regardless of age, gender, or niche passion, gets something out of *Star Wars*. It's a big universe, built around the movies but not limited to them, and all the media elements (novels, comics, children's books, and so forth) fit into a single cohesive time line.

Since the publication of that first edition of *The Essential Guide to Characters*, the *Star Wars* universe has expanded like a well-fed Hutt. Two prequel films have taken their places beside the existing trilogy. Novels such as those in The New Jedi Order series have continued to chronicle the destinies of Luke, Han, Leia, and an entirely new generation against the backdrop of intergalatic war. A new ongoing comic book series—simply called *Star Wars*, a sight not seen on comic racks since the mid-1980s—is fleshing out the adventures in the prequel era, while other tales have gone back hundreds of years to the original glory days of the Jedi. And LucasArts has continued to employ the latest hardware to create totally immersive story-based computer games.

Beyond the familiar stars, a roll call of the *Star Wars* supporting cast would total well over a thousand characters, with twice that number filling the roster of bit players and walk-ons. So it's more important than ever to have an *essential* guide to characters.

This guide is written from the perspective of an in-galaxy scribe, transcribing the biographies of the galaxy's key heroes and villains in the midst of the apocalyptic Yuuzhan Vong invasion (approximately twenty-seven years after *A New Hope*). At the end of the book you'll find a coded bibliography keyed to each character entry.

As the ballpark vendors say, you can't tell the players without a program. Here's the lineup from Ackbar to Zuckuss, and every Vergere in between.

Daniel Wallace
Detroit, Michigan

A GENERAL TIME LINE OF GALACTIC HISTORY

circa 25,000
Before the Battle of Yavin (B.B.Y.)
Hyperspace travel becomes widespread, allowing for galactic expansion and exploration. The Republic is formed and the Jedi Order assembles.

Exploration of the greater galaxy begins along the Corellian Run and Perlemian Trade Route. The Duros colonize the planet Neimoidia.

The First Great Schism between followers of the dark side and the light side occurs. After more than a century, the dark-siders are driven off into the wilds of the galaxy.

circa 17,000 B.B.Y.
The first of the Alsakan Conflicts erupts.

circa 8,000 B.B.Y.
A Republic outpost is established on Malastare. Gran colonists begin to follow but won't settle in earnest for several millennia.

circa 7,000 B.B.Y.
The Jedi Knights lead the Republic through the Hundred-Year Darkness.

circa 5,500 B.B.Y.
Tapani sector merchants establish the first leg of what will later become the Rimma Trade Route.

circa 5,000 B.B.Y.
The Unification Wars. Empress Teta unifies the seven worlds of the Koros system.

The Great Hyperspace War. The Republic successfully fends off an attack by Naga Sadow's Sith invaders, led to the civilized galaxy by Gav and Jori Daragon.

4,250 B.B.Y.
The Vultar Cataclysm. The Jedi weather another schism between dark and light forces.

3,996 B.B.Y.
The Sith War erupts, led by Exar Kun and Ulic Qel-Droma. The Jedi defeat the Sith but suffer great losses, and the Jedi planet Ossus is devastated. The Republic also vanquishes the warlord Mandalore during the conflict.

3,900 B.B.Y.
Naboo is settled by colonists from Grizmallt.

circa 3,000 B.B.Y.
The Hydian Way hyperspace route is blazed, opening the galaxy to much wider colonization. The Tapani sector trade lanes are connected with the Bith route known as the Monedes'mai Hypercanal, forming the modern Rimma Trade Route.

circa 2,000 B.B.Y.
A rogue Jedi Knight falls to the dark side and founds a new Sith Order, which grows in power and wages war against the Jedi over the next millennium.

circa 1,000 B.B.Y.
Following an internal purge, the last surviving Sith are annihilated at Ruusan. Darth Bane goes underground, ensuring the Order's survival and passing the name *Darth* to his successors.

896 B.B.Y.
Jedi Master Yoda is born. He will become a guiding voice in the Jedi Order throughout the coming centuries.

490 B.B.Y.
The Corporate Sector is formed.

350 B.B.Y.
The Trade Federation is founded.

50 B.B.Y.
The Arkanian Revolution. The Arkanian Renegades unsuccessfully try to topple the Arkanian Dominion. Mace Windu later fights rogue Arkanian construct Gorm the Dissolver.

44 B.B.Y.
Qui-Gon Jinn and Obi-Wan Kenobi begin their Master–Padawan partnership.

Plo Koon and other Jedi are victorious in the Stark Hyperspace War.

32 B.B.Y.
The Battle of Naboo. The Trade Federation's invasion of Naboo is thwarted by the Jedi and Queen Padmé Amidala. Naboo Senator Palpatine becomes Supreme Chancellor of the Republic.

Qui-Gon Jinn is killed by Darth Maul. Obi-Wan Kenobi takes Anakin Skywalker as his Padawan.

Count Dooku leaves the Jedi Order, and Jango Fett is selected as the template for a clone army on Kamino.

31 B.B.Y.
The Outbound Flight Project is launched to search for life in other galaxies.

29 B.B.Y.
Anakin Skywalker and Obi-Wan Kenobi attempt to secure living starships from the planet Zonama Sekot.

22 B.B.Y.
The Battle of Geonosis. Jango Fett is killed by Mace Windu. Chancellor Palpatine is granted emergency war powers, and the Clone Wars begin.

Circa 22–10 B.B.Y.
Palpatine declares himself Emperor, and Anakin Skywalker becomes Darth Vader. Imperial rule descends upon the galaxy.

5 B.B.Y.
After Academy graduation and an eight-month stint as an Imperial officer, Han Solo is drummed out of the service when he saves a Wookiee slave named Chewbacca.

0 B.B.Y.
The Battle of Yavin. The first Death Star is destroyed thanks to the efforts of Luke Skywalker, Han Solo, and Princess Leia Organa.

0–3 After the Battle of Yavin (A.B.Y.)
The Rebel Alliance evacuates Yavin 4

and searches for a new base. Kyle Katarn leads the mission to destroy the Empire's dark troopers.

3 A.B.Y.

The Alliance is routed at the Battle of Hoth, but Yoda trains Luke Skywalker as a Jedi. Boba Fett captures Han Solo at Bespin.

3.5 A.B.Y.

Prince Xizor, leader of Black Sun, plots to kill Luke Skywalker but is outmaneuvered by Darth Vader.

4 A.B.Y.

The Battle of Endor. The second Death Star is destroyed by Lando Calrissian and Wedge Antilles. Mon Mothma proclaims the birth of a New Republic.

4-plus A.B.Y.

The truce of Bakura. Imperial and Alliance forces make a temporary pact and join forces to drive off the Ssiruuk.

5 A.B.Y.

A coalition of Grand Moffs and Prophets of the Dark Side tries to usurp Ysanne Isard's position as head of the remaining Empire.

Jerec tries to unlock the power of Ruusan's Valley of the Jedi but is defeated by Kyle Katarn.

7-8 A.B.Y.

Wedge Antilles and the New Republic's Rogue Squadron help capture Coruscant and liberate Thyferra in the Bacta War.

Garik "Face" Loran and other members of Wraith Squadron battle Warlord Zsinj.

8 A.B.Y.

Leia Organa and Han Solo are married following an adventure on Dathomir.

9 A.B.Y.

Grand Admiral Thrawn declares war against the New Republic. Leia and Han Solo's twins, Jacen and Jaina, are born.

Ysanne Isard returns and tries to steal the Super Star Destroyer *Lusankya*.

10-11 A.B.Y.

Emperor Palpatine returns in the body of a clone, and his forces drive the New Republic from Coruscant. Leia and Han Solo's third child, Anakin, is born in exile. After Palpatine's final defeat, former Royal Guardsman Kir Kanos assassinates all members of the Imperial Interim Ruling Council.

11 A.B.Y.

Luke Skywalker founds the Jedi academy on Yavin 4. Imperial Admiral Daala makes terror strikes against the New Republic. Leia takes over from Mon Mothma as Chief of State of the New Republic.

12-13 A.B.Y.

Admiral Daala and other enemies threaten the stability of the New Republic. General Madine is killed by Durga the Hutt.

14 A.B.Y.

Jacen, Jaina, and Anakin Solo are kidnapped by the Empire Reborn movement.

16-17 A.B.Y.

Nil Spaar attacks neighboring star systems with his captured Black Fleet warships. Leia Organa Solo declares war on Spaar's Yevetha and hammers out a victory.

17 A.B.Y.

Kueller and Brakiss, two ex-students from Luke Skywalker's Jedi academy, mastermind a plot to overthrow the New Republic during the Almanian "New Rebellion."

18 A.B.Y.

Thrackan Sal-Solo emerges as the head of the Human League on Corellia and tries to usurp the Corellian insurrection for his own purposes. He is defeated by his cousin Han Solo and Gaeriel Captison's Bakuran navy.

Leia Organa Solo takes a leave of absence as Chief of State.

19 A.B.Y.

The New Republic signs a peace treaty with the Imperial Remnant.

Luke Skywalker and Mara Jade are married.

21 A.B.Y.

Leia Organa Solo is again elected Chief of State.

22 A.B.Y.

Anakin Solo attends the Jedi academy and meets fellow student Tahiri Veila.

23-24 A.B.Y.

Jacen and Jaina Solo train at the Jedi academy and foil Brakiss's Second Imperium, among other threats.

Borsk Fey'lya becomes Chief of State after Leia Organa Solo steps down.

25 A.B.Y.

The Yuuzhan Vong enter the galaxy. Chewbacca is killed on Sernpidal. Yuuzhan Vong forces capture or poison key worlds such as Ithor, Obroa-skai, and Tynna. A miscalculation at Fondor decimates Prince Isolder's Hapan navy.

26 A.B.Y.

The Battle of Duro. Warmaster Tsavong Lah calls for the heads of the Jedi. The Jedi academy is evacuated and the Great Temple is destroyed. Luke Skywalker and Mara Jade's first child, Ben, is born.

27 A.B.Y.

The fall of Coruscant. The Yuuzhan Vong capture the seat of the New Republic government, and Borsk Fey'lya is killed. Anakin Solo is killed.

STAR WARS®
THE NEW ESSENTIAL GUIDE TO
CHARACTERS

Admiral Ackbar

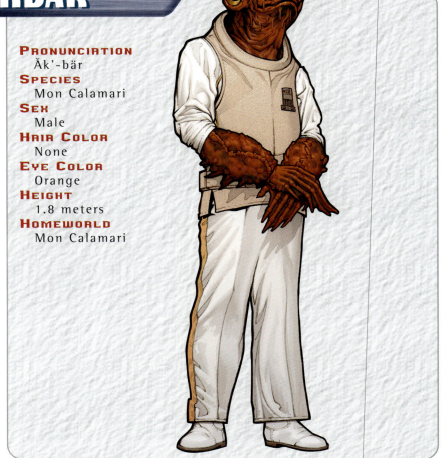

PRONUNCIATION
Ăk'-bär
SPECIES
Mon Calamari
SEX
Male
HAIR COLOR
None
EYE COLOR
Orange
HEIGHT
1.8 meters
HOMEWORLD
Mon Calamari

"T he tide will slacken, the whirlpool will shrink, the krakana will cower. Such is the power of a focused individual."

The Mon Calamari philosopher Toklar wrote those words seven centuries ago, but it almost seems as if he was prophesying the brilliant career of Admiral Ackbar. Easily the most famous Mon Calamari in the galaxy, Ackbar has at last retired after a lifetime of distinguished service.

As a youth on his watery homeworld, Ackbar seemed marked for great things. He became Coral City's representative to the ruling Calamarian Council while barely out of school, and sponsored many of Mon Calamari's extrastellar expeditions. After the rise of the Empire, Ackbar rose to the rank of council leader and attempted negotiations with the Imperial warships that threatened his planet. The talks proved disastrous. The Empire enslaved both the Mon Calamari and Quarren species and exploited the planet's famous shipyards. Ackbar then planted the seeds of a resistance movement, which temporarily drove the Empire offworld. Following Imperial retaliation, Ackbar was captured and presented as "pet" to the up-and-coming Moff Tarkin.

As Tarkin's slave, Ackbar made certain to cultivate an image of placidity, while he accumulated Imperial military secrets for later use. He learned of the Death Star project while it was still in the development phase. Not long before the Battle of Yavin, a Rebel strike team attacked Tarkin's personal shuttle near Eriadu. They failed to assassinate the Grand Moff but succeeded in their secondary goal—freeing Ackbar.

After reestablishing contact with his people—and earning the rank of admiral of the Mon Calamari fleet—Ackbar became an unofficial member of Mon Mothma's Rebel Alliance. Many Mon Calamari followed Ackbar, pressing their huge star cruisers into Alliance service.

Ackbar's inside knowledge of Imperial tactics proved crucial to such early victories as the Battle of Turkana. After the destruction of the first Death Star, Ackbar and the Calamarian Council survived a harrowing Imperial hunt on the planet Daluuj, and the council agreed to formally support the Alliance. Ackbar aided in the evacuation of Yavin and later oversaw Project Shantipole, the Verpine experiment that gave the Rebel Alliance the B-wing starfighter. Impressed, and smarting from General Bel Iblis's resignation, Mon Mothma made Ackbar a full Alliance admiral and put him in charge of all Rebel military forces.

Admiral Ackbar won his greatest victory at Endor, where he defeated Admiral Piett and routed the best elements of the mighty Imperial fleet. Pressing the advantage, Ackbar spent the next few years paring down Imperial space and eliminating warlord kingdoms. At the Battle of Kashyyyk, Ackbar eliminated Grand Admiral Syn in a one-on-one test of tactics.

Ackbar directed the naval battle that freed Coruscant from Imperial rule. Once the planet had been secured, he built a home within a reservoir near Imperial City and named it "Victory

Lake." During the campaign against Warlord Zsinj, Ackbar nearly died at the hands of his own aide, thanks to Zsinj's secret brainwashing of key New Republic personnel.

Despite a political smear campaign orchestrated by Borsk Fey'lya, Ackbar played a key role in the defeat of Thrawn at Bilbringi and Admiral Krennel at Ciutric. Over the next two years, however, Ackbar tasted personal tragedy. The resurrected Emperor drove Ackbar from Victory Lake during his reconquest of Coruscant, then focused his malevolence on Mon Calamari. The waterworld suffered grievous wounds from Palpatine's World Devastators. Thousands of Mon Calamari died, and Ackbar blamed himself.

The following year, another brainwashed aide betrayed Ackbar, causing the admiral's personal B-wing to crash into the Cathedral of Winds on Vortex. Shamed by the lives he had accidentally snuffed out, Ackbar went into self-imposed exile on war-ravaged Mon Calamari, hoping to restore his people and achieve his personal redemption. Leia Organa Solo convinced him of his responsibilities to the greater galaxy, and Ackbar reclaimed his New Republic rank just in time to defeat Admiral Daala.

During the Black Fleet Crisis, Admiral Ackbar befriended a Polneye refugee named Plat Mallar and helped turn the tide of public opinion against the genocidal Yevetha. Ackbar successfully ended the Corellian insurrection by smashing the fleet of the Sacorrian Triad in the Battle of Centerpoint Station, and commanded the New Republic Super Star Destroyer *Guardian* in a series of skirmishes against Admiral Pellaeon, including the Battle of Champala and the Battle of Anx

Minor. In the latter climactic conflict, Ackbar scored a last-minute victory by focusing a hail of concentrated fire on the engines of the Imperial vessel *Glory of Yevetha*. The ship exploded, igniting its volatile antimatter reservoir and annihilating six nearby Star Destroyers. In light of its latest defeat, the Empire was forced to sue for peace.

For years following the New Republic–Imperial treaty, Ackbar lived a quiet life, lending his voice to policy and writing his memoirs at Victory Lake. Nineteen years after Endor, he stepped back into an active role to defeat the forces of the Second Imperium when they threatened the Jedi academy on Yavin 4.

When Borsk Fey'lya was elected New Republic Chief of State, a disappointed Ackbar chose to leave public service altogether. He retired to a small home in Mon Calamari's seatree forest. Now that the Yuuzhan Vong have invaded the galaxy, however, it appears the New Republic is in more need of Ackbar's skills than ever.

PADMÉ NABERRIE AMIDALA

PRONUNCIATION
Păd'-mā Nä-bĕ'-rē
Äm' ē dä-lä
SPECIES
Human
SEX
Female
HAIR COLOR
Brown
EYE COLOR
Brown
HEIGHT
1.65 meters
HOMEWORLD
Naboo

Stubborn, proud, passionate, and wise beyond her years, Padmé Amidala spent her life in service to the people of Naboo. As Queen, she led her planet through its most dire crisis in generations. As Senator, she tried to bring sanity to a Republic on the brink of war.

The citizens of Naboo performed mandatory community service when between the ages of twelve and twenty. Elected Queen at age fourteen, Padmé had already achieved more than some Naboo accomplished in a lifetime. Raised in a mountain village, she was groomed for a higher station from the moment of her birth. Her family—father Ruwee, mother Jobal, and older sister Sola—moved to Theed when Padmé was young. Padmé received instruction at the best schools, taking occasional class retreats to Naboo's lake country.

By age seven she had enrolled in the Refugee Relief Movement, an organization with which her father had a long history. On one mission she traveled with the movement to Shadda-Bi-Boran to relocate the natives before their sun imploded. However, many of the refugees—including one special child, N'a-kee-tula—died when they were unable to adapt to life off their homeworld.

Later Padmé became an Apprentice Legislator. At age twelve she met her first love, a boy named Palo, who went on to become an artist. By contrast, Padmé became a Senatorial adviser and ceremonial "Princess of Theed." In keeping with tradition, Padmé took on a "name of state"—Amidala—when she assumed her royal position.

King Veruna had held the throne

of Naboo for thirteen years, but his dealings with shadowy offworld politicians had eroded public faith in his leadership. He voluntarily abdicated the throne. Amidala and local governor Sio Bibble vied for election to the monarchy. Amidala traveled the countryside giving speeches, winning points for her commitment to reform. In the end, the people elected Amidala in a landslide.

The new head of the Royal Security Forces, Captain Panaka, insisted

that Amidala undergo self-defense and weapons training. He also implemented a time-honored palace trick—the use of look-alikes to act as bodyguards and decoys. Amidala's five handmaidens, Eirtaé, Sabé, Yané, Rabé, and Saché, became her closest friends and were trained to take the Queen's place in times of danger.

A mere five months into Amidala's reign, the Trade Federation blockaded Naboo. Although Amidala could not understand why the greedy conglomerate had chosen to make an example of *her* planet, she nevertheless tried to resolve the conflict without violence. Ultimately, however, Neimoidian droid armies overran Theed. Amidala fled her homeworld in order to obtain help from the Republic.

But the Republic Senate refused to act. Queen Amidala revealed the true measure of her fighting spirit when she called for a vote of no confidence against Chancellor Valorum and returned to occupied Naboo. If those in power could not be bothered to help, she decided she would free her besieged planet herself.

Amidala's shrewd diplomacy won the help of the disenfranchised Gungans on Naboo. Her courage under fire, fighting alongside the Jedi Knights Qui-Gon Jinn and Obi-Wan Kenobi, along with the young boy Anakin Skywalker, brought about the surrender of Neimoidian Viceroy Nute Gunray. Amidala presided over a jubilant victory celebration in the confetti-covered streets of Theed. With her people liberated and Naboo's own Chancellor Palpatine leading the Republic, the future of Naboo looked bright.

Queen Amidala finished an eight-year term and prepared to retire from public service at age twenty-two. The people of Naboo tried to amend the constitution to allow her to remain Queen for life, but she refused, feeling her time as monarch was up. Her successor, Queen Jamillia, asked Padmé to serve as Senator, and she agreed to represent Naboo's interests on Coruscant. When not conducting business on the capital planet, she stayed at her family's home in the Theed residential area.

The Confederacy of Independent Systems troubled Senator Amidala. Count Dooku and his secessionist followers denounced the corruption of the Republic, and while Padmé sympathized with their motives, she wasn't willing to sacrifice a governmental system that had endured for a thousand generations. She served on the Republic negotiating team that tried to forge a peace with the separatists, but suspected that Count Dooku was orchestrating terrorist attacks that threatened to scuttle the negotiations prematurely.

Just before the Battle of Geonosis, Padmé returned to Coruscant to vote against the Military Creation Act, which would commission an army to defend against the separatists. She felt this amounted to nothing less than a declaration of war. Upon her arrival, a terrorist bomb destroyed her Naboo Cruiser and killed her handmaiden Cordé. After a second attempt on her life, she returned to Naboo under the protection of Jedi Padawan Anakin Skywalker.

The last time she'd seen Anakin, he'd been a nine-year-old boy with a child's crush on her. Anakin had grown into a man, and Padmé was unsure of how to handle his obvious interest in her, but once she dropped the professional demeanor she'd been maintaining since her days as Queen, Padmé found herself falling in love.

Padmé and Anakin traveled first to Tatooine, to seek out Shmi Skywalker, then to rocky Geonosis. There they hoped to rescue Obi-Wan Kenobi, who was being held prisoner by Count Dooku, but instead found themselves tossed into a Geonosian execution arena. Padmé narrowly escaped death at the claws of a nexu and watched as the Republic's clone army clashed with Count Dooku's forces—the violent outcome she had worked so hard to prevent.

With the Clone Wars now a reality, Padmé and Anakin married in secret on Naboo. She then watched as Anakin fell deeper into the dark side and became the armored nightmare known as Darth Vader. Padmé bore twin children, Luke and Leia, but hid them away to protect them from the attentions of Emperor Palpatine. Her children grew up in the care of foster families, and Padmé died when they were still very young. She never saw them reverse their father's legacy and bring justice to the galaxy.

NOM ANOR

PRONUNCIATION
Nōm Ä-nōr'
SPECIES
Yuuzhan Vong
SEX
Male
HAIR COLOR
None
EYE COLOR
Blue
(right eye only
—the left is a
plaeryin bol)
HEIGHT
1.77 meters
HOMEWORLD
Unknown

Nom Anor has spent more time in this galaxy—nearly two decades, by some estimates—than any other Yuuzhan Vong. He is also one of the most secular, paying lip service to the goddess Yun-Harla while furthering his own career.

As a member of the intendant caste, Anor was preordained to live his life as a politician. He rose rapidly through the ranks of the intendants; on the day he became an executor, he gouged out his eye with a burning stick to show acceptance of the honor. Since then he has set his sights on the title of high prefect.

But in many ways Nom Anor is more like a member of the shaper caste than an intendant. A brilliant amateur scientist, he bioengineered the coomb spore, the gablith masquer, the naotebe wingling, and other organic tools, in clear defiance of religious protocols governing such innovation. He despises the Yuuzhan Vong traditionalists who cling to the outdated weapons of their ancestors, and believes his breakthroughs will be the key to victory. His tattoos and disfigurements, including a venom-spitting plaeryin bol that sits in the socket that once held his left eye, are evidence of his unique status.

As executor, it was Nom Anor's job to spy on the inhabitants of this galaxy and destabilize their political structure. His first target was the Imperial Interim Ruling Council, formed after the reborn Emperor's defeat. By manipulating council member Xandel Carivus, Anor toppled the power hierarchy and hastened the Empire's collapse.

Over the years he continued to work behind the scenes. On misty Monor II he infected a hundred New Republic diplomats by planting lethal coomb spores in their breath masks. Of the hundred victims, only Mara Jade Skywalker survived, and she suffered for years before beating the disease.

On Rhommamool in the Expansion Region, Nom Anor emerged as the leader of the antitechnology, anti-Jedi "Red Knights of Life." Disguised by an ooglith masquer, Anor whipped his followers into a frenzy of hatred against their sister planet Osarian.

Leia Organa Solo met with Anor in an attempt to defuse the crisis, but she failed to detect his true nature. Anor launched missiles on Osarian, then faked his own death.

By this time the Yuuzhan Vong invasion had begun, at the galactic breach point designated "Vector Prime." The vanguard force, known as the Praetorite Vong, consisted almost entirely of members of the intendant caste. Anor reported directly to Prefect Da'Gara, and Da'Gara's shameful defeat at Helska 4 hurt Anor by association.

Other warriors came in to fix what the Praetorite Vong had bungled, and Anor struggled to regain favor among soldiers who hated his kind. With the priest Harrar—an old friend of Warmaster Tsavong Lah's—he masterminded a plot to dangle the priestess Elan before the New Republic as a defector and, through the priestess's use of a deadly bioweapon, ultimately wipe out the Jedi Knights.

The plan didn't work, but Anor used his knowledge of this galaxy to forge an alliance with the Hutts. Knowing that the treacherous slugs would undoubtedly betray the Yuuzhan Vong, Anor fed them false data—which found its way into the hands of New Republic Intelligence. This misinformation helped the Yuuzhan Vong score a victory at the Fondor shipyards.

After the Fondor battle, Warmaster Tsavong Lah sent Nom Anor to help reclaim the polluted planet Duro as penance for his past failures. Posing as Duros scientist Dassid Cree'Ar, Anor unleashed genetically engineered naotebe winglings, which chewed through the environment domes of the New Republic refugee encampments. By the time Mara Jade Skywalker and Jaina Solo revealed his true identity, it was too late to stop Duro's devastation by Yuuzhan Vong warriors.

Arriving on conquered Duro, the warmaster lifted Nom Anor's penance but pointedly chose not to promote him. Anor continued to struggle to prove himself, infiltrating the ranks of the Givin species, yet failing to win their homeworld Yag'Dhul for the Yuuzhan Vong. Even worse, Tsavong Lah now kept the alien Vergere as his personal adviser. Vergere despised Anor, and the feeling was more than mutual.

Given his long history, Nom Anor came to represent the public face of the Yuuzhan Vong in the eyes of the New Republic government. It was he who met with Leia Organa Solo to convince her to surrender the location of the hidden Jedi refuge. She spurned him even when he threatened the lives of a convoy of refugees. Anor then spoke on the floor of the Senate chamber, trying to convince the legislators to accept the reality of a Yuuzhan Vong victory. Chief of State Borsk Fey'lya denounced him, and when assassins tried to kill Fey'lya, Anor was censured and kicked off Coruscant.

But Nom Anor gained a piece of essential information, which he revealed to Tsavong Lah: Jacen and Jaina Solo were twins. Among the Yuuzhan Vong, such a birth-pairing is rare and highly valued. The warmaster sent Anor to a worldship in the Myrkr system to collect these two presumptuous Jedi for holy sacrifice. He also sent Vergere.

The mission to Myrkr resulted in the death of the youngest Jedi sibling, Anakin Solo, and the capture of half of the twin pairing. Although Jaina Solo escaped, Nom Anor hopes his partial success will elevate him in the eyes of Supreme Overlord Shimrra.

WEDGE ANTILLES

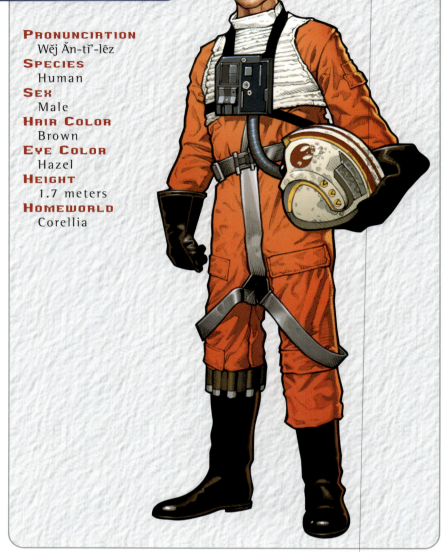

Many of the Alliance's greatest heroes treated the military not as a lifelong career, but almost like a change of clothes. Lando Calrissian and Han Solo resigned and reactivated their commissions at will; Luke Skywalker turned his back on the military in order to devote himself to Jedi instruction.

On the other hand, Wedge Antilles represents the quintessential New Republic soldier. Antilles was there at the very beginning, and through bravery, luck, and leadership worked his way up from greenhorn pilot to New Republic general. Though General Antilles is now retired, junior officers still get tongue-tied when introduced to the man who went up against two Death Stars . . . and lived.

Antilles comes from the same Corellian stock as Han Solo, Corran Horn, and Baron Soontir Fel. His parents, Jagged and Zena Antilles, operated a refueling platform on the Gus Treta Inner-System Market Station that serviced all five Corellian worlds. Wedge spent half of each year on a farm school in Corellia's northern hemisphere, where he studied his lessons in between herding nerfs and shoveling manure. The rest of the year he worked aboard the orbital station, learning to fly and service cargo freighters. Wedge also developed a love for building things, and entertained idle dreams of one day becoming an architect. When he was only seven, his older sister Syal left the family, striking out on her own and eventually earning fame as the holofeature actress Wynssa Starflare.

By the age of seventeen, Wedge Antilles had become an able pilot who frequently worked with smug-

PRONUNCIATION
Wěj Ăn-tǐ'-lēz
SPECIES
Human
SEX
Male
HAIR COLOR
Brown
EYE COLOR
Hazel
HEIGHT
1.7 meters
HOMEWORLD
Corellia

gler Booster Terrik and his daughter Mirax. Wedge was aboard Terrik's ship the *Pulsar Skate* when the pirate freighter *Buzzzer* docked at his parents' refueling platform. Suddenly spooked by a CorSec patrol, the *Buzzzer's* captain, Loka Hask, blasted off without disengaging the fuel lines. The fueling platform erupted in flames; Jagged and Zena Antilles died saving the rest of the station from the same fate.

Shellshocked but hungry for vengeance, Wedge borrowed a Z-95 Headhunter from Booster and caught up with the *Buzzzer* in the Jumus system. He destroyed the freighter with cold precision, but Loka Hask escaped in a flight suit—with a parasitic Corellian limpet attached to his face.

Insurance money from his parents' deaths enabled Wedge to purchase a used cargo freighter. Terrik hooked him up with underground suppliers and customers, many of whom were affiliated with the Rebel Alliance.

Antilles found the work liberating but cash-poor, so he joined the Alliance's starfighter division during an open call for combat pilots. Along with Jek Porkins, Biggs Darklighter, and other early Rebel heroes, Antilles flew an X-wing as part of Red Squadron. He and the other Reds helped procure spare astromechs from Commenor, and returned to Yavin base just in time to go up against the Empire's mighty Death Star. Antilles, flying under the call sign Red Two, scored half a dozen kills in the battle but had to abort his trench run due to a damaged stabilizer.

After the Battle of Yavin, Wedge Antilles and Luke Skywalker jointly founded Rogue Squadron, a flexible starfighter group not bound by standard command channels. Though dismissed at first by Starfighter Command, Rogue Squadron developed a flawless reputation over the next few years. Antilles himself survived several narrow scrapes, including a close encounter with an Imperial bio-weapons lab on Gobindi and a last-minute rescue from a Kessel prison train that would have delivered him to a life sentence in the spice mines. On Thila, site of the relocated Alliance headquarters, Antilles flew into combat in a T-47 airspeeder, not realizing that a very angry Chewbacca was dangling from his fuselage. Both survived.

When the Empire discovered the Rebel headquarters on Hoth, it was Rogue Squadron's mission to stall the enemy's AT-AT walkers. Wedge Antilles and his gunner Wes Janson tripped the first AT-AT using a tow cable and some trick snowspeeder maneuvers. Most of the Rogues escaped, and Commander Antilles assumed leadership of the squadron in Luke Skywalker's absence. Rogue Squadron fought at Gall and Coruscant during the search for Han Solo and the struggle against Prince Xizor.

At the Battle of Endor, Antilles earned a rematch against the super-weapon he'd failed to destroy the first time. Appointed the commander of Red Squadron, Antilles led one of the Rebel Alliance's four main starfighter divisions and flew into the Death Star's reactor core alongside Lando Calrissian. Their torpedoes struck home. Antilles and Calrissian earned joint credit for the annihilation of the second Death Star.

Antilles didn't rest on his laurels. Over the next month he led Rogue Squadron in battle against the Ssi-ruuk, the Nagai, and the Tofs, three new threats from outside known space. The New Republic tried to move Antilles away from the Rogues and into fleet command; in response he engineered a demotion from commander to captain, and remained Rogue Leader.

On a mission to Mrlsst, Antilles once again encountered Loka Hask. The murderer of his parents was now an Imperial negotiator, but Hask met a fitting end when a "planet-slicer" weapon activated above Mrlsst. The device triggered a wormhole that swallowed Hask and his ship. The Rogues then fought at Brentaal, where they accepted a new member—Baron Fel, an ex-Imperial TIE fighter ace and husband to Wedge's sister Syal.

Approximately one and a half years after Endor, Antilles once again reached the rank of commander when

the New Republic temporarily disbanded Rogue Squadron. He spent nearly a year on a publicity tour before rebuilding the Rogues in time for the campaign to capture Coruscant. While undercover in Imperial City, Antilles met Iella Wessiri, a New Republic agent and the former CorSec partner of pilot Corran Horn.

After his maverick military actions during the Bacta War, Antilles formed Wraith Squadron, an experimental group of spies and saboteurs who proved instrumental in the victories over Warlord Zsinj at Kuat and Selaggis. Antilles rejoined the Rogues during the campaign against Grand Admiral Thrawn and fought in the climactic Battle of Bilbringi. Following Thrawn's defeat, Antilles finally accepted a long-overdue promotion to general.

At first his new rank didn't take him away from his squadron mates. General Antilles led the Rogues in battle against Admiral Krennel and killed the clone of Ysanne Isard on Ciutric. But the emergence of the reborn Emperor at last forced him to abandon the cockpit of his X-wing. He com-

manded the captured Star Destroyers *Liberator* and *Emancipator* alongside General Calrissian and led an undercover commando assault on the Emperor's citadel on Byss. Around this time, the New Republic finally launched the captured Super Star Destroyer *Lusankya*. Antilles took command of the warship, directing a restructured Rogue Squadron (incorporating B-wings and A-wings into the traditional X-wing lineup) and scoring a victory against would-be emperor Carnor Jax at Phaeda.

Antilles took advantage of a short stretch of peace by clearing wrecks from Coruscant's orbit and directing the construction droids restoring the damaged cityscape. He volunteered to guard Dr. Qwi Xux following her release from the Imperial Maw Installation, and they quickly fell in love. The two stayed together through the Darksaber affair, after which General Antilles returned to the *Lusankya*. He clashed with Admiral Pellaeon—and with Pellaeon's own Super Star Destroyer, the *Reaper*—in a monthlong brawl for the planet Orinda.

Antilles separated from Qwi Xux

on friendly terms, and ran into Iella Wessiri during a diplomatic mission to Adumar. While leading the lesser nations of Adumar in battle against their bullying neighbor Cartann, he realized Iella was the woman with whom he wanted to spend his life. A few months after the Adumar mission, Wedge and Iella exchanged vows on Coruscant. Two children followed, both of them girls—first Syal, and then Myri.

General Antilles continued to serve the New Republic. He helped contain the Almanian "new rebellion," tried to evacuate Thanta Zilbra before its destruction by Centerpoint Station, and searched for the Caamas Document during the Hand of Thrawn crisis. Finally, in the wake of the Imperial–New Republic peace treaty, he retired from the military.

With the invasion of the Yuuzhan Vong, Antilles returned, helping Kyp Durron destroy a supposed enemy superweapon created from the remains of the planet Sernpidal. And Gavin Darklighter, current leader of Rogue Squadron, will gladly accept any help this old soldier can offer.

DARTH BANE

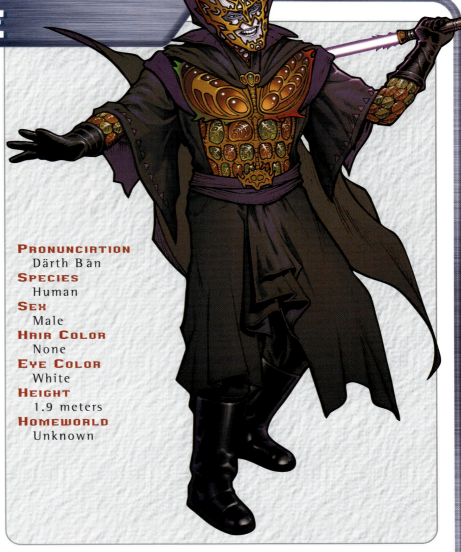

D arth Bane lived a millennium ago, in an age when the "new Sith" had been waging war against the Jedi for a thousand years. The Sith Lords were many; their followers, legion. Bane studied the ways of the dark side under Lord Qordis, and became so confident in his own destiny that he never bothered to complete his formal apprenticeship. Bane believed he had the *right* to rule, and had little patience for titles and hierarchies.

Lord Kaan was the truest object of Bane's scorn. A cruel coward, Kaan preached the philosophy "rule by the strong" to hide the weakness in his spirit. Bane represented a threat to Kaan's leadership, and on the eve of battle against a Jedi battalion, Kaan had his rival poisoned. Darth Bane collapsed on the battlefield. Kaan's Sith army, the Brotherhood of Darkness, left him for dead.

Bane survived. He returned to the Brotherhood of Darkness, and fought Lord Hoth's Army of Light on Ruusan. Seeing Bane alive, Kaan was unnerved, but allowed the other man to sit in on the council of war.

Darth Bane tried to rally the Sith Lords around an aggressive Force technique that, if properly executed, would annihilate the Army of Light. The Lords joined together in meditation, but broke off when they sensed the fearsome anger in Bane's heart. Instead of killing the Jedi, Bane brought about the deforestation of once-lush Ruusan.

Lord Kaan eliminated all his enemies with a "thought bomb," a Force weapon that suicidally consumed all life-energies located within its blast radius. Both the Brotherhood of Darkness and the Army of Light perished

PRONUNCIATION
Därth Bān
SPECIES
Human
SEX
Male
HAIR COLOR
None
EYE COLOR
White
HEIGHT
1.9 meters
HOMEWORLD
Unknown

in the cataclysm, as did Kaan himself.

Bane, the only survivor, flew away from Ruusan in his ship the *Valcyn*. As he headed toward the moon Dxun, the specters of Qordis and Kaan appeared before him, their dead eyes vengeful and accusing.

On Dxun, Bane found the empty tomb of Freedon Nadd, the Dark Jedi whose spirit had led Exar Kun to evil three thousand years earlier. Within the cold iron walls he found a Sith Holocron containing the collected secrets of the dark side. Strange parasites called orbalisks attached themselves to Bane's skin, forming a

suit of organic armor across his torso and feeding adrenaline into his veins.

When he emerged, he maintained a new theory regarding the Force. Previously the dark side had been spread too thin, shared among too many Lords. From that point forward, he decreed, the Sith would never number more than two at a time—one Master and one apprentice, as it had been with Exar Kun and Ulic Qel-Droma. Finding his own apprentice on Onderon, Bane committed the Sith Order to secrecy and began the tradition that would hand the name *Darth* to each of his successors.

JAR JAR BINKS

General Binks! The teachers who knew Jar Jar Binks during his adolescence would one day be amazed to learn that their nightmare pupil had distinguished himself in the Battle of Naboo. "Will lookit yousa!" one remarked upon meeting her former student. "Una *general*, hum?"

While some gushed with pride over Jar Jar's zero-to-hero track, the soldiers thrust under his command—as well as his "fellow" generals—grumbled with private disgust. It wasn't that Jar Jar lacked military experience, for militiagung numbered among Jar Jar's many failed careers. He was just downright dangerous when given a weapon, let alone an entire army.

Even Jar Jar Binks wouldn't have argued with this assessment. When Boss Nass promoted him to general, he fainted. For years, all Jar Jar had wanted was a full belly and the company of friends, but fate seemed determined to thwart even these simple desires.

Kicked out of Otoh Gunga's schools, unable to turn to his parents for guidance, Jar Jar hopped between jobs all during his youth. His klutziness always undercut his enthusiasm. On some days, only a few hours passed before he popped a bubble wall or ignited a plasma drum, rendering himself unemployed before sunset. Jar Jar was working as a vagrant shudderup musician—passersby would pay money to make the music *stop*—when he was discovered by local lawbreaker Roos Tarpals.

Tarpals served as the leader and father figure of a band of young swindlers. Jar Jar became the perfect dupe, distracting security patrols

PRONUNCIATION
Jär Jär Bĭnks
SPECIES
Gungan
SEX
Male
HAIR COLOR
None
EYE COLOR
Orange
HEIGHT
1.96 meters
HOMEWORLD
Naboo

while Tarpals and his crew pulled off scams. Unlike the other thieves, Tarpals treated Jar Jar as a valued team member. Their friendship came to an end, though, when Tarpals enlisted full time in the Gungan Grand Army. The old gang scattered, and Jar Jar again found himself adrift in Gungan society with only his faith in the gods to sustain him.

Fortunately for him, Otoh Gunga ruler Boss Nass possessed a charitable streak. Partly out of respect for

Jar Jar's parents, and partly on the recommendation of now-captain Tarpals, Nass arranged new employment for Jar Jar. It wasn't until *after* Jar Jar accidentally let half the animals escape from the Otoh Gunga Zoo that Nass sentenced Jar Jar to six months hard labor in the Quarry penal colony.

When Jar Jar saved him from drowning in an out-of-control bongo, Nass charitably commuted the sentence. Jar Jar also saved the life of Nass's niece, Major Fassa, who pledged a life debt to her rescuer. Embarrassed by Major Fassa's devotion but excited by the opportunity for romance, Jar Jar was both disappointed and relieved when Fassa's life debt was revoked on a technicality.

Later, Boss Nass threw a lavish party and magnanimously gave Jar Jar a job in the kitchen. Within minutes, Jar Jar exploded the gasser oven. The ensuing rupture in the bubble wall flooded the party, and when Jar Jar tried to save Nass's luxury heyblibber from destruction, he crashed it instead.

This was the final outrage.

Boss Nass ordered Jar Jar banished to the swamps, never to return, upon pain of death. Jar Jar hid within Otoh Gunga, but his old friend Captain Tarpals found him hanging around a restaurant, scrounging for scraps. Tarpals personally escorted Jar Jar to the soggy shores of Lianorm Swamp.

The long months spent in exile were among the worst of Jar Jar's life. Then the invasion of Naboo provided an opportunity for Jar Jar to meet new friends. His adventures with "Annie," "Quiggon," and "Obi-One" exposed him to fantastic worlds and plenty of tasty new foods. On Coruscant, Jar Jar's comments regarding the size of the Gungan Grand Army prompted Naboo's Queen Amidala to consider an alliance between the two cultures of her homeworld. Boss Nass actually agreed to the coalition, and believed Jar Jar to be the one who had orchestrated the Queen's proposal.

Before he knew it, Jar Jar found himself playing the role of heroic Gungan general.

Jar Jar had no intention of staying in the military. He spent a great deal of time with Queen Amidala, learning the language of politics. In time he parlayed his fame as a Gungan general into a diplomatic role as a member of Boss Nass's Rep Council, then as the Gungan ambassador to Theed. When Padmé Amidala stepped down as planetary monarch, Jar Jar followed her in her new role as Republic Senator. Elected to the Galactic Representative Commission, Jar Jar spoke on behalf of the Gungan people and dealt with legislation affecting the Naboo sector. Those who couldn't deal with Jar Jar as a general now had to face him as a politician. But Representative Binks worked hard.

Ten years after his first trip to Coruscant with Qui-Gon Jinn and Anakin Skywalker, Jar Jar Binks had become a respected consultant in the eyes of Supreme Chancellor Palpatine. Representative Binks sat in on closed-door discussions concerning the clone army discovered on Kamino and the threat posed by Count Dooku's separatists. Jar Jar offered to bring forth a measure proposing that Chancellor Palpatine be given emergency war powers, and assured his fellow Senators that Palpatine would give up his power once the crisis had ended.

The emergency measure passed, and the Clone Wars began.

BOSSK

W hen baby Bossk emerged from his egg-sac, he blinked his shiny eyes, yawned to show his tiny fangs, and devoured every last one of his unhatched brothers and sisters. Watching it all, his father Cradossk nearly burst with pride.

Bossk is a Trandoshan, a reptilian species hailing from a planet in the same star system as the Wookiee homeworld of Kashyyyk. Trandoshans hate Wookiees. They also worship a female deity called the Scorekeeper, who rewards successful hunts. Therefore, the killing of Wookiees is more than a satisfying pastime—it's a religious mandate.

Bossk, hatched fifty-three years before the Battle of Yavin, became one of Trandosha's most celebrated Wookiee-hunters while still in his youth. Under the Old Republic, the bloodsport was illegal and practiced furtively, but the Empire's classification of Wookiees as a slave species became a boon to Trandoshan hunters. Bossk scored hundreds of prize Wookiee pelts, further earning his father's respect.

Old Cradossk headed up the Bounty Hunters' Guild—the oldest and largest of the galaxy's hunter fraternities—and he brought his son in as a full member. On Bossk's first guild assignment, he journeyed to war-ravaged Qotile in pursuit of a military deserter from the Stark Hyperspace War who had set himself up as a local King. Bossk nabbed his target, and the terrified natives bestowed upon him the title "monarch of the Qotile system."

Bossk racked up victories and grew quite popular among the

PRONUNCIATION
Bŏsk
SPECIES
Trandoshan
SEX
Male
HAIR COLOR
None
EYE COLOR
Red
HEIGHT
1.9 meters
HOMEWORLD
Trandosha (Dosha)

younger members of the Bounty Hunters' Guild. On Gandolo IV, however, the Trandoshan experienced a rare setback when he tried to capture a pack of Wookiees, including a prime specimen named Chewbacca. The Wookiee's partner, Han Solo, landed his ship, the *Millennium Falcon*, on top of Bossk's parked freighter, crushing it like an empty can. Bossk had to cut his way out of the wreckage and hitch a ride home aboard a manure barge. He sank his

credits into a replacement ship, an advanced YV-666 freighter named the *Hound's Tooth*, and purchased a smaller backup vessel named the *Captivator*. Later, Bossk attempted to claim the priceless statue known as the Yavin Vassilika in a bounty hunter runoff, but lost the prize to his rivals.

After the Battle of Yavin, such setbacks became increasingly common for Bossk, thanks largely to the galaxy's greatest bounty hunter, Boba Fett. Were it not for Fett, Bossk could have recovered a valuable droid barge for Jabba the Hutt and captured Nil Posondum for Kud'ar Mub'at. So when Boba Fett petitioned for membership in the Bounty Hunters' Guild, Bossk reacted with suspicion and outright hostility. His instincts soon proved correct, for Fett had joined the guild in order to destroy it.

After a fiasco of a mission to the planet of the Shell Hutts, Bossk decided to claim his birthright. In the traditional Trandoshan way, he surprised, killed, and ate his father, Cradossk. This played right into Fett's hands, for the Bounty Hunters' Guild split into two warring factions—the Guild Reform Committee, led by

Bossk, and the True Guild, led by Cradossk loyalists. Anxious for money to shore up his power base, Bossk teamed with Fett and Zuckuss to claim the Imperial bounty on the rogue stormtrooper Trhin Voss'on't, but Fett double-crossed the other two hunters and stole their prize captive.

At this point, Bossk accepted the reality that the waning Bounty Hunters' Guild would never again achieve the prominence it had enjoyed under his father's leadership. He began accepting more freelance assignments, on one occasion working with the hated Boba Fett only so he could capture the even-more-hated Han Solo. Bossk, Fett, and other bounty hunters brought Solo to

Ord Mantell, but the Corellian escaped before they could arrange a suitable reward.

At the Battle of Hoth, Bossk numbered among the six elite hunters chosen by Lord Vader to find the *Millennium Falcon*. As he prepared to leave Vader's Super Star Destroyer, Bossk ran into Tinian I'att and her Wookiee partner Chenlambec, two hunters who had failed to make Vader's cut. They claimed to have a lead on Solo's whereabouts, and Bossk accepted them aboard the *Hound's Tooth* as his temporary "partners."

He planned to double-cross them at the earliest opportunity—and skin the Wookiee for his luxurious pelt—but Tinian and Chenlambec had their own double cross in mind. They tricked Bossk into attacking a prison full of Wookiees on Lomabu III that had been set up as a trap for the Rebel fleet. The local Imperial governor, furious at Bossk's interference, threw him in a holding cell. He planned to flay the Trandoshan and make a lizard-skin coat for his lady.

Bossk dug his way out and recaptured the *Hound's Tooth* from Tinian and Chenlambec. Meanwhile, Fett took possession of Solo at Bespin. Since he had already lost out on the Han Solo bounty, Bossk accepted an assignment from Lady Domina Tagge to obtain rare gemstones in the Red Nebula. A short time later, he teamed up with IG-88 on Stenos but failed in an attempt to capture Lando Calrissian for an angry businessman named Drebble.

During a quick stopover on Corellia, Bossk shot and killed CorSec officer Hal Horn. He was imprisoned by Horn's son Corran, but fortunately for Bossk, an Imperial official named Kirtan Loor arranged for his release.

Back in the hunt once again,

Bossk learned that, despite the many weeks that had gone by since Boba Fett had walked away with Han Solo, Fett still hadn't delivered Solo's carbonite slab to Jabba the Hutt. Teaming up with Zuckuss and 4-LOM, Bossk attempted to disable Fett's *Slave I* and hijack its cargo—but only damaged his precious *Hound's Tooth* in the process.

Looking for quick credits, Bossk and several other bounty hunters accepted temporary employment with Quaffug the Hutt on the third moon of Blimph. While there, he was offered the chance to hunt down Lando Calrissian, but the wily gambler outsmarted both Bossk and Quaffug. Bossk, frustrated by his lack of victories, journeyed to Tatooine.

Immediately following the death of Jabba the Hutt, Bossk discovered Boba Fett's *Slave I* drifting in Tatooine's orbit. Believing Fett to be a permanent resident in the Sarlacc's belly, Bossk attempted to steal the ship, but was tricked into thinking the *Hound's Tooth* was wired to explode. Bossk fled in an escape pod. Fett, alive after all, stole Bossk's vessel.

Broke, and without his famous starship, Bossk became the laughingstock of Mos Eisley. He was as surprised as everyone else when Fett returned and offered him a fortune in exchange for some old evidence stored in a droid's data banks—evidence that Fett needed to unravel a conspiracy involving the owner of the Kuat shipyards. Suddenly wealthy, Bossk bought a brand-new ship and returned to the bounty hunting game.

He nearly nabbed Lando Calrissian on Keyorin, with help from the reprogrammed shell of IG-88A, but Calrissian escaped him yet a *third* time.

The years passed, and Bossk grew gray-skinned with age. After the Imperial–New Republic peace accords, he retired from professional hunting—but still killed from time to time for the sheer joy of it. Twenty-two years after the Battle of Endor, Bossk ran into Han Solo on a space station orbiting Ord Mantell. The news of Chewbacca's death on Sernpidal had warmed Bossk's heart, and he couldn't help rubbing the tragedy in Solo's face. Bossk should have seen the punch coming, but he was no longer a young lizard. A broken snout and a mouthful of loose teeth taught him to be a little quicker on his feet next time.

BRAKISS

Although Brakiss is remembered as a villain, his story is a tragic one. Had he been born on a different planet, he might have become a great Jedi Knight.

Imperial occupation troops on the planet Msst identified Brakiss's Force talents when he was only a baby. The Emperor had a standing order for such cases—seize them or kill them. Brakiss scored high enough on the aptitude tests to save his life, but unlike other Force-sensitives such as Shira Brie, he did not earn the personal attention of Emperor Palpatine. Instead, Imperial reprogramming teams associated with the Inquisitorius took custody of Brakiss and turned him into their own weapon.

He was still a teenager when the Empire fell at Endor. His Imperial masters held tightly to their prize, shuttling Brakiss between Imperial warlord kingdoms and their own crumbling headquarters on Msst. Brakiss sat out the campaign of the resurrected Emperor. Then, when Luke Skywalker established his Jedi academy on Yavin 4, the surviving Inquisitorius officers realized they had a perfect opportunity for infiltration. Brakiss was given a false background, and easily passed Skywalker's admission screenings.

Master Skywalker knew Brakiss's agenda from the start, but hoped to win his pupil over to the light. Immediately following the Empire Reborn crisis, after three years of training, Brakiss underwent a Jedi trial in which he faced the darkness in his own spirit. Horrified by the truth, and too ashamed to remain at the academy, he fled back to Msst, where he learned that his masters' power had

PRONUNCIATION
Brǎ'-kǐs
SPECIES
Human
SEX
Male
HAIR COLOR
Blond
EYE COLOR
Blue
HEIGHT
1.83 meters
HOMEWORLD
Msst

dwindled to almost nothing. Brakiss dutifully reported in, but after a brief visit to his mother, he left his homeworld to seek his own fate.

But Brakiss couldn't escape his past. Dolph, another of Skywalker's failed students, set Brakiss up on the moon of Telti. In exchange for subsidizing a droid-manufacturing operation, Dolph forced Brakiss to install remote-triggered explosives in all of his droids. Dolph—under the name Kueller—planned to use the droids in

a revenge plot against Skywalker and the New Republic.

Thirteen years after Endor, Brakiss's droids detonated in the New Republic Senate chamber. Luke Skywalker tracked them back to Telti, where he confronted his former student. Brakiss, conflicted over his role in the deaths of so many, tried to warn Luke of Kueller's plot. Soon after, R2-D2 and C-3PO arrived on Telti and forced Brakiss to flee the moon.

Brakiss made his way to the Deep

Core and reestablished his old contacts within the Imperial warlord kingdoms. The warlords themselves had died in Admiral Daala's mass execution years before, but ambitious power brokers had since sprung up to claim the Deep Core's scant resources. Brakiss became a neutral intermediary between these rival camps.

The peace accords between the Outer Rim Empire and the New Republic, signed by Admiral Pellaeon, were met with sneers by Brakiss and many of the replacement warlords of the Deep Core. Though their forces were minimal, and though they could no longer even call themselves the Empire—that honor had been stolen by Pellaeon—they dreamed of a glorious "Second Imperium." The few surviving Deep Core dominions pooled their resources and created the Shadow Academy, a training center for Dark Jedi.

Brakiss became the Shadow Academy's leader. He operated from a hyperspace-capable space station that boasted an advanced cloaking device. To recruit students, he journeyed to the planet Dathomir and helped found a new order of Nightsisters based in the Great Canyon. Unlike previous Dathomirian Witches, these Nightsisters treated their males as equals and sent their most promising candidates to the Shadow Academy for instruction. One Nightsister, Tamith Kai, became his second in command.

When it appeared that Emperor Palpatine had returned from the dead and thrown his support behind the Second Imperium and its fledgling dark side academy, Brakiss believed the reports wholeheartedly. The Emperor had beaten death before, and Brakiss desperately wanted to believe that he—not Pellaeon—was the true heir to Palpatine's legacy. In truth, the "Emperor" was nothing more than a holographic fabrication perpetuated by a quartet of ersatz Royal Guardsmen.

Four years after Pellaeon's treaty, the Second Imperium began its campaign. Due to its severly limited naval forces, Brakiss was forced to focus on terrorist tactics. Aboard the Shadow Academy, he warned his students against the limiting philosophy of the light side, and urged them to embrace the Force's full continuum. He firmly believed that a new order of Jedi—his Jedi—could bring about an age of glory for the Empire.

Brakiss briefly captured Jacen and Jaina Solo, but the twins escaped before he could convert them. On Coruscant he snatched another Force-sensitive youth, Zekk, and trained him as his protégé. Brakiss gave Zekk a lightsaber, and when Zekk proved his skill in a duel to the death against a fellow student, he became Brakiss's "Darkest Knight."

Brakiss gathered all his forces for an attack on Skywalker's Jedi academy. The defeat of his former Master would be a great propaganda victory.

The fight raged in space and in Yavin 4's steaming jungles. When the tide of battle turned against the Second Imperium, Brakiss cut down two of the false Royal Guards who were guarding the "Emperor," only to learn the truth behind their deception. Enraged by how easily he'd been taken in, Brakiss killed another guardsman, but the final pretender escaped his fury and triggered the station's self-destruct mechanism. Brakiss died as the Shadow Academy burst into fragmented slag.

SHIRA BRIE

Like Mara Jade, Shira Brie was one of the Emperor's Hands. And as with Mara, Shira was assigned to kill Luke Skywalker.

Shira Elan Colla Brie grew up in the Imperial Palace, a top COMPNOR member and Imperial Intelligence recruit under Ysanne Isard. Although the Emperor knew of Brie's talent and Force sensitivity, it was Vader who recommended her for a Rebel infiltration mission. To provide a credible background, the Empire razed the city of Chinshassa on Shalvayne. Posing as a Shalvaynian refugee, Imperial Major Brie joined the Alliance as a lieutenant in Rogue Squadron.

Brie's orders were to kill or discredit Skywalker. In the months following the Battle of Hoth, Shira Brie made herself a hero to the Alliance and a love interest for Luke. On a mission to destroy an enemy communications device, Brie, Skywalker, and a handful of other Rogues flew captured TIEs into the heart of an Imperial armada. Acting on Force-guided instinct, Skywalker shot down Shira Brie's fighter. Though branded with shame for what looked like treason, Skywalker refused to join Vader.

But the Dark Lord wasn't done with Shira Brie. Imperial medics replaced her shattered limbs with cyborg prosthetics. Assuming the name Lumiya, Dark Lady of the Sith, Shira Brie found her Force abilities deepening in direct proportion to her rage. Vader offered the armored cyborg to Palpatine as a new Emperor's Hand.

Just before the Battle of Endor, Lumiya journeyed to Ziost to build an ancient Sith weapon, the lightwhip. She returned from that mission only to discover that both her Masters had

PRONUNCIATION
Shē'-rä Brē
SPECIES
Human
SEX
Female
HAIR COLOR
Red
EYE COLOR
Green
HEIGHT
1.6 meters
HOMEWORLD
Unknown

died. Lumiya committed herself to exterminating the Rebels who had destroyed what she believed was the galaxy's natural order. She allied with the Nagai invaders, promising them the heads of their enemies. On Herdessa she nearly killed Leia Organa, while on Kinooine she dueled with Luke Skywalker and revealed to him her past life as Shira Brie.

Soon the Nagai attacked Endor, forcing the Rebel Alliance leaders to flee. But the Rebels and the Nagai quickly forged a partnership against an even worse enemy, the Tofs. Lumiya switched sides and allied with the Tofs, but their defeat on Saijo left her adrift without allies.

After many months, Imperial ruler Ysanne Isard—Shira Brie's former commander in Imperial Intelligence—enlisted Lumiya's help in hunting down the traitor Mara Jade. Lumiya accepted Isard's warships and stormtroopers, but struck out on her own as a minor warlord. She is believed to have trained would-be emperor Carnor Jax in the ways of the Force. Lumiya has reappeared sporadically since then, but her whereabouts during the Yuuzhan Vong invasion remain a mystery.

C-3PO

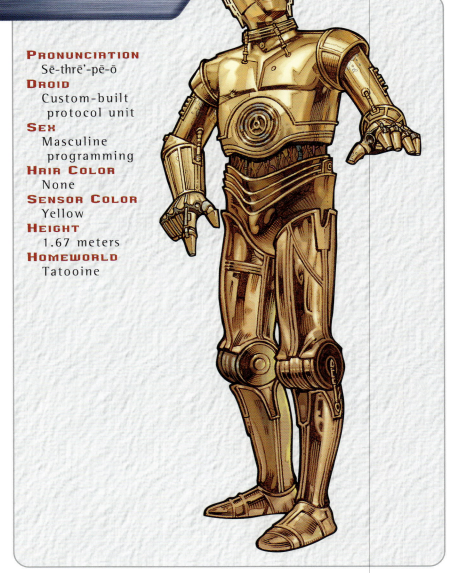

When greeting strangers, the protocol droid still announces, "I am See-Threepio, human–cyborg relations."

As if he needed any introduction. C-3PO is as famous as any of the heroes of the Rebellion, and deservedly so. As much a "son" of Darth Vader as Luke Skywalker, C-3PO overcame his bittersweet origins—and his own innate squeamishness—to help the Alliance vanquish Vader's legacy.

C-3PO the *droid* is built from scavenged parts, taken off sundry Cybot Galactica models more than a hundred years old. But Threepio the *individual* is a one-of-a-kind creation. Nine-year-old Anakin Skywalker assembled the automaton from junk heaps, fusing together a working cognitive module from three scrapped verbobrains. With a uniquely fussy personality both respectful and obstinate, C-3PO came to life on desolate Tatooine.

C-3PO boasted many of the same parts as his factory-made cousins, including a TranLang III communications module, taken from Gardulla the Hutt's destroyed TC unit, which allowed him to understand more than six million languages.

C-3PO met the blue-and-white astromech R2-D2 when Queen Amidala's ship arrived on Tatooine, but shortly thereafter Anakin and R2-D2 left Tatooine in the Queen's company. "Well, Threepio," Anakin remarked, by way of farewell, "I've been freed. I'll make sure Mom doesn't sell you or anything."

The droid stayed behind in Shmi's slave hovel. His exterior plating was completed before he accompanied Shmi to the Lars moisture farm when

PRONUNCIATION
Sē-thrē'-pē-ō
DROID
Custom-built protocol unit
SEX
Masculine programming
HAIR COLOR
None
SENSOR COLOR
Yellow
HEIGHT
1.67 meters
HOMEWORLD
Tatooine

her owner, Watto, sold her to Cliegg Lars. Shmi and Cliegg married, and C-3PO performed simple maintenance tasks around the homestead for Master Cliegg and his son Owen. Ten years after Anakin's departure from Tatooine, Tusken Raiders captured Shmi. Anakin returned with Padmé and recovered his mother's body. Owen presented the finished droid to Anakin, saying it's what his stepmother would have wanted.

C-3PO and R2-D2 reunited on the trip to Geonosis. As the years passed, the two of them ventured out into the galaxy together. Throughout innumerable droid auctions, they stuck together like magnets. A string of owners included personages as distinguished as Ambassador Zell of Majoor and as lowly as a cutthroat glitterstim smuggler. This last owner dumped the droids on the salt flats of Ingo, where they became the property of Jord Dusat and Thall Joben. These young humans dragged the droids into adventures against the Fromm crime family, including a speeder race—versus Boba Fett—on the racing planet Boonta.

C-3PO took pleasure in their next assignment, in which they helped their new master Jann Tosh restore the Tammuz-an monarchy. C-3PO hoped he might remain in the court of Tammuz-an as a translator, but Jann dropped the droids off on Manda on his way to enroll in the Imperial Academy.

On Manda, C-3PO and R2-D2 gained employment with a local hotel, then found themselves caught up in an adventure that took them to Biitu and a confrontation with an immense droid-thing known as the Great Heep. Mungo Baobab, wealthy heir to the Baobab Merchant Fleet, took part in the Heep's downfall and returned with the droids to Manda.

Master Mungo brought his new droids to Roon, where he salvaged

some priceless Roonstones. When he complained that his gems were marred by crystalline etchings, C-3PO informed him that the translated writings represented the oldest-known version of the epic poem *Dha Werda Verda*. C-3PO and R2-D2 traveled to the Baobab Archives to attempt further translation, but due to a mixup in their transfer orders, they were sold to a trafficker in used technological goods.

Governor Wena, a panjandrum representing the Kalarba system, purchased the two droids for his luxury starship. But the governor's extravagances caught the eyes of accountants on Kalarba, who slashed his expense budget. Wena sold his droids to a junk dealer, and the wealthy Pitareeze family picked them up. C-3PO enjoyed this assignment, with the exception of the time Hosk Arena promoters mistook him for the assassin droid C-3PX and tried to make him a gladiator.

Soon after, C-3PO and R2-D2 accompanied a police droid, Unit Zed, on a mission to Nar Shaddaa. When Threepio lost his left leg below the knee, the replacement he received contained a hidden programming module that overrode his personality. Where once he'd been anxious and vacillating, C-3PO was now confident and heroic—and while some might have considered the change an improvement, the "new" C-3PO just wasn't *Threepio*. Once the offending leg was removed, the droid became himself again.

C-3PO and R2-D2 had further adventures with Master Zorneth, an Ithorian botanist, and Master Harthan, a diplomat working the Tion Hegemony. Eventually both droids found lasting employment with the Royal House of Alderaan. C-3PO would have been happy to work at state dinners and ambassadorial receptions forever, but as Princess Leia's personal protocol droid, he was assigned to accompany her on her consular ship, the *Tantive IV*. There he served as interpreter for his astromech counterpart, a certain blue-trimmed R2 unit he knew all too well.

When Darth Vader's Star Destroyer seized the *Tantive IV*, R2-D2 insisted they eject in an escape pod. The two droids became the object of a massive Imperial search and soon found themselves aboard the mighty Death Star. C-3PO breathed an electronic sigh of relief when they finally arrived on Yavin 4, but then watched his faithful friend fly off into battle inside Luke Skywalker's X-wing. C-3PO seized up with panic when Master Luke reported, "I've lost Artoo." Surely there were other astromechs who could have done the job, C-3PO thought to himself.

R2-D2 pulled through, of course, without requiring the donation of any of C-3PO's circuits or gears. Over the next three years C-3PO helped the Rebel Alliance on dismal planets such as Drexel II, Aridus, and Circarpous IV. Finally the Rebels settled on the ice ball called Hoth, with temperatures well outside his operational safety limits. He and R2-D2 took separate paths during the evacuation of Hoth, and C-3PO suffered countless indignities—including total dismemberment and reassembly—while in the company of Captain Solo, Princess Leia, and Chewbacca.

C-3PO's terror reached new heights during the rescue of Captain Solo from the palace of Jabba the Hutt, but his mood lightened considerably on Endor, where the native Ewoks mistook him for one of the most sacred gods in their pantheon. During the historic truce at Bakura, C-3PO translated the musical language of the Ssi-ruuk, which later allowed the Alliance military to mount an offensive aboard the captured enemy flagship *Sibwarra*.

After the Rebel Alliance became the New Republic, Princess Leia frequently required the services of a translator and diplomatic aide. C-3PO was overjoyed to finally execute his primary functions—etiquette and protocol. And when the New Republic captured Coruscant, he was granted the opportunity to ply his trade inside the opulent Imperial Palace and Senate Hall.

Han Solo spoiled this peaceful time in his usual fashion by hijacking Princess Leia and C-3PO to the wilderness planet of the Dathomir Witches. They barely escaped the planet with their lives. Soon thereafter, the droid made a discovery that led everyone to believe General Solo was the hereditary King of Corellia, but this proved to be a fraud.

C-3PO accompanied the Princess to the homeworld of the fierce Noghri during the campaign of Grand Admiral Thrawn, then assumed less hazardous duties as a caretaker for Leia Solo's three young children. Once Jacen, Jaina, and Anakin grew to school age, C-3PO found himself free to adventure with R2-D2 during the "ghost ship" investigation of the Teljkon vagabond. He also helped Chewbacca program Em Teedee, a miniaturized translation droid, for Chewie's nephew Lowbacca.

Following Chewbacca's death on Sernpidal, C-3PO compiled a memorial retrospective from those who'd known the Wookiee best. The somber experience stirred up grim thoughts from deep inside his verbobrain, the kind of thoughts that most droids never ponder for a nanosecond. C-3PO knows the antitechnology Yuuzhan Vong wouldn't hesitate to melt him to slag. Is "death" to a droid merely deactivation, or would it mean the loss of what might be called his spirit? As the alien invaders capture planet after planet, he hopes he never has a chance to find out.

Callista

PRONUNCIATION
Kä-lǐ'-stä
SPECIES
Human
SEX
Female
HAIR COLOR
Blond
EYE COLOR
Gray
HEIGHT
1.7 meters
HOMEWORLD
Chad

A Jedi Knight from the era of Yoda, Callista was trained by a maverick and schooled in unorthodoxy. Yet she defanged the Emperor's first superweapon and saved the lives of dozens of Jedi children.

Master Djinn Altis clashed regularly with the Jedi Council. A scholar of antiquity, Altis argued that Knights and Masters had not always been restricted to a single Padawan, nor had Jedi training always started in infancy.

Several years into Palpatine's term as Supreme Chancellor, Master Altis set out on his starship the *Chu'unthor*—named for the famed Jedi training vessel from an earlier era—seeking Force-sensitive individuals who might have missed their calling. One of his first students was a young man named Geith, and in the watery bayous of Chad he found Callista.

Callista's family worked as deepsea ranchers on Chad's Algic Current, far from the planet's Chadra-Fan settlements. She had been herding tsaelkes and wander-kelp since she could walk, using the Force to communicate with the ocean cetaceans. But since Chad was not a Republic member world, she hadn't been tagged at birth as potential Jedi material.

Callista left her home aboard Djinn Altis's starship, sacrificing everything she knew for the promise of a better life. For five years she trained aboard Altis's hidden complex, floating in the clouds of Bespin. She fell in love with Geith, and decorated her lightsaber handle with a pattern of swimming tsaelkes.

The Clone Wars sorely taxed the Jedi Order. Djinn Altis and his students willingly joined the Jedi cause. Around the time of the Purge, dozens of Temple students, all of them children, were sheltered on Belsavis in the home of Jedi Master Plett. Emperor Palpatine ordered his asteroid-sized battlemoon *Eye of Palpatine* to Belsavis to wipe them all out.

Callista and Geith located and boarded the automated *Eye* in the Moonflower Nebula. Once inside, they realized they couldn't destroy it without help. Geith tried to fly out of the nebula, but the *Eye*'s cannons blasted him to atoms. Left with no other option, Callista attempted a perilous Jedi technique, shedding her corporeal form and merging her spirit with the battlemoon's central computer in order to render the *Eye* powerless.

Thirty years passed.

Roganda Ismaren, one of the former Jedi children of Belsavis and later an Emperor's Hand, returned to the planet of her childhood so her son could call forth the dormant *Eye of Palpatine*. Accompanied by one of his students, Cray Mingla, Luke Skywalker located the battlemoon, still drifting in the Moonflower Nebula, and discovered that an intangible yet vibrant presence existed within the ship's computer. During their "conversations" over a computer screen, Luke and Callista fell in love.

Luke had to eliminate the Emperor's superweapon before it killed again, but by destroying the *Eye*, he would destroy Callista. Before he could take action, Cray Mingla stunned her teacher and loaded him aboard an escape pod. When Skywalker awoke, he watched as the *Eye of Palpatine* exploded.

Cray Mingla slept aboard a second escape pod—or so Luke thought. When "Cray" opened her eyes, Luke realized this was Callista. Just before the explosion, Cray had willingly given her body to Callista. For Cray had suffered the loss of her lover Nichos, and hoped to join him in the afterlife.

A distressing side effect of the spirit transference was Callista's loss of any connection to the Force. She and Skywalker traveled from Dagobah to Hoth in an effort to re-store that connection, and Callista realized with horror that she *could* touch the Force—but only the dark side. Her irregular Jedi upbringing meant that she knew few details regarding the Jedi philosophy espoused by Yoda, but she still became a valuable addition to Luke's Jedi academy.

During Admiral Daala's assault on the academy, Callista single-handedly sabotaged the Super Star Destroyer *Knight Hammer* and boldly faced down Daala. When the *Knight Hammer* burned up in Yavin's atmosphere, Callista was presumed killed. Instead, Luke received a holographic message telling him that she had gone off alone, to seek her powers.

Months passed. Callista traveled with a crew aboard the *Zicreex*, visiting such ports of call as Gamorr, where she solved a murder mystery involving a slain Gamorrean boar and a bloodthirsty kheilwar. She eventually ended up on Nam Chorios in the Meridian sector, a planet infested with plague-carrying insects, and known as a Force nexus. She fell in with a former Jedi named Talseda and the Hutt Jedi Beldorian the Splendid, both petty local washouts. Soon she joined the Theran cultists out in Nam Chorios's barren wastes, where she meditated in the Force presence of the planet's living crystals, and operated the gun stations that prevented anyone from landing on Nam Chorios and carrying away its deadly insects.

When she learned that Seti Ashgad, the leader of Nam Chorios's anti-Theran settlers, planned to meet with Chief of State Leia Organa Solo, Callista sent word urging Leia not to hold any such summit. Her warnings went unheeded, and eight months after the destruction of the *Knight Hammer*, Seti Ashgad kidnapped the Chief of State. Callista helped derail his complicated scheme and save her adopted planet.

Skywalker went to Nam Chorios in search of Callista, and during the aftermath of Ashgad's failed coup the two saw each other again. A single look, however, was all they needed. Without saying a word, both realized their lives were meant to follow divergent paths. With a simple wave, Luke and Callista parted company forever.

LANDO CALRISSIAN

"He's not human, I tell you." So said Barpotomous Drebble, when asked to comment on Lando Calrissian for an unauthorized biography of the gambler-turned-hero. "He's either a mind-controlling alien or a Jedi in disguise." Asked to elaborate, Drebble explained, "It's his luck. No human in the galaxy has a right to be that lucky."

The truth is Lando Calrissian has had as much *bad* luck as good. It's just that his successes are so spectacular, they overshadow his ignominious defeats.

Little is known about Calrissian's early years, and the stories he tells about his youth are so outrageous that nobody knows *what* to believe. Some of the earliest verifiable information dates back to four years before the Battle of Yavin, when Calrissian was approximately twenty-seven years old. He was already a professional gambler, fleecing rich tourists aboard interstellar luxury liners such as the *Queen of Empire*. He didn't even know how to fly a starship, but when he won the YT-1300 freighter *Millennium Falcon* in a sabacc game he vowed to learn, almost on a whim.

He selected a tutor—a hot spicerunner named Han Solo—and arrived on Nar Shaddaa just as the bounty hunter Boba Fett had Solo at gunpoint. Calrissian ended the standoff, earning Boba Fett's enmity, and a grateful Solo offered up piloting lessons at no charge. Had Calrissian foreseen where this partnership would eventually lead, he surely would have refused.

After learning the basics from Solo, Calrissian went to the Central-

PRONUNCIATION
Lăn'-dō Kăl-rĭs'-ē-ŭn
SPECIES
Human
SEX
Male
HAIR COLOR
Black
EYE COLOR
Brown
HEIGHT
1.77 meters
HOMEWORLD
Unknown

ity to make some money at the gambling tables. He won a perky starfish-droid named Vuffi Raa and made a bitter enemy when he crossed Rokur Gepta, the Sorcerer of Tund. Calrissian's discovery of a hidden civilization in the Rafa system made him a hero to xenoarchaeologists and brought him his first taste of fame outside the gaming circuit.

Made rich when he sold a cargo of Rafan life crystals, Calrissian invested his cash in a used-starship lot on Nar Shaddaa. Sadly, he lost most of his inventory when the local smugglers defended themselves against an Imperial attack. Calrissian and Vuffi Raa returned to the Centrality and scored a cool twenty million credits in a botched spice bust, but the gambler lost the prize to the pirate queen Drea Renthal. During his third visit to the Centrality, Calrissian helped the Oswaft defend their home from invasion and was given a pile of precious gemstones in return. Unfortunately, he lost Vuffi Raa when the droid returned to his people in the Unknown Regions, and he lost his gemstone profits when a berubium mining investment proved worthless.

Desperate for credits, Calrissian stole a cache of treasure from the Glottalphib crime lord Nandreeson, earning him a death sentence if he ever returned to Smuggler's Run. Calrissian held high hopes for the sabacc championships in Bespin's Cloud City, and made it to the final round. But second best in sabacc is still a losing hand. Han Solo won both the tournament and the *Millennium Falcon*.

Nearly destitute, Calrissian ran a few successful scams—including hoodwinking an Imperial governor on Pesmenben IV—and ran into Boba Fett a second time aboard the *Queen of Empire*. He replaced the *Falcon* with a sleek new ship, the *Cobra*, and just prior to the Battle of Yavin agreed to participate in a Hutt-sponsored raid on Ylesia. But the smugglers who risked their lives in the raid wound up with nothing to show for it. Like the others, Calrissian believed Han Solo had betrayed them. He and Solo had an angry falling-out and, except for a hostile encounter during the hunt for the precious statue known as the Yavin Vassilika, would not see each other for more than three years.

Five months after the Battle of Yavin, Lando Calrissian again earned fame—this time as an improbable military hero in a slapdash brawl against pirates dubbed the Battle of Taanab. He also continued to expand his business horizons, investigating the amusement park Hologram Fun World as an investment opportunity. But he had no way of knowing that both of his passions—gambling and business—would come to a head a short time

later on the Tibanna gas colony known as Cloud City.

Following an encounter with Barpotomous Drebble, Calrissian entered into a high-stakes sabacc game with Cloud City's Baron Administrator, Dominic Raynor. Calrissian put up the deed to the *Cobra*, but it wasn't enough to cover Raynor's bet. An anonymous benefactor advanced Calrissian five million credits, and when he laid his cards on the table, he had won ownership of Cloud City.

Calrissian soon discovered that the floating city's cyborg liaison, Lobot, and thousands of Ugnaught workers had pooled the five million in order to ensure Raynor's fall from power.

Calrissian worked closely with Lobot for more than two years, battling a bounty hunter when Raynor put out a contract on his life, and stopping the crazed droid EV-9D9 before she destroyed all of the city's automaton population. He also bought a second ship, the luxury yacht *Lady Luck*.

Calrissian prided himself on the colony's small size and out-of-the-way location, factors that made it nothing more than an annoyance to the Mining Guild and all but invisible to the Empire. The citizens of Cloud City, many of them on the run from Imperial forces, looked to him for protection. When Darth Vader and Boba Fett arrived on Bespin, Calrissian sacrificed the few— Han Solo and his companions—for the preservation of the many. But once he realized what he had done to Solo, Calrissian gave up everything he had to get his friend back.

Joining the Rebel Al-

liance, Calrissian teamed up with Chewbacca in his old *Millennium Falcon*, both to strike at Imperial targets such as the *Tarkin* battle station and to search for Han Solo on remote planets like Stenos. On a return visit to Imperial-occupied Cloud City, he was nearly killed by an out-of-control Lobot. Later, Calrissian, Luke Skywalker, and Dash Rendar infiltrated Prince Xizor's castle on Coruscant to rescue Princess Leia. Calrissian destroyed the castle by dropping a thermal detonator down the garbage chute.

Once word came that Solo's carbonite slab had been delivered to Jabba's palace, Calrissian underwent a harrowing ordeal on the moon of Blimph in order to obtain a recommendation from Quaffug the Hutt for membership in the Hutt Guardsman's Guild. Adopting the name Tamtel Skreej, Calrissian infiltrated Jabba's palace to aid in Solo's rescue.

When he returned to the Rebel Alliance, Calrissian received a promotion to general, based largely on his Taanab victory three and a half years prior. As Gold Leader, Calrissian commanded all fighter groups in the Battle of Endor from the cockpit of the *Millennium Falcon*. He fired the shots that collapsed the second Death Star's reactor core, and was hailed a hero.

With the Empire in confusion, Calrissian turned his attention to freeing Cloud City, aided by a group he dubbed "Lando's Commandos." He briefly detoured to help Han Solo squash a Black Sun resurgence, but soon returned to the task at hand. It took months, but eventually the Empire was driven off Bespin and Lando Calrissian came back as Baron Administrator.

Approximately one year after Endor, Calrissian lost Cloud City the same way he'd won it—in a sabacc game. This time, Zorba the Hutt slithered away with the prize. Zorba soon surrendered ownership, but Calrissian gave control to the Ugnaughts and never again served as the city's administrator.

Instead he looked to other opportunities, including Hologram Fun World and the Nomad City mining complex on the planet Nkllon. Nomad City turned a profit, but Grand Admiral Thrawn hit it twice, once to steal mole miners and again to steal dolovite. The complex melted in Nkllon's hot sun, and even though the New Republic replaced most of his equipment, Calrissian lost the deed in yet another round of sabacc.

The next year, Calrissian reactivated his general's commission to fight the cloned Emperor. Following the cessation of hostilities, he helped Luke Skywalker search for Jedi candidates—resulting in a two-million-credit reward from a grateful Duchess. Calrissian invested the money in the spice mines of Kessel. He and Mara Jade also spent years in an on-again, off-again search for Talon Karrde's associate Jorj Car'das in the remote Kathol sector.

Calrissian helped Han Solo find his wife Leia Organa during the Death Seed outbreak in the Meridian sector, and uncovered the mystery of the Teljkon vagabond during the Black Fleet Crisis. In the midst of the Almanian "new rebellion," he returned to Smuggler's Run to help Han Solo, and nearly drowned when he ran afoul of still-angry crime lord Nandreeson. He then sold ownership of the Kessel mines to his old friend Nien Nunb and attempted an underground housing project on Coruscant called Dometown. During the Corellian insurrection, he drew upon his experiences in the Rafa system to unravel the mystery of Centerpoint Station.

He also embarked on a wife hunt that ended when he met Tendra Risant of Sacorria. In the years following the peace treaty between the New Republic and the Empire, Calrissian married Tendra and started a deep-atmosphere Corusca mining operation, *GemDiver Station*, above the gas giant Yavin. The income from *GemDiver* allowed him to open the SkyCenter Galleria on Bespin, which he sold for a huge profit and purchased a controlling interest in two Outer Rim worlds—inhabited Dubrillion and resource-rich Destrillion.

The operation ran well until the Yuuzhan Vong invaded the galaxy. Calrissian asked Han Solo and Chewbacca to make a run to Sernpidal, where Chewbacca died when the Yuuzhan Vong pulled a moon down on the planet. Shortly thereafter, Dubrillion fell to the enemy.

Calrissian bore so much guilt over Chewbacca's death that he refused to attend the Wookiee's funeral. More than a year later he helped Solo set up a Jedi safehouse inside the Maw black-hole cluster, and developed a specialized war droid designed to hunt and kill Yuuzhan Vong.

Lando Calrissian has dedicated most of his life to making amends—first for Han Solo's capture on Bespin, and later for Chewbacca's death at Sernpidal. Now that his investment empire lies in ruins, Calrissian has nothing left to lose.

GAERIEL CAPTISON

PRONUNCIATION
Gă'-rē-ĕl Kăp'-tĭ-sŏn
SPECIES
Human
SEX
Female
HAIR COLOR
Brown
EYE COLOR
One green, one gray
HEIGHT
1.55 meters
HOMEWORLD
Bakura

Gaeriel Captison was once the most prominent citizen on the remote planet Bakura. A lifelong politician, she was a devout follower of the religion known as the Cosmic Balance. Her faith shaped her every action, from her decisions as a leader to her near romance with the Jedi Knight Luke Skywalker.

Followers of the Cosmic Balance believe that affluence is always matched by poverty, happiness by despair. Those who wield excessive power, such as the Jedi, weaken others in the galaxy. On her sixteenth birthday Gaeriel received a white feather from her parents, a sign that she would go on to higher education and a career as a Bakuran Senator. As was required by equilibrium, her younger sister Ylanda received a golden bowl and immediately began a life of starvation and poverty.

Halfway through Gaeriel's four-year curriculum at the Bakur Senatorial Academy, the Empire annexed Bakura by force. Gaeriel's parents—members of the resistance—died in a shootout with stormtroopers. Despite the tragedy, Gaeriel completed her schooling and went on to a year of postgraduate work on Coruscant.

Upon her return she assumed a post in the Bakuran Senate, but had little influence over Bakuran affairs. Even her uncle Yeorg, Bakura's Prime Minister, paid fealty to Imperial Governor Wilek Nereus. It took an army of alien invaders—predating the Yuuzhan Vong by twenty-one years—to upset the status quo.

Just one month into Gaeriel's first term, a species of sharp-clawed saurians targeted Bakura with an overpowering war fleet. Known as the Ssi-ruuk, the aliens had built an empire in the Unknown Regions by sucking life-essences and trapping them in the power batteries of their monstrous machines.

Governor Nereus begged the Empire for help, but Palpatine had just perished aboard the second Death Star, so it was the Rebel Alliance that answered the call. In order to drive off the conquerors, both sides hammered out the first-ever truce between Imperial and Rebel forces.

Gaeriel took a close interest in Luke Skywalker, a member of the Rebel contingent and a self-proclaimed Jedi Knight. The Cosmic Balance viewed all Jedi as greedy scale-tippers, but Gaeriel found herself drawn to Luke despite her religious objections. Luke, bouncing back from the recent revelation that Leia was his sister, latched on to Gaeriel. He sensed her connection to the Force and wanted to forge another, more personal, connection.

In the end, their differences were too great. Although Luke's positive work during the Ssi-ruuk invasion brightened Gaeriel's opinion of the Jedi, her devotion to her homeworld ran too deep. They parted on friendly terms and would not cross paths again for fourteen years.

Bakura chose to join the New Republic. Pter Thanas, former commander of the Imperial garrison, left Imperial service and helped ease the planet's political transition. Gaeriel had never thought much of Thanas, but now she found herself drawn to him during her continued work in the Senate. Before long, the two were married.

Following her uncle Yeorg's retirement, Gaeriel ran for Prime Minister of Bakura and won. She used her new authority to construct four advanced warships—the *Watchkeeper*, *Sentinel*, *Defender*, and *Intruder*—as a preventive measure should the Ssi-ruuk ever return. Approximately eight years after Endor, Gaeriel and Pter had their first child, Malinza.

Malinza was only three when her father contracted Knowt's disease. Gaeriel neglected her reelection campaign in order to minister to Pter. She lost the election, and two days later she lost her husband.

Gaeriel retired, then, to be closer to her daughter. But more than a year later, Luke Skywalker returned to Bakura to ask a favor. The New Republic needed battleships to put down an insurrection in the Corellian system, and the *Intruder* and her sister vessels came equipped with anti-interdiction technology. The Bakuran fleet set out for Corellia under the command of Admiral Hortel Ossilege. Gaeriel, appointed plenipotentiary by the new Prime Minister, accompanied the fleet to speak for Bakura in matters of policy.

Above Centerpoint Station, the Bakuran fleet clashed with the armada of the Sacorrian Triad. The enemy's suicidal robot ramships collided with the *Intruder*, shredding her hull. On the crippled ship's bridge, Gaeriel and Admiral Ossilege—both critically wounded—prepped the *Intruder*'s self-destruct mechanism. When several Triad ships swooped in close like greedy scavengers, Gaeriel punched the button.

Her death brought about a great victory, but that provided little comfort to orphaned Malinza. A well-placed Bakuran family adopted the girl, and Malinza went on to accept a prodigy chair with the Bakuran National Symphony. Luke Skywalker, who felt protective toward Malinza and partly responsible for her mother's death, helped sponsor her education and visited her when he could. After his marriage, both he and his wife, Mara Jade, made the periodic trips to Bakura. Armed with the support of two great Jedi and her own natural gifts, Malinza Thanas must now decide how she will carry on her mother's legacy.

TYCHO CELCHU

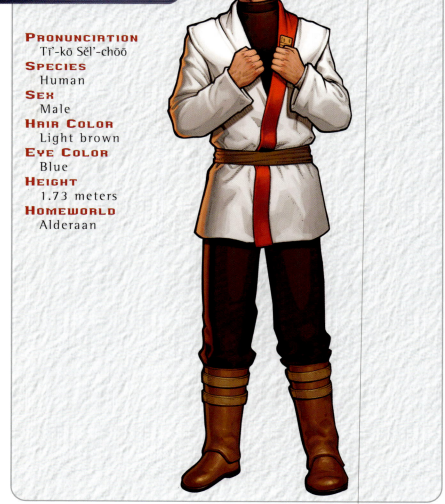

PRONUNCIATION
Tĭ'-kō Sĕl'-chōō
SPECIES
Human
SEX
Male
HAIR COLOR
Light brown
EYE COLOR
Blue
HEIGHT
1.73 meters
HOMEWORLD
Alderaan

Few men have more reason to hate the Empire than Tycho Celchu. And few men have more reason to resent the New Republic than Tycho Celchu. The Empire destroyed his homeworld, and the New Republic nearly destroyed his career.

Born on pacifistic Alderaan, Celchu enrolled in the Imperial Academy on Prefsbelt IV, bent on changing the military from within. He studied under Soontir Fel and graduated to a posting on the Star Destroyer *Accuser* as a TIE pilot. On his twenty-first birthday Celchu called home to his family, only to see the broadcast dissolve in static as Alderaan exploded under the Death Star's superlaser. The millions of Alderaanian casualties included Celchu's fiancée, Nyiestra.

Lieutenant Celchu deserted from Imperial service. It wasn't long before he became a member of Rogue Squadron, the elite X-wing group formed by Luke Skywalker and Wedge Antilles. *Captain* Celchu fought at Hoth and flew an A-wing into the belly of the second Death Star. He earned a third battle patch in combat against the Ssi-ruuk at Bakura.

Tycho's experience as an ex-Imperial came in handy when he infiltrated the TIE garrison on Cilpar. During this mission he met Winter, a fellow Alderaanian and New Republic operative.

A year after the Tatooine mission, Captain Celchu flew a TIE fighter on a reconnaissance and infiltration mission to enemy-held Coruscant. Ysanne Isard captured him, and for months Celchu suffered inside the *Lusankya* prison, though Isard never succeeded in breaking her captive. His jailers then transferred him to a facility on Akrit'tar, from which he escaped back to the New Republic.

But no one in the New Republic trusted Celchu. His fellow officers suspected he'd been brainwashed into becoming a sleeper agent. Wedge Antilles was one of the few who fought for Celchu, installing him as executive officer of Rogue Squadron.

During the capture of Coruscant, Rogue pilot Corran Horn crashed his starfighter and apparently died. Looking to assign blame, prosecutors accused Celchu of murder and put him through a humiliating courtroom trial. When Horn escaped from the *Lusankya* prison where he'd been held by Isard, Celchu received an acquittal and an official apology.

After the Bacta War, Celchu took over as Rogue Leader. He infiltrated Admiral Krennel's forces during Isard's return and earned a promotion to colonel after the resurrected Emperor's campaign. Colonel Celchu led the Rogues against the pirate Leonia Tavira and accompanied Wedge on a mission to Adumar.

Just after the Almanian crisis, Tycho married Winter. Two years later he retired from the military after nearly twenty years of active flight duty.

CHEWBACCA

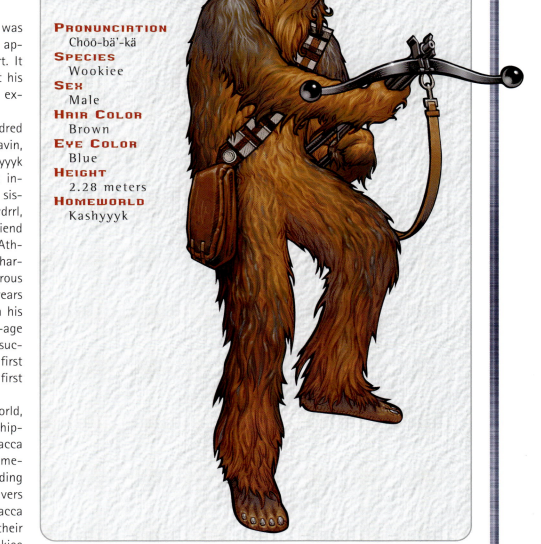

PRONUNCIATION
Chōō-bä'-kä
SPECIES
Wookiee
SEX
Male
HAIR COLOR
Brown
EYE COLOR
Blue
HEIGHT
2.28 meters
HOMEWORLD
Kashyyyk

Everything about Chewbacca was larger than life—his size, his appetite, his courage, his heart. It took a falling moon to snuff out his life, and not even a moon could extinguish his legend.

Born approximately two hundred years before the Battle of Yavin, Chewbacca grew up on Kashyyyk among an extended family that included his father Attichitcuk, his sister Kallabow, and his cousins Jowdrrl, Dryanta, and Shoran. His best friend was the great hunter Salporin. Athletic and popular, Chewbacca harvested the strands of the carnivorous syren plant at age eleven. Two years later, Attichitcuk took his son on his hrrtayyk, the Wookiee coming-of-age ceremony. During Chewbacca's successful hrrtayyk, he built his first bowcaster and used it to kill his first katarn in the Well of the Dead.

Kashyyyk, a seldom-visited world, nevertheless received regular shipments of Republic cargo. Chewbacca learned piloting and starship mechanics at the Rwookrrorro landing pads. Once, when Trandoshan slavers attacked his home city, Chewbacca ripped the leader's arms from their sockets, saving a beautiful Wookiee named Mallatobuck.

At the age of fifty, Chewbacca succumbed to the wanderlust of Wookiee adolescence. He left Kashyyyk and spent long decades roaming the galaxy. The Republic was thriving, and there were plenty of opportunities for a technically skilled Wookiee.

He returned to Kashyyyk occasionally to visit his father and to drop in on the lovely Mallatobuck. On one such stopover, Tojjevvuk, an albino who wanted Malla for himself, ambushed Chewbacca. Their fight spilled over into the lowest levels of the shadow forest, where predators devoured the white-furred Wookiee. Tojjevvuk's father swore vengeance on his son's killer.

Chewbacca went back out into the galaxy, no longer making return visits to Kashyyyk, in order to elude his death mark. Members of Tojjevvuk's clan randomly made attempts on his life, and the rise of the Empire made it difficult for a free Wookiee to travel the space lanes. On one occasion Tojjevvuk's clan arranged for Chewbacca's capture by Trandoshans, but he rallied the other Wookiee captives and escaped from the slave ship. Chewbacca dismembered the head slaver, who survived to regenerate his limbs years later.

Ten years before the Battle of Yavin, the Imperials captured Chewbacca. He escaped and vowed to keep a low profile. But when Wookiee children from several Rwookrrorro clans fell into the claws of slavers half a decade later, Chewbacca risked everything to save them. Exposing himself to vacuum, he transferred the children to a getaway ship, leaving himself behind aboard the slaver vessel. An Imperial TIE pilot, Lieutenant Han Solo, discovered the injured Wookiee slumped in a cockpit chair.

Again a prisoner of the Empire, Chewbacca was transferred to a work detail building a new wing for Coruscant's Imperial Hall of Heroes. His overseer, Commander Nyklas, began beating the Wookiee with a force whip. Lieutenant Solo stepped in and saved Chewbacca. For his insubordination and the loss of Imperial property—one escaped Wookiee slave—Solo was kicked out of the Imperial Navy.

According to Wookiee custom, Chewbacca now owed Han Solo a life debt for saving him from certain death. More than just a pledge to "return the favor," this life debt was meant to extend until the end of Solo's days. Bound by honor, Chewbacca followed Solo to Devaron, where the human eventually accepted him as his partner. It helped that Solo already understood the Shyriiwook language, and soon Han Solo and "Chewie" were running spice for the Desilijic Hutts on Nar Shaddaa.

Chewbacca had nearly two centuries of life experience under his bandoleer and acted as the voice of reason, trying to keep his partner out of suicidal scrapes. Solo joked about his partner's age, but considered Chewie his truest friend. The two had many adventures over the next few years in their vessel, the *Bria*, once defeating a band of Zygerrian pirates and—at Chewbacca's insistence—giving the ship's cargo to the freed slaves.

Solo won the freighter *Millennium Falcon* in a sabacc game, and the two partners headed for the Corporate Sector to make their fortune. On their way they stopped off at Kashyyyk for Chewbacca's first visit home in decades. Because of Chewbacca's selfless rescue of the Wookiee children from slavers, Tojjevvuk's father made the unprecedented move of calling off his death mark. Chewbacca killed a quillarat for the lovely Mallatobuck and she ate from it, signifying their love. The two then married.

But a Wookiee life debt takes precedence even over familial bonds. Chewbacca had no choice but to follow Solo on his further adventures. In the Corporate Sector, Solo saved his partner from incarceration in the Stars' End penitentiary. The pair battled slavers on Ammuud and treasure seekers on Dellalt. When they returned, Chewbacca roared with pride upon learning that Malla had given birth to a son, Lumpawarrump.

Shortly before the Battle of Yavin, Chewbacca ran into Hronk, a member of Tojjevvuk's clan still stubbornly clinging to his father's revoked vengeance pact. Chewie helped Hronk escape from an Imperial prison under the nose of Imperial Captain Quirt, earning forgiveness from the last holdout of a once-hostile clan.

Chewbacca, concerned for his partner's well-being after they lost Jabba's spice cargo, introduced Han to Obi-Wan Kenobi and Luke Skywalker to discuss booking a lucrative charter flight to Alderaan. Chewbacca also convinced Solo to turn around at Yavin and head back into the Death Star brawl to save Luke Skywalker's life.

After the Death Star's destruction, Chewie stuck with his partner, sometimes working with the Alliance and sometimes not. During an attack on one of the Alliance's temporary bases, Chewbacca nearly died when Wedge Antilles took off in his airspeeder while Chewie was still dangling from the ventral maintenance bay. Chewbacca returned to Kashyyyk

when he could, most notably for the Lifeday celebration.

Chewbacca helped destroy the probe droid that uncovered Echo Base on Hoth, and endured torture in a Cloud City holding cell. Han Solo's imprisonment in carbonite, however, was far worse than any torture. With the sacred life debt hanging in the balance, he worked with Lando Calrissian to track down Han, month after agonizing month. To rescue his friend from Jabba's palace, Chewbacca even wore chains and a shackle, a hated indignity he tolerated only to achieve his greater goal. Chewbacca fought alongside his fellow forest warriors, the Ewoks, at Endor, helped save Bakura from invasion by the Ssi-ruuk, and battled Nagai slavers on his homeworld.

When Han Solo and Leia Organa had children of their own, Chewbacca became unofficial guardian of Jacen, Jaina, and Anakin Solo. He rescued Jacen and Jaina when they became lost in the depths of Coruscant,

and when all three children were stolen from his care on Munto Codru he partnered with Leia to rescue them from Lord Hethrir.

During the Black Fleet Crisis, Chewbacca returned to Kashyyyk to participate in Lumpawarrump's hrrtayyk. He was dismayed to discover that his son was apathetic, careless, and afraid to hunt the katarn in the Well of the Dead. He blamed himself for spending so much time away from Kashyyyk. When Chewbacca heard that Han Solo had been captured by the Yevetha, he rushed to the rescue, reluctantly taking Lumpawarrump along.

Together with a Wookiee strike team, father and son boarded the Super Star Destroyer *Pride of Yevetha* and freed Han from the brig. Chewbacca watched with pride as his son faced down dozens of warriors with true Wookiee ferocity. The rescue served as Lumpawarrump's hrrtayyk, and he adopted a new name, Lumpawaroo.

Chewbacca had another reason to celebrate when his sister Kallabow's son, Lowbacca, enrolled in Luke Skywalker's Jedi academy. Knowing how difficult it was for a Wookiee to communicate among Basic speakers, Chewie built Em Teedee, a miniaturized translator droid his nephew could wear on his belt.

At the onset of the Yuuzhan Vong invasion, Han Solo and Chewbacca made a run to Sernpidal as a favor for Lando Calrissian. They had no way of knowing that the Yuuzhan Vong had already targeted the world for destruction. As Chewbacca loaded refugees aboard the *Millennium Falcon*, Sernpidal's moon—pulled down by a Yuuzhan Vong gravity weapon—dipped perilously low in the sky. Chewbacca's last act was to throw Anakin Solo into the *Falcon*. The ship sped away from Sernpidal as the atmosphere ignited. The moon slammed into the planet—but Chewbacca stood unbowed, his final breath a hoarse roar of challenge.

ADMIRAL DAALA

While enemies such as Grand Admiral Thrawn waged war with the gentility of a dejarik player, Daala set upon her targets with the fury of a wounded nek. Ferocious and unpredictable, she was one of the most dangerous opponents the New Republic ever faced.

Daala was born in the wrong era. Under the Old Republic her strategic gifts would have been nurtured, and her destructiveness tempered. But Emperor Palpatine ushered in a culture of intolerance. Women were no longer promoted within the ranks of the Imperial military, and though Daala was accepted to the prestigious Caridan Academy, she seldom received recognition for her accomplishments. The intense training at Carida helped her bury the memories of Liegeus Vorn, her ex-lover, whom she had abandoned in order to pursue her dream.

Upon graduation, she was given rudimentary administrative assignments. Out of frustration, Daala created a false computer persona and competed in strategic games, besting Carida's top instructors. Moff Tarkin uncovered Daala's true identity and took her under his wing—both as a military protégée and as something more personal. Despite Tarkin's prior marriage to a woman of the Motti family, Daala became his lover.

Tarkin promoted Daala to the rank of admiral—an unofficial promotion outside of Coruscant's naval hierarchy, but a legitimate one among Tarkin's forces in the Outer Rim. She assumed command of four new Imperial Star Destroyers—the *Hydra*, *Basilisk*, *Manticore*, and her flagship, the *Gorgon*.

PRONUNCIATION
Dā'-lä
SPECIES
Human
SEX
Female
HAIR COLOR
Copper
EYE COLOR
Green
HEIGHT
1.73 meters
HOMEWORLD
Unknown

She expressed her thirst to crush the Rebel resistance, but Tarkin ordered Daala to guard his secret weapons research facility, Maw Installation, hidden within the Maw black-hole cluster near Kessel. There, the Empire's top scientists developed a working prototype for the Death Star battle station. Just before departing for the finished Death Star, Tarkin ordered Daala to maintain comm silence inside the Maw, and wait for his return.

Unfortunately, Tarkin died at Yavin. Daala's four Star Destroyers waited at Maw Installation for eleven excruciating years, until at last an Imperial shuttle arrived from the outside. But Daala discovered it was carrying only the Kessel fugitives Han Solo, Chewbacca, and Kyp Durron. From them, she learned of Tarkin's death and the Empire's defeat at Yavin. When Solo stole Maw Installation's latest superweapon—the Sun Crusher—and destroyed her Star Destroyer *Hydra*,

Daala chose to abandon her post and begin striking out at the New Republic.

Daala struck at Dantooine and Mon Calamari, but lost two more Star Destroyers in the fierce fighting. Finally, only the *Gorgon* remained. The ship was believed to have been destroyed during the climactic battle to wipe out Maw Installation, but the damaged *Gorgon* limped to High Admiral Teradoc's warlord kingdom in the Deep Core.

Daala tried to reason with the squabbling Imperial warlords, but they seemed more threatened by each other than by the New Republic. Disgusted, she murdered thirteen of the strongest warlords and unified their military forces under her rule. With Vice Admiral Gilad Pellaeon as her second in command and the Super Star Destroyer *Knight Hammer* as her flagship, she executed a terror strike on the Jedi academy at Yavin 4.

The battle went poorly, and sabotage claimed the *Knight Hammer*.

Daala barely escaped with her life. In the aftermath of the latest military fiasco, she transferred all her authority to Pellaeon, then retired to Pedducis Chorios in the Meridian sector. There, she became president of a group of settlers seeking to buy land from a local chieftain.

A year passed, and Daala ignored the activities of Pellaeon's Empire. Then she learned that Moff Getelles, a corrupt Imperial bureaucrat, had masterminded an outbreak of the Death Seed plague in an attempt to control the Meridian sector. Sickened by the thought of an Imperial who would resort to such cowardice, she came out of retirement to help defeat Getelles's forces in the Battle of Nam Chorios. She also reunited with her long-lost lover, Liegeus Vorn.

Grateful for her help, the New Republic made the mistake of letting Daala leave in peace. But now that she had tasted unequivocal victory, she wanted more of the same. She returned to the Deep Core and be-

came the leader of the region's "replacement warlords"—the successors to the thirteen she had murdered more than a year prior. Daala built up the military forces of the Deep Core warlords and received a significant boost when defectors arrived from the Imperial Black Fleet following the conclusion of the Yevethan crisis.

Just prior to the Corellian insurrection, Daala took a huge gamble by striking at neighboring New Republic Core Worlds from her base in the Deep Core. General Garm Bel Iblis led the fleet that opposed her. In the final battle of the campaign, Bel Iblis attempted to trap Daala with a pair of CC-7700 gravity-well frigates. Rather than surrender her ships, she ordered one of them to ram the closest CC-7700, collapsing the gravity cone that prevented her escape. Her damaged flagship *Scylla* then made a blind jump to hyperspace. So far Daala has not returned, but New Republic Intelligence refuses to remove her name from its threat board.

JORI AND GAV DARAGON

Jori and Gav Daragon have been dead five thousand years, but ripples from the events they set in motion still echo today. Had they not led the Sith Empire into war against the Republic, the galaxy might have been spared the horrors of Darth Bane, Darth Maul, and Darth Vader.

During the Daragons' era, the Republic encompassed only a fraction of its current expanse. The Slice between the Corellian Run and the Perlemian Trade Route grew wild out toward the Rim, and most of the galaxy outside the Slice remained unexplored. Jori Daragon and her brother Gav worked as hyperspace trailblazers, seeking safe passages through the brier patch of hyperspace in their ship the *Starbreaker 12.*

The two operated out of the seven-planet Koros system, just inside the Deep Core from Coruscant. Their parents, Hok and Timar, had died running cargo to the outlying planet Kirrek during the Koros Unification Wars. Jori and Gav were forced to sell their home in Cinnagar on Koros Major when hyperspace mapping proved less lucrative than they'd hoped. Soon they were deeply in debt to Aarrba the Hutt, owner of Aarrba's Repair Dock.

Desperate for one big score, Jori and Gav leapt the *Starbreaker 12* blindly into hyperspace. Both siblings had a minor degree of Force attunement, despite their lack of Jedi training, and this sensitivity may have influenced their ultimate destination. The new hyperspace route—now known as the Daragon Trail—took them from Koros Major to Korriban, deep in the Sith Empire beyond the Perlemian Trade Route.

PRONUNCIATION
Jô'-rē and Găv Dă'-rä-gŏn
SPECIES
Human
SEX
Female/Male
HAIR COLOR
Brown/Black
EYE COLOR
Blue/Blue
HEIGHT
1.6 meters/1.8 meters
HOMEWORLD
Koros Major

The Daragons tried to establish trade with the Sith natives and their Force-wielding Lords, but were captured and imprisoned. Sith Lord Naga Sadow secretly freed them, hiding them in his private fortress, then used their "escape" as a tool to fan Sith fears of a Republic invasion. Sadow gathered a vast war fleet and began indoctrinating Gav as his dark-side protégé.

Jori, meanwhile, fled back to the Koros system—inadvertently leading the Sith armada straight to her homeworld. She bravely rallied the armies of Empress Teta for a last-ditch counterattack. Hundreds of thousands of Republic citizens lost their lives in the battle, including Aarrba the Hutt.

Gav, fighting Naga Sadow's dark influence, renounced his position as commander of the Sith fleet. He led Republic forces to the Sith Lord's hiding place above the unstable supergiant Primus Goluud. In the end, Naga Sadow tricked his protégé one last time. A blistering stellar flare incinerated Gav Daragon. After her bitter victory, Jori Daragon returned to the family trade as the new proprietor of Aarrba's Repair Dock.

GAVIN DARKLIGHTER

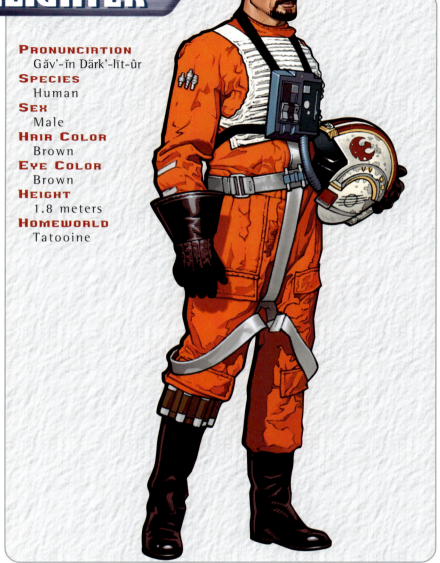

PRONUNCIATION
Găv'-ĭn Därk'-līt-ûr
SPECIES
Human
SEX
Male
HAIR COLOR
Brown
EYE COLOR
Brown
HEIGHT
1.8 meters
HOMEWORLD
Tatooine

Just ten years old when his cousin Biggs fought alongside Luke Skywalker and died a Rebel martyr, Gavin Darklighter heard tales of Biggs's heroism and dreamed of forging a similar path away from the dry sands of Tatooine.

His father Jula—brother of Biggs's father Huff—and mother Silya provided a happy home for their son on their moisture farm, but they never held him back in his strivings for a life offworld. Just as Luke Skywalker had done, Gavin learned piloting behind the yoke of a T-16 skyhopper and moved straight from the bush leagues into the big leagues.

Two and a half years after the Battle of Endor, Commander Wedge Antilles recommended Gavin's recruitment into the rebuilt Rogue Squadron. Although his simulator scores were on par with those of the other squadron members, Gavin knew he had made the cut because of Biggs's reputation—he was only sixteen, and he hadn't even attended the Academy. The sense of having something to prove always pushed Gavin to do his best.

Commander Antilles paired Gavin with Riv Shiel, a Shistavanen Wolfman. Gavin received his own X-wing and named his R2 unit Jawaswag in honor of his Tatooine heritage. The squadron moved to Talasea, and Gavin took a blaster bolt to the abdomen when Imperial stormtroopers invaded the base. A long stint in a bacta tank taught him the value of caution.

Later, during Rogue Squadron's infiltration of enemy-held Coruscant, Gavin went undercover to the "Invisible Sector" ghetto of Imperial City. Many species in the sector, responding to Imperial kidnappings of their kind, had formed the antihuman Alien Combine. When Gavin refused the advances of a beautiful black-and-white-furred Bothan named Asyr Sei'lar, the Combine labeled him a bigot and prepared to execute him.

Gavin escaped when Imperial raiders broke up the Combine's party. Asyr Sei'lar escaped, too, and after the New Republic captured Coruscant—thanks to Gavin's idea of creating a thunderstorm to take down the planetary shields—Asyr joined Rogue Squadron.

Gavin and Asyr grew very close, despite their differences and intolerance from some Bothans—particularly Councilor Borsk Fey'lya. Fey'lya saw Asyr as a potential hero to the Bothan people and didn't want her to sully that image.

While preparing for the Bacta War, Gavin returned to Tatooine to obtain a weapons cache from his uncle Huff. Later, he helped defend a colony on frozen Halanit from attack by Ysanne Isard. He fought alongside the other Rogues during the Thrawn crisis, and when his R2 unit fought off a band of larcenous Jawas, a proud Gavin changed the droid's name from Jawaswag to Toughcatch.

Around the time of the return of Isard, Gavin and Asyr finalized their plans to marry and adopt a Bothan child. Borsk Fey'lya warned Asyr he would do everything in his power to oppose such a union. At Corvis Minor, Imperial forces ambushed Rogue Squadron; Asyr apparently died in the crossfire. Fortunately, Booster Terrik recovered her from the battle scene and allowed her to start a new life as an undercover operative working to change Bothan society from within.

Gavin knew nothing of Asyr's survival. He mourned her, then took steps to ground his life. He began proceedings to adopt two orphan boys who lived near the Rogue Squadron docking bay on Coruscant, and fell in love with the social worker handling the adoption case, Sera Faleur. The two of them were married two years later.

Soon they had a girl of their own, then a boy, then another girl. Gavin continued with Rogue Squadron and spent much of his downtime visiting his wife's homeworld of Chandrila. When his sister's husband died in the Black Fleet Crisis, Gavin welcomed her and her children into his home.

General Antilles and Colonel Celchu retired in the wake of the Imperial–New Republic peace treaty. They turned command of Rogue Squadron over to Gavin and gave him a silver ring bearing the squadron crest. He also received a promotion to colonel, and the honored call sign of Rogue Leader.

With the Yuuzhan Vong invasion, Rogue Squadron suffered serious losses against enemy coralskippers. Gavin filled his roster with new pilots, including young Jaina Solo—who was exactly the same age Gavin had been when he first joined the Rogues. Gavin led Rogue Squadron in battle against the Yuuzhan Vong at Dantooine and Ithor. A squadron of Chiss clawcraft helped out at Ithor, and squadron leader Jagged Fel agreed to remain behind and assist the Rogues. However, their combined efforts failed to save Kalarba from destruction, and Jaina Solo suffered injuries that forced her to take medical leave from Rogue Squadron.

After the Battle of Duro, in light of Warmaster Tsavong Lah's decree that all Jedi be turned over to the Yuuzhan Vong, political pressure mounted on Gavin to leave the Force-strong Jaina out of his squadron. Gavin suggested that she extend her leave of absence indefinitely, but eventually reconsidered. He teamed with Jaina, Kyp Durron, and the legendary Wedge Antilles to destroy a supposed Yuuzhan Vong superweapon created from the remains of the shattered planet Sernpidal.

His squadron helped evacuate Coruscant ahead of the enemy's invasion fleet, and as the New Republic's situation looks more dire than ever, Gavin Darklighter and Rogue Squadron have many battles ahead of them.

Dengar

Not many humans approaching sixty continue working the bounty hunting trade. Those who haven't retired are usually dead.

Dengar is neither retired nor deceased. He has pursued his deadly career for five decades, beginning when he was a young swoop racer on Corellia. Corellian by birth, Dengar had repaired swoops with his father, and translated that familiarity into a spot on the prestigious Ferini racing team. He showed great promise until an illegal race against Han Solo shattered his hopes for the future.

Jockeying for position in a race through Corellia's Agrilat swamps, Dengar smashed into Solo's main repulsor fin. He crashed, and a crystal spike speared his skull. He survived, but his participation in the illegal race marked the end of his professional career.

The Empire saw value in the crippled Corellian. Imperial surgeons removed portions of Dengar's brain and implanted an augmented neurosystem. They gave him cybernetic eyes and ears and burned every emotion from his psyche. Every emotion, that is, except rage—and he had plenty of rage.

In exchange for his "gifts," Dengar worked for the Empire as an assassin. He scored kill after kill, each time fantasizing that it was Solo in his crosshairs. For a time he also worked as a gladiator in the pits of Loovria. Dengar's vessel, a Corellian Jumpmaster 5000 he called the *Punishing One*, became a symbol of terror.

The price Jabba the Hutt placed on Solo's head prompted Dengar to branch out from assassinations into bounty hunting. Although he never joined the Bounty Hunters' Guild, he

PRONUNCIATION
Dĕn'-gär
SPECIES
Human
SEX
Male
HAIR COLOR
Unknown
EYE COLOR
Unknown
HEIGHT
1.8 meters
HOMEWORLD
Corellia

teamed with Bossk and IG-88 to recover the Yavin Vassilika on behalf of Malta the Hutt. After the Battle of Yavin, Dengar ran a job for Jabba that took him from Kubindi to Togoria in search of Solo.

Dengar claimed it was the Empire's order to assassinate the Holy Children of Asrat that convinced him to leave Imperial service. Whether this is true or not, Dengar began going after Imperial targets, earning himself the nickname "Payback."

Teaming up with Boba Fett and other hunters, he captured Han Solo at Hoth, but Solo and the Wookiee escaped during their transfer to Ord Mantell.

Dengar stepped up his anti-Empire activities, killing COMPNOR General Sinick Kritkeen on Aruza and rescuing a beautiful Aruzan woman named Manaroo. Several more high-profile kills convinced a Rebel Alliance agent of Dengar's sincerity. She put him in touch with other Rebels, who soon gave him the coordinates for the main Alliance base—ironically the same place where he'd snatched Solo once before. In the *Punishing One* Dengar set out for the Hoth system.

In truth Dengar didn't care for Rebel ideology; he simply knew this was his best chance to get close to Han Solo. When he arrived, however, the Battle of Hoth was already in full swing. A Star Destroyer seized Dengar's ship, and only the indulgence of Lord Vader saved Dengar from execution for treason.

Given another chance, Dengar tracked Solo's ship to Cloud City, where Boba Fett beat him to the prize. But Dengar discovered the Aruzan woman Manaroo dancing in a Bespin casino. He escaped with her when the city fell under Imperial control, and she used a cybernetic link called an Attanni to restore many of Dengar's lost emotions. The two fell deeply in love.

On Mandalore, supercommando Fenn Shysa captured Dengar, and he barely escaped. On the moon of Blimph, Dengar hunted Lando Calrissian for Quaffug the Hutt, but failed to collect any bounty. Eventually Dengar and Manaroo arrived on Tatooine, where Dengar went to Jabba's palace for work. But Manaroo was enslaved by the Hutt as a dancer. Since Jabba's dancers typically had the life expectancy of a sand fly, Dengar began plotting his employer's demise. Jabba, however, foresaw Dengar's betrayal and staked the bounty hunter out in the desert to die.

Dengar survived, but Jabba didn't return from his trip to the Great Pit of Carkoon. Surveying the aftermath of the battle, Dengar and Manaroo discovered a survivor—Boba Fett, fresh from his ordeal in the Sarlacc. Dengar nursed Fett back to health and Fett, in turn, agreed to a partnership.

Fett wasted no time, going after the powerful industrialist Kuat of Kuat. Manaroo, meanwhile, met with the gambler Drawmas Sma'Da and placed a bet on Dengar's likelihood for survival. The odds against anyone surviving in Fett's company were so great that Manaroo earned a staggering payout when the adventure ended. Flush with success, Dengar and Manaroo married.

Dengar continued his partnership with Fett for years. Lesser bounty hunters tried to trade off his fame, including the hunter Gunner Groth, who posed as Dengar but was killed by Mara Jade on Rishi. The Fett–Dengar partnership came to an end during the cloned Emperor's return. The two tried to capture Han Solo on Nar Shaddaa and failed; a second attempt ended with Fett's *Slave II* bouncing off Byss's planetary shields. Dengar proclaimed that he would never work with Fett again.

As an independent, Dengar freelanced for Grappa the Hutt during the brief reign of the Imperial Interim Ruling Council. More than a decade later, he joined in the quest for the Bornan Thul bounty during the Diversity Alliance crisis. His actions brought him face-to-face with Jacen and Jaina Solo, the children of his old enemy.

Dengar's whereabouts during the Yuuzhan Vong invasion are not currently known. The war, however, has provided plenty of hunt opportunities for those with experience.

GENERAL JAN DODONNA

PRONUNCIATION

PRONUNCIATION
Jăn Dō-dä'-nä
SPECIES
Human
SEX
Male
HAIR COLOR
Gray
EYE COLOR
Unknown
HEIGHT
1.82 meters
HOMEWORLD
Commenor

"To swat a millfly," they say, "use a shovel." Jan Dodonna may be the human equivalent of the millfly, so strong is his will to live. Just when the Empire thought it had broken him, he escaped; just when the Alliance thought it had buried him, he returned to launch a second career.

Dodonna's military service stretches back to the Old Republic. During the Stark Hyperspace Conflict he served as a lieutenant in the Republic police forces, crewing aboard the cruiser *Ardent IV*. Later he became the captain of one of the Republic's first Star Destroyers. Dodonna and his fellow officer Adar Tallon developed revolutionary starfighter and siege tactics that set them on their way to becoming military legends.

After the rise of the Empire, Dodonna retired rather than serve a corrupt regime. But he refused to speak ill of the Empire, still conducting himself as a loyal soldier. The Emperor, in turn, bestowed upon Dodonna his own moon—Brelor, orbiting the planet Commenor.

Dodonna spent years at his estate there, raising his young son Vrad. He stubbornly refused Mon Mothma's overtures to join her resistance movement, even as he watched the Empire use his textbook tactics to commit an ever-growing number of atrocities. But COMPNOR assassins decided that a *dead* hero presented less risk to Imperial security. Mon Mothma sent a messenger to warn him, and though the general scoffed at first, he changed his mind when assassins assaulted his home. Dodonna fled, and joined the Rebellion.

Mon Mothma placed General Dodonna in charge of all starfighter operations. Dodonna's son Vrad became one of the Rebels' most promising young pilots. With Walex Blissex, Dodonna designed the A-wing starfighter by modifying the existing R-22 Spearhead into a fast, agile interceptor. The first prototypes saw use just before the Battle of Yavin. Dodonna also developed the battle analysis computer, though it would be years before the complex device was employed aboard Rebel warships.

Dodonna was also the officer in charge of the Alliance's ground HQ, and he frequently moved the base to avoid Imperial detection. The various command locations included Chrellis, Briggia, Orion IV, Dantooine, and the jungle moon of Yavin 4.

When Princess Leia escaped from the Death Star with the battle station's schematics, it was General Dodonna who discovered the station's sole weakness. He planned the X-wing and Y-wing assault that beat impossible odds and destroyed the Death Star.

Following that victory, the Rebels scrambled to evacuate their Yavin headquarters. However, before the command staff could leave, Imperial Interdictor cruisers blockaded the system. Dodonna maintained the besieged base for six months until Darth Vader moved to crush the Yavin Rebels with his Super Star Destroyer *Executor*. Dodonna's son Vrad volunteered to fly against the Destroyer carrying a shield-draining power gem, but in truth, he didn't have the nerve. Broken by the pressure of living up to his famous father, Vrad planned to bargain with the Empire, in return for his life. Ultimately, however, his cowardice shamed him, and Vrad Dodonna died in a suicide strike that temporarily disabled the *Executor*.

With the base in full evacuation mode, Jan Dodonna received word of his son's death. Consumed by despair, the general felt he had no reason to live. He rigged several of the Massassi temples with explosives, and personally triggered the blast, wiping out a wave of TIE bombers and buy-ing the evacuees more time. Following the escape into hyperspace, the Rebel Alliance held a memorial service for Dodonna aboard the Mon Calamari cruiser *Independence*, and named an assault frigate in his honor.

But Jan Dodonna had not died. Imperial search teams found him buried beneath a pile of rubble. After extensive bacta treatments, he was transferred to the top-secret prison *Lusankya*. Although Dodonna believed he'd been thrown into some Outer Rim hellhole, the *Lusankya* was actually a Super Star Destroyer buried beneath the surface of Coruscant. Despite his frailty, Dodonna emerged as the leader of the *Lusankya* prisoners, and a burly inmate named Urlor Sette acted as his bodyguard.

Under the watchful eye of Ysanne Isard, Dodonna rotted in the bowels of the *Lusankya* for seven years before Isard threw Rogue Squadron pilot Corran Horn in with the others. With Dodonna's help, Horn became the first ever to break out of prison, and though he had the opportunity, Dodonna refused to accompany Horn, knowing that the other prisoners would suffer if he left.

Her cover blown, Isard moved the *Lusankya* and its prisoners to Thyferra, where Rogue Squadron disabled and seized the Destroyer. But by the time of the raid, Dodonna and the others had already been transferred. Isard gave her clone the responsibility of hiding the prisoners, but the twin Isard betrayed her, moving them to Ciutric and allying with Admiral Krennel. Thus, the *real* Isard helped Rogue Squadron free Dodonna's crew from a penitentiary on Ciutric following the Thrawn campaign.

Dodonna got back to work as if he had never left. Together with other "old-timers" such as Yavin's Commander Vanden Willard and his lifelong friend Adar Tallon, Dodonna formed an advisory group jokingly called the "Gray Cadre."

After the Gray Cadre helped topple the resurrected Emperor, General Dodonna went into retirement on New Alderaan. Eventually he passed away, leaving behind a lifelong legacy stretching from the Old Republic to the New.

Count Dooku

PRONUNCIATION
Dōō'-kōō
SPECIES
Human
SEX
Male
HAIR COLOR
White
EYE COLOR
Brown
HEIGHT
1.93 meters
HOMEWORLD
Unknown

Bronzium busts of many great Jedi Masters line the walls of the Jedi Temple's Archives Room. Of these Masters, twenty abandoned their lives of service to walk other paths. Count Dooku was by far the most tragic, for in leaving the Jedi Order he joined the ranks of the Sith.

Although he never sat on the Jedi Council, Dooku earned the respect of his peers through his expertise as a lightsaber instructor and his principled stand on government. Dooku believed that the Republic had grown corrupt, and that the Jedi should no longer serve such a rotten system. Many on the Council sympathized, but argued that to cut ties with the Republic would be to abandon the citizens they'd sworn to protect.

After the Battle of Naboo, Dooku announced his resignation from the Jedi Order, then disappeared. None of his fellow Jedi knew where he'd gone.

Dooku had begun training with Darth Sidious. He'd come to believe that through the dark side, he could shape the galactic order to fit his vision. Sidious, having just lost Darth Maul, knew he didn't have the time to train a new Sith apprentice from infancy, and was happy to have snared such a venerable Jedi.

Renamed Darth Tyranus in the Sith tradition, Count Dooku recruited the bounty hunter Jango Fett to serve as the template for a secret clone army that would be grown on the planet Kamino. He began stirring up anti-Republic sentiment among the outlying systems. Then, Dooku eventually came out of his self-imposed exile. Alleging that Supreme Chancellor Palpatine had done little to curb governmental corruption, Dooku called for systems to create a republic of their own design. Nearly two hundred systems walked out to join him. The Republic, protesting the illegality of the movement, began what would become a two-year debate over the legitimacy of the Confederacy of Independent Systems.

When terrorist bombings began plaguing Coruscant, many Senators blamed the secessionists and debated creating a standing military force. Meanwhile, as the Republic struggled with the concept of raising an army, Dooku simply bought one. He met with representatives from the Trade Federation, Commerce Guild, Inter-Galatic Banking Clan, Techno Union, and Corporate Alliance, promising economic concessions that would line their pockets. In exchange he received their war machines.

Obi-Wan Kenobi, Anakin Skywalker, and Padmé Amidala discovered Dooku's operation on Geonosis. The Count failed in his attempts to kill them, and fled Geonosis—but not before facing his former Master Yoda in a test of lightsabers. His loss to Yoda was of little consequence, for Dooku escaped to his true Master, Darth Sidious.

DROMA

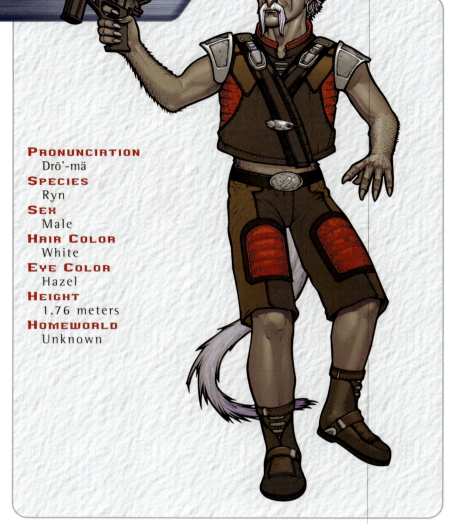

Droma's natural empathy helps him make his way through life, and it helped Han Solo conquer the survivor's guilt that crippled him following the death of Chewbacca.

Droma's species, the Ryn, are wanderers without a world of their own. Some say they descended from a traveling tribe of ten thousand musicians; others claim their ancestors were soldiers who mobilized and never returned home. The nomadic Ryn became fortune-tellers and musicians, whistling melodies through their perforated beaks. But whispered innuendo followed the Ryn from planet to planet. To many they were thieves, swindlers, and child-snatchers.

Droma worked as a pilot and scout in the Corporate Sector, contributing to the support of his large extended family. Shortly after the initial Yuuzhan Vong invasion, a Ryn caravan left the Corporate Sector for the Lesser Plooriod Cluster. The convoy scattered when it was hit by an element of the Yuuzhan Vong's Ithor attack force.

Droma's family ended up on the *Jubilee Wheel*, a space station orbiting Ord Mantell, where they were again caught flat-footed when the Yuuzhan Vong attacked. Droma escaped with help from Han Solo, while the other Ryn fled toward Gyndine.

Determined to locate his family, Droma parted ways with Solo. But fate threw the two together again aboard the starliner *Queen of Empire*.

Soon thereafter they were forced to guard two enemy defectors—Yuuzhan Vong priestess Elan and her "familiar," Vergere. They lost the defectors, recovered them, then barely escaped with their lives when Elan proved to be a double agent.

PRONUNCIATION
Drō'-mä
SPECIES
Ryn
SEX
Male
HAIR COLOR
White
EYE COLOR
Hazel
HEIGHT
1.76 meters
HOMEWORLD
Unknown

On Gyndine, Droma's family split in the face of yet another assault. Uncle Gaph and sister Melisma made it off-world to a Ruan refugee camp; sister Sapha was taken as a slave aboard the enemy vessel *Crèche*. Han agreed to help Droma locate his missing kin, and the Ryn's companionship began to fill a void left by Chewbacca's death.

Seedy smuggling contacts on Tholatin led the two to Ruan, where spaceport officials arrested Droma on charges of forgery. It seemed Droma's relatives had falsified documents in order to gain passage aboard the freighter. However, that vessel was to deposit them into a Yuuzhan Vong war zone at Fondor.

With help from an old BFL labor droid, Han freed Droma, then both raced to Fondor and rescued the refugees from the middle of a full-scale battle. Droma's sister joined them when the *Crèche* was disabled in the fighting.

Droma and his family helped Han Solo establish evacuee settlements on Duro. The devastation of Duro at the hands of the Yuuzhan Vong has once again left the Ryn without a home.

DURGA THE HUTT

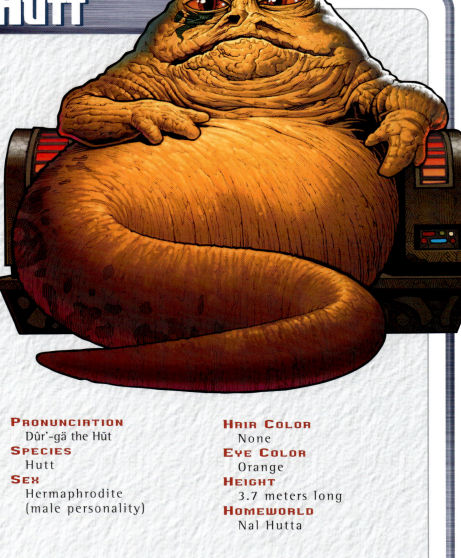

For all his infamy, Jabba the Hutt was a big worm in a small puddle. Durga the Hutt, who had all of Jabba's greed and none of his prudence, gambled on becoming a big worm in the biggest puddle of all—galactic domination.

Durga Besadii Tai, offspring of Aruk Besadii Aora, lived his first century on Nal Hutta enduring the scorn of the other members of clan Besadii. Hutt traditionalists sneered that he should have been killed at birth for the dark, blotchy birthmark that stretched across his face. But old Aruk had no other heir, and Durga proved to be a quick study in the intricacies of clan politics.

Approximately three years before the Battle of Yavin, following the Battle of Nar Shaddaa, Aruk the Hutt unexpectedly died. A grief-stricken Durga suspected foul play and hired the galaxy's best forensics specialists to investigate. At the same time, he fought off rival Besadii members who wanted to usurp control. Needing to solidify his status as clan leader, Durga asked for a favor from Prince Xizor of the crime syndicate Black Sun. Just like that, Durga's rivals "mysteriously" perished.

When Durga's investigations into his parent's death proved fruitless, he again turned to Black Sun. In exchange for the secrets of Nal Hutta's planetary defenses, Durga received the identity of Aruk's murderer. Durga was now firmly in Xizor's pocket, but at last the young Hutt knew that clan Desilijic—clan Besadii's bitter rival—had orchestrated the assassination.

Burning with righteous rage, Durga squirmed over to Desilijic headquarters and challenged clan

PRONUNCIATION
Dûr'-gä the Hŭt
SPECIES
Hutt
SEX
Hermaphrodite (male personality)

HAIR COLOR
None
EYE COLOR
Orange
HEIGHT
3.7 meters long
HOMEWORLD
Nal Hutta

leader Jiliac to personal combat. The two squared off, and Durga used his tail to bludgeon his enemy to death. With Jiliac gone, Jabba became the new leader of clan Desilijic.

Now secure in his power, Durga moved to shore up Besadii's teetering spice-processing operation on Ylesia. Once again he needed to call upon Black Sun—this time for mercenaries to defend against a Desilijic attack. He also hired Boba Fett to kill the traitorous Ylesia overseer Teroenza.

Durga's preparations failed, however, when a combined Desilijic–Rebel Alliance–smuggler assault left Ylesia in ruins. To save Besadii and himself, Durga joined Black Sun full time as one of Xizor's nine lieutenants, or vigos. The move boosted Besadii's finances, but alienated Nal Hutta's rival clans.

Durga didn't care. The other Hutts soon realized that, to this Hutt, power was more important than tradition.

Black Sun's resources gave Durga unprecedented reach. As the years passed he assassinated smaller crime lords, such as Ritinki the Bimm, and established a lucrative ore-stripping corporation, the Orko SkyMine. The deaths of both Xizor and Jabba, scarcely six months apart, followed immediately by the collapse of the Empire, represented an incalculable opportunity, and within eight years of the Battle of Endor, Durga had driven Besadii to dominance over all of Nal Hutta's clans and assumed control of the reorganized Black Sun syndicate.

The extent of his criminal empire intoxicated Durga. He had achieved more than his parent Aruk, and looked for inspiration to the legendary Hutt conqueror Kossak. Giddy with power, Durga vowed to eclipse Kossak's memory and become the greatest Hutt in history. Through Black Sun's spynet he located Bevel Lemelisk, the chief designer for the Empire's Death Star. He then arranged a diplomatic meeting with Chief of State Leia Organa Solo, where his taurill "pets" lifted a copy of the battle station schematics that had once been carried inside R2-D2. Deep in the Hoth asteroid belt, Durga began building his dream—a cylindrical, stripped-down Death Star codenamed Darksaber.

Orko SkyMine provided the raw materials, and Lemelisk engineered the project. The taurill welded together the mighty structure. As the superweapon took shape, Durga imagined using it to ransom planets and annihilate his enemies. With the Darksaber, he would be unstoppable.

Bevel Lemelisk tried in vain to impress upon his megalomaniacal employer one basic truth—a Death Star can't be built on the cheap. Plagued with inferior materials and shoddy taurill workmanship, the Darksaber looked to Lemelisk's eyes as if it would never fire a shot. But an obdurate Durga refused to correct its flaws.

A New Republic commando team tried to sabotage the Darksaber and failed; Durga personally executed their leader, General Crix Madine. But sabotage was hardly necessary—the superweapon was practically falling apart at the welds. When a New Republic war fleet arrived, Durga foolishly chose to use the superlaser to blast an escape corridor through the swarming asteroids. The main weapon sputtered and died, and two huge chunks of rock swooped in to smash the Darksaber into floating debris.

Following Durga's death, Borga Besadii Diori, Durga's cousin, took over the leadership of the Besadii clan. Though she lost control of the Black Sun syndicate, she did maintain Besadii's prominence over the other Hutt clans. During the Yuuzhan Vong war Borga negotiated with the treacherous invaders on behalf of all Hutts—negotiations that later proved disastrous for every planet in Hutt space.

KYP DURRON

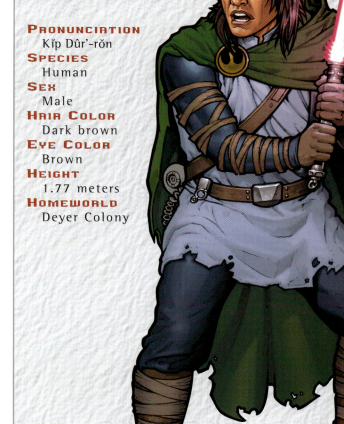

PRONUNCIATION
Kĭp Dûr'-rŏn
SPECIES
Human
SEX
Male
HAIR COLOR
Dark brown
EYE COLOR
Brown
HEIGHT
1.77 meters
HOMEWORLD
Deyer Colony

E asily one of the most polarizing figures in the New Republic, Kyp Durron is considered by some a mass murderer and by others a war hero. Even during the Yuuzhan Vong invasion, Durron has emerged as a divisive force among the ranks of the Jedi.

The son of political dissidents, Kyp Durron grew up in a floating raft city on Deyer Colony in the Anoat system. Even their out-of-the-way location couldn't shield the Durrons from the long arm of the Empire. Stormtroopers invaded Deyer Colony, sending Kyp's older brother Zeth to the Academy planet Carida for military indoctrination. Kyp and his parents, deemed less malleable, were sentenced to life at hard labor in the spice mines of Kessel. Kyp was only a child at the time.

Kyp's parents died at the hands of inmates, former smugglers who did warden Moruth Doole's dirty work. An orphan, Kyp rotted in the galaxy's worst prison for years. His skill with the Force supplied his only edge; the old Jedi crone Vima-Da-Boda offered his only guidance.

Seven years after the Battle of Endor, Han Solo and Chewbacca, imprisoned by a vindictive Doole, met Durron deep in Kessel's spice tunnels. Solo took a liking to the teenager, seeing a little of Luke Skywalker in him. When Solo and the Wookiee escaped, they took Kyp with them.

Durron became one of Skywalker's first students at the Yavin 4 academy. Master Skywalker sensed great power in the young man, but Kyp's long ordeal on Kessel had fueled a soul full of rage and pain. He opened himself to the spirit of the Sith Lord Exar Kun, convincing himself that Kun's power could be harnessed for noble purposes. Instead, the dark energies trampled over Durron's naïveté.

Proclaiming himself a Dark Lord of the Sith, Durron stole the Sun Crusher superweapon. When Skywalker tried to stop him, Durron slammed him with energies so powerful that Skywalker slipped into a near-death limbo. Durron took the Sun Crusher on an anti-Empire rampage. At the Caridan Academy the officials told him that his brother Zeth was long dead; in revenge, he dumped a torpedo into Carida's sun. The supernova could not be stopped, not even when the officials produced Zeth, alive and well.

Carida's sun exploded, annihilating the planet and killing billions, including Kyp's brother. At last, Han Solo tracked Durron down and helped deliver him from Exar Kun's corrupt influence. New Republic officials left his fate in the hands of the recovering

Luke Skywalker. Kyp received no tangible punishment for his crime, but he nearly died battling the Death Star's prototype amid the bottomless singularities of the Maw black-hole cluster.

Guilt and shame tore at Kyp Durron, even after he became a full-fledged Jedi Knight. Many cheered him, claiming that Carida's soldiers would have killed millions over the course of the war. Others condemned him, saying his actions were no better than the genocidal crimes of the Empire. Durron found a way to live with his actions with advice from Fen Nabon, a star pilot he met on Prishardia.

Kyp dedicated himself to the Jedi Order, seeking atonement through action. During the Darksaber crisis, he warned the galaxy of Admiral Daala's attacks and helped defend the Jedi academy from Daala's shock troops. Later, he led the mission to rid a mining colony of the leviathan of Corbos.

Kyp also became a mentor to many younger Jedi students, who admired his hands-on approach. Eventually he took on a single apprentice, Miko Reglia. Kyp returned from time to time to help with academy missions, such as the time he aided in the demilitarization of two warring factions on Anobis.

Kyp Durron and Miko Reglia grew into a formidable team. When Miko reached the rank of Jedi Knight, Luke Skywalker made Kyp one of the few Jedi Masters in the new Jedi Order. Master Durron and Miko Reglia gathered twelve non-Jedi pilots and founded the "Dozen-and-Two Avengers," an X-wing squadron dedicated to eradicating smuggling in the Outer Rim. Durron had never forgotten the faces of the smugglers who had executed his parents.

With his Jedi reflexes, Durron became a hotshot pilot, posting the highest score in Lando Calrissian's "running-the-belt" game at Dubrillion, at least until his time was bested by Jaina Solo. But no amount of maneuvering could save Kyp's squadron from the Yuuzhan Vong. The Dozen-and-Two Avengers were among the first to encounter the Yuuzhan Vong vanguard force. All the Avengers died—except Kyp.

Deeply shaken, Kyp tried to rally the other Jedi into an aggressive, proactive stance. But Master Sky- walker viewed this as the path to the dark side, and struggled to keep the new Jedi Order from splitting into opposing ideological camps. Kyp fought the Yuuzhan Vong at Ithor, and worked to rebuild his squadron. His new group staged a failed mission at Fondor to rescue the Jedi Wurth Skidder from the enemy. He then harried the enemy's flank, single-handedly enabling the evacuation of Kubindi to succeed by holding off a superior force.

Durron's rebuilt squadron returned to the vicinity of Sernpidal, where the enemy had destroyed an entire planet. There they discovered that the Yuuzhan Vong had created a shipwomb amid Sernpidal's remains, and Durron enlisted Wedge Antilles and Jaina Solo to help in destroying it by telling them the enemy had created a superweapon. After the fall of Coruscant, Kyp helped Jaina Solo find her way back after she strayed to the dark side of the Force.

Despite Kyp's flat-out rejection of Jedi passivity, his results are undeniably impressive. It remains to be seen whether his philosophy will tip the fortunes of war—or tip the Force out of balance.

4-LOM

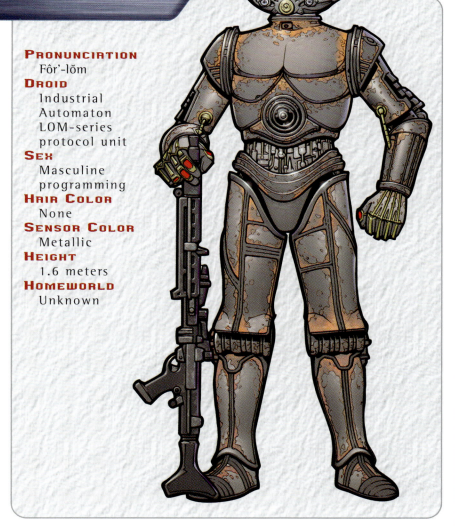

PRONUNCIATION
Fôr'-lŏm
DROID
Industrial Automaton LOM-series protocol unit
SEX
Masculine programming
HAIR COLOR
None
SENSOR COLOR
Metallic
HEIGHT
1.6 meters
HOMEWORLD
Unknown

Four-LOM should never have had a "life" in the first place. As an Industrial Automaton protocol droid from the LOM series, his only purpose was to attend to needs of passengers aboard the *Kuari Princess* starliner. But 4-LOM found no challenge in that.

Over time he began engaging the ship's computer in idle conversation regarding how one might best steal the passengers' valuables. Then, when a careless guest brought aboard the famed Ankarres sapphire, 4-LOM stole the gem, and no one suspected a thing.

The droid began a new career as a master thief. Soon, a lethal-programming upgrade—courtesy of Jabba the Hutt, always eager for new talent—allowed 4-LOM to start working as one of the galaxy's few droid bounty hunters. It was Jabba who suggested he team up with the Gand findsman known as Zuckuss. From Zuckuss—known in the trade as "the uncanny one"—4-LOM hoped to develop the instinct known among organic beings as intuition.

Four-LOM and Zuckuss worked together in the hunt for the Yavin Vassilika, and over the years they achieved fame in bounty hunting circles. But after Zuckuss suffered a life-threatening lung injury, the two hunters accepted a job from the Rebel Alliance that would enable them to pay the medical expenses. Their capture of Imperial Governor Nardix put them in hot water with the Empire.

They hoped to turn things around by accepting Darth Vader's bounty for the *Millennium Falcon*. To infiltrate the Rebel Alliance, 4-LOM and Zuckuss rescued the crew of a Hoth evacuation transport and safely returned them to the Rebel fleet. General Rieekan himself thanked 4-LOM. Moved by the experience, the two hunters threw their original plan to the wind and joined the Alliance.

Four-LOM optimistically calculated a 98.4 percent probability that he would start the New Republic's first bounty hunting guild. Assigned to a Rebel Special Forces unit, 4-LOM and his partner worked as double agents in an attempt to steal Han Solo's carbonite slab from Boba Fett. However, Fett outsmarted them both and, in a tight fight aboard the *Slave I*, blasted 4-LOM into pieces.

Zuckuss repaired his partner. But due to some quirk in his rebuilt processors, or simply the sting of failure, 4-LOM was never the same again. His earlier bout of Rebel idealism vanished like a silicon dream. Four-LOM hunted without regret or pity, working for such clients as Quaffug the Hutt, once nearly capturing Lando Calrissian on the moon of Blimph. Shortly after Jabba's death, 4-LOM again teamed with Zuckuss to capture gambler Drawmas Sma'Da, but from that point on the droid preferred to work alone.

Baron Fel

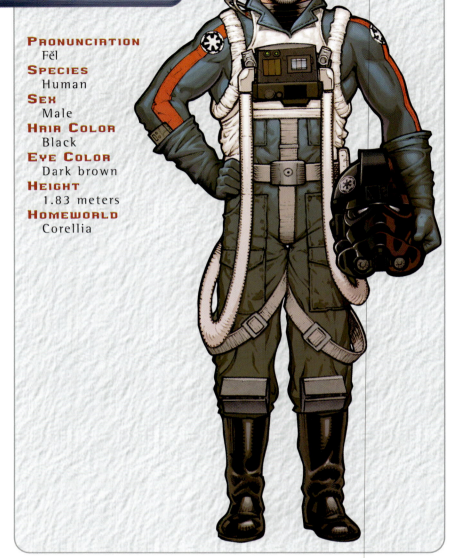

PRONUNCIATION
Fĕl
SPECIES
Human
SEX
Male
HAIR COLOR
Black
EYE COLOR
Dark brown
HEIGHT
1.83 meters
HOMEWORLD
Corellia

Straight-backed, broad-shouldered, and square-jawed, Baron Fel is a man carved from a block of granite. It's easy to see why his heroic profile became the centerpiece for millions of Imperial recruiting posters.

The eldest child of Corellian farmers, Soontir Fel and his family worked for the mammoth agricultural combine Allied Grain and Roughage (AGR). Young Soontir learned piloting in a skyhopper, buzzing over the fields to deliver parts and supplies.

Shortly after his eighteenth birthday, Soontir Fel rescued a girl from the unwanted advances of Ilir Post, son of an AGR board member. To prevent him from testifying at Post's trial, AGR officials pressured Fel to accept an appointment to the Caridan Military Academy. He reluctantly accepted the posting and secured his family's future with AGR.

Fel proved an exceptional cadet, becoming captain of Carida's zoneball team. He flew TIEs even better than he played ball, rivaling Cadet Han Solo in the flight simulators. Although he was a Corellian, too, Solo didn't care to socialize with a hayseed farmboy. Ultimately, Solo graduated at the top of his class; Soontir Fel settled for salutatorian.

Given a lieutenant's rank, Fel joined the 37th Imperial fighter wing as a TIE pilot. During his first tour of duty he helped eliminate the Lortan fanatics who had survived the Resalian Purge. After one year he received a promotion to captain, and volunteered for a second yearlong pilot's tour.

The Empire moved Captain Fel into fleet operations, and for two years he commanded the Dreadnaught *Pride of the Senate*, fighting under Admiral Greelanx in the Battle of Nar Shaddaa. The failure of that engagement left a black mark on Fel's record. Rather than earning a promotion, he was moved to a teaching post at the Prefsbelt IV Naval Academy.

For nearly two years he instructed cadets, and began to harbor hopes of joining Grand Moff Tarkin's elite bodyguard unit. But when two of his graduates, Hobbie Klivian and Biggs Darklighter, mutinied and joined the Rebellion, Fel's hopes of joining Tarkin's unit evaporated. He received a punitive transfer to the 181st Imperial fighter wing, known among pilots as the "One-Eighty Worst." There Fel served under Colonel Evir Derricote.

In a remarkably short time he whipped the second squadron of the 181st into fighting shape. As a result, the Empire sent his squadron into combat at the Second Battle of Ord Biniir, where Fel and his pilots decimated the Rebel fleet. As it turned out, the Death Star died at Yavin that same day. Anxious to propagandize a victory, the Empire gave twenty-eight-year-old Fel a hero's reception on Coruscant. Now a major, Fel met actress Wynssa Starflare, and the two fell in love.

On Coruscant, Major Fel oversaw the reduction of the 181st from a wing to an elite three-squadron group. One year after his victory at Ord Biniir, Fel married Wynssa. She revealed to him her true name—Syal Antilles—and her secret status as the sister of the Rebel Alliance's greatest fighter pilot. Ever the tactician, Fel drew up a contingency plan for Syal's safe disappearance should her relationship to Wedge Antilles ever become public.

At the Battle of Derra IV, Fel distinguished himself again, earned the rank of colonel, and received the title of Baron of the Empire from Palpatine himself. He moved his family off the farm and into his new Baron's holdings on Corellia. Baron Fel's 181st fought at Hoth and Endor. The red stripes decorating the solar panels of the group's TIE interceptors struck terror into the hearts of their enemies.

Over time, Fel found he could not ignore the growing corruption of Ysanne Isard's Empire. Six months after Endor, Isard ordered the 181st into an impossible situation defending Brentaal. Rogue Squadron shot down Fel's interceptor and captured him. Renouncing the Empire, Fel joined Rogue Squadron.

Syal went into hiding before Isard could retaliate. With the Rogues, Fel searched for her for nearly seven months until the couple finally reunited. A few months later Fel helped Rogue Squadron win a key battle against Isard's forces. Enraged, she implemented a plan to remove this thorn from her side—a plan spearheaded by Grand Admiral Thrawn, who was still lying low in the Unknown Regions.

Approximately one and a half years after Endor, Isard captured Fel and shipped him off to Thrawn's hidden base on Nirauan. There, Thrawn revealed to him the dire threats lurking in the Unknown Regions, and the need for skilled warriors to hold them at bay. Fel agreed to join the fight, and Thrawn arranged for Fel's wife to join him.

Syal and Soontir had five children, including their son Jagged, named for Syal's father. When Thrawn returned to lead the Empire, General Fel remained at the Nirauan base to command Thrawn's Chiss squadrons. He provided his genetic template for cloning, and at Thrawn's Mount Tantiss complex, hundreds of the Baron's clones matured in incubators and spread out in underground sleeper cells across the New Republic.

Despite Thrawn's death at Bilbringi, General Fel, Admiral Voss Parck, and Thrawn's Chiss followers never lost faith that their leader would return. Fel lost his right eye in battle against a warlord, but refused a prosthetic replacement.

During the Hand of Thrawn crisis, Fel and Admiral Parck tried unsuccessfully to recruit Mara Jade into their army. Meanwhile, Han Solo and his wife Leia Organa ran into a cell of Fel clones on Pakrin Minor. The Baron himself did not accompany the Chiss force that fought the Yuuzhan Vong at Ithor, but his son Jagged led the squadron with honor befitting the Fel name.

BOBA FETT

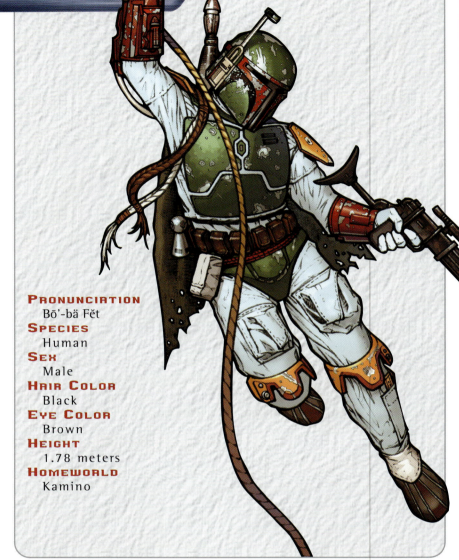

He didn't socialize. He rarely spoke. None of his bounties ever saw his face. Thus Boba Fett encouraged fearful speculation about his past, which sprang up in the absence of facts.

Some said he was Jaster Mereel, a journeyman protector from Concord Dawn who'd been exiled for killing a fellow officer. Others pegged him as an adult during the Clone Wars, fighting as one of the supercommandos on the planet Mandalore.

The true facts, buried beneath a mountain of falsehoods, are that Boba Fett was an unaltered clone of his "father" Jango. Unlike other clones, Boba did not undergo the gene tampering that would lead to docility and growth acceleration. Jango Fett accepted Boba in addition to payment for services he rendered to the Kaminoans, and he raised Boba as his own son. Taun We, aide to the Kaminoan Prime Minister, cared for Boba while Jango hunted bounties offplanet.

Ten years after his birth in a clone incubator, Boba Fett met Obi-Wan Kenobi when the Jedi came to Kamino. Possessing Jango Fett's natural instincts, he instantly knew Kenobi was trouble. The Fetts fled Kamino after a skirmish with the nosy Jedi, then eluded him in the asteroid ring of Geonosis.

But more Jedi invaded Geonosis' execution arena. Jango Fett died in single combat with Jedi Master Mace Windu, and Boba left Geonosis in his father's ship, amid the confusion of battle between Republic forces and Count Dooku's army.

The Clone Wars erupted. The Jedi Order died. Palpatine assumed the throne and authority of Emperor, and

PRONUNCIATION
Bō'-bä Fĕt
SPECIES
Human
SEX
Male
HAIR COLOR
Black
EYE COLOR
Brown
HEIGHT
1.78 meters
HOMEWORLD
Kamino

Boba Fett became what he'd been bred and trained for. He possessed Jango's reflexes, Jango's ship, *Slave I*, and a set of Mandalorian armor that had once belonged to Jaster Mereel, his father's mentor. Boba Fett seemed predestined to become the greatest bounty hunter in the galaxy.

On several early missions he paired with D'harhan, a cyborg with a laser cannon in place of a head. It soon became obvious Boba Fett wasn't the only one operating with a suit of Mandalorian armor. Fenn Shysa and Tobbi Dala, supercommandos from Mandalore, patrolled their planet's space and seldom interfered with Fett's hunts. Jodo Kast, by contrast, competed with Fett for bounties and wore his Mandalorian armor partly to cash in on Fett's reputation.

Fett first met Han Solo while on assignment for Jabba the Hutt; the young Corellian's win in Jubilar's bare-knuckled Free-For-All left an impression on Fett that echoed for years.

Approximately four years before the Battle of Yavin, Fett caught up with Han Solo again, this time as a predator hunting prey. Teroenza, high priest of Ylesia, had hired Fett to capture Solo as revenge for embarrassment the Corellian had caused him. On Nar Shaddaa, Fett nabbed his target, only to have Lando Calrissian turn the tables, free Solo, and send Fett off in *Slave I* under the influence of obedience drugs. Though Jabba eventually talked Fett out of the Solo bounty, Fett's hatred for Calrissian remained. Later, while hunting Bria Tharen aboard a passenger liner, Fett had another bounty spoiled by Calrissian's interference. Only a substantial cash payoff convinced him to leave without retaliating.

Boba Fett took jobs from everyone, including the Empire. Shortly before Yavin, Darth Vader hired Fett to go after Imperial deserter Abal Karda. It didn't take Fett long to discover that Vader's true target was the cask Karda was carrying, containing the decapitated—but still living—head of an Icarii soothsayer. On Maryx Minor, Fett and Vader fought one-on-one for the cask, with Vader emerging the victor by only the slimmest of margins.

Weeks before Yavin, Boba Fett claimed a bounty on High Priest Teroenza, killing him in his Ylesian sanctuary just as the priest prepared to kill Han Solo and Bria Tharen. The rescue meant nothing to Fett—"just business," he said—and indeed a short time later he found himself in direct competition with Solo in a treasure hunt for the Yavin Vassilika. After that affair, Fett remained in Jabba's employ. He accompanied Jabba and several other bounty hunters to Mos Eisley's Docking Bay 94 to provide silent muscle as the

Hutt threatened Solo and his Wookiee copilot.

Jabba soon posted a tremendous bounty on Solo's head, but Fett had other concerns. Several months after Yavin he accepted a job from the arachnid middleman Kud'ar Mub'at to join the Bounty Hunters' Guild and destroy it from within. As planned, after a guild mission against the Shell Hutts of Circumtore—in which Fett's old comrade D'harhan lost his life—the guild split along age lines and tore itself apart. Fett later learned that Prince Xizor had orchestrated the entire affair, with the blessing of the Emperor.

About six months after Yavin, Fett killed the notorious criminal Dr. Evazan, who was experimenting with the reanimation of dead bodies on the planet Necropolis. While there he crossed paths with two children—Zak and Tash Arranda—and their Shi'ido guardian. A few months later he found himself hunting the trio on behalf of Darth Vader. Fett tracked them to Dagobah, where he

ran afoul of a band of shipwrecked cannibals, and he left without collecting the Arranda bounty.

Following the Rebel Alliance's evacuation from Yavin 4, Fett ran into Han Solo and Rebel hero Luke Skywalker on several occasions. First, on a watery moon in the Panna system, Fett unsuccessfully tried to capture Skywalker for Vader. Later, Fett crossed paths with the same group of Rebels while hunting an Imperial spy on ice-covered Ota. Once again, his prey eluded his grasp.

Fett suffered another setback when he was hired by Imperial General Mohc to kill Rebel agent Kyle Katarn. He tracked Katarn to Coruscant but botched the kill, and Katarn went on to destroy Mohc's Dark Trooper Project. To restore his reputation, Boba Fett wiped out an entire Imperial garrison on Vryssa in order to nab a bounty who'd hidden there for protection. The destruction of the

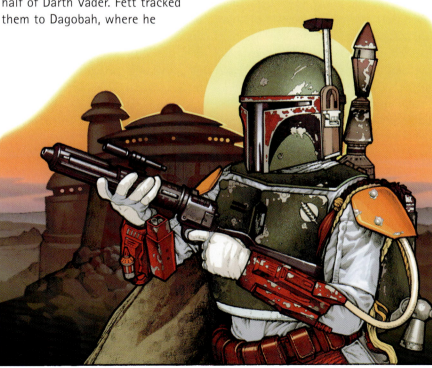

garrison, accomplished without any backup, is considered the most spectacular feat of Fett's career.

Not long before the Battle of Hoth, Boba Fett and several other hunters captured Han Solo and Luke Skywalker, imprisoning them on Ord Mantell. Fett tried to negotiate *two* bounties—one from Jabba and one from Vader—but his captives escaped. He got a second chance when Vader hired him to find the *Millennium Falcon* following its escape from Hoth. Fett beat his fellow hunters to the bounty, and flew away from Cloud City with a carbonite slab containing the hibernating form of Han Solo. Two IG-88 units attacked the *Slave I* as soon as Fett arrived at Tatooine, forcing him to divert to Gall for repairs. After many months, and many attempts by competitors to steal Solo's slab, Fett delivered his cargo to Jabba's palace and received a payoff of a quarter million credits.

During Luke Skywalker's rescue of Solo above the Great Pit of Carkoon, Boba Fett fell into the maw of the Sarlacc. After days of agony he blasted out, barely alive. Fellow hunter Dengar discovered him lying in the sand and saved his life. In return, Fett allowed Dengar to accompany him on a search to untangle a labyrinthine conspiracy orchestrated by wealthy industrialist Kuat of Kuat. For the mission Fett stole the freighter *Hound's Tooth* from his rival Bossk, leaving *Slave I* behind on Tatooine. *Slave I* fell into Alliance hands and rusted in an impound lot on Grakouine.

The galaxy at large thought Boba Fett was a half-digested morsel in the Sarlacc's belly, and he used that to his advantage, flying around in the less recognizable *Slave II* and accepting jobs from only the most discerning clients. When Jodo Kast threatened to blow his cover by encouraging people to believe that *he* was Boba Fett, Fett ambushed Kast and killed him. Dengar continued to work with Fett, often providing the necessary public face for his silent partner. Those in the business knew how to get in touch with Fett. Others, including Han Solo, had no inkling of his survival.

Eventually Fett bought back *Slave I*, keeping it in a parking orbit above Nar Shaddaa. After the grotesque attacks of the reborn Emperor, Boba Fett decided to take a new Hutt bounty on his old nemesis Han Solo. Fett and Dengar surprised Solo on the Smugglers' Moon and chased him to the Emperor's throne-world of Byss, where *Slave II* smashed into the planetary shield.

That was the end of *Slave II* and the termination of the partnership with Dengar. A loner once again, Boba Fett reactivated *Slave I* and took several jobs for Gorga the Hutt. The influx of cash allowed Fett to set up another ambush for Han Solo. He nearly captured Solo in the darkened undercity of Nar Shaddaa, but Chewbacca tore off his helmet and sent him rocketing into a durasteel girder. Fett recovered and lay in wait near a gas cloud, firing on the *Millennium Falcon* when it emerged. In response, he received a circuit-melting blast from the *Falcon's* new "lightning gun." *Slave I* was then replaced by *Slave III*.

Word of Solo's victories over Fett spread far and wide. To erase the stain of failure, Fett accepted a job to kill the insane Imperial overseers of the dungeon ship *Azgoghk*—which he accomplished for only one hundred credits. But he soon needed many thousands of credits, after replacing *Slave III* with *Slave IV* and undergoing surgery to prosthetically replace his right leg, weakened years before in his encounter with the Sarlacc.

Fortunately, fifteen years after Endor, Fett apprehended the Devaronian war criminal known as the "Butcher of Montellian Serat" and earned a staggering bounty of five million credits. His finances bolstered, he moved to secure his pride. On Jubilar, Fett faced off with Han Solo for a final showdown, but both combatants ultimately decided to drop their long-standing feud and go their separate ways.

Boba Fett continued to work the bounty hunting trade as recently as twenty years after Endor. Still flying *Slave IV*, he took a job for Nolaa Tarkona of the Diversity Alliance to find shipping merchant Bornan Thul. Fett eventually found Thul, discovering what he'd been hiding—the coordinates of a plague storehouse—and then transmitting that data to Tarkona. The Diversity Alliance crumbled in battle with the New Republic, and Fett went on to other jobs for other clients. Since the Yuuzhan Vong invasion Fett hasn't been seen, but not even his most hopeful enemies are willing to count him among the dead.

JANGO FETT

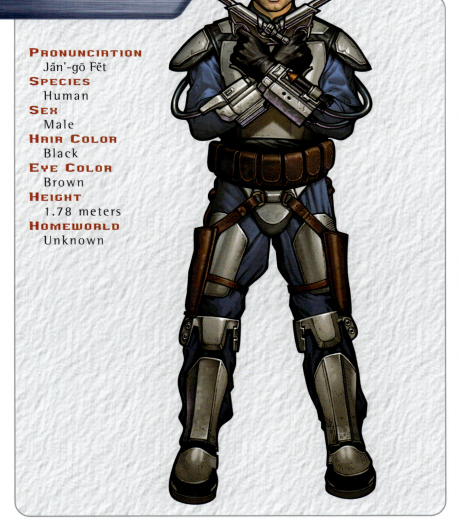

PRONUNCIATION
Jăn'-gō Fĕt
SPECIES
Human
SEX
Male
HAIR COLOR
Black
EYE COLOR
Brown
HEIGHT
1.78 meters
HOMEWORLD
Unknown

Jango Fett cultivated anonymity behind the faceplate of his Mandalorian helmet. Then he served as the template for a clone army, and suddenly Jango was *everywhere*. His clone "brothers" also wore masks, and they spread across the galaxy during the Clone Wars.

Orphaned when his settler parents were killed in an uprising, Jango Fett joined the Mandalorian peacekeepers, a group of nomadic mercenaries with whom he traveled for a few years.

On Galidraan, the Mandalorians found themselves on the wrong side of a battle. The Jedi Knights nearly eliminated their outnumbered opponents. Jango slipped away, preparing to go into business for himself as a hunter-for-hire.

Jango received spectacular payoffs for his successes and earned a reputation as the best in the business. He flew a modified *Firespray*-class F-31 named *Slave I*. Calling himself "just a simple man trying to make my way in the universe," Jango followed no ideologies and accepted jobs from anyone with money. But one private vendetta tortured him—his hatred for his fellow hunter Montross.

Years before, Montross had killed Mandalorian officer Jaster Mereel and mounted his armor—bearing the skull insignia of Mereel's regiment—in his home as a grim trophy. During a job collecting a bounty on the leader of the Bando Gora, Fett confronted Montross and walked away victorious.

Soon after the Battle of Naboo, a man named Tyranus approached Jango on one of the moons of Bogden. Out of all the galaxy's bounty hunters, Jango had been picked to provide the genetic template for a clone army that would be grown on watery Kamino. Fett took up residence in Kamino's Tipoca City and proceeded to provide regular genetic samples. He continued his bounty hunting career from this new base.

The Kaminoans paid well, but Jango also asked for something else. Prime Minister Lama Su gave Jango a newborn clone, unaltered, to raise as his own son. Jango named his clone Boba.

Ten years into Jango's stay on Kamino, Tyranus—really Count Dooku—hired the bounty hunter to eliminate Senator Padmé Amidala on Coruscant. Jango entrusted the job to one of his freelance stringers, Zam Wesell, but killed her when she threatened the security of the operation.

Later, on Kamino, Jango met Obi-Wan Kenobi. His instincts told him the visitor was trouble. Jango and his son prepped their ship to leave Kamino and, after a heated clash with Kenobi, fled the waterworld.

The Jedi Knight followed them through the asteroid rings of Geonosis, and later more Jedi invaded the planet's execution arena. Jango tried to help fight them off, but died in one-on-one combat with Jedi Master Mace Windu.

BORSK FEY'LYA

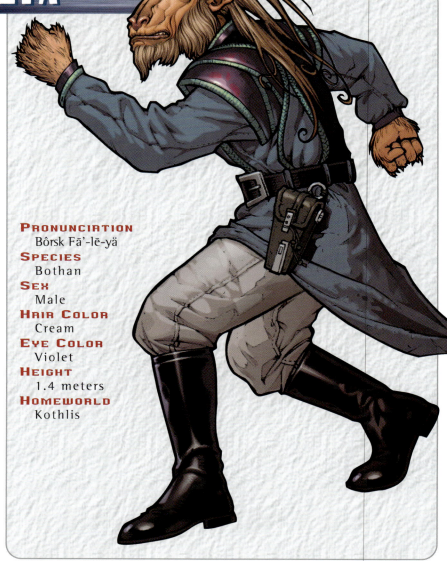

Borsk Fey'lya was like a carnival mirror—how you perceived him depended on where you stood. To the general public, Fey'lya was a hardworking career politician whose tenure as Chief of State was cut short by the Yuuzhan Vong invasion. To his supporters, Fey'lya was a shrewd deal maker, always flexible when compromise would lead to a greater good. To his enemies, Fey'lya was a conniving, amoral traitor.

What's true of Borsk Fey'lya is true of Bothans in general. Some segments of the population actively mistrust the species for its seeming lack of scruples—not to mention its talent for espionage. But Bothans are a complex people with many motivations.

Born into the Alya clan on the Bothan colony world of Kothlis, Fey'lya recognized at an early age that he had little talent for piloting or sports. He worked to become a diplomat, for he felt that politics equaled power. The fact that Fey'lya lived on second-tier Kothlis, and not Bothawui itself, made him push himself even harder. As soon as he acquired wealth through business dealings, Fey'lya purchased a vast spread of land on Bothawui to solidify his image as a legitimate up-and-comer.

According to the "Bothan Way," weaknesses in others should be exploited in order to achieve greater goals. Fey'lya used the Bothan Way like a spleenadder wields its stinger—he kept undercover until the right moment arrived, then he struck without mercy. Fey'lya climbed the political ladder while his rivals fell victim to manufactured scandals and their own lack of charisma. Other Bothans latched on to this rising star, and

PRONUNCIATION
Bôrsk Fā'-lē-yä
SPECIES
Bothan
SEX
Male
HAIR COLOR
Cream
EYE COLOR
Violet
HEIGHT
1.4 meters
HOMEWORLD
Kothlis

soon Fey'lya had a faction at his command. At this point he set his sights on a much more ambitious goal—control of the galaxy.

At the time, Emperor Palpatine ruled with absolute authority, but Fey'lya was certain that even Palpatine could not rule forever. He began making overtures toward the Rebellion, and after the Death Star's destruction at Yavin, he felt confident enough to throw in his lot with the Alliance.

His Bothan faction gave the Re-

bellion an edge in espionage and made Fey'lya one of the most important Alliance figures, particularly after Garm Bel Iblis left the Rebels to fight his own private war. Ever mindful of the balance of power, Fey'lya stayed in contact with Bel Iblis, aiding him financially from time to time.

Just prior to the Battle of Endor, Bothan spies uncovered vital information about the Emperor's second Death Star. Almost all the spies died in the process, and Bothawui's government lionized them as "the Martyrs." Nonetheless, Fey'lya made sure to claim the credit. Despite the fact that the information proved to be bait for a trap, the sacrifice of the Bothans garnered respect from all levels of the Alliance. When the second Death Star exploded over Endor, Borsk Fey'lya became one of the original eight signatories of the Declaration of a New Republic.

The eight individuals comprised the New Republic Provisional Council, and though Mon Mothma was the council's leader, Fey'lya held much of the influence. Always unobtrusive, Fey'lya shaped military strategies for the Trioculus war and the capture of Coruscant.

During Grand Admiral Thrawn's campaign, Fey'lya felt the time was right for an outright grab for power. In what proved to be one of his rare miscalculations, he overplayed his hand by accusing Admiral Ackbar of treason, and by giving an order to retreat at the Battle of the *Katana* Fleet.

Disgraced among the New Repub-

lic Provisional Council, Fey'lya unsuccessfully attempted to shore up his power base with the Bothan people. For a while even his allies distanced themselves from him, and it was years before he climbed back to an equivalent level of power.

In the reconstruction that followed the war against the resurrected Emperor, Fey'lya rose again through the reorganized government. During the Black Fleet Crisis he served as chairman of the Senate Justice Council. The Hand of Thrawn incident could have been devastating for Fey'lya, revealing as it did Bothan complicity in the ruin of Caamas, but he positioned the news as ancient history, and saw that those involved were punished.

Fey'lya stewed when Ponc Gavrisom became Chief of State following Leia Organa Solo's resignation, but vowed to bide his time. Organa Solo resumed service as Chief of State a few years later, but soon ran out her term. Finally, with twenty years' experience and a host of political con-

tacts, Fey'lya became Chief of State in a landslide.

At last, he ruled the civilized galaxy.

Less than a year into his term, the Yuuzhan Vong invaded. Scarcely believing that a threat of this magnitude should appear at the time of his greatest triumph, Fey'lya did little to prevent the enemy from taking bites out of the Outer Rim. But as the invaders swept toward the Core, he did what he could to halt their advance—while preserving such vital worlds as Bothawui. If that meant hanging the Jedi out to dry, he felt, then so be it. But when the Yuuzhan Vong seized *his* Coruscant, Fey'lya stayed behind and died with nobility.

If Borsk Fey'lya were given an epitaph, it might read, "He did what he thought was right." Fey'lya saw even his most selfish actions as noble, for with him in power he believed that all citizens would ultimately benefit. Fey'lya did indeed achieve many positive things in his career, but many New Republic leaders will not mourn his passing.

BIB FORTUNA

PRONUNCIATION
Bĭb Fôr-tōō'-nä
SPECIES
Twi'lek
SEX
Male
HAIR COLOR
None
EYE COLOR
Orange
HEIGHT
1.8 meters
HOMEWORLD
Ryloth

Bib Fortuna served Jabba the Hutt for nearly forty years. Perhaps it's not surprising, then, to learn that no one in the galaxy hated Jabba more than he did.

Born as Bibfort'una into the Una clan on the half-scorched, half-frozen planet Ryloth, he traveled off-world as a mere boy and quickly earned wealth as a trafficker in contraband ryll spice. His actions, however, led slavers to Ryloth, and his fellow Twi'leks sentenced him to death. Bibfort'una barely escaped, though his assets were seized and his name dishonored.

His expulsion from Rylothean culture required the ritual splitting of his personal and clan names. Known as Bib Fortuna from that point forward, he achieved a post in Jabba's organization and worked his way up to the position of majordomo.

Around the time of the Battle of Naboo, Fortuna hatched a plot with a wealthy Coruscant Senator to create a synthesized spice, glitteryll, out of Rylothean ryll and Kessel glitterstim. In part, he orchestrated the scheme to ease market demand for pure ryll and help out an overwhelmed Ryloth, for he still loved his homeworld. With help from Pol Secura, a member of the ruling Twi'lek head clan, Fortuna launched glitteryll production. But Pol Secura's daughter Aayla happened to be Padawan to the Jedi Knight Quinlan Vos, who put an end to the whole operation.

Had Jabba known anything about the glitteryll plot, he surely would have executed his majordomo. As it was, Fortuna fell victim to the Hutt's infamous mood swings, when he mishandled some triviality and found himself demoted to errand boy, replaced by the new majordomo, Naroon Cuthus. Fortuna found himself trapped in Jabba's employ without any of his former influence, and he began to loathe the Hutt even more than he hated so many of his self-righteous Twi'lek brethren.

After the rise of the Empire, Fortuna took revenge on the Twi'leks who had sentenced him to death. Convincing Jabba to loan him a mercenary fleet in exchange for his pick of the spoils, Fortuna returned to Ryloth and left seven cities in ruins. Most of the plunder went to Jabba, but Fortuna took the only item of true value—a small boy, burned and barely alive. The boy was Nat Secura, sole survivor of the powerful Secura clan that had been involved in the glitteryll operation years before. Fortuna imagined himself returning to devastated Ryloth and installing Nat as a puppet ruler.

Praise spilled forth from Jabba's

rubbery lips following the raid on Ryloth. Fortuna became one of the Hutt's two closest lieutenants, alongside the Corellian Bidlo Kwerve. While catering to Jabba's depraved fancies, Fortuna raised Nat Secura within the palace and hired his distant cousin, Firith Olan, to begin orchestrating the plan for taking over Ryloth.

Fortuna knew that Jabba would have to die before the Ryloth operation could be launched, lest the Hutt shove his filthy fingers into the administration of the planet and spoil everything. But before he could initiate his own scheme Fortuna actually had to *save* Jabba from a coup attempt by a vicious pack of freckers, to prevent the Hutt from dying and taking his most valuable secrets to the grave.

Shortly before Yavin, with Naroon Cuthus nearing the end of his usefulness, the rivalry between Fortuna and Bidlo Kwerve heated up. When Kwerve presented Jabba with the gift of a hungry rancor, he earned the "honor" of becoming the monster's first meal. After decades in lesser roles, Fortuna once again became majordomo.

Not long before the Battle of Endor, Fortuna was forced to transfer Nat Secura's brain into a B'omarr spider walker. Jabba had decided to feed Nat to the rancor—which he did, sans brain—and Fortuna could only hope he could somehow clone a new body that would hold Nat's mind. And it had become obvious he would have to move against Jabba very soon.

Fortuna knew he wasn't the only one plotting against the Hutt. He'd counted fourteen assassination plots fermenting within the palace alone, and spotted the obvious Rebel Alliance agent "Tamtel Skreej," who was posing as a palace guard. When Luke Skywalker appeared and made overtures to Jabba, Fortuna met with the so-called Jedi in Mos Eisley. He told Skywalker that the Hutt would never bargain—but if the Rebels could wait until after his coup, he'd be happy to make a fair trade for Solo's carbonite slab.

Fortuna acted as go-between, conveying Skywalker's messages to Jabba. The Hutt refused any deal, ordering his majordomo to bar the Jedi's admittance. Fortuna did as instructed, but fell prey to Skywalker's mind tricks.

When Jabba died aboard his sail barge, Fortuna escaped and sped back to the empty palace, still hoping to salvage his Nat Secura plot. But the spidery B'omarr monks betrayed him, slicing out his brain and sticking it into a spider walker of its own. Fortuna's cousin Firith Olan took advantage of his relative's helpless state, zapping the droid walker with electric jolts each time Fortuna failed to obey his commands.

Olan got in over his head when he tried to take control of Eidolon Base, an Imperial storehouse on Tatooine. Stabbed and left for dead, Olan was dragged back to the palace by Fortuna's spider walker. The B'omarr monks performed one last brain transfer. Bib Fortuna became flesh once again, this time in Firith Olan's much paunchier frame. In his new body, Fortuna worked to rebuild his criminal empire, relying heavily on Firith Olan's network of contacts. None of them had any idea, in their conversations with "Firith Olan," that Olan was actually the brain floating in the jar. Tattooine's reigning crime boss is now the Whipid known as Lady Valarian, and Bib Fortuna has made an alliance with Valarian to figure out a way to profit from the Yuuzhan Vong invasion.

ROKUR GEPTA

R okur Gepta, self-proclaimed Sorcerer of Tund, was no sorcerer at all—just a little Croke spinning illusions. Thanks to Emperor Palpatine, Gepta could have ruled hundreds of stars, but he wasted it all in pursuit of a gambler named Lando Calrissian.

The Crokes are a species of small multilegged slugs hailing from the planet Crakull in the Unknown Regions. Some say Crokes merely fog minds; others claim their disguises are physical creations that can trick scanners.

Rokur Gepta's skills allowed him to infiltrate the secret cabal of dark-side sorcerers on the planet Tund. The sorcerers, believed to have originated during one of the Great Schisms between the dark and light sides of the Force, had refined their beliefs by incorporating Sith teachings. Gepta joined their society, learned their secrets, then annihilated them—and all life on their planet—with the radiation of a unique bioweapon.

Palpatine was known to have studied the sorcerers prior to their destruction. As Emperor, he took a personal interest in Rokur Gepta, making him one of the most powerful individuals in the Centrality region. Were Gepta's powers of illusion so great that he could deceive even Palpatine? Or did Palpatine simply admire the Croke's no-nonsense authority?

Regardless of the reason, Gepta received the decommissioned Imperial cruiser *Wennis* and the authority to supersede most Centrality governmental and military operations. With a crew of cutthroats, Gepta patrolled the Centrality, occasionally returning to irradiated Tund to meditate behind protective force-field barriers.

Gepta's mastery of dark magic was

PRONUNCIATION
Rō'-kûr Gĕp'-tä
SPECIES
Croke
SEX
Male
HAIR COLOR
Unknown
EYE COLOR
Unknown
HEIGHT
1.8 meters
(in illusion form)
HOMEWORLD
Crakull

incomplete at best. Like his appearance, many of his "powers" were illusory. But most Centrality politicians lived in fear of Gepta, including Governor Duttes Mer of the Rafa system. Gepta teamed up with Mer to obtain the legendary Mindharp of Sharu by exploiting Lando Calrissian. When the deal ended in disaster, Gepta declared a vendetta against Calrissian.

The sorcerer killed billionaire Bohhuah Mutdah in the Oseon system and arranged for Lando Calrissian to make a delivery to the dead man's estate. Posing as Mutdah, Gepta captured Calrissian and tortured him.

Interference from a band of raiders allowed the lucky gambler to escape.

Gepta again caught up to Calrissian during the Battle of ThonBoka. Gepta barged into the thick of the fighting and offered a solution—Gepta versus Calrissian, man to man, with the fate of ThonBoka in the balance.

Sealed in flight suits, the two combatants faced off in the vacuum. During the laser duel Calrissian shot Gepta in the ankle, where the actual Croke lay nestled within his larger phantom form. The "body" of Gepta vanished, and Calrissian crushed the tiny Croke between his gloves.

GREEDO

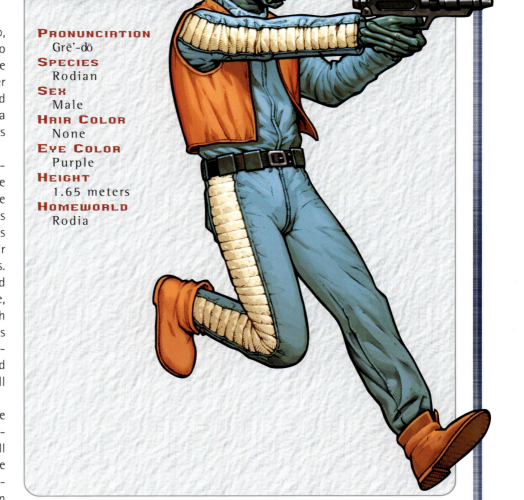

PRONUNCIATION
Grē'-dō
SPECIES
Rodian
SEX
Male
HAIR COLOR
None
EYE COLOR
Purple
HEIGHT
1.65 meters
HOMEWORLD
Rodia

When Greedo told Han Solo, "I've been looking forward to this for a long time," it's a safe bet he wasn't talking about a blaster bolt in the gut. Overconfident and underequipped, poor Greedo gave a bad name to Rodian bounty hunters everywhere.

Ambitious Rodians have long exploited their species' passion for the hunt. Navik the Red, head of the Chattza clan, persecuted those clans that didn't participate in the planet's gladiatorial contests by killing their members and seizing their holdings. Greedo the Elder, a distinguished hunter who'd grown up on Tatooine, died in Navik's purges, along with hundreds of his relatives in the Tetsus clan. His mate Neela fled to a primitive safeworld with her two-year old son, named for his father, and a small band of Tetsus survivors.

They survived on their jungle planet for thirteen years until discovered by Chattza bounty hunters still looking to finish the work Navik the Red had started. Greedo and the others escaped and lost their pursuers in the stew of refugees inhabiting Nar Shaddaa. Teenaged Greedo grew into a petty street punk. His mother hoped to move them off the Smugglers' Moon and into the protection of her brother Avaro Sookcool, a Tetsus who'd earned amnesty from Navik the Red by allying with Black Sun. Instead, Greedo's mother and most of his clanmates—save his cousins Beedo and Chihdo—died in an Imperial attack on Nar Shaddaa's Corellian sector.

Orphaned and alone, Greedo found offworld passage with two bounty hunters. Veteran hunters Dyyz Nataz and Spurch "Warhog" Goa saw in the young Rodian's bulbous eyes his hunger for respect. Warhog Goa pretended to be Greedo's friend, and it was easy—the naive Rodian viewed Goa and his grizzled partner with hero-worshiping awe. But Goa was plotting the most profitable way to get rid of his foul-smelling admirer.

After the group landed on Tatooine, Greedo rented a small ship and tagged along on the search for the Yavin Vassilika, rubbing elbows with the galaxy's greatest bounty hunters. Upon his return, Warhog Goa helped him land a contract for the Han Solo bounty established by Jabba the Hutt. Greedo tracked down Solo twice, each time demanding Jabba's money, and each time receiving humiliation. Finally, upon the urging of Warhog Goa, he confronted Han Solo in the Mos Eisley cantina.

He didn't know that a pair of Chattza bounty hunters, still nursing their clan's grudge against the Tetsus, had paid Goa to set him up for certain death. Greedo talked tough, and even got off a shot, but died when Solo shot him from under their table. As a final indignity, the bartender ground up Greedo's pheromone-laced corpse to flavor a cocktail.

NUTE GUNRAY

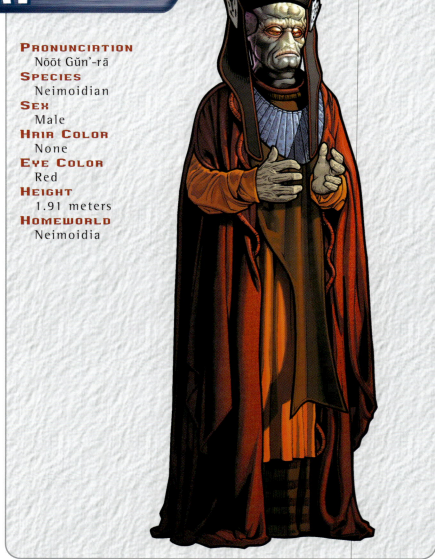

PRONUNCIATION
Nōōt Gŭn'-rā
SPECIES
Neimoidian
SEX
Male
HAIR COLOR
None
EYE COLOR
Red
HEIGHT
1.91 meters
HOMEWORLD
Neimoidia

When the Pulsar Supertanker corporation was under review for Trade Federation expulsion, the final decision hinged on a junior Neimoidian trade officer, who testified of the company's "malicious disregard for profit" and its repeated crimes of "charitable donations lacking discernible reward." Pulsar was duly expelled, which removed Pulsar's CEO from the Trade Federation Directorate and set the testifying officer on the fast track for promotion. The young officer's name? Nute Gunray.

In time, Gunray rose to become Trade Federation Commanding Viceroy, chair of the Trade Federation Executive Board, and leader of the Neimoidian Inner Circle. An exemplary Neimoidian, Gunray described his greed and cowardice as "ambition and prudence."

By striking a bargain with a Sith Lord, Nute Gunray oversaw the Trade Federation's domination by Neimoidian members. Darth Sidious pulled strings to give Gunray lucrative cargo contracts such as the rights to ship lommite from Dorvalla. These deals enhanced Gunray's status as viceroy, but he was still just one leader out of seven. The other members of the Trade Federation Directorate—four humans, one Sullustan, and one Gran—had their own views on how business should be conducted in the free trade zones of the Rim worlds.

That all changed at a trade summit on Eriadu chaired by Chancellor Valorum. Darth Sidious arranged for the assassination of every member of the Trade Federation Directorate— save Gunray. The lucky viceroy filled the directorate's vacancies with Neimoidian puppets, and became the de facto leader of the massive shipping conglomerate.

Rune Haako, Daultay Dofine, and Hath Monchar became Gunray's closest advisers. Lieutenant Haako, settlement officer for the Trade Federation's armed forces, served as Gunray's attaché and legal counsel. He was a cautious Neimoidian, often acting as a brake to Nute Gunray's recklessness. Unlike his commander, Haako had experienced run-ins with the Jedi Knights and respected their power. Captain Dofine commanded the Trade Federation flagship. Under Neimoidian terms, whichever battleship Viceroy Gunray happened to travel aboard automatically became the flagship. Deputy Viceroy Hath Monchar seemed untrustworthy, even for a Neimoidian, and Gunray worried about Monchar's fitness to oversee the secret army being created on Darth Sidious's orders.

The Trade Federation's army boasted battle droids, tanks, starfighters, and STAPs. Gunray, who fancied himself a xenoanthropologist, opened negotiations with the alien Colicoids to obtain a legion of droidekas. But soon Hath Monchar betrayed Gunray, rushing out to auction off the details of the military buildup. Gunray hired a bounty hunter to silence Monchar, but the job was ultimately completed by Sidious's apprentice, Darth Maul. After the incident, Sidious pushed Gunray into ever-more-elaborate schemes, such as a plot to take over Brentaal and control the cargo traffic along the Perlemian Trade Route and the Hydian Way. Sidious eventually scrapped the reckless plan, much to Gunray's relief.

By contrast, blockading Naboo seemed simple and small-scale. Darth Sidious promised Gunray that the Trade Federation's defiance would be a rallying point for the Senate and bring about the repeal of the Republic's trade route tax. Unfortunately, the blockade dragged on and drew unwanted attention. Gunray followed orders, but had private misgivings—several times he considered backing out of the deal, but the all-seeing Sith Lord terrified him.

Finally Gunray put his army to the test by invading Naboo. The opera-tion went better than the viceroy expected. "Victory!" he exulted when he touched down on the conquered planet—but it all fell apart with shocking swiftness. In the final battle Darth Maul proved to be no help at all, and Naboo's Queen Amidala humiliated Gunray in her throne room. Daultay Dofine died when the Droid Control Ship *Profiteer*, known in the Neimoidian tongue as the *Saak'ak,* exploded in orbit. The droid army switched off, and Nute Gunray, Rune Haako, and the other members of the so-called Occupation Council were shipped to Coruscant for trial.

Supreme Chancellor Palpatine promised to bring the Neimoidian instigators to justice, but the courts did little to punish the influential Trade Federation leaders. Even after four trials in the Supreme Court, Gunray retained his position as viceroy under the condition that the Trade Federation surrender some of its war matériel and not expand its army any further. A few influential Senators, claiming that too much scrutiny would be dangerous for the economy, forbade the Jedi from investigating the Trade Federation to determine its compliance with the ruling.

During the years following his shameful defeat at Naboo, Nute Gunray's hatred for Padmé Amidala burned bright. When Count Dooku approached him about allying the Trade Federation with Dooku's own separatist movement, Gunray asked that the Count deliver one special "extra"—Padmé's head. Gunray paid Dooku for the services of Jango Fett, the galaxy's best bounty hunter.

On Geonosis, Gunray met with Count Dooku and representatives from the Techno Union, the Commerce Guild, Corporate Alliance, and the InterGalactic Banking Clan, to discuss using their corporate armies to militarize the separatist confederacy. Gunray ordered hundreds of thousands of new battle droids and super battle droids from the foundries on Geonosis, ensuring that the Trade Federation's new army would dwarf the one that had been assembled for the invasion of Naboo. To his delight, the Geonosians captured Padmé and threw her into the execution arena with two Jedi, to be devoured by monsters.

Against all odds, Padmé survived. Nute Gunray escaped amid the confusion, readying his droid troops for a long and bitter war against the clone troopers of the Republic.

CORRAN HORN

Police officer. Ace pilot. Commando. Martial artist. Jedi Knight. Loving husband. Proud father. Though the list of Corran Horn's achievements seems superhuman, it's not all a result of the Force. Short in stature but long in courage, Corran Horn got where he is today through a mix of hard work and stubbornness.

Corran is descended from a long line of Jedi, dating back to the great Corellian Jedi Keiran Halcyon. All Jedi hailing from the Corellian sector earned a reputation for intransigence, maintaining their own local traditions and often defying the Jedi Council's edict that discouraged marriage and familial bonds. The Halcyon lineage eventually led to Nejaa Halcyon, a famous Master who perished in the Clone Wars fighting an enclave of fallen Jedi on Susevfi.

Halcyon's best friend, Corellian Security Officer Rostek Horn, married Nejaa's widow Scerra and adopted his son Valin. To protect himself from the Emperor's Jedi Purge, Valin assumed the name Hal Horn. In short order Hal Horn married a woman named Nyche, fathered one son, Corran, and graduated from the CorSec academy to follow his adoptive father's career path.

Corran Horn grew up knowing nothing about his Jedi heritage. Like his father, he entered the CorSec academy and graduated approximately two years after the Battle of Yavin. He partnered with his father Hal on many CorSec field assignments, including the arrest of Black Sun kingpin Zekka Thyne shortly before the Battle of Hoth.

Around the same time, Corran's mother died in an accident caused by

PRONUNCIATION
Côr'-rŭn Hôrn
SPECIES
Human
SEX
Male
HAIR COLOR
Brown
EYE COLOR
Green
HEIGHT
1.67 meters
HOMEWORLD
Corellia

an intoxicated speeder driver. Corran moved into the Smuggling Interdiction Division, partnering with officer Iella Wessiri, but tragedy struck again scarcely six months into his new assignment, when his father died at the hands of the bounty hunter Bossk. Kirtan Loor, the division's Imperial liaison officer, set Bossk free without even a fine.

Corran suspected that Loor had arranged his father's assassination, but had no way to prove it. Iella

helped lead him through his grief, and they began discussing their options should they need to slip out from the Imperial noose that was strangling CorSec. Corran met several members of the New Republic's elite Rogue Squadron when they came to Corellia to look for Baron Fel's wife; though the Rogues failed to find her, Corran and Iella helped them rescue Fel's nephew Fyric from kidnappers.

Approximately a year after the Battle of Endor, Kirtan Loor ordered all CorSec officers to crack down on "traitorous" New Republic shipping. Fed up with Loor, and not wishing to suffer Hal Horn's fate, Corran, Iella, Iella's husband Diric, and fellow officer Gil Bastra fled Corellia under false identities.

Corran Horn left in an X-wing fighter he'd claimed from the CorSec motor pool, narrowly escaping an ambush set for him by Loor. Along with his astromech droid Whistler, Corran drifted through a number of low-profile aliases before assuming the identity of Eamon Yzalli, a government official on the Rim planet Garqi. In the year he spent on Garqi, Corran became Imperial Prefect Mosh Barris's personal aide and helped free many political prisoners. He fled Garqi just ahead of Kirtan Loor, and joined the New Republic military.

He arrived just in time for Wedge Antilles's restructuring of Rogue Squadron. Corran passed the tryouts, and flew with the Rogues during the capture of Borleias. Kirtan Loor, now working directly for Ysanne Isard, tried to destroy Corran and his squadron mates. Corran, meanwhile, grew close to Mirax Terrik, daughter of a notorious smuggler whom his father Hal had once sent to the spice mines of Kessel.

Corran and his fellow Rogues went undercover to Imperial-held Coruscant to prepare for the New Republic's invasion of the capital planet. During the fighting, Corran crashed his starfighter and awoke inside the *Lusankya* as a prisoner of Ysanne Isard. The New Republic believed him dead and even put fellow pilot Tycho Celchu on trial for his murder. But Corran escaped from the *Lusankya*, winning two surprises: Nejaa Halcyon's lightsaber from the Imperial Museum, and the welcome news of

Kirtan Loor's death at the hands of one of Isard's sleeper agents.

Eager to explore his heritage as a Jedi, but not yet willing to become Luke Skywalker's pupil, Corran put his Force training on hold. He helped the Rogues topple Isard from her perch as ruler of Thyferra during the Bacta War.

Mirax and Corran were married aboard the captured *Lusankya* and followed that event up with a second, more public ceremony on Coruscant. After a brief honeymoon on Alakatha, Corran joined the

fight against Grand Admiral Thrawn and freed the former *Lusankya* prisoners in the final clash with Ysanne Isard. He lost his home on Coruscant during the war with the reborn Emperor, but returned from that conflict anticipating a stretch of peace.

Instead, he learned that his wife

Mirax had disappeared. Corran enrolled at Skywalker's Jedi academy to hone the skills he would need to find her. He and the other trainees vanquished the four-thousand-year-old spirit of Exar Kun, then Corran left to infiltrate Leonia Tavira's Invid pirate gang. Eventually he rescued Mirax from Tavira's "Jedi advisers"—members of the hidden Jensaarai sect founded by a Dark Jedi whom Corran's grandfather had killed. Armed with a brand-new lightsaber he'd constructed in his time with the pirates, Corran vowed to integrate his life as a Jedi into his career as a Rogue Squadron pilot.

Corran Horn flew with the Rogues for the next eight years. Elegos A'kla, a Caamasi diplomat he'd rescued from the Invid pirates, became a close friend. Approximately two years after her rescue from Tavira, Mirax gave birth to a son, Valin. Following the Hand of Thrawn incident, Corran took advantage of the Imperial–New Republic peace treaty to retire from Rogue Squadron after achieving the rank of colonel. Several years into his retirement, Corran welcomed a daughter, Jysella.

Both Valin and Jysella showed signs of Force sensitivity, so Corran enrolled them at Luke Skywalker's Jedi academy. He spent much of his own time there as a teacher, passing on his lightsaber and piloting skills. Though Corran had no talent for telekinesis, he became one of the academy's experts at projecting images into the minds of others.

The invasion of the Yuuzhan Vong rocked the galaxy and shattered the academy's quiet peace. Master Skywalker dispatched Jedi Knights Corran Horn and Ganner Rhysode to Bimmiel, a wasteland world in the enemy's invasion corridor. They hooked up with a stranded archaeological research team that had dug up the mummified remains of a Yuuzhan Vong scout who had come to Bimmiel fifty years before. The Yuuzhan Vong were also looking for the skeleton, and Corran killed two of them—almost at the expense of his own life. He later learned that the soldiers he had defeated were the kinsmen of Commander Shedao Shai. By killing them and desecrating the bones of the mummified Mongei Shai, he had earned Shedao Shai's personal enmity.

Horn briefly reactivated his military commission to lead a mission to occupied Garqi, now a very different world than the one he'd left twenty years earlier. Corran and his commandos captured several slaves and discovered that Yuuzhan Vong organic armor exhibited a devastating allergy to bafforr tree pollen from Ithor. As the New Republic prepared to defend Ithor against a Yuuzhan Vong retaliation, Shedao Shai sent Corran Horn the jewel-encrusted skeleton of his old friend Elegos A'kla. Knowing his actions skirted dangerously close to the dark side, Corran challenged Shedao Shai to a duel. If Shai won, he would get the bones of his ancestor, Mongei Shai. If Corran won, the planet Ithor would be spared. High atop an Ithor mountaintop, Corran and Shedao Shai battled with lightsaber and amphistaff. Corran won the fatal contest, but Shai's treacherous assistant destroyed Ithor anyway.

Holographic images showing once-beautiful Ithor as a stew of soggy ash horrified the citizens of the New Republic. Egged on by sensationalistic media reports, many blamed Horn for the death of Ithor. To help salvage the image of the Jedi, Corran entered a period of self-imposed exile on his homeworld of Corellia. He soon moved to his father-in-law's ship the *Errant Venture* to stay closer to the action. After the evacuation of the Yavin 4 academy, Horn led Anakin Solo and the Jedi student Tahiri on a mission to prevent the Yuuzhan Vong invasion of Yag'Dhul.

IG-88

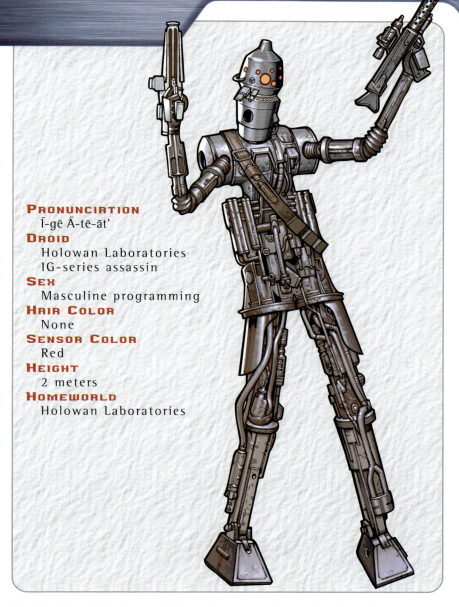

PRONUNCIATION
Ī-gē Ā-tē-āt'

DROID
Holowan Laboratories
IG-series assassin

SEX
Masculine programming

HAIR COLOR
None

SENSOR COLOR
Red

HEIGHT
2 meters

HOMEWORLD
Holowan Laboratories

Some have suggested that IG-88 would have been the perfect weapon to battle the Yuuzhan Vong. His flamethrower, repeating blaster, sonic stunner, paralysis cord, and poison gas canisters would make short work of any opponent, and the finishing touch would be the irony of having a droid decimate the antitechnology Yuuzhan Vong fanatics.

This scenario, however, is academic, since the IG-88 who once racked up bounties is gone forever—and that's undoubtedly for the best.

IG-88 came to life in the laboratories of Holowan Mechanicals several years before the Battle of Yavin. Imperial Supervisor Gurdun had diverted millions of credits into "Project Phlutdroid," an ambitious attempt to build mechanized warriors that would crush the Rebellion. Chief Technician Loruss and her crew constructed five IG-series prototypes.

During a routine test, one of the IG units downloaded sentience programming and suddenly "woke up." Perceiving his creators as threats, the droid killed them within seconds, then copied his consciousness into three identical automatons. The four IG-88s fled the planet, while the fifth droid, IG-72, struck off on his own.

Supervisor Gurdun, horrified by what he'd unleashed, issued a "dismantle on sight" order for the runaway IGs, and it would be years before the Empire scored a mechanized battlefield success with its much more tractable Dark Troopers.

The first IG-88 distinguished himself from his fellows by adopting the designation IG-88A. The others became IG-88s B, C, and D. All four traveled to the droid factories of Mechis III, which they quickly took over by enlisting the local automatons into their army. Their ultimate goal? Galactic domination.

To all appearances Mechis III continued to operate normally. But every droid produced on the assembly lines contained devious, hidden programming. When the activation signal came, the machines would rise up against their organic masters and make IG-88 ruler of the galaxy.

To prevent anyone from stumbling upon the truth, IG-88B assumed a cover identity as a bounty hunter. Far from Mechis III, he tracked and captured dozens of targets. On his first mission to Peridon's Folly, IG-88B eliminated a low-life weapons dealer, then quietly killed an IG design scientist on the side. He continued this tactic across the Empire, earning fame and simultaneously wiping out everyone who might know his weaknesses. Two of IG-88B's hunts, on Tammuz-an and Hosk, mixed him up in the early adventures of R2-D2 and C-3PO.

IG-88B flew the *IG-2000*, a heavily modified Trilon Aggressor assault fighter. With his built-in arsenal he hardly needed to carry a weapon, but he toted around a pulse cannon to intimidate onlookers. Eventually IG-88B joined the Bounty Hunters' Guild and participated in such missions as the search for the Yavin Vassilika and the hunt for Oph Nar Dinnid on the home planet of the Shell Hutts.

IG-72, meanwhile, also became a bounty hunter. For a time he worked with human mercenary Dace Bonearm, and his exploits greatly increased the notoriety of the IG series. Shortly after the Battle of Yavin, IG-72 self-destructed on Tatooine during a mission to capture legendary General Adar Tallon.

Darth Vader eventually visited Mechis III, but the IG-88 units were able to hide the brewing droid revolution even from him. IG-88A modified Vader's production order for probe droids to carry his subversive programming.

Following the Battle of Hoth, IG-88B and five other bounty hunters docked aboard the Super Star Destroyer *Executor* to accept Vader's bounty on the *Millennium Falcon*. Using a tracking device, IG-88B followed Boba Fett to Cloud City, but Fett ambushed the droid in a lower smelting chamber. Paralyzing his opponent with a heavy ion cannon, Fett then blew him to pieces with grenades and left the chunks for the Ugnaughts to fight over.

IG-88s C and D, in identical copies of the *IG-2000*, sped to intercept Fett, but by the time they arrived at Cloud City, Fett had already left. Subsequently, the two droids accepted a number of assignments, including a mission seeking Domina Tagge in the Red Nebula and an attempt to capture Lando Calrissian on Stenos. Eventually, IG-88s C and D set their own ambush for Fett in orbit above Tatooine, but he outwitted the IGs yet again and blasted both starships to scrap. According to some reports, IG-88D survived the explosion and limped to Ord Mantell, where Dash Rendar finished him off.

IG-88A, the last surviving unit, completed his preparations for galactic takeover. He ordered the Mechis III factories to build a duplicate of the second Death Star's computer core, then attacked an Imperial convoy and switched his forgery with the genuine core. Then, with just a hint of nostalgia, IG-88A abandoned his weapons-studded body and uploaded his pure consciousness into the computer core.

Once Imperial techs installed the core, IG-88A *was* the Death Star, able to destroy planets at will. When the Rebel fleet arrived at Endor, IG-88A prepared to transmit the master control signal that would trigger his droid revolution. Lando Calrissian's and Wedge Antilles's destruction of the Death Star's reactor core eliminated IG-88A for all time.

The supply freighter that had delivered the computer core brought IG-88A's empty body back to Mechis III. Without its twisted consciousness, the droid was little more than a drone. At least one individual found the droid shell and reprogrammed it, for IG-88A made one post-Endor appearance on the planet Keyorin. Years later, Tyko Thul found IG-88A's body back on Mechis III and programmed the droid to act as his bodyguard during the Diversity Alliance crisis.

YSANNE ISARD

PRONUNCIATION
Ē-sän' Ī'-särd
SPECIES
Human
SEX
Female
HAIR COLOR
Black and white
EYE COLOR
One red, one blue
HEIGHT
1.8 meters
HOMEWORLD
Unknown

They called her "Iceheart," for she had cold-blooded cruelty to spare. But while one of her eyes shone ice blue, the other burned red as a smoking coal.

Armand Isard, Ysanne's father, became director of Republic Intelligence early in Supreme Chancellor Palpatine's term. After the Clone Wars, Armand's department became Imperial Intelligence, and the director began training his young daughter Ysanne for a career as a field operative. The Emperor's New Order created many dissidents, and traitors needed to be sniffed out and exterminated. The Isards held far more power under the Empire than they'd ever possessed in the Republic.

Ysanne grew into a model field agent, and never used her relationship to Armand as a crutch. But she had inherited the ambition that pulsed through the Isard veins. She formed her own alliances within Imperial Intelligence, plotting her ascension behind her father's back.

Just before the Battle of Yavin, Rebel spies stole a datapack containing the coordinates for the Death Star's construction site at Despayre. Armand Isard dispatched his daughter to Darkknell to retrieve the datapack from the Alliance's transfer agents. Upon planetfall, Ysanne ran into CorSec officer Hal Horn and forced him to help her in her mission. Nevertheless, she failed to recover the Death Star data from Darkknell.

Upon her return to Coruscant, Armand told his daughter that she would not be executed for her failure. Instead of expressing gratitude, Ysanne sprang her trap. Flanked by two of the Emperor's Royal Guards, she accused her father of treason for allowing the datapack to fall into Rebel hands and sending her on a mission from which she was unlikely to return. With his twisted sense of paternal pride, Armand Isard may have admired the skill with which his daughter set him up. But his thoughts on the matter went undocumented, as Palpatine had him executed within the hour.

Now director of Imperial Intelligence, Ysanne worked to demonstrate the usefulness of her office to the only person who mattered—the Emperor. Impressed with her suggestion to build a combination internment center and brainwashing facility, Palpatine gave her the Super Star Destroyer *Executor* from the Kuat shipyards—a twin to Vader's *Executor* from Fondor. She renamed the vessel the *Lusankya*, and, with help from the Emperor's mind-fogging powers, Imperial engineers buried the tremendous battleship beneath the cityscape in Coruscant's Manarai Mountain district. Rebel Alliance General Jan Dodonna, captured during the Rebel evacuation of Yavin 4, became the *Lusankya*'s first prisoner.

When her Emperor died at Endor, Isard ordered troops into a Coruscant plaza to massacre more than a hundred thousand traitorous citizens celebrating the news. But she realized this was a golden opportunity. She curried favor with Grand Vizier Sate Pestage, who had filled the vacant Imperial throne, and captured Emperor's Hand Mara Jade to eliminate this threat to her authority, though Jade escaped Coruscant and disappeared.

Deep in the Imperial Palace, Isard found Emperor Palpatine's personal cloning facility. She transferred one of the Spaarti cloning cylinders to the *Lusankya* and destroyed the rest of the complex. Without anyone's knowledge, Isard grew a clone of herself, which she kept in suspended animation. Meanwhile she acted as Sate Pestage's adviser, pretending to support him while secretly making him look incompetent to his rivals in the Ruling Circle. After Pestage—misled by Isard's advice—allowed the New Republic to capture the planet Brentaal, the Ruling Circle began planning a coup.

Pestage knew his rivals would destroy him. He arranged a series of secret talks with Leia Organa on Axxila to work out a deal for a peaceful transfer of power. In response, the Rul-

ing Circle ordered Pestage's arrest and set itself up as the new voice of the Empire. Pestage fled, and the Circle sent Admiral Delak Krennel to retrieve him from Ciutric. Though Isard tried to recruit Krennel to her cause, he murdered Pestage and became the warlord of the Ciutric Hegemony. With Pestage out of the way, Isard assassinated every member of the Ruling Circle in a single day. At last she ruled the Empire.

Warlord secession and New Republic aggression, however, chipped away at the once-boundless Imperial borders. Eight months after Endor, Is-

ard lost the Imperial Black Fleet when she recalled military forces to defend the Core Worlds against Admiral Ackbar. A year after Endor, the Central Committee of Grand Moffs and the Prophets of the Dark Side staged a coup against her reign. Isard manipulated their downfall and executed the survivors as traitors. A short time later Jerec, a former Jedi who was turned to the dark side by High Inquisitor Treymayne, also failed to topple her regime.

Isard kept her hidden *Lusankya* facility stocked with inmates and periodically updated the memory templates of her sleeping clone. Several months after Jerec's death, Isard captured Rogue Squadron pilot Tycho Celchu at Coruscant but couldn't break his will, not even with the most painful tortures the *Lusankya* had to offer. Isard kept in touch with Grand Admiral Thrawn in the Unknown Regions, and hoped he would not return to challenge her power. When Thrawn expressed his need for Imperial defector Baron Fel, Isard implemented Thrawn's capture plan and gave him Fel as a prisoner.

Three years after Endor, one of Isard's scientists perfected the Krytos virus, a fatal contagion that affected only specific nonhuman species. Realizing that a New Republic invasion of Coruscant was imminent, Isard released the Krytos virus into Imperial City's water supply to spoil her enemies' victory with an outbreak of plague. When an enemy fleet arrived at the capital planet, Isard captured

Rogue pilot Corran Horn—making it appear as if he'd been killed in a crash—and retreated to the buried *Lusankya*. The New Republic settled in above her head.

Horn resisted Isard's brainwashing efforts and eventually escaped from the *Lusankya*. Her cover blown, Isard blasted out through the Coruscant cityscape in her Super Star Destroyer and fled to the bacta planet Thyferra, where she supported a coup and became the planet's head of state. Rogue Squadron went after her in a conflict known as the Bacta War. When defeat seemed inevitable, Isard activated her clone and told it to scatter the *Lusankya* prisoners. Rogue Squadron captured Thyferra, preventing Isard from eliminating her clone as she'd planned, and seized her beloved *Lusankya*. Ysanne Isard did not appear to have survived the Battle of Thyferra.

She had escaped, however, as had her clone. The clone hooked up with "Prince Admiral" Krennel, warlord of the Ciutric Hegemony, and interned the ex–*Lusankya* prisoners on Ciutric. The real Isard spent months putting herself back together mentally, then overthrew a small-time warlord named General Arnothian who controlled a TIE defender production facility. Isard watched from the sidelines as Grand Admiral Thrawn made war against the New Republic. To her shock Emperor Palpatine, reborn in a clone body, contacted her to demand her fealty. Isard feared execution for the loss of Coruscant and promised Palpatine she would reclaim the *Lusankya*.

After Thrawn's defeat, Ysanne Isard's TIE defenders rescued Rogue Squadron from an ambush at Corvis Minor. Isard explained to the Rogues that she wanted their help in bringing down Prince Admiral Krennel and her renegade clone. The Rogues agreed to assist her as long as they got a shot at freeing the *Lusankya* inmates on Ciutric. Posing as TIE defender pilots, the Rogues infiltrated Krennel's planet and freed the prisoners. Admiral Ackbar, meanwhile, put together a fleet from Bilbringi Shipyards and hammered Ciutric's defenses. Both Krennel and the Isard clone died in the fighting.

But the real Isard seized that moment to strike at the undefended Bilbringi Shipyards, where the repaired *Lusankya* waited in dry dock. When she tried to commandeer the gigantic Super Star Destroyer, she found New Republic Intelligence agent Iella Wessiri waiting in her quarters. Wessiri had anticipated Isard's treachery. She shot and killed Ysanne Isard, bringing to an end the reign of "Iceheart."

PRINCE ISOLDER

There's an old proverb: "Men marry women who remind them of their mothers." Isolder of Hapes might have thought that his marriage to a Dathomirian Witch represented a rejection of his aristocratic upbringing, but his bride Teneniel Djo was just as assertive as the Queen Mother of Hapes herself.

Isolder's mother, Queen Mother Ta'a Chume, ruled the sixty-three worlds of the Hapes Consortium with absolute authority. But her empire was a strict matriarchy, and fate had cursed her with two sons. Knowing that her older son, Kalen, lacked the backbone to be prince—or Chume'da—Ta'a Chume arranged to have him killed.

Her younger son, Isolder, was only nineteen at the time of the tragedy. He fled Hapes's Fountain Palace and went undercover as a hyperspace brigand, hoping to find his brother's murderer—the notorious pirate Haravan. It took two years, but Isolder caught Haravan and dragged him back to Hapes. The pirate died suspiciously in prison before he could reveal his motives.

The Queen Mother approved of her son's ruthless persistence. Isolder became Chume'da, and his bride would become the next Queen Mother. But Ta'a Chume disapproved of his first love, Lady Ellian. Isolder discovered his betrothed's body floating in the palace garden's reflecting pool.

Isolder put both tragedies behind him and worked to make a difference—as much as a man could in Hapes's female-dominated society. As Chume'da he commanded the Hapan Battle Dragon *Song of War* and boasted a phalanx of Terephon body-

PRONUNCIATION
Ī'-sōl-dûr
SPECIES
Human
SEX
Male
HAIR COLOR
Blond
EYE COLOR
Blue-gray
HEIGHT
1.88 meters
HOMEWORLD
Hapes

guards led by former bandit Captain Astarta. He patrolled the borders of the Consortium in his custom Miy'til fighter the *Storm*.

Women throughout the Consortium fought over the royal heir, but it was an offworlder who caught the prince's eye. Approximately four years after the Battle of Endor, Princess Leia Organa opened diplomatic talks with the Hapans. Smitten with the Princess, Isolder told his mother of his intention to marry her.

At a reception on Coruscant, the Hapan delegation presented Leia Organa with sixty-three gifts from their sixty-three worlds, each gift more spectacular than the last. The sixty-third gift was Isolder himself.

Her fellow politicians pressured Leia to enter into marriage with the twenty-five-year-old Isolder. To do so would give a financial and military boost to the New Republic.

But Han Solo, jealous of his new rival, kidnapped the princess and brought her to the wilderness planet Dathomir. Isolder followed, and on Dathomir he met the primitive Force-wielding witch Teneniel Djo. Though Teneniel was no princess, she came from a female-dominant society similar to the one in which Isolder had grown up. The Chume'da fell in love and declared his intention to make Teneniel the Chume'la—the future Queen Mother of Hapes.

Isolder also voiced some suspicions he had been developing for quite some time. Ta'a Chume, stung by Isolder's accusations that she had orchestrated the deaths of Kalen and Lady Ellian, grudgingly accepted her son's choice of a betrothed. She soon stepped down, and Teneniel Djo assumed the title of Queen Mother.

Isolder and Teneniel Djo had one daughter, Tenel Ka. She proved to have her mother's blood, demonstrating a profound attunement to the Force. When Tenel Ka reached her early teens, Isolder sent her to Luke Skywalker's Jedi academy on Yavin 4.

Though he had long rejected his mother's mercenary ideals, Isolder still held a traditionalist's view of Hapan society. He began grooming his daughter as the future Queen Mother, despite his wife's objections that Tenel Ka be allowed to choose her own path.

During the Yuuzhan Vong war Isolder again welcomed Leia Organa Solo to Hapes, this time to hear her plea for military aid. He expressed his eagerness to help, driven by a desire to play the hero and by his lingering affection for the Princess. A noninterventionist Hapan ambassador, Archon Beed Thane of Vergill, deliberately insulted Leia in order to provoke Isolder into an honor duel. The two squared off in hand-to-hand combat at Hapes's Reef Fortress. If Isolder won, the Consortium would enter the war. If he lost, the Hapans would remain on the sidelines. Isolder knocked out Thane, and the Hapan navy joined the New Republic for a massive strike against the Yuuzhan Vong at Fondor.

Force-inspired premonitions of disaster plagued Leia's dreams. Her visions proved true. Light-years from Fondor, at Corellia, Centerpoint Station fired a blinding white repulsor beam that shot through space. The misaligned energy pulse damaged the Yuuzhan Vong armada and vaporized the core of the Hapan fleet. Stunned by the cataclysm, Isolder limped back to the Consortium to lick his wounds and prepare for a second strike against the enemy.

Upon his return he learned that Teneniel, who had been pregnant with their second child, had miscarried, when, through the Force, she'd felt the deaths of the Hapan fleet's crew members. While his wife grieved, Isolder searched for ways to protect Hapes from a Yuuzhan Vong attack. The aliens had bypassed the Consortium on their invasion route, but a recent influx of refugees practically guaranteed Hapes would find itself in the crosshairs.

The Yuuzhan Vong attacked against a backdrop of Hapan intrigue. Ta'a Chume plotted to have Jaina Solo marry her son and become the next Queen Mother. To further her plan, she arranged for Teneniel Djo's death.

Isolder helped defeat the Yuuzhan Vong at Hapes. Afterward, he mourned his wife, Teneniel. Though it couldn't make up for the pain in his heart, he made sure that his mother was imprisoned and tried. Isolder's daughter Tenel Ka took over as the new Queen Mother of the Hapan Consortium.

JABBA THE HUTT

Jabba Desilijic Tiure was approximately six hundred at the time of his death. He could have looked forward to many more centuries of spice smuggling, slave trafficking, kidnapping, extortion, and murder, if he hadn't gotten on the wrong side of a human named Leia Organa.

Jabba's family included his uncles Jiliac and Pazda, his nephews Gorga and Grubba, and his father Zorba. Ironfisted ruler of clan Desilijic, Zorba bore Jabba at the age of four hundred and taught his offspring the intricacies of Nal Hutta clan politics. For centuries Jabba managed thousands of Desilijic operations throughout the Old Republic and the glorious expanses of Hutt space. Among his triumphs, Jabba despoiled the forbidden gardens of Nuswatta and survived the infamous orgies of Spunchina.

As a sign of his growing influence, Jabba assumed an offworld posting on Tatooine, a critical smuggling transshipment point despite its uncomfortable climate. Jabba took over the B'omarr monks' fortress in the Dune Sea and subtly battled rival Hutt envoys such as Gardulla of clan Besadii. He raked in credits from the Podracing gambling racket, and boasted his own private viewing box at the Mos Espa Arena.

Jabba's agents were legion. The bounty hunter Aurra Sing was often in his employ, and the ambitious Twi'lek Bib Fortuna acted as his majordomo. Dannik Jerriko, a thousand-year-old Anzati, performed Jabba's silent assassinations. But a Chevin gunrunner named Ephant Mon was Jabba's only true friend. Since Hutts rarely esteem anyone outside their own species, the friendship between Jabba and Ephant

PRONUNCIATION
Jä'-bä the Hŭt
SPECIES
Hutt
SEX
Hermaphrodite
(male personality)
HAIR COLOR
None

EYE COLOR
Orange
HEIGHT
3.9 meters long
HOMEWORLD
Nal Hutta

Mon was unusual and—to some in Jabba's court—inexplicable.

Jabba was always willing to fund Ephant Mon's schemes, such as one just prior to the Battle of Naboo that resulted in the capture of two Cerean women, one of whom was the daughter of Jedi Knight Ki-Adi-Mundi. The Cerean Jedi came to Tatooine to rescue his daughter, and uncovered evidence that Jabba had secretly been arming the Trade Federation for its imminent invasion of Naboo.

Not long after the Naboo incident, Jabba again orchestrated a weapons deal, this time to dump unwanted inventory by inciting a local war between Tatooine's settlers and the Tusken Raiders. Ki-Adi-Mundi opposed him again, and Jabba fought off a takeover attempt raised by his rival Gardulla. At approximately the same time, when Bib Fortuna mishandled some triviality, the notoriously fickle Jabba demoted the Twi'lek to errand boy and made Naroon Cuthas his replacement major-domo.

Fifteen years before the Battle of Yavin, Jabba's father Zorba was arrested for illegal gemstone mining and locked in an Imperial prison on Kip. When bribery failed to free the mighty patriarch, Zorba's sibling Jiliac assumed control of clan Desilijic. Jabba, Jiliac's nephew, became next in the line of clan succession.

Jabba split his time between Tatooine and Nal Hutta. Over the years he experienced many offworld adventures, including his legendary double cross of Gaar Suppoon and his gruesome escape from Princess Nampi. On Nal Hutta he began employing a talented human spice pilot named Han Solo.

When Jabba and Ephant Mon stole guns from an armory on Glakka, their friendship saved both their lives. Ephant Mon shot down the raiders threatening their position, and Jabba returned the favor by wrapping his friend in his fatty coils throughout the subzero night.

Jabba eventually grew weary of the aging Naroon Cuthas and began grooming two candidates for the position of majordomo—the Corellian Bidlo Kwerve and Bib Fortuna, now a top lieutenant entering his third decade of service to the Hutt. During Han

Solo's time in the Corporate Sector, Jabba picked up a new pet on Space Station Kwenn. The Kowakian monkey-lizard Salacious Crumb irritated everyone in the palace but supplied Jabba with an endless store of belly laughs.

Back on Nal Hutta, Durga the Hutt—leader of rival clan Besadii—challenged Jiliac and killed him in a ritualistic death duel. This made Jabba ruler of Desilijic. As he looked at Jiliac's cooling corpse, Jabba saw his uncle's newborn offspring wriggle away from its dead parent. Not about to give up his claim to succession, Jabba rolled over onto the baby Hutt and crushed it.

As ruler of Desilijic, Jabba sponsored Bria Tharen's Alliance raid on Ylesia, destroying Besadii's valuable spice factories. Just before the Battle of Yavin, Jabba received a gift from Bidlo Kwerve—a monstrous, salivating rancor. Jabba made Kwerve the rancor's first meal, then once again

appointed Bib Fortuna his personal majordomo.

Han Solo had once been Jabba's favorite pilot, but he enraged his employer when he dumped a priceless load of Kessel spice. Jabba spent the next three years nursing a vendetta against Solo, offering a fortune for his head. Jabba's agents pinned down the fugitive Corellian on Orleon, but he escaped. Bounty hunters in the Hutt's employ later caught up with Solo on Ord Mantell, but once again he slipped away.

Meanwhile, Jabba sank into ever-greater debauchery. Ephant Mon advised Jabba against this increasingly irrational behavior. After Boba Fett captured Solo, and Jabba hung the carbonized Corellian on his wall, the Hutt wasted millions of credits on a no-holds-barred vehicular demolition contest that resulted in an entertainingly high body count.

Solo's friends in the Rebel Alliance

rushed to rescue him and were swiftly captured. Jabba chose to humiliate the noble Leia Organa by dressing her as a dancing girl and shackling her to his throne. Ephant Mon met with the prisoner Luke Skywalker in Jabba's dungeon and was amazed to discover that the Jedi exuded confidence and peace, even in the face of his death sentence. It was as if he'd already won. Shaken, Ephant Mon tried to caution his old friend against the planned execution. But Jabba, intoxicated with his own omnipotence, viewed the warning as a fatal lack of faith. Declaring their friendship over, Jabba left Ephant Mon behind and sailed out to the Great Pit of Carkoon. He died when Leia Organa strangled him with her own chain.

With word of Jabba's demise, chaos took hold of clan Desilijic. After a round of brutal infighting, two Hutts—Kumac and Jelasi—emerged as joint clan leaders. Meanwhile, Jabba's lesser relatives came to Tatooine to settle his estate. They took what they could, but thieves made off with Jabba's hidden treasure ship the *Spirit of Jabba* and its cargo of priceless funeral urns.

It wasn't until a year after Jabba's death that all of his holdings were discharged. Zorba the Hutt, released from prison via surreptitious orders from Ysanne Isard, returned to Tatooine and found his son's true will and testament. Through the courts, Zorba claimed all that was legally due him as Jabba's father; everything else was soon wrested from the hapless hands of Kumac and Jelasi. In a short time Zorba once again ruled Desilijic, though the clan never achieved its former prominence. Zorba's first official act was to put a death mark on Leia Organa Solo for the murder of his son. The bounty wasn't rescinded until after the New Republic defeated the clone Emperor.

Borga the Hutt is the current head of the Besadii clan—and the de facto leader of Nal Hutta. Other Hutts are openly longing for the glory days of Jabba. Had he survived, they say, the Desilijic clan would have kept Besadii in check. There would have been no Darksaber Project. Black Sun wouldn't have dominated Hutt interests. And Jabba would *never* have brokered a deal with the Yuuzhan Vong—his deviousness ran far deeper than the Yuuzhan Vong's cunning.

JEDI COUNCIL MEMBERS

During the waning years of the Old Republic, the Jedi Council operated out of the Judicial Department under the office of the Supreme Chancellor. Yoda and Mace Windu were both lifelong members. The other ten ever-changing Jedi were less well known, but each had a vital voice in Council debates. Among the more prominent members were:

Depa Billaba
(Dĕ'-pä Bĭl-ä'-bä)

Mace Windu rescued Depa Billaba from space pirates when she was just an infant. Raised within the Temple walls, often under Master Windu's direct instruction, this near-human Chalactan grew to become one of the most pious of all the Jedi. Her unique melding of Jedi philosophy and traditional Chalactan faith made her an authority on spiritual matters.

Adi Gallia
(Ä'-dē Gä'-lē-yä)

Though she looked young, the near-human Adi Gallia was a member of the Jedi Council for more than a decade prior to the Battle of Naboo, and had been a Jedi Master even longer than that. Adi Gallia was a furious combatant, and a political maven with close ties to Coruscant's government. Her parents were Corellian diplomats, but she lived virtually her entire life on Coruscant. She trained a human girl named Siri Tachi to Knighthood in the years before Naboo. Adi Gallia enjoyed a close working relationship with Qui-Gon Jinn and was heartbroken when he died.

Ki-Adi-Mundi
(Kē-ä-dē-mŭn'-dē)

This Jedi hailed from the green world of Cerea, where he had two wives and a daughter. The low birthrate of the Cereans allowed Ki-Adi-Mundi to receive a special exemption from the Jedi edict that discouraged marriage. A Jedi Knight as of the Battle of Naboo, he was the only non-Master on the Council. Ki-Adi-Mundi took up his Council seat following the death of Master Micah Giiett, though he had previously "sat in" on Council meetings when other members were away on missions.

After the Battle of Naboo, Ki-Adi-Mundi traveled to Tatooine to confirm that the great Jedi Sharad Hett had resurfaced as a Tusken Raider chieftain. Though Ki-Adi-Mundi failed to prevent Hett's death at the hands of Aurra Sing, he accepted Hett's son A'Sharad as his Padawan learner. Later he allowed the Dark Woman, one of his old teachers, to take over A'Sharad's training.

As a Jedi Master, Ki-Adi-Mundi

numbered among the few survivors of the Battle of Geonosis.

Plo Koon

(Plō Kōōn)

Plo Koon hailed from Dorin, a cold and dusty world with an extremely thin atmosphere. It lies between two perilous black holes, discouraging visitors and so giving the native Kel Dors an air of mystery and menace among superstitious spacers.

Koon, a long-term Council member, saw all moral issues in terms of black and white—a trait shared by other members of his species, who advocate executions and punitive amputations. He was much more likely than his fellow Jedi to practice "rough justice." Koon could employ the Force Push ability without needing to face his target, manipulated the environment to create fog or ice, and even employed the controversial fingertip-lightning technique, which Koon called "Electric Judgment." He wore goggles and a breath mask in oxygen-rich atmospheres, only doffing the gear in his pressurized quarters, which were accessible via air lock. Had he ever been exposed to pure oxygen, Koon would have suffered immediate blindness or death.

In the Fifth Battle of Qotile, during the Stark Hyperspace Conflict, Plo Koon took up the fallen Republic banner and rallied his forces to victory.

At the time of the Battle of Naboo, Koon was raising a female Trandoshan from Padawan learner to Jedi Knight.

Eeth Koth

(Ēth Kŏth)

The Zabrak known as Eeth Koth was born into the slums of Nar Shaddaa and accepted into the Jedi at the late age of four. Though he was a respected member of the Jedi Council, his fame was eclipsed by that of his first Padawan, the legendary Sharad "Howlrunner" Hett. Koth's outstanding talent was Crucitorn, a Jedi technique for transcending physical pain that goes far beyond his natural Zabrak ability to withstand torture.

Even Piell

(Ē-věn Pē'-ĕl)

Piell, a long-lived Lannik, lost his eye in a battle against seven Red Iaro terrorists who attempted to overthrow his homeworld's government. During the fight he saved the lives of Adi Gallia's parents, who were meeting with the Lannik High Court in their capacity as Corellian diplomats. Piell had a rematch with the Red Iaro terrorists, this time on Malastare, shortly after the Battle of Naboo.

Yarael Poof

(Yăr'-ē-ĕl Pōōf)

Poof, a contemplative Quermian, was a master illusionist able to project visions into the brains of others. One of his lesser-known skills was his ability to trigger spontaneous fires by exciting the molecules of combustible objects. Like all Quermians, Poof lacked a spinal column and could contort his body into impossible shapes. During the Stark Hyperspace Conflict, Yarael Poof's use of Jedi battle meditation helped ensure a victory for the Republic. Poof often served as a calming influence during debates within the Jedi Council chamber.

Oppo Rancisis

(Ŏ'-pō Rān'chē'-sĭs)

Rancisis, 174 years old as of the Battle of Naboo, was incredibly ancient for a snake-bodied Thisspiasian. His mother was the Blood Monarch of Thisspias, but Rancisis was offered to the Jedi Order as a baby, where he was accepted by Master

Yaddle as a Padawan. When Rancisis reached the age of twenty, his younger sister was killed when agitators stormed the Thisspias alcazar in Ratamesh. The monarchy reverted to Rancisis but he refused it outright, preferring his life as a Jedi.

Following his role as fleet battle strategist during the Stark Hyperspace Conflict, Rancisis received a position on the Jedi Council. He was also an instructor of Malacia, a Force ability that induces dizziness and nausea.

Saesee Tiin
(Sā'-sē Tē'-ŭn)

This telepathic Iktotchi from Iktotch, the moon of Iktotchon, was trained by Master Omo Bouri, the great Wol Cabbashite who orchestrated the Treaty of Trammis. Master Bouri perished a decade before the Battle of Naboo, and Tiin devoted himself fanatically to the Jedi, hoping to gain the skills necessary to communicate with his Master on the spirit plane. He didn't train a Padawan, and Mace Windu privately questioned the value of this loner, since he rarely contributed to Council discussions.

The *Sharp Spiral*, a customized SoroSuub Cutlass-9, was Tiin's personal starfighter, given to him by a grateful Coruscant diplomat. Tiin was an expert pilot, and served as the official liaison between the Jedi Council and Freedom's Sons, a civilian group of non-Jedi who assisted the Knights on special projects.

Yaddle
(Yă'-dŭl)

Four hundred seventy-seven years old as of the Battle of Naboo, Yaddle trained dozens of Padawans in her life, including Oppo Rancisis. According to popular legend, Yaddle ascended to the rank of Master after spending more than a hundred years in an underground prison on Koba. One of her students, the vain and confident Empatojayos Brand, passed the trials for Knighthood after Naboo. After Brand, Yaddle did not take another apprentice.

As head of the Librarians' Assembly, Yaddle worked with curator Ashka Boda to maintain the Temple's collection of Holocrons, scrolls, and Sith tomes. She was skilled with Jedi healing techniques, and was a master of Mortichro, a forgotten Jedi art that slowed the body functions of other beings. Yaddle split her time between Coruscant and Kamparas, where she taught at an auxiliary training center for Jedi Knights who did not live at the Temple full time.

JEDI FROM THE BATTLE OF GEONOSIS

The Battle of Geonosis was a dark day for the Jedi, their gravest blow since the Battle of Ruusan a thousand years prior. Though scores fell under the weapons of Geonosian battle droids, individual Jedi distinguished themselves with extraordinary heroism.

Kit Fisto

(Kǐt Fǐs'-tō)

This Nautiloid Jedi Master hailed from the Sabilon region of Glee Anselm, a gentle, watery world in the Mid Rim. His outlook on life was laid-back and accepting, and he believed it was his Jedi mission to use nature's gifts for the betterment of the people of the galaxy. His acute sense of smell allowed him to read the emotions of other beings. Prior to the Battle of Naboo, Kit Fisto took a Mon Calamari named Bant as his Padawan after her previous Master became one with the Force.

Barriss Offee

(Bǎr'-rǐs Ō-fē')

A female human Jedi Padawan, Barriss Offee was born to unknown parents aboard a passenger liner, and taken into the Jedi Order at infancy. She called no world home and exhibited a rigid adherence to the philosophy that her life belonged to the Jedi Order.

Shaak Ti

(Shǎk Tē)

Jedi Master Shaak Ti was a Togruta from the overcrowded planet Shili. Unlike most Togrutas she chose a solitary life as a Jedi, but still felt stabs of loneliness despite the Force training she used to keep her emotions in check. Her natural ability to sense other bodies in close proximity to her own served her well in combat situations. Shaak Ti trained two Padawans in her career, only to see both fall victim to criminal killers shortly after their graduations to Knighthood.

Luminara Unduli

(Lōō-mǐn-ä'-rä Ǔn-dōō'-lē)

Luminara Unduli hailed from the same planet as the notorious space pirate Arwen Cohl, who had once freed her people from oppression at the hands of a neighboring world. Unlike Cohl, Luminara had dedicated her life to justice, and became a Jedi Master more than a decade prior to the Battle of Geonosis.

Jerec

Jerec betrayed the Jedi Order. He schemed to betray his own Master, Emperor Palpatine. Motivated by nothing besides his obsessive self-interest, Jerec would happily have subjugated everyone, everywhere, and ruled over a galaxy of slaves.

At the time of the Clone Wars, Jerec was a full-fledged Jedi Knight, blind since birth, and tasked with seeking out rare artifacts in far corners of the galaxy. Upon his return to Coruscant, he discovered that the Jedi Order had been all but exterminated. He fled to the Unknown Regions, but Imperial High Inquisitor Tremayne tracked him down and offered him a chance for survival in the New Order. In the end Jerec did not believe in his ideals enough to die for them, and when faced with Tremayne's offer he eagerly turned traitor.

Jerec used the Force to enable him to perceive his surroundings. He wore a thin strip of leather over his eyes and was quick to take advantage of those who were unaware of his sensory advantage. Jerec bore Sith tattoos on his face, as Darth Maul had before him, though Palpatine never named Jerec a Sith Lord. Darth Vader already held that title.

Instead, Jerec shared the Imperial Palace with many other dark-siders—some former Jedi, others Force-sensitive youngsters. Some served Palpatine, others Vader, but none of them ever stopped scheming for advantage over the others. Jerec outranked the Dark Side Adepts such as Hethrir, Sedriss, and Kadann, but they viewed him as a turncoat waiting for the right opportunity to stab them in the back. Palpatine trusted Jerec so

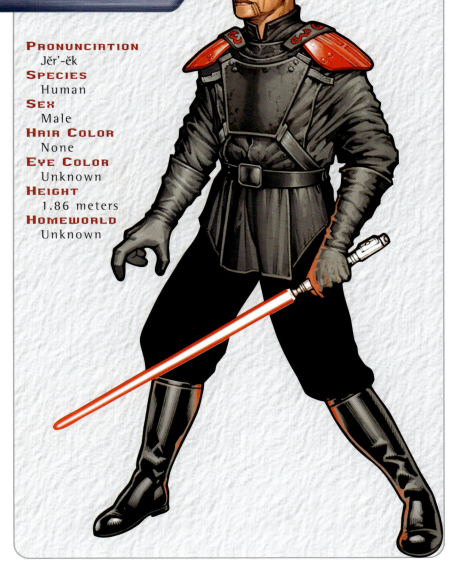

PRONUNCIATION
Jĕr'-ĕk
SPECIES
Human
SEX
Male
HAIR COLOR
None
EYE COLOR
Unknown
HEIGHT
1.86 meters
HOMEWORLD
Unknown

little that he frequently assigned Captain Thrawn to command Jerec's Star Destroyer the *Vengeance*. Jerec embarked on several long-range missions to find other "lost" Jedi and turn them to the dark side of the Force.

Jerec knew that intimidation alone would not give him what he craved. He needed power, but he also needed funds. Wielding the bargaining tool of exemption from Inquisitorius audits, Jerec attracted silent corporate backers and quietly be-

came a billionaire.

Not long before the Battle of Yavin, Jerec led a mission to eliminate a Rebel cell on Sulon. He killed Morgan Katarn, father to Imperial Cadet Kyle Katarn, then a short time later Jerec decorated Kyle at the Caridan Academy's graduation ceremony. Had he possessed a deeper connection to the unifying Force, Jerec might have foreseen the role Kyle Katarn would play in his downfall.

Approximately ten months after Yavin, Jerec took the *Vengeance* to Ithor and released an ancient menace named Spore. A self-aware, highly contagious parasite, Spore had the power to infect and enslave millions. Jerec planned to use Spore's contaminated army to overthrow the Emperor, but space slugs in Ithor's asteroid field destroyed the *Vengeance*.

Though he survived, Jerec became more cautious, and he postponed further coup attempts. He built a tower in Baron's Hed on Sulon and ruled there as a conquering governor.

But the Emperor's death at Endor, and the sudden splintering of the Empire into warlord fragments, provided an opportunity he couldn't resist. He began angling for the Imperial throne itself, relying on help from his corporate partners. With his wealth, Jerec purchased a Super Star Destroyer variant from Kuat Drive Yards and named it the *Vengeance*, for his former command.

As he watched Yasanne Isard and Sate Pestage scheme for Imperial control, Jerec also stepped up his efforts to locate the Valley of the Jedi. This battlefield on Ruusan held thousands of trapped Force spirits and represented a bottomless well of energy. With the Valley's power, Jerec was certain he would be mightier than Palpatine.

A year after Endor, Jerec tracked down a hidden Jedi of the old Order named Qu Rahn. Probing Rahn's mind for data on the Valley's location, he learned that a map could be found in Morgan Katarn's old homestead on Sulon. Then Jerec finished the purge he had begun two decades earlier by executing Rahn.

Jerec's dark-side underlings, along with the droid 8t88, located the map. Jerec quickly took the *Vengeance* to Ruusan, wiping out the planet's only settlement, and constructed a headquarters tower. But Kyle Katarn moved to stop him. Katarn had already defeated three of Jerec's allies, Yun, Gorc, and Pic, and Jerec set a trap for the Jedi initiate at the Ruusan tower, threatening the life of Katarn's partner in the hope of luring Katarn to the dark side.

The gambit failed, but Jerec trusted in his surviving lieutenants to kill Katarn. Meanwhile, Jerec cracked open the unfathomable power of the Valley of the Jedi, only to have Kyle Katarn prevent him from successfully tapping into the Valley's central Force stream.

In the end, it came down to a face-off between Jerec and Katarn—one charge, one cut. Jerec was sliced nearly in two. As he lay dying, he watched the spirits of the Valley escape forever into the light, never again to be exploited by a would-be tyrant.

Qui-Gon Jinn

PRONUNCIATION
Kwī'-gŏn Jĭn
SPECIES
Human
SEX
Male
HAIR COLOR
Gray
EYE COLOR
Blue
HEIGHT
1.93 meters
HOMEWORLD
Unknown

People who commented on Qui-Gon Jinn always ended up revealing a lot about themselves. To hidebound conservatives he was an anarchic bomb-thrower. To free-thinkers he was as stubborn and set in his ways as a bantha. To a stranger off the street he could be as warm as an old friend, while to his own Padawan he could sometimes be distant and hard to know.

Qui-Gon Jinn, fatally run through by Darth Maul's lightsaber, was cremated with full honors at the Theed Funeral Temple. In attendance were Supreme Chancellor Palpatine, the members of the Jedi Council, dignitaries from all over Naboo, and Obi-Wan Kenobi, Qui-Gon Jinn's Padawan learner for more than twelve years.

Obi-Wan thought it ironic to see the Jedi Council at the funeral, considering his Master had always given them such fits. Throughout Qui-Gon Jinn's long career, he cultivated a reputation as a maverick who ignored the rule book and followed his heart. Qui-Gon possessed a keen attunement to the "here-and-now," but didn't adhere to the big-picture perspective of the unifying Force. This myopia—Qui-Gon called it "insight"—brought him into direct conflict with Yoda and other old-guard Jedi. Plo Koon tried to convince his comrade to join him on the Jedi Council, but Qui-Gon refused to be tied down to their orthodox philosophies.

Qui-Gon Jinn was a member of the Jedi Order all his life, raised from infancy in the Temple on Coruscant. He maintained some ties with his original homeworld, and once obtained a special rock as a keepsake from his planet's River of Light. Qui-Gon's Master considered his apprentice the most skilled swordsmaster he had trained, though he was at times frustrated by Qui-Gon's tendency to go off on side quests to help powerless creatures.

Qui-Gon's first Padawan was a brilliant young man named Xanatos. Their Master–Padawan bond grew strong, but Xanatos gave in to anger when he joined his birth father, the governor of Telos, in violently suppressing a Telosian insurrection. Feeling he had no choice, Qui-Gon killed the corrupt governor, and Xanatos furiously quit the Jedi Order.

Qui-Gon obsessed over his failure for years, vowing to never again train a Padawan, but forged a connection with thirteen-year-old Obi-Wan Kenobi while on a mission to Bandomeer. Obi-Wan became Qui-Gon's second and final apprentice. Though Obi-Wan briefly abandoned the Jedi Order to help end a civil war on Melida/Daan, he soon rejoined his Master and the two became a powerful pair. Qui-Gon and Obi-Wan fought together on planets all across the Republic, finally catching up with the rogue Jedi Xanatos and fighting to save the people of Telos from his corrupt influence. Though he could have allowed despair to claim him, Qui-Gon did not blame himself for the evils perpetrated by his former Padawan. In their final confrontation, Xanatos killed himself by stepping into a pool of acid. Qui-Gon closed a painful chapter of his life.

Qui-Gon and Obi-Wan also performed a mission on Ord Mantell in which Qui-Gon used his connection to the living Force to befriend the native Mantellian savrip. Later, both Jedi went into action against the anti–Trade Federation terrorist organization known as the Nebula Front.

Warned that the Nebula Front planned to assassinate Supreme Chancellor Valorum on Eriadu, they overlooked the assassins' true target—the members of the Trade Federation Directorate. It was one of their few failures.

The two Jedi tried to mediate the Trade Federation's blockade of Naboo, but Neimoidian treachery forced them to flee. Eventually they ended up on Tatooine. Qui-Gon's discovery of Anakin Skywalker on that desert world perfectly illustrates the frustrations that others had with this self-assured rule-breaker. So confident was he that this boy was the Chosen One that he gambled everyone's fates on Anakin's freedom. He employed mind manipulation and dice cheating to achieve his goals, and allowed nine-year-old Anakin to risk his life in a perilous Podrace. When the Jedi Council refused Qui-Gon's request to train Anakin as a Padawan, he immediately began crafting a way to subvert their authority.

The final battle with Darth Maul in the Theed power generator was fast, furious, and fatal. Qui-Gon, a master duelist by anyone's standards, no longer had the stamina of youth. The Sith Lord stabbed him through the chest. Nevertheless, with his dying breath, Qui-Gon made Obi-Wan promise to train Anakin Skywalker, despite the Jedi Council's orders.

Dozens of offworlders came to Naboo for Qui-Gon's funeral. While many of them had had differences with him in the past, everyone in attendance knew that he died a hero.

Kir Kanos

PRONUNCIATION
Kēr Kā'-nōs
SPECIES
Human
SEX
Male
HAIR COLOR
Brown
EYE COLOR
Unknown
HEIGHT
1.83 meters
HOMEWORLD
Unknown

K ir Kanos is a fanatic. At one point he valued his loyalty to Emperor Palpatine more than he valued his own life, and today the last Royal Guardsman continues to eliminate those who do not live up to his impossible standards of honor.

Kanos began his career in the Imperial armed forces and earned sufficient honors to enroll in Royal Guard training on Yinchorr.

As a graduation exercise, Kanos and his training partner Lemmet Tauk stood before Emperor Palpatine and battled to the death. As Kanos stood over his partner's broken body, Darth Vader attacked and defeated the victorious guardsman, leaving Kanos with a jagged facial scar—and a reminder of his place in the Emperor's hierarchy. "Always remember," Vader warned, "that you are weak before the power of the dark side."

After Palpatine's death at Endor, Kanos and most of his fellow guards continued to serve the Empire. They knew Palpatine's power was great, and their faith was rewarded when the Emperor returned from death in a clone body. But then Palpatine died a final death on Onderon.

As the surviving Royal Guards gathered on Yinchorr to mourn, one of their brethren arrived with shocking news. Palpatine had died, in part, because of damaged clones arranged by fellow guardsman Carnor Jax. In the next instant, Carnor Jax's stormtroopers burst in and murdered everyone in the room. Only Kir Kanos survived.

If he could no longer serve Palpatine, Kanos vowed he would at least take vengeance on the clone Emperor's killer. Carnor Jax, having become leader of the Imperial Interim Ruling Council, put everything he had into finding and eliminating the seemingly unstoppable guardsman. After a clash on Phaeda, where Kanos met New Republic operative Mirith Sinn, Jax and Kanos faced off in their old training arena on Yinchorr. Kanos won the duel, and in doing so became the last Royal Guard.

Kanos set his sights on the Imperial usurpers of the Interim Ruling Council. On Baramorra he established a bounty hunter alias, "Kenix Kil," an anagram of his name in guard battle language.

Kanos abandoned his plans when Mirith Sinn was captured by Grappa the Hutt. He dropped everything to rescue Mirith from the savage Zanibar aliens on Xo. Mirith Sinn got closer to Kanos than anyone in ten years, but he resumed his mission and executed "Emperor" Xandel Carivus. Under his Kenix Kil alias, Kanos continued his grim work.

The ersatz "Royal Guards" promoted by Admiral Daala and the clone guardsman Major Tierce enraged Kir Kanos. He worked behind the scenes to undermine and eliminate such pretenders, including the false guards who ruled the Second Imperium's Shadow Academy.

TALON KARRDE

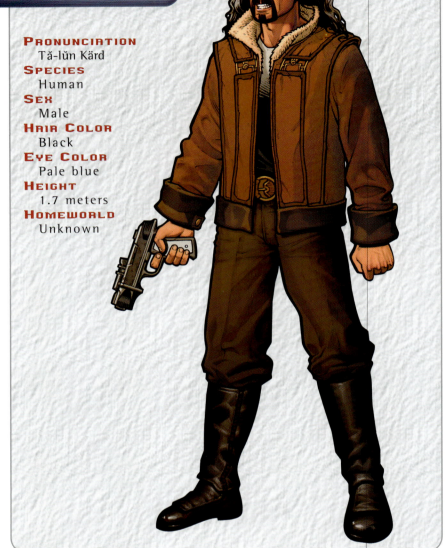

PRONUNCIATION
Tă-lŭn Kärd
SPECIES
Human
SEX
Male
HAIR COLOR
Black
EYE COLOR
Pale blue
HEIGHT
1.7 meters
HOMEWORLD
Unknown

In theory, smuggling kingpins inhabit the fuzzy gray zone between the Empire's evil and the Rebel Alliance's idealism. In practice, none is truly neutral. Jabba the Hutt was as villainous as Emperor Palpatine, while Talon Karrde is clearly on the side of the heroes.

Karrde began his career working within the organization of Jorj Car'das, one of the Hutts' chief rivals in the competitive smuggling industry. Business was good under the trade-restrictive Empire, and Karrde gained shipboard experience on the many freighters in Car'das's fleet.

Six years before the Battle of Yavin, Karrde was serving as a navigator aboard one such vessel when the ship's captain, Hoffner, made a blind hyperspace jump in order to escape a pair of Carrack cruisers. The freighter emerged in the vicinity of the long-lost *Katana* Dreadnaught fleet, a fact that went unrealized by all but Karrde and Hoffner. Both men filed away the location for later use.

Shortly before the Battle of Yavin, Jorj Car'das dropped out of sight following a life-changing encounter with Yoda on Dagobah. Karrde assumed control of Car'das's organization, and after Jabba the Hutt's death he picked up hundreds of new contacts and markets, making his group the most influential operation in the Outer Rim.

Four years after Endor, Talon Karrde rescued Quelev Tapper's smuggling group from Imperial extermination and absorbed it into his own organization. Tapper accepted the job of Karrde's second in command, and Melina Carniss, one of Jabba's ex-agents became a valued lieutenant. Karrde and Tapper bid against New Republic agents on Kaal for control of a sunken treasure ship that had once belonged to an Emperor's Hand. Later, Karrde helped Booster Terrik obtain weapons used for overthrowing Ysanne Isard in the Bacta War. During that operation, he realized Melina Carniss was a traitor and had her eliminated.

Approximately six and a half years after Endor, Karrde and Quelev Tapper landed on Varonat to investigate a safari operation run by a local Krish. The Krish's hyperdrive mechanic, a redheaded human female, went by the name Celina Marniss. Recognizing the uncanny similarity between her name and that of his ex-lieutenant, Karrde knew there was more to this woman than met the eye.

The investigation on Varonat went sour. Quelev Tapper died in a shootout, but "Celina" saved Karrde, and on their way out she provided her real name—Mara Jade. She had encountered Melina Carniss years earlier inside Jabba's palace and had taken her alias from that name.

Mara Jade filled the vacancy left by Quelev. Karrde and his command staff operated from a base on Myrkr, deep within the Great Northern Forest. During Grand Admiral Thrawn's war against the New Republic, Karrde stumbled across Luke Skywalker's X-wing, drifting in space. He contemplated turning Skywalker over to Thrawn, but decided instead to help him escape the Grand Admiral's forces. This brought him to Thrawn's attention and cost Karrde his Myrkr base.

Skywalker repaid his debt by rescuing Karrde from a prison cell aboard the Star Destroyer *Chimaera*. Karrde, in turn, gave the New Republic the coordinates of the *Katana* fleet. Now set firmly against Grand Admiral Thrawn, Karrde convinced several rival smuggling kingpins to work with him against the Empire. Their efforts proved vital in Thrawn's defeat at the Battle of Bilbringi.

The smugglers' cooperation at Bilbringi led directly to the formation of the Smugglers' Alliance, a coalition of several major contraband traffickers nominally headed by Karrde. He took this opportunity to announce his retirement, but in fact it was a ploy to fool his rivals into thinking he'd left the business.

Karrde had long remained curious about Jorj Car'das's disappearance so many years before, and sponsored an expedition by Mara Jade and Lando Calrissian to determine Car'das's whereabouts. It took years, but they learned that he had settled on the remote planet Exocron.

Karrde helped Han Solo obtain the ysalamiri used to defeat the tyrant Kueller during the Almanian crisis. Soon thereafter, a wealthy industrialist forced Mara Jade to rescue his daughter from slavers, but Karrde turned the tables by demanding that the industrialist give up his experimental star yacht as compensation. Karrde presented the ship to Mara—who named it the *Jade's Fire*—and set her up with her own business to better prepare her for leadership within his organization.

Fifteen years after Endor, Karrde decided to seek out Jorj Car'das himself, in order to obtain a copy of the famed Caamas Document. With Shada D'ukal, a Mistryl Shadow Guard, he traveled to Exocron. Though Car'das tried to deceive him by posing as a decrepit old man, he later dropped the charade and praised Karrde for treating his former employees with dignity and respect. Though Karrde didn't secure the Caamas Document, he obtained information that helped expose the con artist posing as Grand Admiral Thrawn.

After the Hand of Thrawn incident, Mara Jade married Luke Skywalker. Although he participated in the wedding, Karrde knew he had lost Mara to the Jedi Order. Fortunately, he had a new lieutenant—Shada D'ukal. He also had a new mission. With peace existing between the Empire and the New Republic, Karrde worked to establish a joint intelligence-gathering service that would cater to both sides.

The new organization saw its greatest test during the Yuuzhan Vong invasion. When the enemy threatened several worlds at once, Karrde studied spice shipments planned by the Yuuzhan Vong–allied Hutts and realized they had ceased deliveries to Corellia, Bothawui, and Tynna. But this intelligence proved to be intentional misinformation when the Yuuzhan Vong attacked Fondor instead. As a result, Karrde's organization lost favor with the New Republic. Still, he earned points by helping evacuate the Jedi children from Yavin 4.

KYLE KATARN

On Danuta, he mowed down a base full of stormtroopers. He went toe to toe with a Phase Three Dark Trooper and won, then defeated seven Dark Jedi, each one more powerful than the last.

Kyle Katarn, born on the Sullustan colony moon known as Sulon, lived a hard farmer's life with his father Morgan. He enrolled in the Imperial Military Academy on Carida at age eighteen. But as he trained to be an Imperial officer, he failed to realize the extent of his father's involvement with the Rebel Alliance.

For nearly four years, Morgan Katarn worked in subtle ways against local Imperial control. Ultimately, he helped relocate dissident refugees to uninhabited Ruusan, where he located the Valley of the Jedi, lost for a thousand years. Realizing that the Valley contained Jedi spirits of unimaginable power, Morgan kept the location secret. On advice from a Jedi in hiding named Qu Rahn, Morgan carved the Valley's coordinates into the ceiling of his home and secreted away Rahn's lightsaber, keeping it for Kyle.

Several months later, in a raid against Sulon's local Rebel cell, the Dark Jedi Jerec decapitated Morgan Katarn with a vibroknife.

Kyle, meanwhile, neutralized an enemy-held asteroid on behalf of the Empire, but spared a beautiful Rebel named Jan Ors. For heroism in the Rebel pacification, Katarn received the Medal of Valor from Jerec during Carida's graduation ceremonies. Moments after graduation, Kyle learned that his father was dead—"killed by Rebels," as the official Imperial report stated.

PRONUNCIATION
Kī'-ŭl Kŭ-tärn'
SPECIES
Human
SEX
Male
HAIR COLOR
Brown
EYE COLOR
Brown
HEIGHT
1.8 meters
HOMEWORLD
Sulon

Imperial Second Lieutenant Kyle Katarn boarded a passenger liner en route to his first military posting. On board, Jan Ors gave him proof that the Empire, not the Alliance, had executed Morgan Katarn. Kyle threw his medal in the recycling bin and joined the other side.

Mon Mothma allowed Kyle to go after the plans for the Death Star. Kyle requisitioned a battered ship—the *Moldy Crow*—and stole the readouts from a top-secret Imperial complex on Danuta. When combined with data from other spies, they provided a complete technical blueprint for the seemingly invulnerable battle station.

Katarn's success prompted Mon Mothma to give him a second mission. Months after the evacuation of Yavin 4, he went after General Mohc's automated Dark Troopers. Katarn followed the trail from a bombed-out Rebel outpost on Talay to Mohc's ship the *Arc Hammer*. Along the way he rescued Crix Madine from prison and battled Boba Fett to a standstill. Katarn was a one-man wrecking crew, sometimes lugging five or six weapons at once. In the end, he killed Mohc and destroyed the *Arc Hammer*, making the construction of more Dark Troopers impossible.

Over the next few years Katarn continued running missions for the Alliance. One year after Endor, he learned from the droid information broker 8t88 that Jerec—the same Dark Jedi who had awarded him his Imperial medal—had been the one who'd killed his father. Unfortunately, 8t88 was *working* for Jerec, and Katarn battled both the droid and Jerec's minions in his quest for revenge. Guided by the spirit of Qu Rahn, Katarn returned to his homestead on Sulon and found Rahn's lightsaber. The map to the Valley of the Jedi, however, had already been stolen by Jerec. Katarn obtained a copy, and the race was on.

Jerec's six underlings—Yun, Gorc, Pic, Maw, Sariss, and Boc the Crude—proved no match for Katarn, inexperienced though he was. He cut them all down except for Yun and Sariss,

whom he spared. In gratitude, Yun saved Kyle from Sariss's blade, but died at her hands. When Boc the Crude pulverized Katarn's lightsaber with a rock, the Jedi took Yun's lightsaber as his own.

Throughout the fighting Katarn skirted dangerously close to the dark side of the Force. In the final showdown with Jerec, in the Valley of the Jedi, he put aside his hatred, refusing to kill Jerec in cold blood and defeating him in fair combat. Jerec's death released the Jedi spirits trapped in the Valley, fulfilling a thousand-year-old prophecy: "A Knight shall come, a battle will be fought, and the prisoners go free."

Katarn refused Luke Skywalker's offer to become an apprentice. Instead he joined the New Republic military, working his way up to the rank of captain. He also met another maverick Force user, Mara Jade, and together they helped each other develop their abilities.

During the resurrected Emperor's campaign, Captain Katarn helped defend a New Republic outpost on Altyr 5. Ancient inscriptions led him to the

swamps of Dromund Kaas, a long-forgotten Sith world. The pure Sith evil permeating the swamp planet's temples overwhelmed him, pulling him into the dark side. Mara Jade found him and brought him back to the light by forcing him to choose between the darkness and her own life.

Shamed by his failure, Kyle Katarn enrolled in the first class of Luke Skywalker's Jedi academy. After a brief stay he turned his back on the Force, fearing that he might slip to the dark side again. He gave his lightsaber to Luke and let his Force skills atrophy. For years he worked as a mercenary, acting as an operative for Mon Mothma.

Katarn eventually returned to the Force, becoming a combat instructor at the academy. His students fought the invading Yuuzhan Vong with valor at Ithor, Obroa-skai, and Gyndine. Katarn has since seen many of them die, betrayed by enemy collaborators or sniffed out by Jedi-hunting voxyn. He fears the Yuuzhan Vong may succeed where Jerec did not.

OBI-WAN KENOBI

PRONUNCIATION
O-bē-wän Kĕ-nō'-bē
SPECIES
Human
SEX
Male
HAIR COLOR
Brown
EYE COLOR
Blue-gray
HEIGHT
1.79 meters
HOMEWORLD
Unknown

Your knowledge is impressive, Obi-Wan, but information can be a burden. Feel, don't think, and knots will untie themselves." This was a typical lesson from Qui-Gon Jinn—frustrating and seemingly contradictory. Qui-Gon's death not only robbed Obi-Wan Kenobi of his beloved friend and role model, but also forced Obi-Wan to come up with his *own* style of teaching as he molded Anakin Skywalker into a Jedi.

He melded Qui-Gon's kindness and openness with Yoda's discipline, but with mixed results. As Obi-Wan later told Anakin's son, "I thought that I could instruct him just as well as Yoda. I was wrong." Late in life Obi-Wan acted very much like Qui-Gon, bending the rules whenever it served his goals.

By contrast, at the time of his ascendance to Knighthood, Obi-Wan had a reputation as a stern and serious Jedi, always urging caution upon his impulsive Master, or chiding the reckless behavior of his Padawan. The roots of his complex character can be traced back to his own days as a Padawan, when his rebelliousness led him to temporarily quit the Jedi Order.

Born fifty-seven years before the Battle of Yavin, Obi-Wan Kenobi lived from infancy through adolescence within the walls of Coruscant's Jedi Temple. Until the age of twelve, he received Jedi tutelage under Master Yoda and other Temple instructors. But no Jedi Knight or Master took him on as a Padawan learner, and just before his thirteenth birthday the Jedi Council decided Obi-Wan's fate for him. Kenobi was to receive a backup career in the Jedi Agricultural Corps—a bitter disappointment. After his as-

signment to the planet Bandomeer, however, Kenobi helped Master Qui-Gon Jinn foil a plot by Qui-Gon's former apprentice Xanatos. An impressed Qui-Gon accepted the youth as his new Padawan learner.

Intoxicating—that was the only word to describe hopping across the galaxy, after having lived so sheltered a life on Coruscant. During Obi-Wan's third official mission with Qui-Gon, he allowed his youthful zealousness to get the better of him. On the

planet Melida/Daan, Kenobi joined forces with the Young, a group of young adults about his own age, who were fighting their elders to end a planetary civil war. To help them, Kenobi turned his back on his Master and quit the Jedi Order. However, his rebellion proved short-lived, and it was only upon returning to the Temple that Kenobi realized how much he had hurt the other Jedi students and Padawans. When Qui-Gon Jinn finally reaccepted him as his

Padawan, Kenobi vowed to become the consummate Jedi.

By all accounts he succeeded. Kenobi and Jinn made an impressive pair, whether overseeing planetary elections or battling terrorists. The two of them soon caught up with Xanatos on the planet Telos, foiling the rogue Jedi's scheme and watching as Xanatos killed himself in a pool of acid. Later they paired on several missions with Master Adi Gallia and her Padawan Siri Tachi. Obi-Wan even saved Qui-Gon's life when he rescued his Master from Dr. Zan Arbor, an insane scientist who plumbed the nature of the Force through evil experiments.

As the years passed Kenobi grew skilled in Force techniques including speed, healing, and telekinesis. He exhibited a natural affinity for the "big picture," the unifying Force espoused by the Jedi Council. But sensitivity to the "here-and-now"—the living Force—sometimes eluded him. Kenobi remained slightly bewildered by, and a little envious of, the attention his Master lavished on what he termed "pathetic life-forms." On a mission to Ord Mantell, for instance, Qui-Gon befriended the native Mantellian savrip when Obi-Wan would have initially dismissed them as monsters.

Approximately a year before the Battle of Naboo, Obi-Wan Kenobi joined his Master and several members of the Jedi Council in ending an uprising by the reptilian Yinchorri. Neither Kenobi nor anyone else realized that the disturbance had been secretly arranged by Darth Sidious. The Sith Master had taken the first steps in his scheme to rule

the galaxy, and Obi-Wan unwittingly played a part. When Chancellor Valorum gave a speech on Eriadu, Obi-Wan's efforts to protect Valorum from assassins allowed Sidious to eliminate his true target, the members of the Trade Federation Directorate. Later, Obi-Wan and Qui-Gon helped recover a shipment of droid starfighters from Bartokk assassins before they could be delivered to the Trade Federation.

On Sidious's orders, Nute Gunray and the Trade Federation blockaded Naboo to protest a shipping tax. Chancellor Valorum, anxious to resolve the situation, asked for Jedi ambassadors to "persuade" Gunray to back down. Mace Windu sent Jinn and Kenobi. The Naboo mission

proved to be a crucible for Obi-Wan Kenobi, who slew Darth Maul in lightsaber combat and held Qui-Gon in his arms as his Master breathed his last. Impressed with his skill in striking down a Sith Lord, the Jedi Council promoted the twenty-five-year-old Kenobi to the rank of Jedi Knight.

Kenobi honored his Master's last request by taking on Anakin Skywalker as his Padawan learner. A student all his life, Kenobi was suddenly a teacher. Skywalker lacked the foundation of a Temple education, so Kenobi had to teach the boy Jedi fundamentals he'd mastered himself by age two. In addition, Anakin's raw power and buried rage made for a dangerous combination. Nightmares of his mother, still a slave on remote Tatooine, plagued Anakin and disturbed Obi-Wan. Kenobi tried to rein in his Padawan's recklessness, but still found himself chasing after Anakin—such as when the boy snuck out of the Temple to the racewing competitions in Coruscant's garbage pits.

Three years into their partnership, Obi-Wan Kenobi and Anakin Skywalker confronted Kad Chun, the brother of a Jedi student Obi-Wan had inadvertently killed more than a decade earlier. Earlier that same year they went on a fact-finding mission to the mysterious Outer Rim world Zonama Sekot. Enemy forces belonging to Commander Tarkin and Raith Sienar attacked the planet, while Anakin laid bare the anger in his heart by brutally killing an enemy agent.

Kenobi, shaken by the experience, devoted himself even further to his Padawan's training. Not long after, the two Jedi went after Krayn, a notorious pirate and slave trader. Showing little restraint, Skywalker killed Krayn with his newly built lightsaber.

Seven years after the Krayn mission, following their mediation of a border dispute on Ansion, Obi-Wan and Anakin received an assignment from the Jedi Council to protect Senator Padmé Amidala of Naboo. After chasing would-be assassin Zam Wesell through the traffic lanes of Coruscant, the two caught her only to witness her death before she could reveal the identity of her employer. The Jedi Council thought it best that Padmé return to Naboo. Anakin accompanied her, while Obi-Wan Kenobi followed the trail of the assassin to watery Kamino.

There he learned that someone had commissioned an army of clones, all grown from the genetic template of bounty hunter Jango Fett. Kenobi tracked Fett to Geonosis, where he discovered a massive droid army being assembled for the Trade Federation. He warned the Jedi Council, just before being captured and thrown into an execution arena. With Padmé, Anakin Skywalker rushed to Geonosis to help his Master, and the two Jedi battled Count Dooku, almost losing their lives in the process. The Battle of Geonosis ended with no clear victory, marking as it did the beginning of the Clone Wars.

Given the rank of general, Obi-Wan Kenobi fought alongside Bail Organa and other famous figures in defense of the Republic. For Kenobi, the war's greatest tragedy wasn't the establishment of a galactic dictatorship, but the loss of his apprentice to the dark side of the Force. After suffering terrible injuries, Anakin Skywalker donned the black armor of Darth Vader and became Palpatine's Sith disciple. The Jedi who survived the Clone Wars saw their numbers decimated by the Emperor's Jedi Purge. Obi-Wan Kenobi, along with Yoda, went into hiding.

But first Kenobi ensured the safety of Anakin's twin children, planting the seeds for the return of the Jedi. Anakin and Padmé's daughter, Leia, entered the home of Bail Organa on Alderaan. Their son, Luke, went with Kenobi to Tatooine, where Anakin's stepbrother Owen Lars agreed to raise the boy on his moisture farm. Obi-Wan moved into a hermitage out by the planet's Jundland Wastes. The last thing he wanted was to draw attention to himself.

As Luke Skywalker grew into a young adult, Kenobi kept a close watch. Both he and Yoda believed that Luke, given the proper guidance, had the potential to undo Vader's evil. When Luke and his friend Windy got lost in a sandstorm, Kenobi rescued the boys from a hungry krayt dragon. When he brought them back to the moisture farm, Owen Lars ordered him to leave. Owen knew Kenobi's plans for his nephew, and didn't like them one bit.

Eventually, the Force set destiny in motion. Luke's uncle and aunt died under the guns of Imperial stormtroopers. The young man agreed to follow Kenobi to Alderaan to meet Bail Organa. Kenobi hired a disreputable smuggler—Han Solo—for passage to Alderaan, and then used Jedi mind manipulation to net two thousand credits from the sale of Luke's landspeeder.

But the Empire's Death Star destroyed Alderaan before they could arrive. With that tragic turn of events, Kenobi sensed he was destined to play one last role in the Galactic Civil War. On a solo mission inside the enemy battle station, he confronted his former Padawan in a contest of lightsabers. Knowing Luke held the key to ultimate victory, Kenobi gave up his life to allow the young Rebel the opportunity to escape.

Luke Skywalker heard Kenobi's voice during his trench run against the Death Star and knew his mentor had not vanished forever. Later, in the presence of the Kaiburr Crystal on Mimban, Kenobi's spirit inhabited Luke's body and guided his limbs in combat against Vader.

In a blizzard on Hoth, Kenobi appeared to Luke in ghostly form for the first time. On Dagobah, it almost seemed as if he'd never passed on, as he answered Luke's questions and offered sound advice. Luke later saw the spirits of Kenobi, Yoda, and Anakin Skywalker at the Endor celebration, but Kenobi wasn't finished with his otherworldly assistance. He appeared to Luke after Endor to warn him of the threat of the Ssi-ruuk, and later guided him in a dream to the location of the Lost City of the Jedi. Finally, five years after Endor, Kenobi's spirit informed Luke that the distance between their worlds had become too great. He bid his student a fond farewell, reminding him that he was the first of a new generation of Jedi.

KUELLER

Luke Skywalker first knew Kueller as Dolph, a Force-sensitive young man from the distant planet Almania. Since the time of Grand Admiral Thrawn, Almania had suffered under the merciless regime of the Je'har. After having trained at the Jedi academy for less than a year, Dolph received news from home. He returned to find that his parents had been murdered by the Je'har, their bodies staked outside the governmental palace.

Dolph's training as a Jedi was raw and unfinished. He knew just enough of the Force to be dangerous. Insane with rage and grief, he fell deeply into the dark side. Dolph donned a Hendanyn death mask and became Kueller—an avenging demon determined to save Almania.

As a Dark Jedi, Kueller wielded supernatural powers of destruction. He soon attracted a reverent army, and their war against the Je'har claimed millions of lives. After many months, Kueller contacted Brakiss—another of Skywalker's failed students—and initiated the second phase of his plan.

Kueller helped heal the psychological scars Brakiss had suffered, and set him up as operator of the Telti droid plants. In return, Brakiss installed a remote-activated bomb inside each droid his factories produced. For two years, Kueller ensured that the rigged droids fell into all the right hands. Meanwhile he mopped up the last of the Je'har, then massacred tens of thousands of suspected "sympathizers" in a string of bloody purges.

Thirteen years after Endor, Kueller made his move against the New Republic. His droids exploded on the Almanian moon of Pydyr and in the New Republic Senate chamber.

PRONUNCIATION
Kōō-ĕl'-ûr
SPECIES
Human
SEX
Male
HAIR COLOR
Brown
EYE COLOR
Brown
HEIGHT
1.9 meters
HOMEWORLD
Almania

Luke Skywalker followed the trail of bombing deaths to Almania, where he recognized his former pupil as the terrorist mastermind. Kueller captured Skywalker and ordered his sister, Leia Organa Solo, to surrender New Republic executive power to him. To underscore his demand, he exterminated the population of the moon Auyemesh with more booby-trapped droids.

In response, Leia stepped down as Chief of State. She flew to Almania with a small armada under the command of Wedge Antilles.

Skywalker had already escaped from Kueller's dungeon, but Kueller intercepted him and forced a lightsaber duel. When he lost the advantage, though, Kueller activated a control designed to detonate every rigged droid. Fortunately, R2-D2, on Telti, intercepted and deactivated the signal.

Before Kueller could unleash any more surprises, Leia took aim and shot him. The butcher of Almania lay sprawled lifeless in the dust. Leia bent down and removed Kueller's grinning death mask—revealing, for the last time, the boyish face of the aspiring Jedi known as Dolph.

EXAR KUN

PRONUNCIATION
Ĕk'-sär Kōōn
SPECIES
Human
SEX
Male
HAIR COLOR
Black
EYE COLOR
Gray
HEIGHT
1.9 meters
HOMEWORLD
Unknown

Marka Ragnos's spirit survived for a millennium. The shade of Freedon Nadd clung to its tomb for centuries. Palpatine himself came back from death more than once.

But Exar Kun topped them all.

For four millennia he sustained himself in a state beyond death. It took a legion of Luke Skywalker's new Jedi to eliminate this veteran of the Sith War for all time.

Four thousand years before the Battle of Yavin, this gifted Jedi Knight thought he knew the dark side better than his own Master, Vodo Siosk-Baas. Abandoning his training, Kun traveled to the tomb of the Sith Lord Freedon Nadd, where Nadd's withered life-essence led Kun to the Sith mausoleums on Korriban. There, faced with death under a ton of crushing stone, Exar Kun opened his spirit to the dark side.

Fully committed now, Kun journeyed to Yavin 4, where the descendants of Naga Sadow's Massassi warriors waited for a new Dark Lord to lead them. After obliterating Nadd's lingering spirit, Exar Kun made Yavin 4 the new fulcrum of Sith power.

Kun intended to kill fallen Jedi Ulic Qel-Droma, whom he saw as a potential rival. Before that could occur, the ghost of Dark Lord Marka Ragnos named Kun the newest Dark Lord of the Sith and made Ulic his apprentice. Emblazoned with a Sith tattoo on his forehead, Exar Kun swayed more Jedi Knights to his cause. Kun strode into the heart of Coruscant and slew his former Master Vodo Siosk-Baas on the floor of the Senate chamber.

At his Yavin 4 base, Kun ordered the Massassi to build new temples dedicated to his glory. He dabbled in dark side magic, creating two-headed animal monstrosities and imprisoning the Massassi children inside a mystical golden orb.

Using ancient Sith technology, Kun's agents triggered a multiple supernova in the Cron Cluster that devastated the planet Ossus. When Ulic Qel-Droma revealed the location of Exar Kun's base on Yavin 4, a Republic war fleet arrived at the jungle moon. Knowing he couldn't survive a bombardment, Kun left a "night beast" behind as guardian and drained the collective life force of the remaining Massassi, preserving his own spirit within the temple walls.

For four thousand years he remained there, driven half mad by the unthinkable isolation. When Luke Skywalker's Jedi academy set up shop in the same Massassi temples, Exar Kun took possession of Luke's most powerful student, Kyp Durron, driving Skywalker into a state of near death. Kun also toyed with the other trainees —including the particularly troublesome Corran Horn—before the students united with the spirit of Vodo Siosk-Baas to vanquish the Sith Lord for all time.

WARMASTER TSAVONG LAH

The creator god Yun-Yuuzhan sacrificed his body parts to birth the lesser gods. In honor of this severe pantheon, Tsavong Lah has endured countless mutilations—but such devotion should come as no surprise. Tsavong Lah is warmaster.

The commander of the Yuuzhan Vong invasion effort and elite protector of Supreme Overlord Shimrra, Tsavong Lah has nearly duplicated the physical appearance of Yun-Yammka the Slayer, his patron god. And he has seen to it that the Chosen Land has provided many candidates for sacrifice.

Hundreds of larval armor scales grow into the skin of Tsavong Lah's torso, to provide him with extraordinary protection in battle. He carries a serpentine tsaisi—a half-length amphistaff—as his baton of rank, and wields command from the bridge of the battleship *Sunulok* instead of from the massive worldships of the Yuuzhan Vong fleet.

Only two individuals have earned any measure of affection from Tsavong Lah: Seef, his female attendant, and Harrar, a priest who was once attached to Lah's training division. Khalee Lah, Tsavong's son, acts as the warmaster's henchman among the rank-and-file troops.

The hot blood of the warrior caste roars through Lah's veins, and he shows nothing but contempt for the devious bureaucrats of the Praetorite Vong. He found his prejudices confirmed when the invasion stalled under the guidance of the Praetorite, and his warrior armies were forced to take up the reins. He assumed command following the defeat at Helska 4, and since then Lah has led his

PRONUNCIATION
Sä'-vŏng Läh
SPECIES
Yuuzhan Vong
SEX
Male
HAIR COLOR
Black
EYE COLOR
Black
HEIGHT
1.96 meters
HOMEWORLD
Unknown

troops to such great victories as those at Dantooine and Ithor.

Tsavong Lah's immediate subordinate, Supreme Commander Nas Choka, directed most of the early victories, including the ecological transformation of Tynna and the attack on Fondor. The Battle of Fondor was to have given the Yuuzhan Vong a vital foothold for a Core World strike. Instead, the fleet retreated with heavy losses after an energy beam from Centerpoint Station smashed through

their formation. Though the Fondor clash was certainly no defeat—the New Republic suffered even greater losses than the Yuuzhan Vong—the encounter prompted Tsavong Lah to take a more active role.

When the New Republic started shipping refugees to the planet Duro, the warmaster was certain he could turn the situation to his advantage. The polluted world sat at the edge of the Core Worlds on the Corellian Run, and would make a fine staging area for an assault on Coruscant. Furthermore, the ritual sacrifice of civilian refugees had been a key element of the Yuuzhan Vong battle plan since Tsavong Lah had taken command.

Nom Anor, executor from the intendant caste, had already set up shop on Duro under the warmaster's orders. Disguised as a native scientist, he sabotaged the refugee settlements and worked to purify poisoned Duro—all to atone for his past failures in the eyes of Tsavong Lah. Meanwhile, Lah himself led a devastating assault on Duro that swept through the enemy resistance as if it were vapor. Duro's gigantic orbital habitats plummeted to the surface, the fiery deaths testifying to the glory of the gods.

Leia Organa Solo was among the survivors, and she was soon captured. The warmaster planned to make a special sacrifice out of such a worthy opponent, and tortured her to the brink of death. It was her son Jacen who rushed to rescue her. Tsavong Lah had heard that Jacen Solo was a pacifist, but "the Craven One" attacked with unchecked ferocity. Jacen's Force whirlwind tossed a roomful of objects aloft; a heavy metal desk smashed Lah out a window and tore loose his left foot.

Standing painfully on the surface of conquered Duro, Lah broadcast an ultimatum to the citizens of the New Republic. The warmaster promised to halt the Yuuzhan Vong invasion, in exchange for the lives of every Jedi Knight. One Jedi in particular, Jacen Solo, was declared worthy of sacrifice at Tsavong Lah's own hands.

In a sacrificial ritual the warmaster fought and defeated a vua'sa creature, cutting a talon from the animal's corpse to replace his lost foot. He then took on a new adviser—Vergere, an alien who had once belonged to a Yuuzhan Vong priestess. Though Vergere's appearance triggered revulsion in the warmaster's heart, he recognized the value of her insight regarding the inhabitants of this galaxy. The fact that Executor Nom Anor hated Vergere was an amusing bonus. And when Lah learned of Jacen and Jaina Solo's special status as twins, a phenomenon believed by the Yuuzhan Vong to be the province of the gods, he dispatched Nom Anor and Vergere to capture them in the Myrkr system.

Once the war entered its third year, Supreme Overlord Shimrra called for decisive results. With a hint of trepidation, Tsavong Lah authorized Battle Plan Coruscant. One Yuuzhan Vong war fleet was to advance on the New Republic capital from the direction of Reecee; the other pincer was to strike from Borleias. Though Tsavong Lah lost his Reecee fleet in a shameful defeat, he boldly struck at Coruscant with only half his planned forces. The gamble paid off, for Coruscant's defenses crumbled and Yuuzhan Vong shapers began remaking the world in the image of their gods. And Tsavong Lah, warmaster, prepared to govern the transformed planet.

OWEN LARS AND BERU WHITESUN LARS

PRONUNCIATION
Ō-wĕn Lärs and
Bĕ-rōō' Whīt'-sŭn
SPECIES
Human
SEX
Male/Female
HAIR COLOR
Brown/Brown
EYE COLOR
Blue/Blue
HEIGHT
1.7 meters/
1.65 meters
HOMEWORLD
Tatooine

O wen Lars, a lifelong farmer, thought sand weevils were the most bothersome pests in the galaxy. He held roughly the same opinion of Jedi.

The first time Owen met Anakin Skywalker, his Jedi stepbrother was frantically searching for his missing mother, with tragic results. And Anakin went downhill from there. Beru Whitesun tempered Owen's bitterness with warmth and love as she and her husband raised Anakin Skywalker's son into adulthood.

Owen Lars developed a tough attitude early in life. Though his father, Cliegg, owned one of the most successful moisture farms by the Dune Sea, moisture farming was hard, dirty work.

Cliegg Lars married Shmi Skywalker, a slave he'd purchased from the junk dealer Watto, and then freed. Shmi spoke often of her son Anakin and how he'd been taken offworld by a Jedi Master.

Ten years after the Battle of Naboo, Owen's stepmother disappeared while gathering vaporator mushrooms. The Tusken Raiders who'd snatched her decimated a rescue party and crippled Cliegg. Accompanied by Padmé Amidala, Anakin Skywalker arrived in the wake of the tragedy, bent on vengeance. Anakin returned with Shmi's dead body, the bloodlust of murder still brimming in his eyes.

Beru, meanwhile, spoke to Padmé of the galaxy's many worlds. She revealed that she never wanted to travel away from Tatooine's double suns.

Soon thereafter, Owen and Beru married. Anakin Skywalker turned to the dark side of the Force and became Darth Vader. Another Jedi, Obi-Wan Kenobi, brought Anakin's infant son Luke to Tatooine to be raised away from the clutches of Emperor Palpatine. Owen had never shirked a duty in his life and worked to raise Luke as a grounded, responsible young adult. Above all, "Uncle" Owen tried to prevent his nephew from following the Jedi path that had led to his father's damnation. He told Luke that Anakin had been an undistinguished freighter crewer and that Ben Kenobi, out in the Jundland Wastes, was a "crazy old wizard."

He indulged Luke's passion for speed, helping his nephew buy a landspeeder, as well as a beat-up T-16 skyhopper. But Owen refused Luke's repeated requests to leave Tatooine and enroll in the Academy.

Owen's misgivings proved correct when he purchased two droids from a party of Jawas. One of them had actually been owned by Shmi Skywalker more than two decades before, though if either Owen or Beru realized it, neither showed any sign. Within days, Darth Vader's stormtroopers arrived at the homestead where Anakin Skywalker had once buried his mother. They reduced the homestead to cinders.

BEVEL LEMELISK

Bevel Lemelisk wasn't the only scientist behind the creation of the Death Star, but he perpetuated the planet-killing concept to create no less than six different superweapons. To this day, he remains one of the only individuals executed by the New Republic for war crimes.

Anything as complex as the Death Star necessitated contributions from many branches of engineering. Raith Sienar first conceived of the battle station concept nearly thirty years before its ultimate completion. Tol Sivron administered the Maw Installation where the Death Star became a reality; Qwi Xux served as one of Sivron's most talented scientists.

As chief engineer, Bevel Lemelisk outranked everyone. Lemelisk's career began in the final years of the Old Republic, when he helped the Geonosians produce their attack craft and assisted Walex Blissex with the design of the Victory Star Destroyer. After years of service to the Empire, Lemelisk began work for Tarkin in the Maw Installation. Emperor Palpatine approved the construction of a Death Star prototype—the first weapon ever to wield a superlaser—and later gave his blessing to a production version.

Lemelisk left the other Maw scientists behind when he took charge of the construction. The Death Star worked as planned, but fell victim to a design flaw at Yavin. As a result, the Emperor punished the engineer with the torture of flesh-eating piranha-beetles. Lemelisk died in agony, then awoke in the body of a clone. Motivated by fear, he set to work designing the second Death Star, and also built the *Tarkin* superlaser. Lemelisk died seven times in to-

PRONUNCIATION
Bě'-věl Lě'-mě-lǐsk
SPECIES
Human
SEX
Male
HAIR COLOR
White
EYE COLOR
Brown
HEIGHT
1.67 meters
HOMEWORLD
Unknown

tal, dark side magic shuttling his consciousness through seven clones.

The second Death Star was destroyed at Endor—taking Palpatine with it—and Lemelisk joined the Imperial design team at Kuat. He applied his superlaser expertise to the construction of the gigantic Star Destroyer *Eclipse*.

When the New Republic captured Kuat, the *Eclipse* team fled to the Deep Core. Lemelisk didn't join them—he'd heard rumors of the Emperor's resurrection and wanted to stay as far away as possible. Instead he fell in with Durga the Hutt.

In Durga's employ Lemelisk designed the Darksaber, a stripped-down Death Star similar to the *Tarkin*. But Durga's reliance on substandard materials doomed the project, and Lemelisk fled the Darksaber just before its destruction.

The New Republic captured Lemelisk, tried him for war crimes, and sentenced him to death. He spent four years incarcerated on Orinackra, with one research furlough to study Lord Hethrir's captured worldcraft. Bevel Lemelisk's last words before facing the firing squad were, "At least make sure you do it right this time."

LOBOT

L obot could have become a swashbuckling pirate and slaver king. But he no longer remembers the firing of his pirate flash-guns. Life before he received a cyborg brain implant is a dream within a dream.

Lobot's father terrified millions as an Outer Rim slaver. His son aspired to earn even greater notoriety. But right around the time of the Clone Wars, rival pirates killed Lobot's father and took the fifteen-year-old Lobot prisoner. After two years of imprisonment, he escaped to Bespin's Cloud City and became a thief. When the law caught up with Lobot, Baroness Administrator Shallence offered him a fifteen-year term as the city's computer liaison. Cloud City techs shaved Lobot's head, drilled holes in his skull, and fitted him with a Biotech Aj^6 cyborg headband.

The device kept him in constant contact with the city's central computer and boosted his intelligence, strength, and reaction time. It also eroded his emotional and linguistic centers. At the end of his fifteen years Lobot chose to remain on Bespin as Cloud City's permanent liaison. He served as chief aide to many Barons, but the corrupt Baron Administrator Raynor was the worst. So Lobot took up a collection from the city's workers totaling five million credits, then gave it to the gambler Lando Calrissian to put up in a sabacc game. With a little electronic cheating arranged by Lobot himself, Calrissian won Cloud City and took over as the new Baron Administrator.

Lobot and Calrissian became friends, working together to free Princess Leia Organa and Chewbacca when Darth Vader's stormtroopers in-

PRONUNCIATION
Lō'-bŏt
SPECIES
Human
SEX
Male
HAIR COLOR
None
EYE COLOR
Blue
HEIGHT
1.75 meters
HOMEWORLD
Unknown

vaded the city. Calrissian left, but Lobot remained behind as Cloud City came under the control of Imperial Captain Treece. The Ugnaught workers, angered by Treece's cruelty, planted bombs throughout Cloud City and sabotaged Lobot's cyborg headband so the Imperials couldn't use him to disarm the bombs. Calrissian and Luke Skywalker returned to save the city, and a repaired Lobot resumed control—just in time for the Empire to retake everything.

After the Battle of Endor, Calrissian returned to kick the Imperials out for good, with the help of a group he dubbed "Lando's Commandos." Lobot's expertise made him Cloud City's de facto administrator.

Twelve years after Endor, a visit from Calrissian prompted Lobot to leave Cloud City and experience adventures in the greater galaxy. He helped solve the riddle of the Teljkon vagabond, went to Bastion to search for the Caamas Document, and worked with Calrissian to open the *GemDiver* mining station above Yavin. Since the Yuuzhan Vong onslaught he has returned to administer Cloud City, well away from the aliens' invasion corridor.

GARIK "FACE" LORAN

PRONUNCIATION
Gă'-rĭk Lō-răn'
SPECIES
Human
SEX
Male
HAIR COLOR
Black
EYE COLOR
Green
HEIGHT
1.78 meters
HOMEWORLD
Pantolomin

Old Imperial propaganda holovids such as *Jungle Flutes* and *The Black Bantha* offer a certain nostalgic charm for modern citizens, but to wink at such productions is to ignore the damage they caused. *Win or Die* is said to have boosted Imperial recruitment significantly.

No one understands this more than Garik Loran, star of the above blockbusters. This former child actor grew up, shed his naïveté, and became a dedicated fighter against the Empire he once glorified.

Originally from Pantolomin, Loran earned fame in a string of smash hits honoring Emperor Palpatine. Rival child star Tetran Cowall chipped away at his popularity, but Loran, nicknamed "the Face," remained an idol to billions of young girls.

Shortly before Yavin, Rebel extremists captured Loran and would have executed him, but an Imperial commando squad burst in amid a storm of blasterfire. Injured and terrified, Loran hid from his rescuers and quietly returned home. His parents secretly shipped him to their birthworld of Lorrd, and the newsnets somberly reported the death of the holovid star.

Among the Lorrdians, Loran—now bearing a jagged facial scar—refined his gift for mimicry. With his wealth he bought an A-wing and became an exceptional pilot. After the Battle of Endor, Loran joined the New Republic's Comet Squadron, but soon received a demotion for insubordination.

Wedge Antilles was looking for washouts to join Wraith Squadron, an experimental X-wing team of spies and saboteurs. Flight Officer Loran joined up as Wraith Eight and became the squadron's infiltrator and master of disguise.

After the Wraiths captured the corvette *Night Caller* from Warlord Zsinj's forces, Loran posed as the corvette's captain in a series of tense missions behind enemy lines. He earned a promotion to lieutenant for bravery against Zsinj's forces during a skirmish above Talasea.

Of all his fellow Wraiths, Loran formed his closest friendship with Ton Phanan. His friend's death at Halmad hit him hard. Loran had his facial scar removed with the money left to him in Phanan's will.

After Kuat, Loran received a promotion to brevet captain. For heroic actions while attached to General Han Solo's task force, New Republic Starfighter Command made Loran a full captain.

With the Zsinj threat seemingly over, General Cracken decommissioned Wraith Squadron, and re-formed it as a New Republic Intelligence unit. Over the years Loran continued to lead the team.

Today, Loran is unrecognizable to fans of his old holodramas. Bald-headed, he wears a false mustache, false beard, and counterfeit facial scar.

GENERAL CRIX MADINE

PRONUNCIATION
Krĭkhs Mā-dēn'
SPECIES
Human
SEX
Male
HAIR COLOR
Reddish blond
EYE COLOR
Unknown
HEIGHT
1.7 meters
HOMEWORLD
Corellia

Imperial officers explained away their atrocities by claiming they were "just following orders." That wasn't good enough for Crix Madine. Consumed with guilt over his role in a genocidal war crime, he switched sides and dedicated his life to making amends. In the end, he died a martyr to the Rebel cause.

A son of Corellia, Crix Madine enlisted in the Imperial military like many men his age. His fiancée Karreio was a vocal supporter of Emperor Palpatine's New Order. Young and in love, it was hard for Madine to distinguish ideology from infatuation. He dreamed of a future as a heroic Imperial officer, with Karreio at his side.

Madine's superior officers found that he excelled at sabotage and guerrilla-style tactics, exactly the type of warfare practiced by the Rebel Alliance. An innovative guerrilla team called the Imperial Storm Commandos was formed as a direct counterpunch to the Rebel threat. Madine was given the rank of colonel and assumed command of the new unit.

Based on Carida, the Storm Commandos struck at dozens of Rebel targets, with spectacular success. Colonel Madine took pride in "clean" strikes, but grew sick at heart when Imperial forces took part in civilian massacres.

When one of his fellow Carida officers, General Rom Mohc, built an army of wantonly lethal Dark Troopers, Madine secretly slipped word of the project to the Rebel Alliance. Though he told himself he was doing the right thing, putting the brakes on Mohc's madness, Madine knew his actions amounted to treason. He

could never tell Karreio.

Soon after, his Storm Commandos were ordered to Dentaal to punish the revolutionary Independence Party there. Following orders handed down from the highest levels, Madine's soldiers unleashed the incurable Candorian plague, which ultimately annihilated more than ten billion people. Horrified that his devotion to the Empire had led him to such slaughter, Madine faked his death and fled in a stolen shuttle.

Madine wanted to find a Rebel-held world and give himself up, but General Mohc intercepted his shuttle and recaptured the betrayer for the Empire. Found guilty of treason, Madine was locked in a maximum-security prison on Orinackra, to await execution. But Rebel agent Kyle Katarn sprang Madine from under the Empire's nose and transferred him to a Rebel safehouse on Corellia. Imperial AT-STs tried to recapture the defector, but Luke Skywalker and

Rogue Squadron covered Madine's successful extradition.

Many members of the Alliance didn't trust an ex-Imperial war criminal, but Mon Mothma saw enough promise in Madine to make him a general and the commander of Alliance Special Forces. General Madine proved his worth in daring commando raids such as the liberation of Gerrard V and the destruction of a weapons depot on Loronar's Jade Moon.

General Madine planned the assault on Endor's shield generator, employing a stolen Imperial shuttle to slip through the Empire's sentry net. His handpicked commando team would then take down the generator itself. Many expected him to lead the ground crew, but he assigned that task to General Han Solo. During the legendary Battle of Endor, Madine commanded an Alliance fleet element and helped bring down the Super Star Destroyer *Executor*.

In the post-Endor years, Madine led special operations to capture key Imperials and support planetary revolutions. On one mission to Kintori Madine briefly met Mara Jade. He declared a truce with the former Emperor's Hand so Mara could expose the local Imperial governor as an embezzler.

When the New Republic captured Coruscant, Madine received word that his ex-fiancée Karreio had been among the Imperial casualties. Saddled with guilt over Dentaal, and the death of the woman he'd once loved, Madine buried himself in his work. By the time of the Darksaber incident he held the title Supreme Allied Commander for Intelligence, overseeing both General Cracken of NRI and Admiral Drayson of the top-secret Alpha Blue division.

Though he hadn't accepted a field assignment in some time, General Madine took a hands-on approach to the Darksaber crisis. Those who'd known him the longest suspected that he needed to exorcise his demons through action. Madine went undercover in the slums of Nal Hutta, releasing an artificial "moon moth" droid that planted a tiny tracking device on Durga the Hutt's ship. The trail led to the Hoth asteroid belt, where Durga's Darksaber superweapon was taking shape. Madine picked two of his best commandos—Korenn and Trandia—and the three hopeful saboteurs flew to the Hoth asteroids in their A-wings.

Korenn died on the way in, crushed by one of the drifting rocks. Madine and Trandia penetrated the asteroid screen and infiltrated the Darksaber, but Durga's goons discovered them. The henchmen killed Madine's partner and dragged the general before the Hutt. Durga, furious that anyone would challenge his ultimate weapon, executed General Crix Madine with a single blaster shot.

Durga's Darksaber met an explosive end, taking Madine's body with it. Back on Coruscant, the New Republic held a hero's funeral for a champion of the Rebellion.

DARTH MAUL

PRONUNCIATION
Därth Mäl
SPECIES
Iridonian Zabrak
SEX
Male
HAIR COLOR
None
EYE COLOR
Yellow
HEIGHT
1.75 meters
HOMEWORLD
Iridonia

Darth Maul was a weapon forged for one purpose only—the destruction of the Jedi. And Maul's Master, Darth Sidious, held no sentimental illusions about his apprentice. To Sidious, Maul was neither a friend nor a surrogate son—he was simply an implement. When Maul was struck down on Naboo, Sidious cast him aside like a broken blade and quickly obtained a replacement.

Maul was a Zabrak from Iridonia, but details of his early life are nonexistent. He was taken from his home planet as an infant by Darth Sidious, who wanted to claim the Force-sensitive child as his own before Maul could be discovered by the Jedi. Sidious was a cruel teacher. Maul had no true childhood; he spent every moment pushing himself to become stronger, harder, smarter, and faster. The physical training was exhausting, and the psychological indoctrination terrifying. On one occasion, as punishment for flinching at a dinko's bite, Sidious filled young Maul's quarters with scores of dinkos and locked him in the room until he had killed every last one.

In Sidious's hidden Coruscant lair and on deserted training planets across the galaxy, Maul practiced martial arts, marksmanship, and the handling of melee weapons. He mastered the lightsaber and the Sith lanvarok, and learned the art of dueling with two blades—one in each hand—in the Jar'Kai style. He was ever mindful of the here-and-now, and was thus acutely attuned to the living Force—albeit the Force's dark side.

Several years before the Battle of Naboo, Darth Maul reached the final step in his training. His Master sent him to an Outer Rim planet covered with deserts, swamps, and mountains and ordered him to survive for a month against a legion of assassin droids.

Maul persevered, but his final test was to battle his Master in a lightsaber duel. Sidious goaded Maul into opening himself to the vast power of the dark side, and in that moment Darth Maul became a Dark Lord of the Sith.

Maul was ever respectful of his Master and the ancient traditions of the Sith. The dark side was all he knew; without it he possessed nothing. While many former Sith—from Naga Sadow to Exar Kun—had borne Sith tattoos on their foreheads, Maul covered his entire body with jagged patterns of red and black. In his Master's Sith Holocron, Maul found patterns for Sith speeders, probe droids, and a double-bladed lightsaber, and reproduced them with faithful precision. Using the Force mechanical skill *mechu-deru*, Maul customized a protocol droid named C-3PX into a formidable guard droid to serve as a personal sentry.

Maul was Sidious's "Hand," used to perform secret missions of assassination and intimidation. On the orders of his Master he journeyed to the lommite-mining planet Dorvalla, where he secretly pitted two rival mining companies against each other. The ensuing chaos left Dorvalla ripe for takeover by the Trade Federation. It also allowed Maul to use his new double-bladed lightsaber against living opponents instead of training droids, an experience he relished.

After Dorvalla, Darth Maul received from his Master the gift of a cloak-capable Sith Infiltrator starship. Armed with this new weapon, Maul crippled the Black Sun crime syndicate by journeying to its headquarters on Ralltiir and murdering every last member of the ruling board. Later, Maul destroyed a Bar-

tokk fortress on the same planet, simply because the insectoids had gotten in his way.

When a Neimoidian, Hath Monchar, fled the Trade Federation, carrying information on Darth Sidious's long-term invasion plans, Sidious dispatched Maul to eliminate the traitor. The job proved more difficult than expected. Darth Maul killed Monchar with ease, but as more people exposed themselves to the Neimoidian's information, Maul had to add more bodies to the pile. Before long he was hunting a Jedi Padawan named Darsha Assant, and Lorn Pavan, an information broker. Maul chased them across Coruscant's cityscape, but in the end he fulfilled his Master's wishes by tying up all of the "loose ends."

While Darth Maul enjoyed his field missions, his true goal was to exterminate the Jedi and burn their Temple to the ground. Maul had no

ambitions to overthrow his Master, but he knew that under the Sith "rule of two," Sidious would have to die before Maul could take on his own apprentice. Such thoughts had a way of entering his mind during quiet moments of meditation.

Maul's heart burned with anticipation when his Master instructed him to hunt down two Jedi, Qui-Gon Jinn and Obi-Wan Kenobi, on Tatooine and Naboo. Had he not run into Togorian pirates and Sand People along the way, perhaps he would have been at full strength for the final conflict inside the Theed power generator. Instead, after killing Qui-Gon, Darth Maul fatally underestimated the Jedi's Padawan, Obi-Wan Kenobi. Qui-Gon's apprentice cut Maul in half and cast his body into the melting pit. Thus ended his ambitions, and the way was cleared for a new Dark Lord of the Sith.

MON MOTHMA

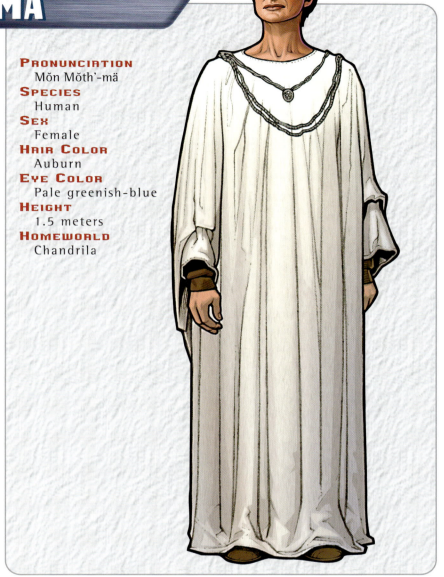

PRONUNCIATION
Mŏn Mŏth'-mä
SPECIES
Human
SEX
Female
HAIR COLOR
Auburn
EYE COLOR
Pale greenish-blue
HEIGHT
1.5 meters
HOMEWORLD
Chandrila

We, *the beings of the Rebel Alliance, do this day send forth this Declaration to His Majesty, the Emperor, and to all sentient beings in the galaxy, to make clear to all the Purposes and Goals of this Rebellion."* Every galactic citizen recognizes the opening line of the Declaration of Rebellion, and everyone knows its author. Never a warrior, Mon Mothma overturned an Empire not with weapons, but through the conviction of her words.

Born on the Core World of Chandrila, Mon Mothma grew up in a port city on the shores of the Silver Sea. Her mother, the city's governor, taught her to love her homeworld. Her father, a Republic arbiter-general, showed her the wonders of the galaxy. While still in her teens, Mon Mothma became Chandrila's sector representative in the Republic Senate. The Chandrilans had a reputation for political idealism, and those Senators who dismissed Mon Mothma at a naive child quickly discovered that her keen political mind could put most of them to shame.

After the chaos of the Clone Wars, Palpatine ascended to the throne of Emperor. It wasn't long before Imperial atrocities such as the Ghorman Massacre occurred, and Palpatine seemed to encourage further abuses of military power. Knowing it could mark the end of her career, but unwilling to remain silent, Mon Mothma became one of the New Order's fiercest critics. She attracted a like-minded supporter in Alderaanian Senator Bail Organa. The two met secretly in Organa's Coruscant quarters to discuss organized resistance in the early political discussions that are now known as "the Cantham talks."

Even the birth of her daughter Lieda didn't slow Mon Mothma. Bail assigned her an Alderaanian aide, Malan Tugrina, who was so devoted to her that he became almost a surrogate son. Still working in secret, Mon Mothma persuaded retired general Jan Dodonna to join her growing resistance movement, and enlisted unofficial help from anti-Imperial radical Cody Sun-Childe.

Her double life as a Senator and seditionist couldn't last forever. A few years before the Battle of Yavin, Mon Mothma's activities came to the attention of Emperor Palpatine. Branded a traitor and facing certain execution, she fled Coruscant and disappeared into the Rebel underground. Months later Mon Mothma, Bail Organa, and Corellian Senator Garm Bel Iblis united the three largest resistance groups under the Corellian Treaty. Shortly thereafter,

Mon Mothma broadcast the famous Declaration of Rebellion via the galaxywide HoloNet.

Commander in Chief of all Rebel Alliance activities, she persuaded planets such as Agamar to join the fight. She personally recruited many commandos and special agents, including Kyle Katarn, who helped obtain the first Death Star plans. Garm Bel Iblis, for one, thought Mon Mothma's authority reached too far—that she had the potential to become a dictator like Palpatine. After the Battle of Yavin, following an angry clash with her over the proposed attack on Milvayne, Bel Iblis withdrew from the Alliance. Undaunted, Mon Mothma fought on with new allies, until one triumphant day . . .

"We, the members of the Rebel Alliance, formally announce our intention to restore the glory of the Old Republic . . . to create a New Republic." Mon Mothma issued this second document one month after the death of the Emperor at Endor. A ruling council governed the New Republic, and Mon Mothma served as Chief Councilor. She orchestrated the New Republic's liberation of the Core Worlds, including her homeworld of Chandrila, and soon governed from Coruscant itself. On Chandrila, where the people welcomed her home as a hero, Mon Mothma built a private dacha on the banks of Lake Sah'ot.

During the New Republic's campaign against Warlord Zsinj, Mon Mothma became an assassination target in Zsinj's Project Minefield brainwashing scheme. Malan Tugrina, her loyal aide for decades, died with a knife buried in his heart—one that had been meant for her.

A year later, Grand Admiral Thrawn rattled the foundations of the New Republic and prompted Garm Bel Iblis to return after a nine-year absence. Bel Iblis had realized his error in thinking Mon Mothma's ruthless streak could ever translate into tyranny. But even his forces could not hold off the armies of the resurrected Emperor Palpatine. The New Republic suffered great losses, but survived.

Concerned for the future of the democracy she'd created, Mon Mothma designed a new structure for the government and became the New Republic's Chief of State. She also appointed admiral Hiram Drayson, a fellow Chandrilan, the head of a secret intelligence agency called Alpha Blue.

Not even a year into her term as Chief of State, Mon Mothma survived a second assassination attempt, this time by Ambassador Furgan of Carida. Furgan's weapon was molecular poison, but it didn't kill her. Nevertheless, Mon Mothma never truly fully regained her health. She retired, and appointed Leia Organa Solo to be her successor as Chief of State.

Six years later, Mon Mothma returned as Chief of State during the Almanian crisis, but only as a temporary stand-in. Once Leia defused the emergency, Mon Mothma returned to her main home on Coruscant, and with her daughter lived the quiet life she had earned. Shortly before the invasion of the Yuuzhan Vong, she passed away peacefully in her sleep.

BOSS NASS

PRONUNCIATION
Bŏs Năs
SPECIES
Gungan
SEX
Male
HAIR COLOR
None
EYE COLOR
Orange
HEIGHT
2.06 meters
HOMEWORLD
Naboo

Boss Nass wasn't content to be the one who united the Gungans and the Naboo. He wanted to be remembered as the ruler who gave his people the stars.

Boss Nass made cunning decisions all his life, long before he became boss of Otoh Gunga and Commander in Chief of the Gungan Grand Army. In his youth he was known as a bright but uncontrollable risk-taker. While still in school, Nass ventured off to find a sando aqua monster and somehow survived the encounter.

New bosses were often chosen from the ranks of the Rep Council, but Nass never served as a Rep. In his hodgepodge career he spent time as an army sergeant, an engineer, an energy miner, and the head of several small businesses. It seemed inevitable that he would then become Otoh Gunga's Boss—by that point, Nass knew *everyone*, and his forceful, almost bullying personality was perfectly suited for a position of supreme authority.

Nass was rarely diplomatic, but he was always honest. He trusted his instincts more than the advice of his Reps, and thus his decisions could seem mercurial and unfair. He was fiercely protective of those he loved, particularly his only niece, Major Fassa.

Boss Nass showed uncharacteristic tolerance with Jar Jar Binks. He first placed the troublemaker on probation after a zoo accident, then banished him after Jar Jar flooded Nass's mansion and crashed his luxury heyblibber. It wasn't until Jar Jar broke exile and brought outlander Jedi to Otoh Gunga that Nass sentenced the lawbreaker to be pounded to death. Only Qui-Gon Jinn's skills at Jedi mind manipulation saved Jar from the Boss's wrath.

When the Trade Federation's "mackineeks" invaded Otoh Gunga, Boss Nass ordered the city's evacuation to the Gungan sacred place. There, after Queen Amidala humbled herself in a symbolic gesture to prove that the Naboo had put aside their arrogance, Nass agreed to commit his army to the Queen's cause.

At great cost, the Gungan Grand Army diverted the Trade Federation's attention so the viceroy could be captured. During the victory celebration, Queen Amidala gave Boss Nass the Globe of Peace. Nass remarked that the sphere resembled Ohma-D'un, shining brightly in the night sky of Naboo. That satellite was the source of the Boss's next great scheme.

Only a ruler of Nass's stature could have persuaded thousands of Gungans to forsake their homes and resettle on Ohma-D'un, Naboo's largest moon. And only a ruler of Nass's shrewdness could have foreseen how effectively the move would silence all his critics. When the Naboo looked up at the moon they saw a *Gungan* moon, and for Gungan hard-liners that was more than enough compensation for lives lost in battle.

Nien Nunb

PRONUNCIATION
Nīn Nŭnb
SPECIES
Sullustan
SEX
Male
HAIR COLOR
None
EYE COLOR
Black
HEIGHT
1.6 meters
HOMEWORLD
Sullust

"Nunb? He kicked the scarns outa the Empire real good." So say the young of Sullust in describing one of their most famous heroes. Nunb's staggering feats have become legendary—some real, most mythical.

Humans give credit for the destruction of the second Death Star to Lando Calrissian. Sullustans say Nien Nunb, Calrissian's copilot, deserves the true credit for the liberation of the galaxy. Nunb's fame began years before Endor, when he left his job as a cargo pilot for Sullust's SoroSuub Corporation, in protest over SoroSuub's Imperial allegiances. The company tried to have him killed, and he responded by becoming a pirate.

In his ship the *Sublight Queen* Nien and his sister Aril raided outgoing SoroSuub shipments and turned the merchandise over to the Rebel Alliance. The Sullustan people, already angry with SoroSuub for dissolving the planetary government, applauded Nunb's actions. Soon he had attracted a score of like-minded followers. SoroSuub formed a protective Home Guard, composed of native pilots who weren't too vigilant about hunting their local hero.

Councilor Sian Tevv, an old friend of Nunb's and a prominent member of the Rebellion, arranged for his admittance into the Alliance navy. Although many of his ships didn't make it past the Imperial blockade on their way out from Sullust, Nien Nunb gained a reputation as one of the Rebels' most trusted pilots. In the Battle of Endor, Nien Nunb copiloted the *Millennium Falcon* into the skeleton of the unfinished Death Star. For its destruction, he earned the Kalidor Crescent for his heroism.

Nunb helped cover the Alliance's evacuation from Endor when the alien Nagai invaders threatened that world. Later he flew with Han Solo in the *Falcon* to escort two royal children to the metalworks of Vandelhelm. When Lando Calrissian formed a team of raiders called "Lando's Commandos," Nien Nunb joined the group in a dangerous operation on Abraxas and in the liberation of Cloud City from the Empire.

In later years Nien Nunb moved away from piloting, even as he watched his sister Aril Nunb become a fighter ace in Rogue Squadron. After the first war with Admiral Daala, Nunb took a position as Chief Administrator of the Kessel mines when his friend Calrissian took ownership of the spice planet.

Shortly before the Yuuzhan Vong invasion, Czethros, leader of Black Sun, took over the Kessel mines. Nunb, along with the Jedi Knights Jaina Solo and Lowbacca, defeated Czethros and booted his henchmen off Kessel for good. With the Yuuzhan Vong offensive so close to Kessel, Nien Nunb has turned the spice world into a fortress to protect his assets and the lives of his workers.

NYM

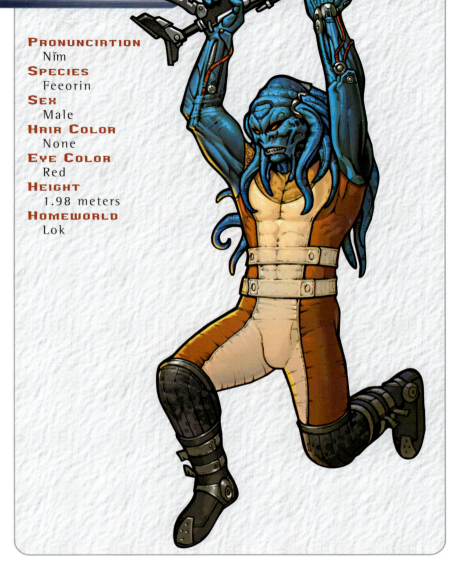

It's a well-known fact that the Battle of Naboo hinged on a Queen, a Gungan, two Jedi, and a nine-year-old boy. But the newsnets package the truth for easy consumption, omitting the accolades belonging to a thuggish space pirate from Lok.

Nym the pirate captain was a Feeorin, one of the last of his breed. Orphaned at an early age on the mean streets of Lok, he joined up with the pirate crews who hung around the landing pits. After earning respect as a pilot, mechanic, and hand-to-hand combatant, Nym gathered his own crew and practiced piracy along the heavily trafficked hyperlanes between the Core Worlds.

Five years before the Battle of Naboo, Nym and his crew pulled off the daring heist of a prototype Scurrg H-6 bomber from a storage silo on Nubia. A Bith engineer modified the vessel far beyond its original specs, and—newly christened the *Havoc*—the starfighter became Nym's personal raider, ripping up the opposition with its experimental bomblet generators.

Nym returned to Lok and built a stronghold there. For years his pirate crew harassed Trade Federation shipments up and down the Rimma and the Corellian Trade Spine. When Nym made off with a cache of secret weaponry, the Trade Federation hired mercenary Vana Sage to capture him. Not realizing Sage's true intentions, Nym used the mercenary as a go-between when he tried to sell the weaponry. He wound up in the brig of a Trade Federation freighter.

His loyal crew rescued him before the torturers could arrive, and he returned to Lok, but a vengeful Trade

PRONUNCIATION
Nĭm
SPECIES
Feeorin
SEX
Male
HAIR COLOR
None
EYE COLOR
Red
HEIGHT
1.98 meters
HOMEWORLD
Lok

Federation—testing its new war equipment just prior to the invasion of Naboo—pounded his Lok base to powder with AATs, MTTs, and droid starfighters. Nym barely made it out alive. Afire with hatred for his persecutors, he joined forces with two unlikely partners. The first was Naboo starfighter pilot Rhys Dallows. The other was Vana Sage, betrayed by the Trade Federation and thirsting for her own brand of revenge.

Nym and his new allies hit Trade Federation targets like a cyclone, finally taking the fight to Naboo itself. In the *Havoc*, he helped destroy one arm of the battle droid army. With the Trade Federation's flanking forces decimated, the Gungans survived long enough for Anakin Skywalker to destroy the Droid Control Ship.

Supreme Chancellor Palpatine pardoned Nym for his past crimes. The ex-pirate took a job with a Republic Special Task Force, advising its own pirate-fighting patrols.

Ric Olié

PRONUNCIATION
Rĭk Ō-lē'
SPECIES
Human
SEX
Male
HAIR COLOR
Light brown
EYE COLOR
Unknown
HEIGHT
1.83 meters
HOMEWORLD
Naboo

Before he became the best star pilot on all of Naboo, Ric Olié was a lanky fourteen-year-old offering short flights in his Sandtek Skyflipper for ten credits a hop. When he plowed the flying machine into a grassy hill, the residents of his home village figured "Reckless Ric's" piloting days were over.

Not a chance. When he crashed his Skyflipper, Olié learned how to fit the shattered parts back together so he could assemble a replacement. After graduation from public school, he enrolled in the sector piloting academy, where graduates took jobs as cargo captains or home guard pilots. Deep down he suspected he was as good as any Republic flier, but his patriotism for Naboo kept him from proving his talents in the employ of some other world. He enrolled in Naboo's Space Fighter Corps and worked his way to the top.

This internal conflict haunted Olié, even though he was indisputably Naboo's top pilot. When he had opportunities to fly among offworld pilots, especially *Republic* pilots, he tended to be a show-off. Such chances were rare, but Olié and his fellow fliers participated in Republic-sponsored sorties against sector pirates and flew many escort missions to Coruscant and back.

As head of the Space Fighter Corps, Ric Olié was in charge of Echo, Alpha, and Bravo Flights, which collectively comprised Naboo's complement of defensive starfighters. Bravo Flight, housed in Theed, was the most prestigious of the three, and Olié naturally bore the call sign of Bravo Leader. Because the Space Fighter Corps was one of the three branches of the Royal Security Forces, Olié took his orders directly from Captain Panaka. Most of the pilots in the Space Fighter Corps had been barge drivers or employees of small passenger charters. Only a few had graduated from the sector academy. In addition to his job as a fighter jockey, Ric Olié also piloted the Royal Starship.

During the Battle of Naboo, Ric Olié and his pilots knew the Trade Federation's Droid Control Ship outgunned them. Despite the odds, they fought on for the sake of their homeworld.

Olié was proud of Bravo Flight's success against the Trade Federation's droid starfighters, and was just a little amused that a nine-year-old boy with no combat experience brought about ultimate victory. But Ric Olié knew there would be other opportunities for battle, and over the next few years he showed the galaxy what Bravo Squadron could do.

EMPEROR PALPATINE

PRONUNCIATION
Păl'-pä-tēn
SPECIES
Human
SEX
Male
HAIR COLOR
Brown-silver
EYE COLOR
Unknown
HEIGHT
1.73 (in Jedi) meters
HOMEWORLD
Naboo

In just a few decades Palpatine went from savior to demon in the public consciousness, but the depth of his evil reveals that he was a demon all along. At a time when the galactic government seemed to be disintegrating under the acid drip of corruption, he earned accolades as the man who could save the Republic from itself. The public never suspected it had elected an evil man who would fashion a dark regime in his own twisted image.

Early in Palpatine's career, no one ever thought that this subdued politician from backwater Naboo could ascend to the most powerful office in the galaxy. Still, disappointing as his initial political life may have been, Palpatine discovered that legislative bodies operated under the same basic rules that governed company boards and military regiments. Members of any group, he observed, could be merged into exploitable partnerships given the proper motivation. Like a colossus astride a mountaintop, a leader has power over those beneath him, but becomes a target for their barbs and arrows. Palpatine's writings on the nature of power from this period became popular political texts. (Much later, Palpatine merged political theory with Sith doctrine in *The Book of Anger*, volume one of a vast dark side compendium.)

Though most of his peers left public service at age twenty, Palpatine remained in local politics. The people of Naboo soon elected him as their sectorial Senator, representing Naboo and many neighboring planets in the Republic Senate. Because of Coruscant's wild dissimilarity from Naboo, his fellow delegates expected the newcomer to be swallowed up in the Senatorial shark pool. But Palpatine's doubters underestimated his political savvy. His rustic background lent him an air of uncorrupted promise, and beneath the surface his hunger for success dwarfed the ambitions of any of Coruscant's lazy incumbents.

Palpatine's tenure as Senator extended for two decades, bolstered by reelection after reelection. He was a private man, seldom emerging from his private apartment to appear at social functions, but at work he always operated at 100 percent. He forged alliances with key personalities, including Commander Screed of the Republic Judicial Department and Jedi Master Jorus C'baoth. Palpatine had under-the-table allies in every organization from the Techno Union to Freedom's Sons, and cultivated friendships with the leaders of the Caamasi delegation to enhance the public's perception of his moral authority. Sate Pestage and Kinman Doriana, Palpatine's two loyal aides, kept the Senator's schedule and clandestinely handled his dirty work.

Approximately six months before the Battle of Naboo, Palpatine attended a trade summit on Eriadu to discuss Chancellor Valorum's proposal to tax the shipping lanes within the outlying free trade zones. Although most of the delegates didn't realize it, Palpatine had been pushing Valorum for months to pass the tax despite the predictable resistance of the Trade Federation. The summit ended in disaster when the non-Neimoidian members of the Trade Federation Directorate died in an assassination plot. In the wake of the deaths, Nute Gunray and his fellow Neimoidians assumed exclusive control over the Trade Federation.

Concurrent with the Eriadu summit, King Veruna of Naboo announced his abdication of the throne. Years earlier Palpatine had established a tense working relationship with Veruna, and despite some mutual animosity the King had heeded Palpatine's advice to become involved in offworld politics. Veruna even built a series of underground storehouses on Naboo for Palpatine where—according to rumor—the Senator disposed of his political enemies. Veruna's corruption at last alienated the people of Naboo, and a short time after his abdication Veruna died at the hands of assassins.

Young Queen Amidala took the throne in Veruna's place, and the Trade Federation invaded Naboo six months later. When the Queen escaped to Coruscant, Senator Palpatine manipulated her to in effect be his mouthpiece, delivering a motion of no confidence against Supreme Chancellor Valorum. Partly out of sympathy for his besieged homeworld, Palpatine received the most votes in the election to succeed Valorum.

As Supreme Chancellor, Palpatine surprised many with his take-charge attitude. Others complained that his reforms lacked teeth—his partial disarmament of the Trade Federation, for example, amounted to little more than a slap on the wrist.

The Senate reelected Palpatine to a second term. After eight years in office he managed to extend his stay beyond its traditional limits by agreeing to deal with Count Dooku's separatist movement before he would consider retirement.

Dooku's Confederacy of Independent Systems had announced its secession from the Republic, and for two years the Senate debated the separatists' right to secede. Eventually a group of Senators proposed the Military Creation Act to defend the Republic against secessionist aggression. When Obi-Wan Kenobi discovered a clone army on Kamino, Palpatine's supporters suggested the Chancellor be given emergency war powers to commandeer the clones and use them against the droid armies of the confederacy. Calling it "the saddest day of my life," Palpatine acceded to the motion brought forth by Naboo Representative Jar Jar Binks and assumed dictatorial powers. At the time, he asked only that he be allowed to retire in peace once the crisis had ended.

Of course, Palpatine planned to do no such thing. He used the chaos of the Clone Wars to grab even more power for himself, eventually declaring himself Emperor. Anakin Skywalker, a Jedi whom Palpatine had watched carefully for more than a decade, became the black-armored Darth Vader and devoted himself to the Emperor's service in the dark side of the Force. Vader helped Palpatine exterminate the surviving Jedi and spearheaded the creation of a staggering new military, anchored by numberless stormtroopers and mighty Star Destroyers. Because the Senate still oversaw Palpatine's actions, he kept his greatest horrors a secret, such as the battlemoon *Eye of Palpatine* and its mission to exterminate Jedi children.

Emperor Palpatine named Sate

Pestage his Grand Vizier. Pestage instituted the social policies of the Emperor's New Order, including the concept of "High Human Culture," which led to the persecution and enslavement of alien species. The Caamasi, for example, nearly died out when their world was firebombed shortly after the Clone Wars. But Palpatine also exploited talent wherever he could find it, bringing the alien Mitth'raw'nuruodo into the Empire and molding him into the fierce Grand Admiral Thrawn.

Palpatine ruled from the Imperial Palace on Coruscant, but soon opened a "resort world" in the restricted Deep Core. Imperial ships ferried millions of immigrants to the planet Byss, where the Emperor fed off their life-energies through the dark side. The palace on Byss became home to Palpatine's dark side subordinates, for while Palpatine and Vader fulfilled the "two Sith" rule, the Emperor found uses for other Force-sensitive underlings. These included the Jedi-hunting Inquisitors and dark side elite—a semigeneric term encompassing the Emperor's Mages and the Emperor's Hands. Jerec, Kadann, and Mara Jade were representative members of each of these three classes.

After torturing Jedi librarian Ashka Boda, one of the last surviving Jedi Masters, Emperor Palpatine learned the secret of spirit transference via the Force. This allowed him to offset the dark side's physical ravages by transferring his consciousness into healthy clone bodies. Palpatine built three cloning complexes—one on Coruscant, one on Byss, and a third in his secret military storehouse in Mount Tantiss on Wayland.

The Emperor had little regard for the Rebellion that organized against his rule. He believed that his reign would extend for a thousand years, and approved toys such as Grand Moff Tarkin's Death Star to blast naysayers to atoms. Eventually he disbanded the Senate, silencing the last remaining outlet for political criticism.

The Rebel Alliance, however, proved itself a viable threat by destroying the Death Star at Yavin. Palpatine ordered another battle station, and tortured designer Bevel Lemelisk to make sure the replacement had no flaws similar to the exhaust port that led to the destruction of the original. Palpatine commissioned the vast flagship *Eclipse*—though it would be years before his vessel would see completion—and survived a coup attempt when Grand Admiral Zaarin tried to kidnap him on Coruscant. He also enjoyed pitting Darth Vader against Black Sun leader Prince Xizor, a game that ended when Vader vaporized his rival.

But Xizor was just a warm-up. Palpatine dreamed of replacing Vader with someone even more powerful—Anakin Skywalker's son, Luke. When Mara Jade failed to kill Luke Skywalker at Jabba's palace, Palpatine decided to convert the young Rebel and make him the new Dark Lord of the Sith. In the end, he miscalculated the love of a father for his son. Vader threw Palpatine down the Death Star's reactor shaft, where his body disintegrated in a cloud of energy.

But like certain Jedi of the light side, Palpatine retained his identity in the realm beyond death. His spirit journeyed to Byss to inhabit the body of a healthy young clone. Rejuvenated, he waited on Byss with his World Devastators and his surviving Dark Side Adepts, waiting for the right moment to strike.

After the fall of Grand Admiral Thrawn, Palpatine contacted his various Imperial fleet commanders, receiving their renewed pledges of loyalty and launching a stunning attack from the Deep Core. Even when the fleet's factions turned on one another, Palpatine allowed it as a way to exterminate the weak. Luke Skywalker went to Byss to stop the Emperor, and instead joined his cause, hoping he could defeat the dark side from within. Skywalker fell so far he nearly became the new Vader, but his sister Leia Organa brought him back to the light. The Emperor died aboard his flagship the *Eclipse* when brother and sister turned Palpatine's all-consuming Force storm back on its maker.

His spirit had survived disembodiment once before, so Palpatine had little difficulty inhabiting a fresh clone on Byss and returning to menace the New Republic. He used a new superweapon, the Galaxy Gun, to cow hundreds of star systems. But in the midst of his victories he discovered that his clone supply was dying due to suspicious genetic tampering. Palpatine hoped to overcome the deterioration of his clone stock by transferring his life-essence into a host with Skywalker blood—namely, the infant Anakin Solo, son of Han Solo and Vader's daughter, Leia Organa. On Onderon, Palpatine tried to take possession of the baby, but Han Solo shot him dead. Jedi Knight Empatojayos Brand intercepted the Emperor's departing life-essence, binding it to his own as Brand passed into the light of the Force. Thus it was ensured that the true Palpatine could never again return from beyond death.

CAPTAIN PANAKA

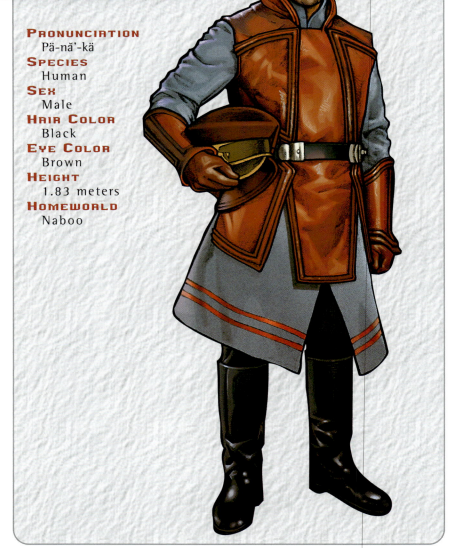

Panaka, head of the Naboo Royal Security Forces and captain of the Queen's guard, was often called "the quickest eyes on Naboo." So during the cleanup after the great ground battle between the Gungans and the Trade Federation, Captain Tarpals of the Gungan Grand Army found Panaka standing amid a contingent of Naboo officers. "Daza cullin yous da quickest eyes un Naboo,'" Tarpals said, "boot mesa figgerin me peepers gotta built-in edge." A friendly marksmanship contest followed, using a target painted on the side of a disabled AAT. According to witnesses, Panaka won with five bull's-eyes to Tarpals's three.

The anecdote is especially illuminating in light of Panaka's established dislike of Gungans. Like most of the Naboo, he was raised to think of the amphibious natives as barbarians. In his career as a security officer, the few Gungans he encountered were criminals, outcasts from their underwater communities, which only served to reinforce the stereotype. During the Queen's flight from Naboo, Panaka was opposed to bringing Jar Jar Binks along—he was certain that the Gungan would only bring trouble, and for the most part Panaka was right. But Jar Jar also brought military aid from the Gungan Grand Army, and postbattle accounts of Gungan bravery opened Panaka's eyes. What were once unknowns—and therefore potential threats to the Queen's security—proved instead to be assets and allies.

Panaka was born on Naboo, but had an extensive offworld education at a series of guilds specializing in personal combat and threat analysis.

PRONUNCIATION
Pä-nă'-kä
SPECIES
Human
SEX
Male
HAIR COLOR
Black
EYE COLOR
Brown
HEIGHT
1.83 meters
HOMEWORLD
Naboo

His instructors drilled him in a broad curriculum covering everything from politics to vehicle maintenance. To gain actual combat experience, Panaka joined a Republic Special Task Force and fought in several skirmishes against sector pirates. Upon returning to Naboo he enlisted in the Royal Security Forces. His guild education, as well as his combat experience, gave him an edge over his fellow officers, most of whom had never left Naboo.

While he served offworld, Panaka's older sister—an officer in the Palace Guard—died in a live-fire exercise. In dealing with his grief, Panaka dedicated himself to his job and the service of King Veruna. He tried to form friendships, but to Panaka, who viewed his job as the summation of his character, outside interests merely provided unwanted distractions. Frustrated by his inability to connect with his fellow officers, he vowed to win their respect instead.

Years passed, and Lieutenant Panaka served with distinction under the command of Captain Magneta, head of the Royal Security Forces. He was paired with a female partner, Sergeant Bialy, but still kept to himself. In lieu of socializing, he thought up ways to improve security force procedures, in the process inventing a liquid-cable grappling hook shooter to scale walls.

On one mission to oversee the removal of a beached sando aqua monster from the Naboo shoreline, Panaka discovered a secret underground chamber filled with decomposing bodies and enigmatic locked rooms. Both King Veruna and Senator Palpatine seemed to have some connection to the chamber, but Captain Magneta ordered the area "cleansed" with a proton torpedo strike before Panaka could examine all the evidence.

Six months before the Battle of Naboo, King Veruna abdicated the throne in the wake of his implication in a corruption scandal. Subsequently, Captain Magneta failed to prevent the former King's mysterious death, and resigned in disgrace. Panaka took her place as head of the Royal Security Forces, and became responsible for the safety of fourteen-year-old Queen Amidala. He insisted that the Queen employ a handmaiden/decoy ruse and undergo self-defense training. Panaka also tried to beef up Naboo's defenses, but the Advisory Council rejected his recommendations.

The captain held responsibility not only for the Queen, but for every volunteer soldier in the Security Forces as well, including the Security Guard, the Palace Guard, the Security Officer Corps, and the Space Fighter Corps. On any other world Panaka would likely have borne the rank of general, but Naboo's security forces were so small that Panaka held only the title traditionally given to the captain of the royal monarch's personal guard.

Naboo's security officers often complained that their boss was humorless, and they were absolutely right. In his new position Panaka could be downright grim. He trained his security squads relentlessly in the effort to make up for their lack of combat experience—prior to the Battle of Naboo, less than 1 percent of all Naboo guards had fired their weapons in the line of duty.

Captain Panaka valued security above all else, and while he could take orders from others, he wouldn't hesitate to speak up when he thought those orders were absurd. He repeatedly warned Amidala that his security forces could not hope to withstand the numerically superior droid army of the Trade Federation, and he stood up to Qui-Gon Jinn and Obi-Wan Kenobi when he felt their advice was inappropriate. Panaka always prepared for the worst.

Though he would have never admitted it, during the final assault to free Naboo from the Trade Federation Panaka felt exhilarated. At last he was doing what he was trained for, what he was *good* at. Outwitting Viceroy Nute Gunray and recapturing the Palace was a sweet feeling indeed.

After the Battle of Naboo, Panaka protected the Queen as she continued her term, and continued to serve Queen Jamillia as head of security. Captain Typho, Panaka's nephew, took over his former responsibilities as protector of Padmé Amidala following Amidala's election to the Senate.

ADMIRAL GILAD PELLAEON

Rebel propagandists were fond of demonizing their Imperial enemies—and to be honest, it wasn't that hard. From Tarkin to Ozzel to Screed, Imperial officers were cruel, careless monsters. But Admiral Gilad Pellaeon is respected by his allies and enemies alike as the fair-minded leader of the post-treaty Empire.

Pellaeon began his career during the Old Republic, and was so eager to become an officer that he lied about his age in order to get into the Raithal Academy. Upon graduation, Ensign Pellaeon served aboard an escort vessel for a convoy near Garvyn. When pirates attacked, Pellaeon used the planet's powerful magnetic pole to confuse his enemies and destroy them. For his quick thinking, Pellaeon earned a string of swift promotions.

During the Emperor's reign, Pellaeon was transferred to the crew of the Imperial Star Destroyer *Chimaera*. By the time of the Battle of Endor, he had become the *Chimaera*'s second in command. The fierce fighting above the forest moon decimated the Imperial fleet and killed the Destroyer's captain. Realizing the battle was lost, Captain Pellaeon assumed command and ordered all surviving warships to retreat to Annaj.

With the death of Admiral Piett and the absence of any Grand Admirals, Pellaeon's order made him the de facto fleet leader at Annaj. However, many warship commanders refused to follow his lead, and left Annaj to form warlord kingdoms.

Pellaeon was no warlord, though. He brought the surviving fleet back to Coruscant and served for several years under Ysanne Isard. Despite his favorable reputation within the fleet, Isard

PRONUNCIATION
Gǐ'-lăd Pěl'-lā-ŏn
SPECIES
Human
SEX
Male
HAIR COLOR
White
EYE COLOR
Brown
HEIGHT
1.7 meters
HOMEWORLD
Corellia

refused to promote him to admiral.

After Isard's defeat and the loss of Coruscant to the New Republic, Pellaeon tried to hold the main Imperial fleet together in the face of warlord factions and Republic aggression. The Empire seemed doomed, and then Thrawn—the Emperor's last Grand Admiral—returned from the Unknown Regions.

Thrawn made the *Chimaera* his command vessel and Pellaeon his close confidant. The Empire swiftly recaptured much of its lost territory, and when Thrawn fell to an assassin's blade, Pellaeon's fleet withdrew as the Empire imploded. Captain Pellaeon was as shocked as anyone when the dark forces of the resurrected Emperor launched from the Deep Core.

For a time, Pellaeon fought under the clone Emperor's banner, and almost died carrying out his brutal offensive. He was forced to abandon his beloved *Chimaera* during Operation Shadow Hand; most of his senior staff lost their lives. When the reborn Emperor died on Onderon, Pellaeon had little choice but to join High Admiral Teradoc's warlord kingdom in the Deep Core to protect his surviving crew. Teradoc promoted Pellaeon to vice admiral and placed him in command of a strike force of crimson-hulled *Victory*-class Star Destroyers.

Admiral Daala brought an end to the Empire's fragmentation. She executed the thirteen strongest warlords and united their forces, appointing Pellaeon her second in command. But Daala made the poor tactical decision to attack Luke Skywalker's Jedi academy. Her defeat at Yavin 4 elevated Pellaeon to the rank of admiral and gave him supreme control over all Imperial military forces.

Pellaeon transferred Imperial units out of the Deep Core and expanded Imperial holdings in the Mid and Outer Rims. His annexation of the Imperial holding known as the Pentastar Alignment gave him the Super Star Destroyer *Reaper* as his new command vessel. From the bridge of the *Reaper*, Pellaeon spearheaded a major Imperial victory at Orinda and bombarded the planet Adumar when its inhabitants took up arms against the Empire. Pellaeon lost his Super Star Destroyer, however, in an effort to stem the New Republic's incursion into Imperial space through the Antemeridian sector.

Years passed and the Empire continued to wilt, though Pellaeon scored a personal victory when he recaptured the *Chimaera* from Ackbar at the Battle of Gravlex Med. Thirteen years after Endor, Pellaeon gambled the Empire's future on one aggressive strike, and lost. The New Republic's Third and Fifth Fleets, including the Super Star Destroyer *Guardian*, decimated the Imperial Navy. Pellaeon's surviving ships retreated, and the Empire shrank to a mere eight sectors in a backwater corner of the Outer Rim.

Pellaeon realized the Empire could no longer win by force, and proposed a peace treaty with the New Republic, but one Imperial Moff sabotaged his efforts by creating a Grand Admiral Thrawn impersonator in an attempt to rule the Empire. Pellaeon exposed the false Thrawn and signed the historic armistice between Imperial and New Republic forces.

Though he was technically subordinate to the Moffs, Pellaeon ruled the so-called Imperial Remnant for six peaceful years. The Yuuzhan Vong shattered that tranquillity. The invaders bypassed Imperial space, but Pellaeon recognized the threat they posed and committed his navy to a joint Imperial–New Republic offensive alongside Bothan Admiral Traest Kre'fey. Their forces fought with valor at Ithor, but neither admiral could prevent the Yuuzhan Vong from releasing a bioweapon that turned the vibrant planet into a blackened husk. The death of Ithor terrified the citizens of the Imperial Remnant and Pellaeon's fleet went home, more to keep the peace than to actively defend Imperial worlds.

Life in Pellaeon's Imperial Remnant is much like life in the New Republic—slavery is forbidden, and blatant alien prejudice is rare. The admiral deserves much of the credit for these advances. But Pellaeon *could* have defected to the Rebellion during the Emperor's New Order, as did Jan Dodonna, Crix Madine, Tycho Celchu, and countless others. Instead he knowingly served a regime responsible for some of the worst atrocities in galactic history. For some citizens, Pellaeon's "good deeds" will never bring him absolution.

SATE PESTAGE

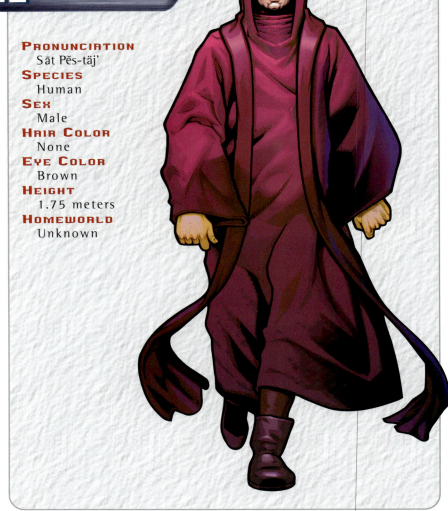

PRONUNCIATION
Sāt Pĕs-täj'

SPECIES
Human

SEX
Male

HAIR COLOR
None

EYE COLOR
Brown

HEIGHT
1.75 meters

HOMEWORLD
Unknown

If anyone truly understood Emperor Palpatine, it was Sate Pestage. He stood at Palpatine's side from his days as Naboo's Senator to his resurrection on the hidden throneworld Byss. Rumors dogged him, some of them surely untrue—that he was a relative of Palpatine's, for instance, or that he was one of the earliest clones.

He emerged into public view several years before the Battle of Naboo as one of Senator Palpatine's aides, alongside Kinman Doriana. Pestage covered up the Senator's illegal doings on Naboo during the term of King Veruna; on one such mission he ran afoul of then-lieutenant Panaka.

During Palpatine's tenure as Chancellor, Pestage controlled the executive agenda. When Palpatine became Emperor, Pestage was named Grand Vizier. He handled everything from managing Palpatine's calendar to tasting his food for poisons. In return, the Emperor gave Pestage stewardship of a cluster of wealthy worlds known as the Ciutric Hegemony.

By the time of the Battle of Hoth, Pestage was, in fact, running the Empire. Palpatine, consumed with dark side studies, had surrendered the day-to-day responsibilities of rule to his Grand Vizier. Which is why, when Palpatine died at Endor, many assumed Pestage would be heir apparent to the Imperial throne.

Ysanne Isard did not share that view. She began pitting Pestage against the Imperial Interim Ruling Council, hoping to eliminate both parties and rule as Empress. Isard used the New Republic's invasion of Brentaal to make Pestage look weak and ineffectual.

Pestage realized his hold on the throne was tenuous. His Eidolon Base on Tatooine—created years earlier as a secret safehouse—had already been destroyed by Rogue Squadron. Soon Coruscant itself would no longer welcome him. So he approached Leia Organa on Axxila and offered a deal—if he would be allowed to keep his twenty-five worlds in the Ciutric Hegemony, he would surrender Coruscant to the New Republic.

The plan never took wing, as the Imperial Interim Ruling Council issued an order for his arrest. Pestage fled, but was apprehended on Ciutric. A New Republic operation to rescue him failed, and Imperial Admiral Delak Krennel snapped the neck of the former Vizier.

But had Sate Pestage truly died? Emperor Palpatine had cloning facilities on Coruscant. Pestage is believed to have grown a clone of himself. He either sent the clone to Palpatine's citadel on Byss, or went to Byss himself, leaving the clone behind to take the fall. On Byss, Pestage helped bring about Palpatine's own resurrection through cloning. Finally, though, he died on Byss when the planet was consumed by the devastating energies of the Galaxy Gun.

ADMIRAL FIRMUS PIETT

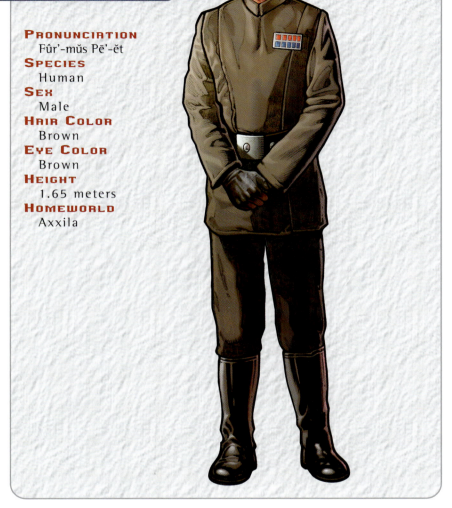

PRONUNCIATION
Fûr'-mŭs Pē'-ĕt

SPECIES
Human

SEX
Male

HAIR COLOR
Brown

EYE COLOR
Brown

HEIGHT
1.65 meters

HOMEWORLD
Axxila

Y ou are in command now, Admiral Piett." Few captains ever achieve the rank of admiral; elevation to that lofty rank is normally cause for celebration. But when such promotions occurred aboard Darth Vader's *Executor*, junior crew members formed pools for betting on their new admiral's life expectancy.

Firmus Piett was the last to receive such an honor from Lord Vader. Born on Axxila, Piett began his naval career in the first years of the Emperor's New Order. His lack of Core World connections doomed him to a posting in his home sector. But under Piett's leadership, the Axxila antipirate fleet soon patrolled the most buttoned-up sector in the Outer Rim.

Vader assigned Piett to his personal fleet of Star Destroyers, to command the *Accuser* under the fleet leadership of Admiral Griff. The Super Star Destroyer *Executor* soon joined the fleet, and Griff perished during the Rebel evacuation of Yavin 4. In the resulting power vacuum, Captain Ozzel became admiral of Vader's fleet, and Piett took over as captain of the *Executor*.

For years Captain Piett hunted for the new Rebel base. When one probot reported an intriguing find in the Hoth system, Piett made sure Vader was present on the bridge before he brought the matter to Ozzel's attention. As expected, Vader overruled Ozzel's objections and acted on Piett's recommendation.

That embarrassment, combined with a critical mistake Ozzel made exiting hyperspace at Hoth, spelled the end for the admiral. Piett watched his commander fall dead under Vader's mystical grip, then—with some foreboding—took command of the fleet. Captain Kallic became captain of the *Executor*.

Piett's detractors pointed to the high turnover rate among Vader's officers as evidence of Piett's unfitness for the admiralty. But Lord Vader gathered many of the Empire's best officers around him, without regard for their political standing. With the exception of Thrawn, Vader had little use for Palpatine's Grand Admirals, and Piett had exhibited genius to match any of the Emperor's twelve.

Though Piett failed to capture Luke Skywalker at Bespin, Vader allowed his admiral to live. When Vader returned with the *Executor* to Coruscant during the Black Sun affair, he brought with him the Emperor's toady, Admiral Okins. This allowed Piett to continue the work of Vader's fleet from the bridge of the *Accuser*.

Months later, Piett and the *Executor* arrived at Endor to take part in Palpatine's ambush of the Rebels. Hamstrung by the Emperor's orders to hold back, Piett's fleet fell prey to Calrissian's point-blank tactics.

When an A-wing plowed into the bridge, the decapitated *Executor* went down with all hands on board.

Podracer Pilots

C For every winner on the Podracing circuit, there are a hundred also-rans, each with a tale to tell. Anakin Skywalker's upset victory in Tatooine's Boonta Eve Classic enraged Sebulba, the bookmakers' favorite, and stunned the other sixteen competitors.

Aldar Beedo

(Äl'-där Bē'-dō)

Many Podracers had wild nicknames, but Aldar Beedo's handle of "Hit Man" was chillingly accurate. Beedo, a Glymphid from Ploo II, was a professional assassin responsible for murdering Elan Mak's father and countless other individuals. He entered the Boonta for the money—specifically, for the cash advance offered by Wan Sandage to kill Sebulba. Beedo tried to pick off his quarry in midrace, but his Manta RamAir Flat-Twin Turbojet was too slow to catch Sebulba before the Dug's last-minute crash. Aldar Beedo finished third overall in the Boonta Eve race and went on to compete in the Phoebos Memorial Classic on Malastare.

Dud Bolt

(Dŭd Bōlt)

Dud Bolt was one of the few Vulptereens who wasn't working for the Trade Federation on his species' homeworld of Vulpter. Hundreds of thousands of Vulptereens toiled beneath the decaying industrial surface of their planet, operating colossal driller machines so the Trade Federation could store cargo in the resulting warrens. Bolt enjoyed a much better life than most, piloting a "hometown" Vulptereen RS 557 in competitions across the galaxy. But unlike other Podracers, Bolt didn't care about winning—he made his money by acting as Sebulba's midrace bodyguard. During the Boonta Eve Classic he intentionally steered his racer into Ark "Bumpy" Roose's path, bringing down both machines and earning a hefty under-the-table bonus from Sebulba.

Ebe Endocott

(Ē'-bē Ĕn'-dō-cŏt)

Originally from Triffis, Ebe Endocott began his racing career as a land-speeder driver on the planet Boonta, the famous world that lent its name to Tatooine's Boonta race and planetwide holiday. On the advice of his cleric, Endocott shifted to the more lucrative career of Podracing, finishing first in three semipro tournaments on Malastare. He was cocky and flashy, piloting a new Jak Racing J930 Dash-8, and finished fourth in the Boonta Eve Classic, unwittingly preventing Elan Mak from taking a clear shot at Aldar Beedo.

Gasgano

(Gäs-gä'-nō)

This four-armed Xexto was Gardulla the Hutt's personal champion, piloting a Hutt-sponsored Ord Pedrovia Podracer. Many expected Gasgano to beat Sebulba in the Boonta Eve Classic. As it turned out, he *did* beat the unlucky Sebulba, but still finished second behind Anakin Skywalker. In his off hours, Gasgano was a fastidious fellow who considered himself intellectually superior to his fellow racers. Ironically, he transformed into an ugly bar brawler whenever he'd had too much to drink.

Mars Guo

(Märs Gōō'-ō)

Mars Guo didn't make it off Tatooine. A skilled Phuii Podracer from the gaming planet of Phu, Guo had an unbearable ego. Prior to the Boonta Eve race, he placed just behind Sebulba in the Baroonda Fire Mountain Rally. The Dug, threatened by Guo's skill and enraged at the Phuii's interest in Sebulba's masseuse Ann Gella, tossed a piece of metal into the right engine of Guo's Collor Pondrat Plug-2 Behemoth during the race. The machine shredded like meat on a grater as it plowed into the desert floor. Believe it or not, Guo survived.

Clegg Holdfast

(Klĕg Hōld'-făst)

Holdfast was a Nosaurian from New Plympto. The planet was home to an exotic species of arboreal crablike spiders, whose eggs were a vital ingredient in many intoxicants. When the Republic enacted a "protected species" statute, it turned most Nosaurians into poachers overnight. Holdfast left this life at an early age, and despite his total inexperience, he took a job writing for *Podracing*

Quarterly. When his bosses assigned him the role of "participatory journalist," he had to learn the ropes fast.

Holdfast was sponsored by Biscuit Baron, a string of restaurants owned by Trade Federation associate TaggeCo, a frequent advertiser in *Podracing Quarterly*. During the Boonta, Sebulba torched Holdfast's Keizar-Volvec KV9T-B Wasp with a blast from his flame jets. Not wanting to offend a star of Sebulba's magnitude, the editors of *Podracing Quarterly* changed the official record to show that Holdfast had completed the race with a time of nearly half an hour, effectively burying the incident.

Neva Kee

(Nā'-vä Kē)

This Xamster from Xagobah was a Podracing revolutionary. His experimental Farwan & Glott FG8T8-Twin Block2 Special Podracer had no cables—the entire machine was one solid unit. Kee's Podracer could turn tighter corners and endure greater punishment than more traditional machines. Racing traditionalists tried to ban him from the sport, but the rebellious Xamster attracted a loyal fan base. During the Boonta Eve Classic, Kee left the course in midrace and mysteriously vanished.

Elan Mak

(Ē'-län Mäk)

Though race fans knew him as Elan Mak, this racer's given name was Kam Nale. Hailing from Ploo IV in the Ploo sector, the amphibious Fluggrian was driven by a hot thirst for vengeance.

Aldar "Hit Man" Beedo had killed Mak's crime lord father and Mak entered the Boonta in order to assassinate the assassin. Although the sharp-reflexed Fluggrians made nat-

ural Podracers, Elan Mak's KRT 410C Podracer was slow and outdated. He finished fifth in the race, unable to catch Aldar Beedo and exact his revenge. He has since reinvented himself as a hard-core Podracer.

Ody Mandrell

(Ō'-dē Măn-drĕl')

This racer was a reptilian Er'Kit, short and squat by the standards of his species. Mandrell, born on Tatooine, piloted a punishing Exelbrok XL 5115 that was designed to smash his competitors and force them out of his way. The other racers, convinced that young Mandrell carried a death wish, tended to steer clear of him lest he bring them bad luck. During the Boonta Eve race, Ody Mandrell made a risky maneuver pulling into the pits, and paid for it when his engine sucked in a pit droid.

Mawhonic

(Mäw-hŏ'-nĭk)

Mawhonic the Gran hailed from Hok, one of a dozen Gran colony worlds scattered throughout the galaxy. Like most offworld Gran, Mawhonic had nimble fingers that distinguished him from his club-handed brethren on the Gran homeworld. Mawhonic was large for a Podracer pilot, but his Galactic Power Engineering GPE-3130 was balanced to compensate.

In the Boonta Eve race, Sebulba smashed Mawhonic's machine into the side of a mesa, where it exploded in a fireball. Shortly after, Mawhonic raced in the Phoebos Classic on Malastare no worse for wear. Sebulba, certain he caused a *fatal* crash, suspected that Mawhonic had been replaced by an impostor.

Teemto Pagalies

(Tēm'-to Pä'-gä-lēz)

The moralistic Veknoids of Moonus Mandel banished Teemto Pagalies from their midst when he refused to enter an arranged marriage with the daughter of an influential trader. Unlike his leisurely fellows back on the homeworld, Pagalies became obsessive about time, since Podrace victories were often decided by a fraction of a second. He was disappointed when his cycling-electromagnet stabilizer and IPG-X1131 Longtail engines were damaged by a Tusken Raider's potshot; nevertheless he continued in his Podracing career after recovering from his injuries. Pagalies had a dangerous infatuation with Sebulba's masseuse Ann Gella, which only became stronger when his rival for Ann's affections, Mars Guo, perished in the Boonta.

Ben Quadinaros

(Bĕn Kwä-dĭ-nä'-rōr)

Ben Quadinaros and his large extended family were refugees. Toong'l, homeworld of the Toongs, had suffered suffered environmental poisoning due to a pair of comet strikes. Quadinaros and his parents, cousins, uncles, aunts, and their children fled Toong'l and skipped across the galaxy, purportedly living for a time on the mysterious sorcerers' planet of Tund. They arrived on Tatooine mere weeks before the Boonta.

Although Quadinaros had previously raced on the amateur Pouffra Circuit, he was a raconteur by trade, not a professional Podracer. But he accepted a wager from Boles Roor and entered the race in a rented Balta-Trabaat BT310, coming out five million peggats richer despite the fact that he never crossed the starting line. He used the money to support his family and further his improbable racing career.

Boles Roor

(Bôls Rōōr)

Boles Roor's fame as a glimmik singer far outshone his meager ability as a Podracer. Although the Sneevel had twice won the Boonta Eve Classic, those triumphs had occurred in an earlier decade. By the time of Anakin Skywalker's historic race, the wealthy Roor competed only as a hobby, and often substituted flashiness for competence. His Bin Gassi Quadrijet 4Barrel 904E Podracer, for example, sported ornate detailing that concealed a poor weld job by lazy mechanics. Roor lost five million peggats when he wagered that Ben Quadinaros was too timid to enter the Boonta Eve classic, then finished sixth in the race and made up his monetary losses in a sold-out, year-long club tour.

Ark "Bumpy" Roose

(Ärk Rōōs)

Ark Roose, better known as "Bumpy," was a hopeless dimwit. The restrictive government of Sump, Roose's homeworld, permitted Roose's participation in the Galactic Podrace Circuit purely for publicity purposes. However, the blockheaded Roose did little to improve the image of Nuknogs. Just prior to the start of the Boonta Classic, the paranoid Roose attempted to sabotage Anakin Skywalker's Podracer—but damaged Ben Quadinaros's machine instead. During the race he accidentally crashed his Vokoff-Strood Plug-8G 927 into Dud Bolt's Podracer. Both pilots failed to finish.

Wan Sandage

(Wän Săn-däj')

Wan Sandage, a Devlikk from Ord Radama, came from a family of 128 brothers and sisters. Six years old at the time of the Boonta, he was well past middle age and desperately wanted to eliminate Sebulba before succumbing to senility at age nine. Many Devlikks were active on the Podracing circuit, but all were female—Sandage was the only male Devlikk to race in more than thirty generations. All Devlikks possess an inherent attunement to the magnetic poles of Ord Radama and can never be lost in its labyrinthine cities. On Tatooine, however, Sandage couldn't rely on his magnetic sense and was easily disoriented. He learned the twists and turns of the Boonta only through relentless practice runs in his Elsinore-Cordova TurboDyne 99-U.

Ratts Tyerell

(Răts Tĭ-rĕl')

Also known as the "little scrapper," Ratts Tyerell was well liked by his fellow Podracers, but to outsiders he seemed boastful, bullying, and rude. His family often followed him from race to race, cheering wildly from the stands. His species, the Aleena, maintain a strong warrior tradition and are often outraged that many of the galaxy's larger species don't take them seriously. The diminutive Aleena were bred for wide physical variation—some are white, some are striped, some have tails, some have long necks, and some are half the size of Ratts Tyerell.

Tyerell, infuriated with Sebulba's blatant cheating, vowed to fight fire with fire. Before the Boonta Eve race he named his Vokoff-Strood Titan 2150 the *Scatalpen*—after a predator from Aleen that slashes open the belly of its prey, causing it to trip on its own entrails—and hired an outlaw tech to outfit his Podracer with illegal weaponry. But before he could jockey into a strategic position, Tyerell fatally collided with a stalactite.

ULIC QEL-DROMA

I s there a more tragic figure than a fallen Jedi? Ulic Qel-Droma's life went from one of heroism to barbarism, followed by shame and exile. He achieved redemption only moments before his death.

In Ulic's time, four thousand years before the Battle of Endor, the Jedi Council's laws governing training were much more liberal. Master Arca Jeth of Arkania had three Padawans—Ulic Qel-Droma, Ulic's brother Cay, and the Twi'lek Tott Doneeta—and he continued to teach them after they'd been appointed Jedi Knights. On one of their first missions together, the three Knights rescued a princess from Onderon and uncovered ancient Sith malevolence planted centuries earlier.

When the corrupt influence of Onderon's Sith spirits spread offworld thanks to two meddling Tetan nobles, Qel-Droma decided to go undercover within the new Tetan "Krath" society to, as he put it, "conquer the dark side from within." After Qel-Droma's beloved Master Arca died under the cannons of a Krath war droid, there was no turning back.

The Sith seductions he enjoyed as a Krath disciple overwhelmed Ulic. When another fallen Jedi, Exar Kun, arrived with the intention of eliminating him, the two men instead joined forces. Kun became Dark Lord of the Sith; Qel-Droma was his apprentice. Historians call their campaign of conquest the Sith War.

Qel-Droma commanded the armies of the Krath. After he defeated the warlord Mandalore in single combat, he controlled the Mandalorian army, too. Their combined forces executed a strike on Coruscant, but Ulic was captured by his fellow Jedi.

PRONUNCIATION
Ōō'-lĭk Kĕl-drō'-mä
SPECIES
Human
SEX
Male
HAIR COLOR
Brown
EYE COLOR
Brown
HEIGHT
1.77 meters
HOMEWORLD
Alderaan

Exar Kun rescued his comrade before a death sentence could be carried out. It wasn't until the invasion of Ossus that Qel-Droma's actions caught up with him. When Cay Qel-Droma tried to reach his brother through the Sith's influence, Ulic murdered him with a lightsaber. Shellshocked with horror, Ulic didn't resist when Nomi Sunrider cast a spell that blocked his access to the Force—seemingly forever.

Captured again by the Jedi, living in silent penance, Ulic led Republic forces to Exar Kun's base on Yavin 4, where Kun's forces perished in a conflagration. The Sith War was over. Exiled by the Jedi Knights, Ulic wandered alone for ten years. Eventually he chartered a vessel to dump him on empty, frozen Rhen Var, where he hoped to live out his last days.

But Vima Sunrider, Nomi Sunrider's thirteen-year-old daughter, sought out her mother's friend and persuaded him to become her mentor. In Vima's instruction Ulic found his redemption. When he finally died a senseless death—shot in the back by a no-name freighter pilot trying to be a hero—Ulic's body vanished into the light of the Force.

R2-D2

The blue and white paint on his chassis masks the dents, and therefore few people realize that R2-D2 has been fighting the good fight longer than any of the New Republic's more conspicuous champions. Before Luke Skywalker was ever born, R2-D2 helped free Naboo—and he's still going strong more than half a century later. This little droid has Chewbacca's heart, Princess Leia's courage, and Han Solo's colorful vocabulary whistled in an electronic argot.

R2-D2 is an aftermarket-modified R2 astromech droid manufactured by Industrial Automaton. He began his career as the property of the Royal House of Naboo. The Naboo techs altered all their astromech droids, including R2-D2, with add-ons such as small internal repulsorlift coils, magnetized treads, and retractable booster rockets.

The rockets, designed for controlled maneuvering in weightless space, soon became the props for a common astromech prank. R2-D2 was the first droid to discover that, if he dumped all his fuel in a single sustained burn, he could overcome Naboo's gravity and "fly" high above the ground. Other astromechs quickly followed R2-D2's lead, and the little blue-and-white droid earned a reputation as a troublemaker.

R2-D2 served the Royal Security Forces, initially under King Veruna. As a plug-in counterpart for Bravo Squadron's N-1 starfighters, Artoo accompanied the squadron on escort missions to planets across the galaxy.

Following Veruna's abdication and Queen Amidala's ascension to the throne, R2-D2 spent most of his time

PRONUNCIATION
Är'-tōō Dē'-tōō
DROID
Industrial Automaton R2-series astromech
SEX
Masculine programming
HAIR COLOR
None
SENSOR COLOR
Red
HEIGHT
0.96 meter
HOMEWORLD
Naboo

working aboard the Royal Starship as a maintenance and repair unit. During the Queen's escape from the Trade Federation, R2-D2 and four of his fellow astromechs rolled out onto the ship's hull to repair the shield generator. As turbolaser bolts shredded his friends, Artoo stuck to his task and saved the ship. He accompanied the Queen to Tatooine, where he met a home-built protocol droid named C-3PO. Though dissimilar in appearance and personality, the two droids struck

up an instant rapport during this brief encounter.

During the battle to reclaim Naboo from the Trade Federation, Artoo and young Anakin Skywalker flew together inside an N-1 starfighter—firing the proton torpedoes that destroyed the enemy's mightiest battleship.

For the next ten years R2-D2 remained in the service of Padmé Amidala, even after she stepped down as Queen and took on a new life as a Senator. He accompanied Padmé and

Anakin back to Tatooine and once again hooked up with C-3PO. The two formed a partnership at the Battle of Geonosis.

In the years following the Clone Wars, they drifted into the possession of a succession of offworld masters. New owners stripped off much of R2-D2's RSF equipment, including the booster rockets, and installed miscellaneous accessories such as laser pointers and underwater propellers. One master, who operated a one-man refueling station, taught R2-D2 how to play dejarik holo-chess.

While obviously amused by C-3PO's hyperbole, not to mention his neurotic fussiness, Artoo genuinely cared for the auric protocol droid. He knew the sentiment was mutual. The two droids stayed together through many owners, experiencing adventures on every planet from Ingo to Kalarba. Eventually both of them became the property of the Royal House of Alderaan. It was during this time that Princess Leia loaded R2-D2 with the plans for the Empire's Death Star battle station and ordered him to find Obi-Wan Kenobi on Tatooine. The subsequent quest brought R2-D2 and C-3PO to Yavin 4, where R2-D2's data was used to plan a counterattack against the Imperial superweapon, and when Luke Skywalker flew into battle, it was with R2-D2 plugged into his X-wing.

As R2-D2 and Luke roared along the battle station at top speed, preparing to fire proton torpedoes, the droid had no way of knowing that Anakin was also present at the current engage-ment, shrouded in the armor of Darth Vader. From behind the controls of his TIE fighter, Vader buried several laser bolts in R2-D2's head dome. Only the heroic efforts of Rebel technicians saved the astromech from permanent shutdown.

For the next three years R2-D2 worked alongside C-3PO in the service of the Rebel Alliance. After the Battle of Hoth, however, he separated from C-3PO when Luke Skywalker journeyed to Dagobah. From Dagobah onward R2-D2 became Luke's droid almost exclusively, while C-3PO was more frequently found in the service of Princess Leia.

Following Skywalker's rescue from Cloud City, Alliance High Command established a new base on the forested planet Arbra. R2-D2 and C-3PO did their best to help out, saving the Rebel fleet from burning up in Arbra's sun and volunteering for a mission to the unfriendly "droid world" of Kligson's Moon. On Coruscant, during Leia's attempts to rescue Han Solo, R2-D2 and C-3PO had to fly the *Millennium Falcon* in order to save their masters from imminent death at Prince Xizor's castle. R2-D2 did his best, but with C-3PO at the control yoke the smuggling ship barely survived its swerving, lurching journey.

R2-D2 suffered as a drink server aboard Jabba's sail barge during the Tatooine mission to rescue Solo. As part of the mission he had to keep his friend C-3PO in the dark regarding the rescue plan, for C-3PO's ignorance was vital in the overall strategy. Later, during the shootout at the Imperial bunker on Endor, R2-D2 took a blaster bolt in the line of duty.

In the years following Endor, as R2-D2 spent most of his time in the service of Luke Skywalker, he became so familiar with the systems of Luke's X-wing that the starfighter exceeded all specifications for a vessel of its class—but only when R2-D2 was in the astromech socket.

After Grand Admiral Thrawn's debilitating attacks, the reborn Emperor lashed out from the Deep Core and pummeled the vulnerable New Republic. R2-D2, close beside Master Luke, became a prisoner on the Emperor's throneworld of Byss. Even while Skywalker knelt before Palpatine, he secretly loaded the command codes for the Empire's World Devastators into R2-D2's memory banks. Much as the droid had done with the Death Star plans, R2-D2 returned to the New Republic with the critical information and brought about a victory in the Battle of Mon Calamari.

Luke Skywalker soon opened a Jedi academy on Yavin 4, and seldom flew in his X-wing after that, but R2-D2 still stayed with him. Over the years he rarely saw his friend C-3PO, though the two droids reunited during Lando Calrissian's exploration of the Teljkon vagabond, and carried their partnership into the investigation of the Almanian "new Rebellion." On the droid-manufacturing moon of Telti, R2-D2 and C-3PO uncovered evidence of an Almanian scheme to rig the galaxy's

droids with explosive detonators. At the last instant R2-D2 intercepted the master detonation signal, saving the lives of millions.

After the Almanian crisis R2-D2 returned to the academy. Several years later, during the Hand of Thrawn crisis, he accompanied Luke to distant Nirauan to rescue Mara Jade. The droid infiltrated an enemy complex and downloaded a copy of the Caamas Document, which proved crucial in defusing interspecies tensions than had been plaguing the New Republic. In later years, R2-D2 took on many of the administrative responsibilities of the Jedi academy. When young Anakin Solo enrolled as a student, R2-D2 tried in vain to keep

Anakin and his friend Tahiri out of trouble.

Since the onset of the Yuuzhan Vong invasion, R2-D2 has stayed out of the spotlight, strategically a good move in view of the invaders' fervent hatred of droids. Following the death of Chewbacca on Sernpidal he helped C-3PO compile a retrospective documentary on the Wookiee hero.

The fall of Coruscant forced the New Republic into exile, making their defensive war all the more difficult. C-3PO keeps telling R2-D2 that no place is safe for droids, but R2-D2 has never backed down from a challenge. As long as his friends are threatened, this little droid is in the fight to the end.

DASH RENDAR

PRONUNCIATION
Dăsh Rĕn'-där
SPECIES
Human
SEX
Male
HAIR COLOR
Red
EYE COLOR
Green
HEIGHT
1.8 meters
HOMEWORLD
Corellia

Han Solo knew Dash Rendar for years, but wasn't around to see his friend's turn in the galactic spotlight. When Rendar joined the fight against Prince Xizor, Solo was frozen stiff in carbonite; by the time he thawed out, Dash had died.

Or so state the official files regarding the Black Sun incident. Rendar has been spotted many times since his "death" at Coruscant, and the most recent reports have placed him at the crest of the Yuuzhan Vong invasion wave, sabotaging the enemy collaborators of the Peace Brigade.

Like so many others who aided the Alliance, Dash Rendar is Corellian. His parents owned RenTrans, a wealthy Core World shipping concern, and Dash enrolled in the Caridan Academy to prepare for a career as an officer. But Prince Xizor of Black Sun sabotaged a RenTrans freighter and the vessel crashed into the Imperial Museum, killing Dash's brother.

An enraged Emperor Palpatine gave all of RenTrans's assets to Xizor, banished the family, and expelled Dash from the Academy. Forced to make his own way, Dash became a freelance pilot, smuggler, and gun for hire.

He crossed paths with Han Solo, whom he'd known from Carida, and worked jobs with Katya M'Buele and Lando Calrissian. He amassed enough credits to purchase the Corellian YT-2400 freighter *Outrider*. During a stopover on Rodia a comedian gave him a droid in exchange for passage offplanet, and LE-BO2D9 ("Leebo") became Rendar's copilot.

While Solo became entangled with the Rebel Alliance, Rendar remained independent. His success allowed him to purchase a second ship, the *Out-* *runner*. Approximately a year after Yavin, Rendar worked with Zak and Tash Arranda to defeat the artificial intelligence of the passenger liner *Star of Empire*. Following the incident, he started shipping cargo for the Rebels, but more for credits than ideology.

Rendar had just finished a food delivery to Hoth's Echo Base when the Empire attacked. He hopped into an unused snowspeeder and took down one of the advancing AT-ATs. After Han Solo's capture at Cloud City, Rendar joined in the rescue effort as a favor to Lando Calrissian. He tangled with IG-88D on Ord Mantell and located Boba Fett's ship at Gall.

At Bothawui, Rendar and Luke Skywalker helped the Bothan spynet capture the plans for the second Death Star from the Imperial freighter *Suprosa*.

Later, on Coruscant, Rendar helped Skywalker and Calrissian infiltrate Prince Xizor's castle. On their way off the capital planet, the *Outrider* struck a chunk of debris and apparently exploded. Months later, however, the human replica droid Guri encountered Rendar in a cantina on Hurd's Moon. The cocky Corellian looked no worse for wear.

NAGA SADOW

PRONUNCIATION
Nā'-gä Sä'-dō
SPECIES
Sith
SEX
Male
HAIR COLOR
Brown
EYE COLOR
Green
HEIGHT
1.88 meters
HOMEWORLD
Ziost

The First Great Schism between the light and dark sides of the Force occurred in the early years of the Old Republic. Certain Jedi turned to the dark side, and when defeated, they fled the civilized galaxy and conquered a primitive species—the Sith. They made themselves the Lords of the Sith, and named the greatest among them the Dark Lord.

Naga Sadow, heir to this wicked tradition, became the first Sith Lord in nearly twenty millennia to reestablish contact with the forgotten Republic, setting in motion a chain of disastrous events.

Sadow's Jedi lineage was among the purest in the empire, containing minimal Sith blood. Like the other Sith Lords, he used dark arts to keep his body alive for centuries.

The death of Dark Lord Marka Ragnos set off a power struggle in the Sith Empire. Sadow schemed to become the next Dark Lord by discrediting his rival Ludo Kressh, and the arrival of Republic explorers Jori and Gav Daragon provided the needed catalyst. Sadow fanned imaginary fears of an invading Republic war fleet. Fearing for the empire's survival, the other Sith Lords named him their new Dark Lord.

With a Sith tattoo of rank newly etched into his forehead, Dark Lord Naga Sadow prepared a vast Sith armada to conquer the unsuspecting Republic. Jori Daragon inadvertently led the Sith forces to her home system, where the invaders attacked the seven Koros worlds, and exploded up the Koros Trunk Line to Coruscant.

The Sith Empire was smaller than the Republic, but far wealthier and in possession of bizarre technology. Naga Sadow sat in his meditation sphere, generating illusions that made his military appear ten times as large.

Gav Daragon, whom Sadow had molded into his dark protégé, shrugged off Sadow's influence and led the Republic fleet to the Dark Lord's hiding spot. Sadow fled for his life, back to the Sith Empire. The armies he abandoned crumbled under a Jedi assault.

When Sadow arrived back among the Sith worlds, he found his rival, Ludo Kressh, waiting to crush him. Sadow sacrificed hundreds of Sith warships to cover his escape. Flying between the unstable binary star known as the Denarii Nova, Sadow triggered a stellar flare that vaporized his final Republic pursuer, then limped to an obscure jungle moon called Yavin 4. There he entombed his flagship and placed himself in suspended animation. Sadow's Massassi guards populated the jungles and built towering temples of stone.

Six hundred years later a Jedi Knight named Freedon Nadd came to Yavin 4 and reawakened Naga Sadow. After teaching Nadd the secrets of the Sith, Sadow is believed to have died at his student's hands.

THRACKAN SAL-SOLO

PRONUNCIATION
Thrǎ'-kǎn Sǎl-sō'-lō
SPECIES
Human
SEX
Male
HAIR COLOR
Brown
EYE COLOR
Brown
HEIGHT
1.8 meters
HOMEWORLD
Corellia

Han Solo was an orphan. Raised by a cruel stranger since the age of two, young Han wanted more than anything to uncover some link to his vanished family. When he finally found one—his cousin Thrackan Sal-Solo—he immediately wished he hadn't.

The Solo lineage is a tangled one. Korol Solo, a pretender to the Corellian throne, fathered the infamous pirate Dalla Solo, also known as Dalla the Black. Some believe Dalla is Han's grandfather, but a more compelling line of evidence points to Denn Solo and his wife Tira Gama. During a bandit raid on Tralus in the Corellian system, Denn and Tira were separated, each protecting one of the couple's two children. Denn's son, possibly named Jonash, fathered Han Solo. Tira Gama's daughter Tiion married Randil Sal on Corellia and had one son, Thrackan Sal-Solo.

Randil Sal died when Thrackan was just a baby. Devastated, his wife Tiion shut herself up in the decaying Sal-Solo estate, refusing to socialize with anyone except the servant droids. Thrackan grew up friendless and angry, yet fiercely protective of his mother.

At the age of seventeen, Thrackan caught an eleven-year-old boy trying to sneak into the walled Sal-Solo compound. The boy gave his name as Han Solo, and Thrackan couldn't deny the family resemblance. Thrackan figured out Han's likely parentage, and the two spent the next six weeks together. Thrackan constantly bullied the younger boy, but couldn't take it when Han finally fought back. He locked Han in an empty room, learned that he had escaped from the custody of a con artist named Garris Shrike, and sold Han back to the vengeful Shrike for a tidy sum.

The following year Thrackan took a job in Corellia's Imperial government, where his cruelty proved useful. His dream was to attend the Imperial Naval Academy and become an officer, but Han's dishonorable discharge reflected badly on the Solo name. When ruling Corellian Diktat Dupas Thomree died a few years before the Battle of Yavin, Diktat Gallamby filled his office. Thrackan Sal-Solo became Gallamby's second in command.

But Thrackan wanted to be diktat *himself*. He chafed under Gallamby's rule during the crumbling, isolationist post-Endor years. Gallamby disappeared into the Outlier systems and the New Republic appointed a governor-general to rule the Corellian sector—an *alien*. Thrackan, who believed in the superiority of humans, went underground. He formed the anti-alien group known as the Human League and proclaimed himself its Hidden Leader.

Approximately fourteen years after Endor, Thrackan received a communication from the Triad rulers on the outlying Corellian planet Sacorria. The Triad planned to use Centerpoint Station—a weapon that could destroy stars—to bully the New Republic into recognizing the Corellian sector as an independent state. The Triad wanted to use Human League members as disposable troops, and Thrackan Sal-Solo recognized that this might be his last chance for power.

When the Triad started destroying stars, Thrackan activated Centerpoint's jamming field, crowned himself Corellian diktat, and tried to pass himself off as the mastermind behind the whole plot. Han Solo and his family found themselves trapped in the Corellian system in the midst of the crisis. Thrackan and Han confronted one another, and Han realized that not much had changed in thirty-six years. His cousin was just as mean-spirited as he'd been when they were youths.

Han escaped from Thrackan's custody by befriending a native Selonian and fleeing into the tunnels. Thrackan struck back by capturing Han's three children, Jacen, Jaina, and Anakin, in a repulsor chamber on Drall. The Solo children slipped past Thrackan's Human League henchmen and flew off in the *Millennium Falcon*. Thrackan gave chase, but the Bakuran warship *Watchkeeper* seized his vessel. Thrackan, held temporarily in the ship's brig, was transferred to Corellia before the *Watchkeeper* went into battle against the Triad's forces. The New Republic earned a victory in the Battle of Centerpoint Station and prevented the secession of the Corellian sector. As for Thrackan Sal-Solo, the Corellian courts sentenced him to life imprisonment in Sacorria's Dorthus Tal prison.

Less than eight years into his sentence, the New Republic freed Thrackan in exchange for his help in arming Centerpoint against the Yuuzhan Vong. Optimistic commanders hoped that Centerpoint could end the war with a single blow and considered the commutation of Sal-Solo's sentence a small price to pay.

Thrackan stood in Centerpoint's control center as Anakin Solo debated whether or not to fire the station's devastating repulsor beam. Light-years away, at Fondor, the Yuuzhan Vong and Hapan war fleets prepared to clash. Believing that the Force would not want him to wield such power, Anakin acceded to his brother Jacen's wishes and relinquished the controls.

Shoving Anakin aside, Thrackan grabbed the trigger and activated Centerpoint himself. The station's misaligned beam wiped out *both* fleets, friend and foe alike. Despite the cost in Hapan lives, Thrackan earned praise for striking the first decisive blow against the invaders. Within a year, he had been elected the new governor-general of the Corellian Sector.

Sebulba

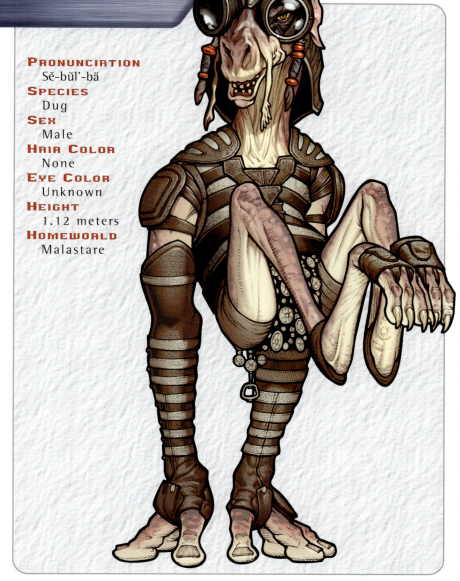

In its official publicity holos the Galactic Podracing Promotional Board offers up many noble reasons for the Podraces—speed, excitement, strategy, sportsmanship. But the real lure of Podracing is much more primal. People go to see the crashes.

And Sebulba the Dug was one of the most popular racers in the history of the sport. Wherever Sebulba went throughout his long career under the Old Republic, crashes were sure to follow. Even when some of those high-speed wrecks looked a bit suspicious, race organizers were loath to penalize their most popular superstar. It would have jeopardized the bribes he paid them.

Sebulba's dirty dealings on and off the course ensured that his fellow Podracers hated him with the same conviction with which the general public loved him. Other racers would have sooner drunk a bottle of frinka venom than said one kind word about Sebulba.

Sebulba rose to fame piloting a Split-X Collor Pondrat Plug-F Mammoth Podracer, an intimidating flame-orange machine built for speed. It was also built for *sabotage*. At one time or another, Sebulba's racer sported illegal flamethrowers, razor saws, nail spitters, and sensor jammers, and the engine housings were reinforced to serve as battering rams. On average, Sebulba was suspected of causing more than three dozen crashes per year, many of them fatal.

Ego was the foundation of Sebulba's psyche. Dugs were treated badly on Sebulba's homeworld of Malastare, and he knew what it felt like to be the victim of prejudice. Throughout the galaxy Dugs had a

PRONUNCIATION
Sĕ-bŭl'-bä
SPECIES
Dug
SEX
Male
HAIR COLOR
None
EYE COLOR
Unknown
HEIGHT
1.12 meters
HOMEWORLD
Malastare

justified reputation for viciousness and bullying, springing from a deep cultural sense of self-pity. They viewed themselves as embattled warriors, always fighting to maintain what was theirs and always getting beaten back unfairly by the Republic, the Gran, or the ZeHethbra. Jailers on frontier worlds liked to joke, "Half the Dugs on my planet are already in jail, and the other half—well, just give 'em time." Hearing this sort of "joke" only made the average Dug angry and

more likely to do something violent, and hence more likely to prove the jester correct by landing himself, behind bars.

Spurred by such bias, Sebulba always acted as if he had something to prove. He relished his fame and liked to linger in public places to draw a crowd. When his admirers fawned over him he basked in the praise, but when they became *too* fawning he would suddenly beat them aside in disgust.

Sebulba was born in Pixelito, a

Gran city on Malastare's eastern continent. Many Dugs in Pixelito were virtual slaves, forced by exploitative labor contracts into serving their Gran masters. Sebulba rose above this to become a rare Dug superstar. One Podracing track on Malastare's southern continent was designed by Sebulba himself, and bore the grandiose name Sebulba's Legacy.

Because they knew that other species wanted nothing to do with them, Dugs developed an inward and self-congratulatory culture. Most claimed to trace their ancestry back to great warriors, heroes, and patriots. Sebulba traced his own lineage back to Statesman Surdu of the Black Shred Water clan, an honor that further inflated his ego. Exploiting his fame, he fathered several children on Malastare in fleeting dalliances with Dug females.

Dug culture promoted many superstitions about death—for example, when preparing a body for funeral services, hooks were driven beneath the deceased's skin, inscribed iron balls were festooned onto the hooks, and the decorated corpse was dropped into the choppy waters of Malastare's Ghoop Ocean. Sebulba owned a number of "lucky" items to ward off the specter of death, including a leather racing suit decorated with flashy coins, and a custom-built massage chair. He purchased the blue Rutian Twi'lek twins Ann and Tann Gella because they were trained *yobanas*—a Twi'leki word loosely translating as "masseuses."

If murdering, cheating, and arrogance didn't provide enough strikes against his character, Sebulba also lived a double life as a part-time slave trader. His employees, including a clumsy Abyssin henchman and a deadly Sakiyan tracker named Djas Puhr, rounded up children for resale in Outer Rim slave markets. His clients included Gardulla the Hutt and the Zygerrian Slavers' Guild.

Anakin Skywalker's upset victory in the Boonta Eve Classic wounded Sebulba's pride and destroyed his Split-X Mammoth. He immediately purchased Anakin's remarkable Podracer, repainted it, and entered it in the Phoebos Memorial Classic on Malastare. Following a rare suspension for "indiscretions" during the Boonta race, his victory on Malastare allowed him to requalify for the Galactic Circuit. Eight years later, Sebulba showed up all those who had bested him in the past by embarking on a cutthroat "revenge tour" around the Podracing circuit.

Though Sebulba was vile, his villainy seems almost trivial compared to the pure, archetypal evil manifested in Darth Maul and Darth Vader. But this provided no comfort to the families of opponents he murdered or children he enslaved. Amid Sebulba's throngs of cheering fans, a small but passionate group busily plotted the Dug's long-overdue comeuppance.

He eventually met a fatal end, much to the joy of his detractors, but his legacy survived even into the Imperial era. Shortly before the Battle of Endor, Sebulba's grandson Pugwis earned fame in Jabba the Hutt's brutal demolition tournaments. Pugwis, one of several young Dugs who traced their lineage back to Sebulba, piloted a beefed-up Podracer based on the same basic design that his grandfather had employed.

EXECUTOR SEDRISS

PRONUNCIATION
Ĭg-zĕk'-yĕ-tĕr Sĕd'-rĭs
SPECIES
Human
SEX
Male
HAIR COLOR
Black
EYE COLOR
Brown
HEIGHT
1.8 meters
HOMEWORLD
Unknown

When an amoral mercenary turns out to be Force-sensitive, the result is something like Sedriss. Not even thirty, Military Executor Sedriss commanded all the forces of the resurrected Emperor, from the largest World Devastator to the lowliest stormtrooper.

Unlike many of the Emperor's Dark Side Adepts, from Jerec to Mara Jade, Sedriss remained loyal even after the Emperor's death at Endor. While the others made grabs for power or abandoned the Empire altogether, Sedriss journeyed to Byss and waited for his Master's return. When Palpatine awoke in a new clone body, he rewarded Sedriss by absorbing him into his will and making him the leader of the Dark Side Elite.

Palpatine's Dark Side Elite consisted of seven warriors completely subsumed into the Emperor's volition. Sedriss, possessing slightly more autonomy than the others, was also leader of Byss's military. He orchestrated the assaults that pushed the New Republic from the Core Worlds—and then his Master died again.

Sedriss never lost faith. In Bast Castle on Vjun he prepared the Dark Side Elite for Palpatine's return, but one of their number—Kam Solusar—defected to the light side during an encounter with Luke Skywalker. Undaunted, Sedriss continued to execute Operation Shadow Hand, gaining territory in Palpatine's name and disciplining recalcitrant worlds such as Balmorra.

Returning to Byss, Executor Sedriss surprised two of Palpatine's dark-side mages, Nefta and Sa-Di, in the act of smashing the Emperor's clone tanks. Sedriss executed them as traitors, and a newly reborn Palpatine praised his servant's devotion. He ordered Sedriss to capture Luke Skywalker and the turncoat Kam Solusar on Ossus.

Sedriss and fellow Dark Side Elite Vill Goir landed troops on Ossus, but the native Ysanna shamans beat them back. Finally, Sedriss grabbed an Ysanna hostage and backed up against a tree. The "tree" was Jedi Master Ood Bnar, awakened after four millennia. When Sedriss called down electricity from the atmosphere, Ood drew up power from Ossus' core. The two combatants annihilated each other.

Palpatine had seven Dark Side Elite, and during the events of Operation Shadow Hand he appointed two replacements for members lost in battle. All of the nine members of this cabal—save for the defector Kam Solusar—are confirmed dead. Sedriss and Vill Goir perished on Ossus, Zasm Katth's and Baddon Fass's Star Destroyer crashed on Nar Shaddaa, and Krdys Mordi, Kvag Gthull, and Tedryn-Sha fell in battle on New Alderaan. Xecr Nist was later captured by Luke Skywalker on Onderon and died in prison.

SENATOR VIQI SHESH

A mbition minus morality equals Viqi Shesh. Though not sadistic like Palpatine, Shesh's evil springs from her simple overriding selfishness. The death and enslavement of billions mean nothing to her, as long as she comes out on top.

Born into a wealthy family on Kuat, Shesh considered power her birthright. She was only a girl when the ruling industrialist Kuat of Kuat killed himself by destroying a section of the planetary stardocks. The Shesh family lost status during the subsequent reconstruction, and worked to forge underground alliances with the New Republic. When Imperial control of Kuat finally collapsed four years later, the family received so many shipbuilding offers from eager New Republic clients that they rejected sight unseen any job grossing less than a billion credits.

Shesh took a job in Kuati corporate marketing. Her career taught her the value of appearances and the importance of information control. It also inured her to the fears and hopes of the galaxy's inhabitants. Individuals and ideologies appeared to her as colored icons on a strategy sheet. She understood *how* to give consumers what they wanted. She just didn't *care*.

She kept her indifference private, for as a salesperson she certainly knew how to sell herself. Viqi Shesh entered politics less than six years before the Yuuzhan Vong invasion, and paid for her campaign with family money. After her election, her Senatorial inexperience became a public asset, for the media hailed her as a breath of fresh air. She deftly manipulated the newsnets into devoting hundreds of hours of coverage

PRONUNCIATION
Vĭ'-kē Shĕsh
SPECIES
Human
SEX
Female
HAIR COLOR
Black
EYE COLOR
Brown
HEIGHT
1.67 meters
HOMEWORLD
Kuat

to her pet cause—helping impoverished refugees. In short order she earned a seat on the board of the Senate Select Committee for Refugees (SELCORE) and earned a reputation in the Senate chamber as a fair-minded deal maker.

Considered the New Republic Senate's fastest-rising star, Shesh received a high-level appointment to the Security and Intelligence Council. And after the beginning of the Yuuzhan Vong invasion and the extermination of Ithor, she became a member of Chief of State Fey'lya's Advisory Council.

The popular Senator now held one of the most influential stations within the New Republic government, yet she harbored grave doubts over her side's ability to win the war. Sernpidal, Dantooine, Ithor, and hundreds of other planets fell like two-legged stools. The invaders from outside the galaxy seemed unstoppable. Viqi Shesh decided her skills as a deal maker could ensure her survival, and vault her to the head of a new collaborationist government.

Disguised as a Kuati telbun, she met with Reck Desh of the Peace Brigade. Desh's troops had already thrown in their lot with the Yuuzhan Vong. Senator Shesh provided him with the secret route by which New Republic Intelligence would be transporting two enemy defectors. She hoped that after the Peace Brigade recaptured the defectors, the Yuuzhan Vong would recognize her willingness to play by their rules.

Shesh's plotting caught the attention of Yuuzhan Vong agent Nom Anor. Following the New Republic's defeat at Fondor, Anor met with Shesh in her office on Coruscant. He thanked her for her attempt at returning "stolen property" to his people. Shesh, in turn, made clear her interest in a mutual alliance. Soon she received a Yuuzhan Vong villip that enabled her to communicate with her new partners, and an ooglith masquer to disguise her appearance when necessary.

Viqi Shesh knew the Yuuzhan Vong wished to sacrifice thousands of "infidels" to their pantheon of gods. She used her position in SEL-CORE to arrange massive refugee shipments to Duro, a world targeted for invasion by the enemy. When Warmaster Tsavong Lah contacted her via villip, she manipulatively spoke to him in fawning tones, and failed to realize the scorn the Yuuzhan Vong directed at all infidels, herself included.

Following Duro, Senator Shesh worked even harder to ingratiate herself with the warmaster. Rotated off SELCORE, she won a posting with the New Republic Military Oversight Committee. Shesh then gave the Yuuzhan Vong a Force-sensitive vornskr from Myrkr, which the aliens bioshaped into a pack of Jedi-hunting voxyn. In the New Republic Senate, she helped persuade many of her fellow delegates that the refusal of the Jedi to surrender to Tsavong Lah was endangering the galaxy. Soon she had split the Senate along pro- and anti-Jedi lines.

Chief of State Fey'lya worked hard to unify his government, and Shesh suggested to the warmaster that a covert assassination would clear the way for her own ascension to that post. Tsavong Lah put her in touch with a local cell of Yuuzhan Vong infiltrators, but the attempt failed. In fact, she only unified the Senate behind Fey'lya.

As the invasion of Coruscant commenced, the warmaster ordered Viqi Shesh to prove her worth. She tried to distract the Jedi by kidnapping the Skywalker baby, but led her infiltrators into an ambush.

Exposed as a traitor, Senator Shesh tried to steal the Skywalker infant a second time by disabling the escaping refugee shuttle, but Mara Jade intercepted Shesh and shot down her ship.

DARTH SIDIOUS

L ike a dejarik grandmaster, the shadowy Sith Lord known as Darth Sidious played his game without revealing any hint of his strategy. His moves were subtle, but his objective was no less than domination of the galaxy.

Sidious, who operated on Coruscant right under the noses of his Jedi enemies, was heir to the ancient Sith tradition. Under Darth Bane's "rule of two," Sith ranks were limited to a single Master–apprentice pairing. The identity of Sidious's own Master remains a mystery, but since Sidious already had his own apprentice as of the Battle of Naboo, it can be presumed that his Master was long dead. Sidious broke Darth Bane's *second* rule, however, when he revealed the existence of the Sith to the Jedi, ending a thousand years of silence.

The Neimoidians were his pawns. Early on, Sidious consolidated their power by arranging for the assassination of all non-Neimoidians who belonged to the Trade Federation Directorate. Exploiting the Neimoidians' two greatest weaknesses—fear and greed—he pushed Viceroy Nute Gunray into blockading the planet Naboo. Then, when the time was right, he ordered Gunray's droid armies to invade and overrun Naboo.

Darth Maul was Sidious's tool. A finely honed weapon of burning fury and cold precision, Maul was raised from infancy to be Sidious's apprentice and fellow Dark Lord of the Sith. In the hidden lair on Coruscant, Maul was tested and tortured, broken down and rebuilt into a projectile that would one day be aimed at the Jedi and fired.

On the surface, Lord Sidious's

PRONUNCIATION
Därth Sĭ'-dē-ŭs
SPECIES
Human
SEX
Male
HAIR COLOR
Unknown
EYE COLOR
Unknown
HEIGHT
1.78 meters
HOMEWORLD
Unknown

schemes surrounding Naboo looked like failures. His pawns were captured by Queen Amidala; his apprentice was cut down by Obi-Wan Kenobi. And the Naboo events led to repercussions in other areas, most notably the election of Senator Palpatine to the office of Supreme Chancellor.

Following the events on Naboo, Sidious went underground once again, this time to train a new apprentice to replace Maul. He had no time to train another student from infancy, and so convinced the great Jedi Master Count Dooku to join him as the galaxy's new Sith Lord. According to the tradition of

Bane, Sidious bestowed upon Dooku the new name Darth Tyranus. The two Sith spent the next decade assessing the growth of a clone army on Kamino and launching a secessionist movement that threatened the stability of the Republic.

After the Battle of Geonosis, Sidious watched with great interest as the Republic's clone army prepared for a protracted war against the droid armies of the secessionists' corporate allies. Only time would tell if this would lead to the end of the game for Darth Sidious—or checkmate for the Republic.

RAITH SIENAR

PRONUNCIATION
Rāth Sē'-när
SPECIES
Human
SEX
Male
HAIR COLOR
Black
EYE COLOR
Blue
HEIGHT
1.8 meters
HOMEWORLD
Unknown

For Raith Sienar, life was an engineering problem. Passionate emotions were design flaws. Though not actively wicked, Sienar possessed a dispassionate moral neutrality that, in the end, made him an accessory to evil.

Unlike Bevel Lemelisk or Umak Leth, Raith Sienar didn't limit himself to colossal Death Stars or profligate World Devastators. Many of his inventions were smaller, but still deadly—the TIE fighter, the Interdictor cruiser, the Sith Infiltrator. Billions died under the lasers of his war machines, yet Raith Sienar is undeniably considered one of the most ingenious engineers in galactic history.

Sienar came from a long line of starship builders. Five millennia ago, his ancestors constructed warships for Empress Teta during the Unification Wars, earning enough credits to ensure that the Sienar lineage would remain wealthy for generations. Approximately a century before the Battle of Yavin, the Sienar family united with the wealthy Santhe family—owners of Santhe Security—through an arranged marriage. More powerful than ever, the Sienars were guaranteed financial and technological dominance over their competitors.

Born about sixty years before the Battle of Yavin, Raith Sienar strove to be the most unpredictable member of the secretive clan. In his youth, he turned his back on the family business and became a hyperspace explorer. Using his inheritance to fund a small scouting operation, he mapped dozens of new hyperlanes and discovered exploitable systems in the Unknown Regions. By the age of twenty, Sienar had amassed his *own* fortune.

Confident that he had proven himself, he returned to the fold.

In light of his son's success, Raith's father Narro groomed his son to become CEO of Sienar Technologies. The family's most profitable company, Sienar Technologies produced grand vessels for the Republic and the Trade Federation, including the *Marauder*-class cruiser. To prepare himself for the pressures of the boardroom, Raith assumed a false identity and went undercover at several major competitors, including Corellian Engineering Corporation, Baktoid Armor Workshop, and Incom.

Later he spent time among the Xi Char of Charros IV, to master the secrets of precision engineering. When the devout Xi Char discovered the presence of a "nonbeliever" among them, they hired four bounty hunters to kill the spy. Sienar led the assassins on a long chase through hyperspace before exiting near an uncharted black hole—one that he had discovered (but intentionally failed to report) some years earlier. The unsuspecting bounty hunters plunged into the singularity and vanished.

When he returned to Sienar Technologies, Raith was rewarded with his own internal workshop, Sienar Design Systems (SDS). Under his hands-on leadership, SDS specialized in one-of-a-kind contracts for wealthy clients. SDS's secret Advanced Projects Laboratory pushed ion drive technology to its limits, modifying stock vessels into fast, unique starships. Sienar also befriended Wilhuff Tarkin, an up-and-coming officer in the Republic Outland Regions Security Force.

Six years before the Battle of Naboo, the Xi Char made a second attempt on Raith's life. Both Raith and his father were attacked by mercenaries during a pleasure cruise near Dantooine. Raith fled in an escape ship, but the family vessel exploded, killing Narro Sienar. When news of Narro's death reached Sienar Technologies, the board of directors gave Raith full control of the company.

As CEO, Raith diverted funds from Sienar Technologies to Sienar Design Systems. Complaining of "uninspired" Republic contracts, he indulged in experimentation. With a small hand-picked crew, he designed Darth Maul's cloak-capable Sith Infiltrator under contract to the mysterious Darth Sidious. He also began to design an "expeditionary battle planetoid," a theoretical moon-sized battle station.

Three years after the Battle of Naboo, Commander Tarkin convinced Sienar to lead a task force that would secure living starships from the planet Zonama Sekot. However, Sienar worked to subvert Tarkin's authority on the mission, and ultimately their expedition failed, thanks in part to interference from Obi-Wan Kenobi and his Padawan Anakin Skywalker. In the aftermath of the Zonama Sekot debacle, Tarkin took credit for Sienar's battle planetoid—after Sienar no longer expressed interest in the design. In modified form, Sienar's brainchild would one day become the Death Star.

Sienar continued to develop ion drive technology, following design cues from the Sith Infiltrator to produce the first Twin Ion Engine (T.I.E.) starfighter. When Palpatine ascended to the Emperor's throne, he nationalized Sienar Technologies. Under the new company known as Sienar Fleet Systems (SFS), Raith's T.I.E. morphed into the mainline TIE fighter, then later the TIE bomber, infiltrator, Advanced, and other TIE variants. Other successful SFS products that were incorporated into the Imperial Navy included the Skipray blastboat, the Interdictor cruiser, and—in conjunction with Cygnus Spaceworks—the *Lambda*-class shuttle.

Still brilliant in his advancing years, Sienar died in an assassination presumably orchestrated by jealous rivals in his own company. Following his death, the company fell under the control of the Santhe family. From her headquarters on Lianna, Lady Valles Santhe kept SFS running even after the Empire's collapse at Endor. During the rise of the reborn Emperor, Lady Santhe created Sienar Army Systems to supply the Imperial ground forces with new assault vehicles. The TIE crawler, or "century tank," was one of the last products to be released under the Sienar brand name.

AURRA SING

The Anzati are horrifying vampiric monsters, so frightening that many prefer to dismiss them as children's fables. The bounty hunter Aurra Sing was not an Anzati, but she was the only outsider ever to earn their respect.

An Anzati education would be more than enough to make anyone an untouchable killer, but Sing had no less than *four* distinct educations in the science of combat. Hands down, she was one of deadliest fighters in the galaxy.

Though humanoid, Aurra Sing's species was never cataloged. Her skin was much paler than the human norm, and unusual black patches ringed her eyes. Each of her fingers exhibited an extra phalange.

Sing's first combat education began at birth, when she was born to a spice addict mother in the stinking slums of Nar Shaddaa. Though she remembered little of this nightmarish period, the abuse she suffered at the hands of various hooligans left an indelible impression on her psyche. Even at this early age, she learned the rules—or lack thereof—that governed street fighting.

After two years, Aurra Sing was discovered by the notorious Jedi Master known only as the Dark Woman. The grim Jedi sensed the Force power in young Aurra, and convinced the girl's mother to give her daughter over to the Jedi Order. Aurra Sing departed aboard the Dark Woman's starship, and her second education began.

Most of Sing's next seven years were spent in the sterile confines of the Jedi Temple on Coruscant, where the Dark Woman and other Jedi in-

PRONUNCIATION
Ô'-rä Sĭng
SPECIES
Unknown
SEX
Female
HAIR COLOR
Reddish brown
EYE COLOR
Unknown
HEIGHT
1.74 meters
HOMEWORLD
Nar Shaddaa

structed her in lightsaber combat and the use of the Force. Ki-Adi-Mundi, one of the Dark Woman's former pupils, helped train Aurra and worried about her troubled spirit.

At age nine, while on Ord Namurt for offworld training with the Dark Woman, Aurra Sing was tricked by a young Twi'lek girl and captured by star pirates. She was convinced by the pirates that the Dark Woman had arranged to sell her into slavery, and so she allied herself to the pirate crew,

from whom she learned the tricks of buccaneers and cutthroats. Piracy was Aurra Sing's third education.

The pirate captain took a liking to his newest acquisition and taught her many tracking and ambush techniques, but after several years he grew jealous of her skills and began to fear she might one day usurp his power. For a few thousand credits, the captain sold Aurra Sing to Wallanooga the Hutt.

The Hutt wanted his own personal

assassin, so he apprenticed Sing to a group of Anzati who owed him a debt. The vampires taught her their forbidden arts and implanted a Rhen-Orm biocomputer inside her skull to augment her situational awareness. After four years with the Anzati, Aurra Sing's fourth and final education came to an end.

Complete at last, Sing took her revenge on all those who had used her. She killed her Hutt owner. She killed the pirates who had stolen her and took their blockade runner as her own. When she crossed paths with Jedi Knights she killed them, too, keeping their lightsabers as grim trophies. More than anything she wanted to catch up with the Dark Woman and take revenge for the "betrayal" on Ord Namurt.

Aurra Sing took up work as a freelance bounty hunter. She refused membership in the Bounty Hunters' Guild, but accepted side jobs from guild leader Cradossk. Sing piloted a customized swoopbike and carried many weapons, including twin blaster pistols, a projectile rifle, and her original red-bladed Jedi lightsaber.

She spent a great deal of time on Tatooine around the period of the Battle of Naboo. She witnessed Anakin Skywalker's victory in the Boonta Eve Podrace, and later returned to hunt the Jedi-turned-pirate Reess Kairn. Later still, Sing accepted competing jobs from Jabba and Gardulla the Hutt that pitted her against the rogue Jedi Sharad Hett and Tatooine's native Sand People. She killed Hett, but his son A'Sharad survived and became the Padawan learner of Ki-Adi-Mundi.

Approximately two years after the Battle of Naboo, Aurra Sing attracted the attention of the Jedi Council when she killed two Jedi Masters in the undercity of Coruscant. Ki-Adi-Mundi, A'Sharad Hett, and Adi Gallia agreed to track her down and put an end to her string of murders. Sing, meanwhile, accepted a contract on two lives—the Quarren Senator Tikkes and her former teacher, the Dark Woman. She joked that she would have taken the second job for free.

On a jungle world in the Kamdon system, Sing attacked her targets and other Jedi sent to take her down. She failed to kill either Senator Tikkes *or* the Dark Woman. Padawan A'Sharad Hett—who nursed the pain of his father's death—beat her badly in single combat. Sing slunk away to fight another day.

Her career continued, though her public profile dimmed as the years passed. For a time she worked as a contract stringer for the bounty hunter Jango Fett. Much later, between the Battles of Hoth and Endor, rumors swirled that an aging Aurra Sing had accepted a job as a combatant in Jabba the Hutt's vehicular demolition contests. So it would seem that, as long as there are targets to hunt and bounties to claim, there will always be work for Aurra Sing.

ANAKIN SKYWALKER/DARTH VADER

They called him the Chosen One. Then he murdered billions and they gave him other names. Found by Qui-Gon Jinn, trained by Obi-Wan Kenobi, corrupted by Emperor Palpatine, and saved by his own son, Anakin Skywalker died fulfilling a prophecy nearly as old as the Jedi Order itself.

Anakin Skywalker spent his early years as a piece of human property, purchased by Gardulla the Hutt of Tatooine when Anakin was approximately three years old. The slave dealers implanted in Anakin's body a tracking device that would explode should he ever escape. Fortunately, Gardulla had also bought Anakin's mother, Shmi, and their strong bond made it possible for Anakin to survive his enslavement with remarkable good humor. In Gardulla's fortress, Anakin met other slaves his own age, including a dark-haired boy named Kitster.

When Gardulla lost big on the Mos Espa Podraces, she lost both Anakin and Shmi to Watto, a Toydarian junk dealer. Anakin's fortunes improved, but only marginally. Watto was less cruel than the Hutt, but he was still a hard master. Despite his youth Anakin proved adept at fixing machinery, finding rare parts, and negotiating deals with local Jawa traders. He even built his own protocol droid, whom he named C-3PO.

On one occasion Watto ordered his slave to take a used Podracer for a test spin, and in the process discovered Anakin's potential as a Podracer. From then on Anakin doubled as Watto's pilot, flying the Toydarian's Podracer even as he secretly built his own racing machine in the boneyard behind the Mos Espa slave quarters.

PRONUNCIATION
An'-ä-kǐn Skī'-wälk-ûr / Därth Vä'-dûr
SPECIES
Human
SEX
Male
HAIR COLOR
Blond
EYE COLOR
Blue
HEIGHT
1.85 meters/ 2.02 meters (as Vader)
HOMEWORLD
Tatooine

Anakin developed a flair for heroics, clandestinely freeing a number of Ghostling slaves from Gardulla's fortress, and earning fame in racing circles as one of the youngest winners of the Boonta Eve Classic. Ironically, this victory ended Anakin's Podracing career when Jedi Master Qui-Gon Jinn won the boy from Watto in a bet on the outcome. Jinn took the boy with him to Coruscant, and soon thereafter Anakin flew a starfighter in the Battle of Naboo, thus earning the right to be trained as a Jedi Padawan under Obi-Wan Kenobi—though over the objections of several members of the Jedi Council. It was during this time in his life that Anakin met—and developed a childhood crush on—Queen Padmé Amidala.

Anakin's defenders pointed to prophecy. The boy's raw power indicated he was the one who would be destined to bring balance to the Force. Those who tutored Anakin in the Temple, however, proclaimed the reckless boy the embodiment of *imbalance*. At nine years of age, Anakin found himself in the curious position of being both too young and too old to be a Padawan. Most Jedi students weren't accepted as learners until they were nearly thirteen; on the other hand, those students had been trained in the Jedi way since infancy. Lacking a secure foundation, Anakin became a source of great frustration to Kenobi, but he also proved a source of great pride. For despite his penchant for behavior such as flying parawing gliders in Coruscant's garbage pit races, Anakin became a gifted Padawan.

Since he never knew a father, Anakin displayed a deep-seated need for a mentor. Kenobi worked to fill the voids left in Anakin's life by the absence of Qui-Gon, Shmi, and, to a much lesser degree, even Watto. Nevertheless, Anakin suffered from nightmares that showed a horrible fate for his mother back on Tatooine. Three years into his Jedi apprenticeship, Anakin received an official mission with Obi-Wan from the Jedi Council, to investigate cult leader Kad Chun. A second mission took him to the planet Zonama Sekot, where he killed an alien Blood Carver in a furious rush of the Force's dark side. The incident deeply troubled Obi-Wan.

After his return from Zonama Sekot, Anakin constructed his first lightsaber in a cave on the ice planet of Ilum. The Jedi Council dispatched Kenobi and Anakin on a mission to take down Krayn, an infamous Outer Rim slave trader. Anakin knew Krayn from his former life as a slave, and when he had the opportunity, he stabbed the depraved pirate through the heart with his lightsaber.

After ten years as a Padawan, the teenaged Anakin Skywalker received his first solo assignment—to guard Senator Padmé Amidala. Though he hadn't seen the former Queen of Naboo in a decade, Anakin found his childhood crush supplanted by the deep, spiritual love of adulthood. At first Padmé resisted his advances, but she soon fell under the same spell.

Anakin and Padmé journeyed to Tatooine to quell Anakin's nightmares about his mother, but Anakin learned that Shmi had been kidnapped by Tusken Raiders. He rode all night through the Dune Sea, only to find his mother mere moments before she died. Consumed with rage and grief, he slaughtered every man, woman, and child in the Tusken Raider camp.

Anakin had no opportunity to come to terms with what he had done. Part of him blamed Obi-Wan for restricting his Jedi training, seemingly out of jealousy. Nonetheless, Anakin left Tatooine for Geonosis to rescue his Master from the enemy forces of Count Dooku. Anakin, Padmé, and Obi-Wan were captured and sentenced to die in the. Geonosian execution arena. Using his prisoner's chain, Anakin roped the reek and rode it to safety. He and Obi-Wan cornered Count Dooku in the Sith's hidden starship docking bay, battling him two-on-one with lightsabers. Dooku, far superior to Anakin in the art of the duel, severed the young man's right arm, which would later be replaced with a crude metal one.

Like all of the Jedi, Anakin could sense that the Clone Wars would be a time of apocalyptic devastation. His future uncertain, he rebelled against Jedi rules and chose to seize what happiness he could by marrying Padmé in a secret ceremony on Naboo. A few years later, after suffering near-fatal injuries that required him to don nightmarish armor and a life-support system, Anakin Skywalker renounced his former life and became Darth Vader, Dark Lord of the Sith.

Vader helped Emperor Palpatine hunt down and exterminate the Jedi, though Yoda and Obi-Wan Kenobi escaped his grasp. Vader also enlisted allies to his dark cause, including the deadly Noghri of Honoghr, and the Force-sensitive Firrerreos known as Hethrir and Rillao. As the Emperor's right hand, Vader wielded nearly as much power as Palpatine himself. But the Dark Lord expressed few personal desires. His rare indulgences included several residences on Coruscant, and a private retreat on the storm-scoured planet Vjun, which he called Bast Castle.

On Falleen, Vader's scientists accidentally released a lethal bioagent, and the Dark Lord ordered the "sterilization" (by turbolaser) of two hundred thousand natives, making a bitter enemy of Black Sun's Prince Xizor—a Falleen—in the process. Vader also antagonized the notorious bounty hunter Boba Fett, but after battling to a stalemate on Maryx Minor they worked out a respectful truce. Shortly before the Battle of Yavin, Vader killed the Dark Woman, one of the last stragglers from the Jedi Purge and a woman who'd known Anakin when he was still an uncorrupted boy.

When the Death Star plans were stolen by Rebel agents, Vader worked to retrieve them, and his flagship *Devastator* captured Princess Leia Organa's vessel. He took the captive Princess to the battle station, never realizing he was tormenting his own daughter. In due time, Obi-Wan Kenobi arrived on the Death Star and Vader slashed him out of existence, gloating, "Now *I* am the Master." Shortly thereafter, the Rebels attacked the battle station, and from the cockpit of his custom TIE Advanced fighter, Vader sensed a Force-strong pilot—his son, Luke Skywalker, he later learned—who destroyed the Death Star and spoiled the Empire's chance for victory at Yavin.

His fighter damaged, Vader limped away and found his way back to the Empire. He oversaw many missions against the Rebels, including a capture operation at the Wheel gambling station, before discovering the true identity of the pilot who'd destroyed the Death Star. Vader set plans in motion to capture Skywalker and sway him to the dark side of the Force. Luke barely escaped from three separate traps on Jazbina, Fondor, and Aridus. Meanwhile, Vader became involved in events such as the Bounty Hunter Wars, but kept his primary focus on the Yavin Rebels.

At Fondor, the Super Star Destroyer *Executor* was launched six months after the Battle of Yavin. Vader made the mighty vessel his flagship and roared to Yavin to annihilate the Rebel base. To his disgust, the Rebels were able to make a full evacuation thanks to the incompetence of Vader's top officer, Admiral Griff.

While he searched for the new Rebel headquarters, Darth Vader returned to the types of experiments he'd enjoyed on Falleen. Besides the infamous Project Starscream, he oversaw the development of mind-altering pacifog on Kadril, and funded General Mohc's plan to build the robotic Dark Troopers. When his underlings captured Luke Skywalker and Princess Leia on Mimban, Vader rushed to the world and engaged both Rebels in combat, but the spirit of Obi-Wan Kenobi, fighting through Skywalker, defeated Vader and cut through his mechanical right arm.

Shortly before the Battle of Hoth, Vader enlisted Grand Admiral Thrawn's help in damaging Xizor's Black Sun operations on Corellia. In return, the Dark Lord gave Thrawn the use of his Noghri death commandos. Thrawn also helped Vader plan strategy for the Battle of Derra IV, a key Imperial victory that paved the way for the rout at Hoth.

Next, the *Executor* forced key Rebel heroes to Bespin's Cloud City, where Vader faced his son in combat and revealed the truth of their relationship. Rather than join his father, Luke fell into an open air shaft. Vader later recovered his son's lightsaber—which had once been his own—and Luke's severed hand. He presented both to Palpatine for the Emperor's trophy chamber on Wayland.

Vader again caught up with Luke Skywalker aboard the *Tarkin* battle station, but lost him when several traitorous officers tried to assassinate the Dark Lord. Thereafter, outside complications prevented Vader from concentrating exclusively on Skywalker. Admiral Harkov and Grand Admiral Zaarin both turned traitor; the latter tried to kidnap Palpatine at Coruscant, but was foiled by Vader's skillfull piloting of a TIE defender.

Prince Xizor's long-simmering vendetta finally flared up when the Black Sun chief tried to assassinate Luke Skywalker. Vader refused to allow anyone to touch Skywalker before he had a chance to recruit him, and he punished Xizor by vaporizing the Falleen crime lord aboard his luxury skyhook.

Darth Vader and Luke Skywalker faced their final showdown in the presence of the Emperor, aboard the second Death Star. Luke tried to reach the core of goodness that had once been Anakin Skywalker, but when Vader learned he had a daughter and threatened to drive her to the dark side, an enraged Luke overwhelmed his father and cut off Vader's right hand. Palpatine urged Luke to kill his dying father, and his refusal to do so brought the spirit of Anakin Skywalker to the fore. As Palpatine tortured the younger Skywalker with Force lightning, Anakin seized the tyrannical sorcerer and cast him down the Death Star's reactor shaft.

Anakin Skywalker died, again fulfilling the ancient Jedi prophecy, restoring balance to the Force by eliminating the greatest evil the galaxy had ever known. His spirit appeared to both of his children—to Luke on Endor and to Leia on Bakura—and then he disappeared into the life beyond.

LUKE SKYWALKER

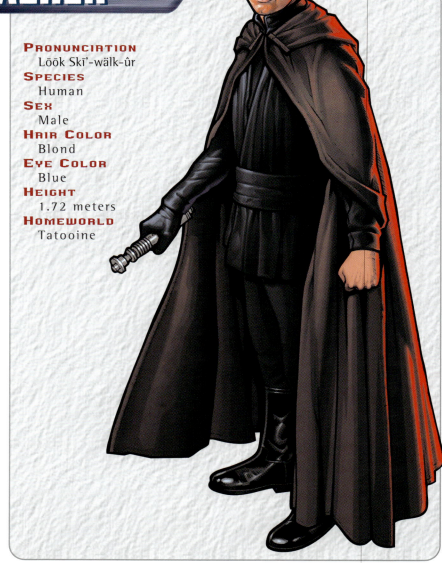

PRONUNCIATION
Lōōk Skī'-wälk-ûr
SPECIES
Human
SEX
Male
HAIR COLOR
Blond
EYE COLOR
Blue
HEIGHT
1.72 meters
HOMEWORLD
Tatooine

Tragedy has shaped much of Luke Skywalker's life. He has been orphaned no less than three times—first when his Tatooine guardians were murdered, again when his mentor Obi-Wan Kenobi was cut down, and a third time when his father became one with the Force.

Luke has experienced tragedy from the other side as well, watching many of his Jedi students—from Kyp Durron to Brakiss to Kueller—fall to the dark side or die in battle. Even now, the Yuuzhan Vong threaten to destroy the Jedi Order Luke has worked so hard to restore.

The son of Anakin Skywalker and Padmé Amidala, Luke was spirited away to desolate Tatooine and the farming household of Owen and Beru Lars. Wishing to protect the boy from his father, who'd become the Sith Lord Darth Vader, Obi-Wan Kenobi watched over Luke from a hermitage in the Dune Sea. Well into his teens Luke believed that his father had been an undistinguished navigator aboard a spice freighter, a lie manufactured by Owen to prevent the boy from seeking out the truth. Luke shared his father's reckless streak and his innate Jedi reflexes. Instead of Podracers, young Luke flew skyhoppers through the zigzags of Beggar's Canyon at white-knuckle speeds.

Immature and easily excitable, he received little respect from his friends in Anchorhead, who called him Wormie. As the years passed, several of Luke's more ambitious friends—including Biggs Darklighter and Tank—left Tatooine for the Imperial Academy, but for Luke it was always "one more season" on the farm.

The adventure he longed for even-tually arrived, but brought with it a bracing slap of reality. Two droids—C-3PO and R2-D2—fell into his care, and prompted by a mysterious holographic plea, Luke brought them to Obi-Wan Kenobi, even as stormtroopers burned the Lars home-stead to cinders. In the ensuing events, he met new allies, including Han Solo and the Wookiee Chew-bacca, but Luke also witnessed more deaths, such as the sacrifices of Kenobi and Biggs Darklighter. At the behest of Princess Leia Organa, he joined the Rebel Alliance and de-stroyed the Empire's Death Star, thus becoming the Alliance's newest hero.

At first, Luke worked harder at be-coming a pilot than at becoming a Jedi. With fellow ace Wedge Antilles he founded Rogue Squadron, and found time for other missions, slip-ping through the Imperial blockade of Yavin 4 to challenge Darth Vader on Jazbina, risking his life aboard the Wheel gambling station, and discovering the out-of-the-way ice planet called Hoth.

Skywalker helped cover the Alliance's evacuation from Yavin 4, and was given a field promotion to commander by General Dodonna. However, Dodonna was captured during the evacuation and the promotion was never logged. While the Alliance fleet hopped across the galaxy, Luke volunteered for missions to worlds such as Mimban, where he and Leia Organa faced Vader with unusual help from the spirit of Obi-Wan Kenobi, who actually possessed Luke's body during a duel.

Luke worked with pilot Keyan Farlander on the rollout of the B-wing starfighter. Rogue Squadron, meanwhile, continued to rack up victories, but Luke gradually surrendered his responsibilities as squadron leader to Wedge Antilles.

The Alliance soon settled on frozen Hoth. Luke assumed a commander's rank after his superior officer, Commander Narra, died in the Battle of Derra IV. It wasn't long before Darth Vader located the Hoth outpost, and Luke battled AT-AT walkers to help cover the command staff's evacuation. Guided by a ghostly command from Obi-Wan, he journeyed to Dagobah and underwent formal Jedi instruction under the tutelage of Master Yoda. But he rushed off without finishing his training in order to rescue his friends from Cloud City, where *they* had to rescue *him* from a precarious perch on a weather vane. Luke had suffered a stinging defeat from the Dark Lord, and in the process learned that Darth Vader was his father.

Fitted with a prosthetic hand to replace the one that Vader had severed on Cloud City, Luke threw himself back into Alliance service as a way to block out his anguish. He flew many missions with Rebel pilot and double agent Shira Brie, and was nearly court-matialed when it appeared he had killed her in a dogfight. He flew with Rogue Squadron at the Battle of Gall and infiltrated Prince Xizor's castle to rescue Leia Organa. Later, after he'd been captured by the Empire during a diplomatic mission to Abridon, Luke escaped with help from Imperial defector Brenn Tantor.

Having built a new lightsaber to replace the one Obi-Wan Kenobi had given him, Luke began to believe he was now a full Jedi Knight. His rescue of Han Solo from Jabba's palace did little to dispel his conceit, but when he returned to Dagobah, Yoda told him the truth—unless he confronted Darth Vader, he would never be a full Jedi. Obi-Wan Kenobi's spirit further gave Luke the news that he had a twin sister—Leia Organa. Aboard the second Death Star, Luke Skywalker confronted Emperor Palpatine and brought his fallen father back to the light. Alone, on Endor, Luke burned Vader's cape and armor.

In some ways Luke had never felt more alone than after the defeat of the Empire and the redemption of his father, but there was no time for contemplation. Obi-Wan Kenobi appeared once more to give Luke an urgent directive—stop the Ssi-ruuk invasion of the planet Bakura. Luke led the task force that freed Bakura and found a Force-strong young man named Dev Sibwarra, who did not survive the fighting. Luke later trained an Iskalonian named Kiro, who eventually abandoned the Jedi ways to lead his native people.

Luke began to realize that he might bring back the Jedi Order, if he located and trained other Force-sensitive individuals. After a mission on Tandankin, he officially resigned from Rogue Squadron, vowing to spend more time in the study of the Jedi. The New Republic, however, wasn't willing to give up Commander Skywalker's military skills altogether. Luke continued to command naval units, and one year after the Battle of Endor he was promoted to general. A brutal campaign to free the Inner Rim from Lord Shadowspawn followed, and Luke watched thousands of his soldiers die. Convinced this was not the way of the Jedi, Luke resigned from the military altogether.

He devoted himself full time to finding apprentices. Already turned down by New Republic agent Kyle Katarn, Luke approached Rogue Squadron pilot Corran Horn, but was again rebuffed. His adventures with the Witch clans of Dathomir revealed a possible source of many new Jedi, and during Grand Admiral Thrawn's campaign, he met Mara Jade, a former assassin of Emperor Palpatine's. Like the others, though, Mara wasn't yet ready for formal training.

Six years after Endor, the reborn Emperor nearly subjugated the New Republic for good. As the most powerful light-side Jedi in the galaxy, Luke Skywalker seemed preordained to oppose the Emperor's clone, but he remained haunted by thoughts of his father, who had served Palpatine only to destroy his Master when Palpatine had least expected it. Luke decided to conquer the dark side from within.

On Byss, the new Imperial center, Luke knelt before Palpatine's clone and declared, "My father's destiny is my own." He endured many horrors on Byss, including the replacement of his prosthetic hand with a duplicate, but eventually fell too far into the dark side. It took the strength of his sister Leia to bring him back, and the heroism of another Jedi—Empatojayos Brand—to banish Palpatine's spirit forever.

Having endured a crucible, Luke had no older Jedi to rely on, for even Obi-Wan Kenobi's spirit had passed on. After his experiences on Byss, Luke truly became a Jedi Master, the first of the new Jedi Order. In a speech before the New Republic, he asked permission to establish a Jedi academy. From Yavin 4 he attracted Force-strong candidates from across the galaxy, even including those who had earlier turned him down.

Luke chose Yavin 4 in part because he had earlier discovered an ancient Jedi structure there, a subterranean "lost city" beneath the jungles. What Luke didn't realize was that trapped within the stone walls of many of the buildings on Yavin 4 thrived the spirit of Dark Lord Exar Kun, who soon killed one of Luke's students. Still another trainee was driven to the dark side before the Jedi collectively banished the evil spirit.

The Jedi academy, or praxeum, became the center of Luke Skywalker's life. While several of his students failed in their training, many more succeeded. Only a year after its inception, the academy graduated its first class of Jedi Knights.

Luke tried to make time for a personal life, but the demands on his time were too great. During the *Eye of Palpatine* crisis he met Callista, a holdover from the previous era of Jedi Knights. The two fell in love, but when Callista lost her connection to the Force, she chose to find her way back on her own, and left Luke. A second, Akanah, became involved with Luke during the Black Fleet Crisis, but Luke broke the relationship off when he learned Akanah was manipulating him.

During the Hand of Thrawn incident, Luke at last found lasting love. Mara Jade, who had once tried to kill him, now agreed to join him in marriage. On Coruscant, Luke and Mara participated in two ceremonies—a Jedi service and a public wedding that was nearly disrupted by Imperial agitators.

Luke's academy curriculum fluctuated as he learned more about the old Jedi Order through the *Chu'un-thor*'s records and other links to the past. He began placing the older students in Master–apprentice pairings, and made the academy a place for younger initiates, much as Coruscant's Jedi Temple had once been.

Mara didn't share Luke's devotion to the academy, and so spent much of her time on New Republic missions while Luke taught his Jedi hopefuls. Soon, the ranks of students included his niece and nephews, Han and Leia Solo's children Jacen, Jaina, and Anakin. Luke promoted the three to Jedi Knight and helped them battle the Second Imperium, the Diversity Alliance, and Black Sun.

Twenty-one years after the Battle of Endor, the new Jedi Order numbered approximately one hundred Knights and Masters. Luke petitioned the New Republic government to allow for the reestablishment of the old Jedi Council, but soon had more pressing things on his mind.

Yuuzhan Vong invaders, seemingly existing outside the Force, plowed through the New Republic and decimated the Jedi. Luke had to eventually fight simultaneously on *three* fronts—against the Yuuzhan Vong, against the New Republic citizens who came to view the Jedi with suspicion and fear, and against discord within the Order itself as aggressive Jedi like Kyp Durron threatened to form breakaway factions. In the midst of the war, his wife Mara gave birth to their first child, Ben.

Luke Skywalker has long held the opinion that it was his destiny to bring back the Jedi. Palpatine couldn't stop him, nor could the warlords of the Empire, but his triumphs may be torn from him by the Yuuzhan Vong. For the sake of his students—and his infant son—he has vowed not to let that happen.

MARA JADE SKYWALKER

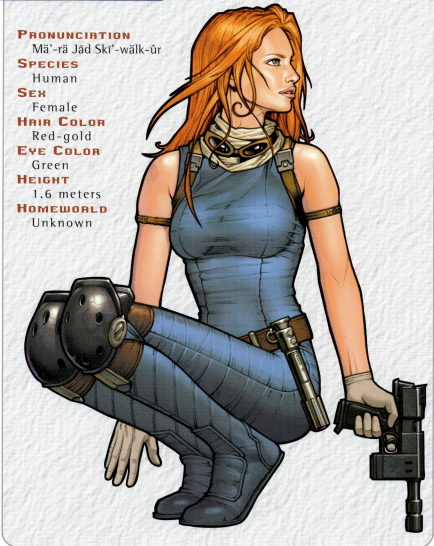

PRONUNCIATION
Mä'-rä Jäd Skī'-wälk-ûr
SPECIES
Human
SEX
Female
HAIR COLOR
Red-gold
EYE COLOR
Green
HEIGHT
1.6 meters
HOMEWORLD
Unknown

The Empire's deadliest agent, married to the Rebel Alliance's greatest hero. The irony is thick, but many on both sides relish the symbolism.

As Luke Skywalker's wife and one of the few Jedi Masters of the new Jedi Order, Mara Jade finds it hard to stay out of the public's eye. But for most of her life she was invisible. As one of the secretive Emperor's Hands, Mara went unnoticed by most and unrecognized for what she truly was.

Emperor Palpatine discovered Mara when she was just a girl. She was so young that she has few memories of her former life. Raised on Palpatine's estate, Mara became an expert combatant, spy, and assassin, and an excellent blade duelist wielding her blue-hued lightsaber. Through the Force, she could hear Palpatine's commands from anywhere in the galaxy.

Mara proved her skills by breaking into Grand Moff Tarkin's private quarters, after which Palpatine named her Emperor's Hand—an elite agent sworn to do his bidding. The Emperor had other Hands, but led each to believe that he or she was the only one. Only a few high-ranking Imperials, including Darth Vader and Grand Admiral Thrawn, knew of Mara's true role. Others assumed she was simply one of Palpatine's concubines.

As Hand, Mara received her own starship and a protocol droid named K3. She stretched the Empire's iron grip across the galaxy and helped stamp out the sputtering flame of the Jedi. Rumor has it that she located the legendary Jedi Master known as the Dark Woman hiding on Cophrigin V, but the Emperor gave that particular extermination job to Darth Vader.

After the Battle of Yavin, Mara familiarized herself with the dossiers of her Rebel Alliance enemies, particularly the X-wing ace and budding Jedi Knight called Luke Skywalker. When Vader failed to convert Skywalker at Cloud City, Emperor Palpatine gave Mara secret orders to assassinate the young Rebel. She infiltrated Jabba the Hutt's palace as the dancing girl Arica, but Melina Carniss, one of Jabba's own counteragents, foiled her first attempt on Skywalker's life. Then Jabba refused to allow her to board his sail barge, and she watched in frustration as her target floated off over the dunes toward the Great Pit of Carkoon.

Her mission a failure, Mara accepted Palpatine's alternate assignment to assassinate Dequc, a criminal underlord who'd been trying to fill the power vacuum left behind after Darth Vader killed Prince Xizor. She accomplished the mission, or so she thought, and returned to Coruscant, where she felt a scream of rage tear through the Force. Her worst nightmare had come true—her Master, Emperor Palpatine, had died. A vision flashed behind Mara's eyelids, of Skywalker and Vader, murdering her Emperor. Deep in her subconscious echoed Palpatine's last command: *"You will kill Luke Skywalker."*

Imperial Intelligence director Ysanne Isard moved to wrest power from Sate Pestage, the Emperor's de facto successor. Isard was among those who knew Mara Jade's true status, and that Mara had the power to make her life difficult. So Isard imprisoned her in a holding cell on Coruscant. Mara escaped. Relying on her undercover training, she disappeared into the galaxy's dregs in a harried effort to shake all Imperial pursuers.

Hopping from world to world behind dozens of false identities, Mara performed the occasional clandestine mission to honor her dead Master. On Qiaxx she discovered that her earlier assassination of Dequc had only eliminated a decoy, so she corrected her error. On Kintori, Mara crossed paths with New Republic General Crix Madine when she silenced a treasonous Imperial governor.

She took the name Chiara Lorn on the planet Phorliss during the Dequc affair. Later she became Merellis, a comeup flector for a Caprioril swoop gang. After several years, Mara landed on Varonat and took a mechanic's job under the alias Celina Marniss—a play on Melina Carniss, the agent who had thwarted her mission in Jabba's palace. Four and a half years after Endor, the smuggling chief Talon Karrde arrived on Varonat and

ran afoul of the local crime boss. Mara saved his life, and out of gratitude Karrde offered his rescuer a place in his organization.

For the first time since the death of Palpatine, Mara felt as if she belonged. But through fate or the Force, the man she considered her worst enemy practically dropped into her lap. She discovered Luke Skywalker's X-wing drifting in space, and Karrde brought the Jedi to his Myrkr base. While Karrde contemplated turning Skywalker over to Grand Admiral Thrawn, Mara fought the Emperor's *"You will kill Luke Skywalker"* command as it reasserted itself in her brain. Instead of killing Skywalker, she found herself *helping* him escape Thrawn's forces on Myrkr.

A short time later, Grand Admiral Thrawn seized Mara and revealed to her the truth she had never known—she had been but one of many Emperor's Hands in service to Palpatine. When Thrawn double-crosssed her and captured her employer Talon Karrde, Mara again swallowed her hatred for Luke Skywalker and enlisted the Jedi's help in rescuing Karrde.

The New Republic government, suspicious of this ex-Imperial agent, jailed Mara for a short time on Coruscant. But Luke and his friends sprang her from her cell so she could help them eliminate Thrawn's cloning facility on Wayland. Inside Wayland's Mount Tantiss complex, Mara killed two clones—the mad Jedi Master Joruus C'baoth and a clone duplicate of Luke Skywalker, thus fulfilling—on a technicality—the Emperor's final command.

Luke Skywalker gave Mara his old blue-bladed lightsaber, lost at Cloud City but recovered at Wayland. She used it to replace her violet saber, lost during the years she'd spent on the run from Isard and Isard's freelance enforcer, Lumiya. Mara thought about becoming a full Jedi Knight, but didn't want to do so as a byproduct of Skywalker's charity. She sought out Kyle Katarn, a Force user who had rejected Skywalker's teachings, and the two of them agreed to a mutual exchange of information. She also built her own lightsaber, a new violet one balanced for the techniques with which she was familiar.

When Emperor Palpatine came back in a new clone body, Mara refused to believe it was really him. For his part, Palpatine spurned his treasonous former Hand and replaced her with Executor Sedriss and his Dark Side Adepts.

Mara continued to aid the New Republic, assisting in the evacuation of Coruscant and securing vital cargo shipments for the government-in-exile. During the worst of the fighting, Mara traveled to Dromund Kaas to free Kyle Katarn from the Sith-induced darkness into which he had plummeted.

Restored to the light, Katarn conceded he still had much to learn about the Force. Mara reluctantly admitted that she did, too. Katarn became one of Skywalker's first academy students, and Mara visited the academy on occasion, while keeping Talon Karrde's newly formed Smugglers' Alliance up and running.

After Admiral Daala's first defeat, Mara entered into a partnership with Lando Calrissian for the administration of the spice mines of Kessel. Their partnership extended into other business dealings, but despite Calrissian's best efforts it never grew into a romantic pairing. On behalf of Talon Karrde, Mara and Lando Calrissian spent years investigating the whereabouts of Karrde's former associate Jorj Car'das.

As a representative of Karrde's Smugglers' Alliance, Mara had any number of starships at her disposal—her modified Z-95 Headhunter for speed, the nimble *Shrike* for stealth, and the *Hunter's Luck* or *Starry Ice* for transporting cargo. But she never had a starship that was truly her own until she rescued an industrialist's daughter from the dungeon of a Drach'nam slaver. Thanks to Karrde, an armed experimental SoroSuub star yacht was offered up by the tycoon as payment for services rendered. Mara christened the vessel the *Jade's Fire*.

Using the *Jade's Fire* as her home base, Mara briefly went into business for herself, as part of Karrde's plan for her to gain experience in a variety of disciplines. While visiting customers in the Corellian sector, Mara got caught up in the Corellian insurrection, helping Leia Organa Solo escape from imprisonment despite suspicion from some quarters regarding her motivations.

After Corellia, Mara returned to Karrde's organization. During the supposed return of Grand Admiral Thrawn, she investigated mysterious alien messages that were originating from the planet Nirauan on the fringes of the Unknown Regions. When Mara's own signal abruptly cut off, Luke Skywalker followed her to Nirauan, and together they infiltrated the Chiss outpost known as the Hand of Thrawn. In order to prevent Thrawn's followers from reaching the outer galaxy, Mara remote-steered the *Jade's Fire* into the base's docking bay, destroying her most cherished possession.

During their adventure on Nirauan, Mara and Luke realized that—despite their past animosity—they were a perfect match. Upon their return to Coruscant they were married in the Reflection Gardens, though their public ceremony was nearly spoiled by Imperial troublemakers.

To replace the *Jade's Fire*, Luke presented Mara with the *Jade Sabre*. Over the next few years Luke spent most of his time at the academy, while Mara spent hers adventuring with Mirax Terrik or assisting Jedi academy graduates during offworld assignments.

While escorting a diplomat to Monor II, Mara became infected with deadly coomb spores planted by Yuuzhan Vong agent Nom Anor. Mara used her Jedi abilities to sustain herself, but the effort proved debilitating. Nevertheless, Mara took on Jaina Solo as her apprentice. Luke, knowing the extremes of light and dark Mara had traversed over the course of her life, bestowed upon her the title of Jedi Master.

During the initial Yuuzhan Vong invasion, a weakened Mara tried to recuperate on Dantooine. When the ruthless aliens attacked that world, she lost the *Jade Sabre*. She fought bravely at Ithor, and rejoiced when a vial of tears obtained from the alien called Vergere sent her disease into remission. Mara secured her third personal star yacht, the *Jade Shadow*, and helped battle the Yuuzhan Vong when the invaders struck at Duro.

It was during the Duro incident that Mara, through the Force, sensed something growing inside her body. Initially fearing that the disease had returned, she realized with amazement she was pregnant. She carried the child to term despite a recurrence of her disease, and gave birth to a baby boy. She and Luke named their son Ben, and Mara has become more determined than ever to drive out the Yuuzhan Vong, for a galaxy under alien occupation is no place to raise the next generation of Skywalkers.

Anakin Solo

Named for his grandfather, Anakin Solo constantly struggled to live up to—and live down—the legacy of Anakin Skywalker. The pressures of his heritage drove him to become one of the greatest Knights of the new Jedi Order. They may also have led to his tragic death.

Anakin was born late in the sixth year after the Battle of Endor, one and a half years after the births of the Solo twins Jacen and Jaina. He came into the galaxy during tumultuous times—which seemed to suit him. Whether threatened by Palpatine's life-essence on Onderon or snatched away from his fortified nursery on Anoth by Caridan Ambassador Furgan, baby Anakin remained serene.

He grew up on Coruscant under the care of the droid C-3PO. His mother, Leia Organa Solo, had full-time responsibilities as New Republic Chief of State; father, Han Solo, was also occupied with governmental duties. While Jacen and Jaina enjoyed the closeness of twins, Anakin developed a quiet, focused introspection that others mistook for daydreaming. While he lagged slightly behind in reading and verbal skills, he excelled at mathematics and engineering like his grandfather before him. By the age of three he could dismantle and reassemble his nanny droids.

Anakin's connection to the Force seemed primal, much more profound than that of either of his siblings. This talent was also recognized by his enemies. Palpatine and Furgan were the first, but Lord Hethrir of the Empire Reborn movement realized that the three-and-a-half-year-old child would provide the ideal sacrifice to

PRONUNCIATION
Ăn'-ä-kĭn Sŏ'-lō
SPECIES
Human
SEX
Male
HAIR COLOR
Brown
EYE COLOR
Blue
HEIGHT
1.73 meters
HOMEWORLD
Nespis VIII (born), Coruscant

the extra-dimensional being called Waru. His parents and his uncle Luke saved him from that grim fate, but Anakin's status as a nexus of the Force remained undeniable.

The Corellian insurrection further reinforced that belief. Separated from their parents, in the company of their tutor and the Wookiee Chewbacca, the three Solo children located a planetary repulsor chamber buried beneath the surface of Drall. Without knowing anything about the ancient alien technology, Anakin divined its purpose and activated the repulsor just by touching it. The hidden architecture of the Corellian system—including Centerpoint Station and all five planetary repulsors—imprinted itself on Anakin and responded to his prodding. Seven and a half years old at the time, Anakin saved billions of lives by blocking a supernova blast fired from Centerpoint Station.

As he grew older, Anakin became more outgoing and mature. Midway through his eleventh year he began formal instruction at Luke Skywalker's Jedi academy on Yavin 4. He made a friend, a nine-year-old Tatooine girl named Tahiri, and showed his reckless side by embarking on an unsupervised excursion to the Palace of the Woolamander. There he discovered a mystical golden globe containing the spirits of Massassi children, trapped for four thousand years by the Sith Lord Exar Kun. Anakin's power in the Force allowed him to free the spirits. He also discovered a hibernating, four-legged Jedi Master named Ikrit—a living link to the old Jedi Order—who became Anakin's informal mentor.

On a visit to Dagobah, Anakin entered the same dark-side cave his uncle had endured during his training with Yoda. Within the blackness Anakin faced down the fear of following in his grandfather's footsteps, and emerged a stronger, more confident Jedi. Later, he helped recover Obi-Wan Kenobi's lost lightsaber from Darth Vader's castle on Vjun, though the brooding emptiness of his grandfather's retreat weighed heavily on his mind.

As his training continued, Anakin alternated between Jedi sessions on Yavin 4 and regular schooling on Coruscant. He was away from the academy when his siblings battled the Second Imperium, but helped rebuild the damaged Great Temple and provided information that prevented a resurgence of the Black Sun crime syndicate.

Luke Skywalker promoted Anakin to the rank of Jedi Knight and took him and his brother Jacen as apprentices for further training. The bold, brash style practiced by Kyp Durron appealed to Anakin, and he toyed with the idea of joining Kyp's

"Dozen-and-Two-Avengers" fighter squadron. To Anakin, the Force was a hammer that should be employed whenever possible, to shatter the fortifications of evil. This philosophy put him into direct conflict with Jacen's measured pacifism.

In the twenty-first year after the Battle of Endor, the Yuuzhan Vong struck at the Outer Rim planet Sernpidal by pulling its moon down into a fatal orbit. Just before the satellite's impact, Chewbacca threw Anakin

aboard the *Millennium Falcon*, but could not climb on board himself. Knowing that hesitating would only kill them all, Anakin piloted the *Falcon* away from ground zero. Sernpidal's falling moon killed Chewbacca.

Han Solo dearly loved his son—Anakin had nearly been named for him—but blamed him for the death of his oldest friend. It was months be-

fore they reconciled. Meanwhile, Anakin spent time on Dantooine, where Mara Jade taught him not to over-rely on the Force. The teenager assisted Luke and Mara in a search for lost Imperial superweapons, at which time a con man named Chalco and a rogue Jedi named Daeshara'cor taught him the value of humility. Anakin also fought in the Battles of Dantooine and Ithor.

Just before the Battle of Fondor, Anakin returned to the Corellian system to reactivate Centerpoint Station as a defensive weapon. Though he could have used Centerpoint to eliminate the Yuuzhan Vong fleet that was menacing Fondor, Anakin gave in to his brother's wishes that the station not be used as a tool of mass destruction. Instead, their uncle Thrackan Sal-Solo seized the controls, then mistakenly wiped out both the Yuuzhan Vong fleet *and* the friendly Hapan navy. Outwardly Anakin blamed Jacen for the debacle, but privately he blamed himself for hesitating when he should have acted.

Despite Warmaster Tsavong Lah's demand that the New Republic surrender its Jedi, Anakin remained a dashing public figure. Many assumed that the charismatic young man would one day assume Luke Skywalker's role, and a part of Anakin began to believe the hype.

Soon it became apparent that the Jedi academy on Yavin 4 could no longer be protected from the Yuuzhan Vong enemy collaborators of the Peace Brigade. Anakin rushed off alone to rescue the young Jedi students, including his friend Tahiri. He arrived in time to hold off brigade forces until Talon Karrde arrived with reinforcements, but Master Ikrit died in the fighting.

A Yuuzhan Vong fleet then arrived at Yavin 4, transforming the Great Temple and the surrounding jungle into a shaper colony. Enemy forces captured Tahiri and prevented Anakin from escaping the system. To save his friend, Anakin teamed up with Vua Rapuung, a former Yuuzhan Vong warrior who had become a Shamed One when his body rejected ritual implanting. Rapuung died during the rescue of Tahiri, but he provided Anakin a new understanding of the complexity of the enemy.

Tahiri suffered badly during her time in captivity. Anakin worried that enemy brainwashing might drive her to the dark side. The two young Jedi fought under Corran Horn's command at Yag'Dhul, where they helped drive off a Yuuzhan Vong invasion force. During a quiet moment aboard the Yag'Dhul station, Anakin and Tahiri exchanged a kiss, and vowed to become more than just friends.

Nearly two years into the war, Anakin spearheaded a bold mission into the heart of enemy territory. The three Solo children, along with a Jedi strike force, commandeered a Yuuzhan Vong vessel and infiltrated an enemy worldship near Myrkr. Anakin led the charge through the training labyrinth to eliminate the cloning labs that grew Jedi-hunting voxyn. He fought with passion, but without hatred, allowing the Force to guide him rather than shaping it to his own purposes.

In the end he sacrificed himself to help destroy the last bit of voxyn genetic material. Anakin's death brought his parents to the brink of despair, forced Jacen to question the path of a Jedi, and temporarily pushed Jaina into the grip of the dark side.

HAN SOLO

PRONUNCIATION
Hän Sō'-lō
SPECIES
Human
SEX
Male
HAIR COLOR
Brown
EYE COLOR
Brown
HEIGHT
1.8 meters
HOMEWORLD
Corellia

I 've flown from one side of this galaxy to the other," Han Solo once boasted, "but I've never seen anything to make me believe there's one all-powerful Force controlling *everything*."

Solo no longer denies the existence of the Force. His wife is Force-sensitive; so are his children. His brother- and sister-in-law are Jedi Masters. Han Solo an island in a Jedi family, and perhaps this is one reason why he spent so much of his time with his *Millennium Falcon* copilot Chewbacca. Now that his oldest friend is dead, Han must face a life without certainties, trusting his gut to help him in the war against the Yuuzhan Vong.

Even if he hadn't married Leia Organa and fathered a new generation of Jedi, Han Solo would have gone down in history as one of the key figures of the Galactic Civil War. Yet his origins were humble, and if the historians could have seen Han as an abandoned orphan on Corellia, they would have pegged him not as a future champion, but as a criminal-in-training.

In fact, Han Solo *was* a criminal for many years—a pickpocket, a con artist, and a spice smuggler. His disreputable career began when he was taken in as a very young child by a felon named Garris Shrike. Aboard the freighter *Trader's Luck*, Han learned the finer points of thievery from the other children kept aboard to further Shrike's scams. The *Trader's Luck* orbited Corellia, but visited many planets across the galaxy, and young Han became a polylinguist. Dewlanna, Shrike's Wookiee cook, taught Han to understand the growling Shyriiwook tongue and acted as

his surrogate mother.

As he grew older Han longed to escape, but the cruel Shrike refused to give up any of his "employees." During one adventure on Corellia, Han met a cousin, Thrackan Sal-Solo, but was unable to uncover any hard information about his own birth parents. He was amused by old genealogy charts that linked him to Dalla the Black, a criminal who had lived many years earlier, and had proclaimed himself "King of Corellia."

Shrike discovered that Han possessed the instincts of a pilot and trained him as a swoop racer. Han won huge cash prizes—which immediately went to Shrike—and also won the lifelong enmity of future bounty hunter Dengar, when he caused Dengar to crash in an illegal race.

At the age of seventeen Han came to the attention of another famous bounty hunter while competing in the bare-knuckles All-Human Free-For-All on Jubilar. Boba Fett, on assignment for Jabba the Hutt, witnessed the young Corellian's fight from a distance. Han won the contest, but Shrike abused him just the same.

By age nineteen, Han had had enough. He escaped from the *Trader's Luck* as a stowaway on a cargo barge and wound up on the Hutt spice-processing world Ylesia. The Besadii Hutts hired the young Corellian to pilot their spice cargoes, and he fell in love with one of the human spice workers, a beautiful girl named Bria Tharen. His love for Bria inspired him to take her away from Ylesia aboard a stolen Hutt yacht, earning him a death mark courtesy of clan Besadii.

Han and Bria made it all the way to Coruscant, but their romance didn't last long. Bria left Han to find her own path. Brokenhearted, Solo enlisted in the Imperial Navy. For the next four years he trained at the Military Academy on Carida alongside such famous classmates as Soontir Fel and Mako Spince. He graduated at the top of his class and began service as a naval officer and TIE pilot.

While investigating a slaver freighter that had been carrying Wookiee slaves, Lieutenant Solo refused to kill the sole survivor when ordered to do so by his superior officer. Soon after, on Coruscant, Solo saved the same Wookiee from a savage beating at the hands of a construction overseer. For this second act of insubordination, he was drummed out of the Imperial Navy.

His career in ruins, he found new employment in the criminal underworld of Nar Shaddaa. Chewbacca, the Wookiee he'd saved, swore a life debt to him and followed him everywhere. They began running spice for the Desilijic clan, whose members included Jabba the Hutt. At first they flew company vessels, but in time Solo purchased his first ship—the *Bria*. He coveted the hot-rod freighter owned by his new friend Lando Calrissian, and in a high-stakes sabacc tournament on Bespin he won ownership of Calrissian's cherished *Millennium Falcon.*

Solo and Chewbacca took their new ship to the Corporate Sector and the Tion Hegemony. Upon their

return, Solo partnered with his former love Bria Tharen—now a leader in the Rebel Alliance—in a raid on Ylesia's spice factories. When Bria double-crossed him by seizing all the spice for the Rebels, she broke his heart a second time. On the heels of that debacle, Han botched one of Jabba's critical Kessel runs when he was intercepted by Imperials. The furious Hutt placed a bounty on Solo's head.

On Tatooine, an incompetent Rodian criminal tried to collect that bounty and failed fatally. Solo took a charter to fly four passengers to the Alderaan system, hoping to raise enough money to mollify Jabba. But en route, the *Falcon* was captured by the most terrifying battle station ever known. Alongside a farm boy and a former Jedi Knight, Solo rescued a Princess, fought his way out of the Death Star, and helped destroy the battle station. Thus began his career as a Rebel.

On several occasions Solo tried to break away and pay Jabba, but he always came back to the Rebellion—and the Princess. After the Battle of Hoth he realized his deep love for her, but by then it was too late. He was trapped at Bespin by Darth Vader, frozen in carbonite, and claimed by Boba Fett. Hanging on Jabba's palace wall, Han hibernated for many months before Leia Organa and her friends freed him from the ordeal he described as a "big, wide-awake *nothing*."

Back with the Rebellion, Han accepted a promotion to general and led the successful assault on the Imperial shield generator on Endor resulting in the destruction of the second Death Star. Over the next month he helped thwart invasions from the Unknown Regions by the Ssi-ruuk, as well as the Nagai and the Tofs.

Solo spent years aiding the emerg-

ing New Republic, but despite his general's rank he rarely commanded soldiers. His relationship with Leia Organa lurched through several starts and near stops.

During the New Republic's effort to unseat Warlord Zsinj, Han was absent from Coruscant for five months, commanding a naval task force that wiped out much of Zsinj's fleet. Upon his return to Coruscant, he discovered that Leia and the handsome Prince Isolder of Hapes were discussing a political marriage that would unite their two powers. In a fit of jealousy, Solo kidnapped the Princess to the wilderness of Dathomir. His harebrained courtship had an improbably happy ending, for upon their return to Coruscant the two were finally wed.

Han and Leia saw the birth of their first children, the twins Jacen and Jaina, during Grand Admiral Thrawn's war against the New Republic. One and a half years later, after the New Republic High Command fled Coruscant at the time of the reborn Emperor, Leia gave birth to their third child, Anakin, on the space city Nespis VIII.

The New Republic government then recaptured Coruscant, returning some normality to life. Curious to revisit his old smuggler's haunts, Solo agreed to make a diplomatic call on Kessel. Instead, Kessel's vengeful warden captured Solo and Chewbacca and imprisoned them in the spice mines. They escaped by stealing a ship and flying into the Maw's black-hole cluster, but in doing so unleashed Imperial Admiral Daala on the New Republic. Stopping Daala—and foiling the Besadii Hutts' Darksaber scheme—took another year.

The following five years hit Han Solo hard. First, a megalomaniacal politician from Nam Chorios kidnapped his wife. Later, the leader of an Empire Reborn movement kidnapped all three Solo children. Both incidents ended happily, but the thought of losing a loved one shook Solo to his core. On a policing mission against the Yevetha species, he was captured and brutally tortured before his eventual escape. When Kueller of Almania tried to foment a "new Rebellion," Solo suffered the effects of a political smear campaign that painted him as the instigator behind a terrorist bombing. Finally, during the Corellian insurrection, his cousin Thrackan Sal-Solo resurfaced to stir up trouble.

The Hand of Thrawn incident brought about a lasting peace between the New Republic and the Empire. Solo was finally able to settle down, though his natural wanderlust gnawed at him from time to time. He participated in the wedding ceremony of Luke Skywalker and Mara Jade, and proudly watched his three children grow into young adults and gifted Jedi Knights.

When he was fifty-four, the Yuuzhan Vong invaded the galaxy. Solo didn't even realize there *was* an invasion, however, when he and Chewbacca made a supposedly routine delivery to Sernpidal for Lando Calrissian. But when Sernpidal's moon crashed into the planet, he lost his oldest friend . . . forever. He needed someone to blame for the death of Chewbacca, and for a time he accused his son Anakin, whom he felt had taken the *Falcon* out of harm's way too early. In truth Anakin's quick actions

had saved everyone aboard the ship, but that didn't matter. Han would rather have died at Sernpidal than been forced to live with the aftermath.

Lost in grief, Han Solo hit rock bottom. For a time he returned to his old devil-may-care smuggler's lifestyle, abandoning his wife and battling the Yuuzhan Vong on his own terms with a blaster at his side and the *Falcon* under his feet. Droma, an itinerant Ryn, helped Solo work through his personal war and temporarily filled the *Falcon*'s copilot seat. Solo's cold attitude, however, drove a wedge between him and Leia. The two separated, but later reconciled when the Yuuzhan Vong threatened Duro.

Their reunion came just in time, for without each other and the strength of their union, Han and Leia would never have endured what lay ahead. For a year after the fall of Duro the two helped create a "Great River," a saferoute designed to enable the Jedi to move undetected after the Yuuzhan Vong called for the extermination of their kind. The New Republic was losing the war, so Solo and Leia reluctantly gave permission for their three children to lead a Jedi strike force against a Yuuzhan Vong worldship in the Myrkr system.

Through the Force, Leia sensed Anakin's death. Their youngest son had become a casualty of war, and his parents were devastated.

Han Solo has now lost two of the most important people in his life, and both deaths are due to the Yuuzhan Vong. He has grown less reckless in his advancing age, and closer to his remaining family, but he can never forgive the invaders for what they have done. They have cost him too much.

JACEN SOLO

PRONUNCIATION
Jā'-sĕn Sō'-lō
SPECIES
Human
SEX
Male
HAIR COLOR
Brown
EYE COLOR
Brown
HEIGHT
1.79 meters
HOMEWORLD
Coruscant

For Jacen Solo, the Force is much more than a simple light-versus-dark equation. He openly wonders if good and evil might coexist within a single individual. While his younger brother Anakin once viewed the Force as a hammer, Jacen has expressed the opinion that it might be best not to use the Force at all. By focusing his energies inward, he hopes to forge a more personal connection with the Force than could ever be explained in a Jedi academy course.

Since birth, Jacen understood the living Force. When the spirit of Exar Kun drove his uncle Luke into a state near death, Jacen was able to communicate with the world beyond. Luke linked his spirit with his nephew's, and the two-year-old boy took up a lightsaber and killed several attacking Sith battle hydras.

By the time he was five, it was impossible to deny that Jacen had an affinity for living things. When Lord Hethrir kidnapped the Solo children, Jacen spoke to Hethrir's sand dragon through the Force and rode on the creature's back. His talents, so different from the mechanical aptitude exhibited by his twin Jaina and his brother Anakin, often baffled his father, who mistook Jacen's lack of interest for laziness. The boy bonded more easily with his mother, who understood his need for connection.

During the Corellian insurrection, Jacen showed that he could adapt. He flew his father's *Millennium Falcon* for the first time at the age of nine, piloting with such skill that he deftly outmaneuvered Thrackan Sal-Solo. Along with Jaina, he began Jedi training at the Yavin 4 academy, and built his own lightsaber at fourteen.

In a training exercise, Jacen accidentally cut through the arm of fellow student Tenel Ka. Shocked by his lack of control, and shamed that he had caused such pain to a girl he considered more than a friend, Jacen dedicated himself to Tenel Ka's rehabilitation. Tenel Ka, however, got along fine without her arm—and, it seemed, without Jacen as well.

Jacen and the other students fought the Second Imperium and the Diversity Alliance. Though Jacen hoped to build a deeper bond with Tenel Ka, their relationship never progressed beyond a meaningful friendship. When the young Jedi Knights met Anja Gallandro during Black Sun's resurgence, Jacen experienced a brief infatuation with the attractive and much older woman.

In the months before his sixteenth birthday, Jacen began questioning his role as a Jedi. Overt use of the Force had stopped the Diversity Alliance, but it had done nothing to address the root causes of evil. When he found that he wasn't getting the answers from his uncle Luke, he turned his thoughts inward.

During Jacen Solo's sixteenth year, the Yuuzhan Vong invaded the galaxy. Jacen flew alongside his siblings in the Battle of Dubrillion, and he bravely rescued the beautiful Danni Quee from a Yuuzhan Vong ice prison on Helska 4. But the fighting only intensified Jacen's spiritual search. On a mission with Luke Skywalker to occupied Belkadan, Jacen tried to free a group of slaves and was captured by the enemy. The Yuuzhan Vong would have transformed him into a slave himself, had his uncle not freed him.

Jacen participated in Corran Horn's slave extraction mission on Garqi and later fought in the disastrous attempt at the defense of Ithor. Prior to that battle, Jacen partook of an Ithorian religious purification ceremony in which he surrendered "the need to know now what I will become later."

His admission in no way tempered his quest for meaning. During the Yuuzhan Vong attack on Fondor, Jacen persuaded his younger brother Anakin not to wield Centerpoint Station against the enemy. When Centerpoint was then fired by Thrackan Sal-Solo—vaporizing thousands of friendly soldiers—the philosophical schism between the two brothers deepened.

At the Battle of Duro, Jacen reached a turning point. The Force spoke to him in a vision, urging him to "stand firm" lest the galactic balance be tipped in favor of the invaders. When Warmaster Tsavong Lah threatened his mother, Jacen at last connected with the unifying Force and confronted the warmaster's evil head-on. In a furious rush of power, Jacen defeated Tsavong Lah, earning himself a Yuuzhan Vong death mark.

Over the next year Jacen worked with his mother and father in their efforts to create a "Great River" saferoute for the hunted Jedi. When Han started using the *Millennium Falcon* to harass Yuuzhan Vong ship-ping, Jacen butted heads with his father over the morality of piracy. Han admitted that while he didn't always understand his son, he never stopped being proud of him.

Anakin Solo continued to use the Force in a manner Jacen considered reckless and wasteful. More to keep an eye on his brother than anything else, Jacen accompanied a Jedi strike force on a mission behind enemy lines. Aboard a Yuuzhan Vong worldship near Myrkr, Anakin died in order to destroy the enemy's voxyn genetic storehouse.

Jacen, rocked by his brother's death, experienced a second shock when his twin Jaina fell into the angry current of the dark side. Unable to escape the worldship, Jacen was captured by enemy troops. The enigmatic alien named Vergere—a former Jedi living among the Yuuzhan Vong—would prove to be the only figure who might protect him and guide his future use of the Force. Regardless, Jacen's quest for understanding is far from over.

JAINA SOLO

PRONUNCIATION
Jā'-nä Sō'-lō
SPECIES
Human
SEX
Female
HAIR COLOR
Brown
EYE COLOR
Brown
HEIGHT
1.49 meters
HOMEWORLD
Coruscant

Jaina Solo has her mother's looks and her father's panache, but the family member she most takes after is her uncle Luke. Already a Jedi Knight and an X-wing pilot in Rogue Squadron, Jaina has unfortunately taken steps toward the dark side of the Force.

Born during the war with Grand Admiral Thrawn, Jaina Solo and her twin Jacen found themselves targets for assassination while still in the womb. From the beginning would-be conquerors tried to use the young Solo twins to their advantage, so it wasn't long before Jaina's mother Leia shuttled her children off to safeworlds—New Alderaan and Anoth among them—where she entrusted others with their care.

It was for their own protection, Leia claimed, but Jaina often wondered if it wasn't simply because her mother had no time for children. Even when the twins were present at their parent's home on Coruscant, Leia had twenty-four-hour responsibilities as New Republic Chief of State. Thus, despite living a life of privilege, Jaina's upbringing was a difficult one.

Early on, she proved to have a contrary streak, sometimes to her advantage, other times not. Left unattended for an instant during a visit to Coruscant's Holographic Zoo, two-year-old Jaina led her brother into the terrifying depths of the feral undercity. And only three years later, when Lord Hethrir of the Empire Reborn movement kidnapped all three Solo children, Jaina stubbornly defied him and broke out of her cell.

By the time she reached fourteen Jaina Solo had been the target of more plots than a Hutt heir, yet she survived them all with her confidence and sense of humor intact. At her uncle Luke's Jedi academy she met new friends and found innovative ways to use her innate knack for piloting and engineering. When a TIE fighter from the original Death Star was discovered in the Yavin jungles, she patched up the twenty-year-old ship and touched off the first of several encounters she and her fellow Knights would have with the villainous Shadow Academy.

Jaina alternated her time between Yavin and Coruscant. On the capital planet she got to know a young street tough named Zekk, who proved to be perfect material for Brakiss's Shadow Academy. Kidnapped by Brakiss and transformed into his Darkest Knight, Zekk faced off with Jaina during the battle for the Jedi academy. Zekk couldn't bring himself to fight his friend, though, and gave himself up instead. Jaina spent many weeks helping him return to the light.

The two grew closer during the Diversity Alliance affair, though Zekk frequently disappeared to pursue jobs as a bounty hunter. Eventually he agreed to finish his Jedi training under Master Skywalker's tutelage. He and Jaina became fellow students in the Force.

Following Black Sun's resurgence, Jaina agreed to hone her skills under Jedi Master Mara Jade. In Mara, Jaina found a surrogate mother—someone who spent time with her and shared her connection with the Force.

Leia Solo considered her daughter the most grounded and least complicated of her three children. However, she didn't see the gulf that had opened between the two of them, and the invasion of the Yuuzhan Vong drove them even farther apart, although it ultimately became the catalyst for their reconciliation.

The invasion also provided plenty of chances for Jaina to prove herself as a starfighter ace. Just prior to the attack on Sernpidal, Jaina flew Lando Calrissian's "running-the-belt" asteroid game, easily beating Kyp Durron's record. Following the Battle of Helska, Rogue Squadron leader Gavin Darklighter accepted Jaina as one of his pilots. Though she was only sixteen, she was no younger than Gavin had been when he'd debuted as a Rogue.

As Rogue Eleven, Jaina and her wingmate Anni Capstan fought in the Battle of Dantooine. She nicknamed her astromech droid "Sparky," and earned her own nickname—Sticks. Before the Battle of Ithor she met the handsome Jag Fel, a pilot for Grand Admiral Thrawn's former Chiss forces in the Unknown Regions. Jag flew several missions with Jaina after Anni Capstan died at Ithor.

But Jaina suffered a near-fatal accident during the fight for Kalarba. Temporarily blinded, she traveled to Duro for recuperation and angrily confronted her mother. All the frustrations of a lifetime boiled up in both of them. Shortly thereafter, Leia and Jaina both had their heads shaved during Duro decontamination, and Jaina began to see and respect her mother's humility. When Warmaster Tsavong Lah nearly killed Leia in a gruesome bloodletting ritual, Jaina helped move her mother to safety.

With the Yuuzhan Vong calling for the death of the Jedi, Jaina was asked to extend her leave of absence from Rogue Squadron indefinitely. She sought out Kyp Durron, who was planning an attack against an enemy superweapon constructed from the remains of the planet Sernpidal. Jaina enlisted help from Gavin Darklighter and Wedge Antilles in destroying the construct, which proved to be nothing more than an elaborate worldship.

During the Jedi mission to destroy the Yuuzhan Vong voxyn laboratories, Jaina watched her younger brother Anakin die before her eyes. Grieving, she lashed out and blamed Jacen's "philosophy of weakness" for failing to prevent the tragedy. Jaina vowed to make Anakin's death count for something—by never again giving a centimeter to the Yuuzhan Vong.

Her aggressive stance was echoed by many of her fellow Jedi. But none of them realized just how far into the dark side Jaina had slipped. After the fall of Coruscant she traveled to the Hapes Cluster, where the former Queen Mother Ta'a Chume tried to maneuver her into becoming Prince Isolder's new wife. Ta'a Chume even had Isolder's current wife, Queen Mother Teneniel Djo, killed in order to further her scheme. Jaina overcame the Hapan intrigue, and began the road back from the dark side, accepting advice from Kyp Durron that has helped her in her quest for the light.

LEIA ORGANA SOLO

PRONUNCIATION
Lā-yä Ôr-gǎ'-nä Sō'-lō
SPECIES
Human
SEX
Female
HAIR COLOR
Brown
EYE COLOR
Brown
HEIGHT
1.5 meters
HOMEWORLD
Alderaan

While her brother Luke has restored the Jedi Knights, Leia Organa Solo has made her own, equal (if not greater) impact on the state of the galaxy and the lives of its citizens. Rebel, diplomat, ambassador, and Chief of State, the charismatic Princess of Alderaan has embodied both the Rebellion and the post-Imperial reconstruction for more than two decades.

Born to Anakin Skywalker of Tatooine and Padmé Amidala of Naboo, Leia never knew her birth parents. She claims to have a shadowy memory of her mother as a beautiful but sad woman, but nothing more. In the effort to hide their latent Force abilities from Emperor Palpatine, Leia and her brother Luke were separated at birth and raised in secret among foster families. Obi-Wan Kenobi, having served with Bail Organa of Alderaan during the Clone Wars, placed Leia with the Organa family, where she would be raised as a member of the Royal House.

Like her mother, who served as Queen, and later Senator, of Naboo, Leia enjoyed the benefits of a palace education. She had the finest tutors and the most advanced equipment. Bright, outspoken, and more than a little rambunctious, Leia was often mistaken by visitors for a domestic girl, so little did she exhibit upper-crust gentility.

Bail Organa exposed his adopted daughter to as many experiences as he could. He brought her to Senate meetings on Coruscant and to the Great Meet herd ceremony on Ithor. He encouraged her to attend Alderaanian debates and palace receptions for offworld personnel. When his daughter was old enough, Organa hired weapons master Giles Durane to train her in the art of self-defense.

Leia became the youngest member of the Imperial Senate while still a teenager. As she criticized Emperor Palpatine's policies from her platform in the Senate chamber, she secretly helped her father, Mon Mothma, and Garm Bel Iblis expand the underground Rebel Alliance. On one "mercy mission" to deliver relief supplies to the blockaded planet Ralltiir, Leia learned that the Empire was constructing a terror weapon more horrific than any that had ever been conceived.

Rebel spies captured the blueprints to this superweapon—the Death Star—and Leia intercepted the secret data transmission at Toprawa. This act of espionage marked her vessel, the *Tantive IV*, as suspect and Darth Vader's Star Destroyer *Devastator* captured her corvette above Tatooine. Leia was transferred to the Death Star, where she watched her home planet of Alderaan perish in a flash of superlaser fire.

A team of rescuers, including Leia's as-yet-unrevealed brother and her future husband, rescued her from her prison cell and helped her to deliver the Death Star's schematics to the Rebel base on Yavin 4. Above the jungle moon, the Rebels assaulted the Empire's battle station, and succeeded in destroying it.

After this, the Rebel Alliance's first major victory, the galaxy at last viewed the band of freedom fighters as more than just guerrillas. Leia took over the Alliance's diplomatic efforts and won planets over to the cause. On one mission to Circarpous IV, she lost control of her Y-wing over Mimban and crash-landed in the swamps. She escaped with help from Luke Skywalker, but only after enduring excruciating torment in a lightsaber battle at the hands of Darth Vader, whom she knew only as a mortal enemy.

Prior to the establishment of the base on Hoth, Leia spent much of her time with Luke Skywalker and Han Solo, which sometimes took her away from the Alliance High Command for weeks at a stretch. Once the Rebels established their ice planet headquarters, she vowed to spend less time on such distractions. But Imperial snowtroopers forced the evacuation of Hoth's Echo Base, and Leia found herself stranded aboard the *Millennium Falcon* with its irritatingly cocky captain. The close quarters generated sparks, and by the time Solo descended into the carbonite pit on Cloud City, Leia openly admitted that she loved him.

Rescuing Han Solo became her highest priority. While searching for Boba Fett—who was to deliver Han's carbonite slab to Jabba the Hutt on Tatooine—Leia investigated the crimi-

nal syndicate Black Sun and its charismatic leader, Prince Xizor. Xizor captured and attempted to seduce her, but Leia escaped and Xizor died under the guns of Darth Vader's flagship.

Always a fighter, Leia went undercover as the bounty hunter Boushh and infiltrated Jabba's palace. When her rescue attempt failed, Jabba humiliated her by dressing her as one of his slave girls and chained her to his dais. Leia bided her time until Luke Skywalker made his move at the Sarlacc pit, then took her revenge on the Hutt by strangling him with the very chain that bound her.

On the forest moon of Endor, Leia learned an amazing secret—and a terrifying one. Luke Skywalker revealed that not only was he her brother; but her birth father was Darth Vader! Her preconceptions shattered, the Princess had only a few hours to digest these revelations; then the climactic battle for the galaxy's freedom was under way. As a general, Leia fought alongside Han and the Ewoks on Endor and witnessed the explosion of the second Death Star. In the postbattle victory celebration, Leia shared her revelations with Han, and reaffirmed her love for him.

She now knew that the Force ran strong in her bloodline. Perhaps it was the Force that had enabled her to withstand torture at Vader's hands, or perhaps it had guided her career with the Alliance. Regardless, Leia vowed to explore the path of a Jedi, but politics kept her much busier than either she or her brother would have liked.

At Bakura, Leia negotiated the first-ever truce between the Alliance and the Empire, though it proved short-lived. She helped arrange the cease-fire between the Alliance and the Nagai, and six months after the Battle

of Endor, Leia nearly worked out a deal with Sate Pestage that would have given the New Republic control of Coruscant. Unfortunately, Ysanne Isard's ascension to the Imperial throne put an end to further deal making.

Leia's busy schedule frequently kept her away from Solo. She helped plan the New Republic's strategy to retake Coruscant, and opened talks with the Hapes Consortium—the first such negotiations in more than three thousand years.

The Hapes visit ultimately led to marriage for Leia and Han. Stung by the attention she showed Hapes's Prince Isolder, Solo kidnapped Leia and brought her to the wild planet of Dathomir. His far-fetched plan rekindled their love, and upon their return they exchanged vows on Coruscant. The next year, during the war against Grand Admiral Thrawn, Leia gave birth to the twins Jacen and Jaina. It was during this time that Noghri bodyguards—the finest in the galaxy—were assigned to protect the Princess and her family.

Too soon after this happy event, the resurrected Emperor forced the New Republic to flee from Coruscant, and turned the Core Worlds into war zones. Leia sheltered the twins on New Alderaan, but was already pregnant with a third child. On the space city Nespis VIII she gave birth to her second son, Anakin. Leia named him for the father she had learned to forgive.

Following the Emperor's final defeat, Leia placed all three children on the safeworld of Anoth. She worked to rebuild Coruscant and dealt with many self-important political delegates like Ambassador Furgan of Carida. Noghri bodyguards shadowed her everywhere, always well out of sight. When Mon Mothma narrowly survived a grave illness, she appointed

STAR WARS: THE NEW ESSENTIAL GUIDE TO CHARACTERS

Leia as her successor as New Republic Chief of State.

Ratified by a popular vote, Leia Organa Solo became a hands-on leader. She negotiated with Durga the Hutt in the Darksaber crisis and endured a kidnapping during the Death Seed outbreak. But when the Empire Reborn movement led to the capture of her three children, she abandoned her governmental post and went undercover to rescue them. She declared war on the Yevethan species during the Black Fleet Crisis, and temporarily resigned as Chief of State in order to go after Kueller and help end his "new Rebellion."

After the Corellian insurrection Leia felt she had to escape from the incessant infighting of government and took an indefinite leave of absence. Ponc Gavrisom became Chief of State in her stead. Still, fifteen years after she first hammered out the truce of Bakura, it was Leia who negotiated a permanent peace agreement between the New Republic and the Empire. The incident made Leia realize that perhaps the world of politics was where she belonged. Two years after the peace treaty, the people of the New Republic once again elected Leia Organa Solo Chief of State.

While she attended to executive matters on Coruscant, her children grew into Jedi Knights at the academy on Yavin 4. After nearly four additional years as the head of the government, Leia announced her permanent retirement from politics, and Borsk Fey'lya succeeded her as Chief of State.

Few expected the "retirement" to stick, and they were right. But no one anticipated the event that would spur her return. The Yuuzhan Vong invasion took the New Republic by surprise, and when Fey'lya proved too slow to counter the threat, Leia took an active

role. She convinced many planets to join the fight, including the Hapes Consortium, though Hapes's decision to enter the war proved disastrous. Leia accepted a position in SELCORE, the Senate Select Committee for Refugees, to relocate New Republic citizens displaced by the invasion.

All this activity kept her away from her husband. Reeling from the death of Chewbacca, Han had sunk into a self-destructive behavior pattern, and Leia ultimately decided to let him work out his demons in his own way. For a year they saw each other only rarely, and the marriage was strained, but they crossed paths during the Yuuzhan Vong attack on Duro and recommitted their lives to each other shortly after.

At Duro Leia tried to help SELCORE manage the refugee settlements being built on the polluted planet's surface, but soon found herself fighting for her life against a Yuuzhan Vong invasion force. Warmaster Tsavong Lah captured her and put her through agony, crippling her legs until she could no longer stand. The warmaster would have sacrificed her to the gods had it not been for her son Jacen. The young Jedi injured Tsavong Lah and helped Leia

make it offplanet on the *Falcon*. After several treatments in a bacta tank she regained the complete use of her legs.

Over the next year she and Han Solo helped Luke Skywalker create a "Great River"—a saferoute for Jedi to travel in defiance of Tsavong Lah's edict calling for their heads. Once again Leia's diplomatic skills came to the fore in enlisting help from wary partners and suppliers.

When the Yuuzhan Vong's Jedi-hunting voxyn were traced to the Myrkr system, Leia hesitantly permitted her three children to lead a Jedi strike force and destroy the voxyn threat. Through the Force, she felt a devastating psychic blow as her youngest child, Anakin, died in battle.

To Leia, the fall of Coruscant seemed trivial by comparison. Though it was at times difficult for her to show it, her children had always been the most important things in her life. With Anakin dead, Jacen captured, and Jaina flirting with the dark side of the Force, the brave Princess will be hard-pressed to keep despair at bay.

KAM SOLUSAR

Kam Solusar has beaten the odds twice: as a former Jedi who escaped the Imperial Purge, and a former Dark Jedi who fought his way free from the Emperor's influence.

The great Jedi Master Ranik Solusar earned many reprimands from the Old Republic Jedi Council when he married and fathered a son. Following the Clone Wars, Ranik met his end at the hands of Darth Vader.

His son, Kam, had learned some Force skills from his father, but lacked formal training. Rather than die with the other Jedi—or turn traitor and join the executioners—he fled to the isolated star systems that lay beyond the galaxy's spiral arms.

For nearly thirty years he lived among unknown peoples, cut off from the Empire and the New Republic that supplanted it. Finally he returned to the stars of his birth, only to run into the spiritual successors of those who had destroyed the Jedi.

The reborn Emperor Palpatine enlisted special dark side warriors as living extensions of his will. The leader of these Dark Jedi, Executor Sedriss, tortured the Force-strong Solusar until he submitted. Psychologically shattered, Kam Solusar became one of Palpatine's seven Dark Side Adepts.

After Palpatine's defeat and apparent death at the New Republic's Pinnacle Base, Solusar encountered Luke Skywalker on the abandoned space city Nespis VIII. Skywalker sensed the goodness the Emperor had smothered, and bested Solusar in the ancient Jedi game of lightsider. Solusar renounced the dark side and returned with Luke to the New Republic.

PRONUNCIATION
Kăm Sō'-lōō-sär
SPECIES
Human
SEX
Male
HAIR COLOR
White
EYE COLOR
Unknown
HEIGHT
1.9 meters
HOMEWORLD
Unknown

Palpatine returned from death in a fresh clone, but this time Kam Solusar fought against his former dark-side comrades. On Ossus he cut Vill Goir in half, and battled more of the Dark Side Adepts on New Alderaan.

Mon Mothma gave Solusar a temporary general's commission, and he led the assault team that infiltrated the Emperor's flagship *Eclipse II*. Kam Solusar became one of the first twelve students at Luke Skywalker's Jedi academy. After the Corellian insurrection, Solusar married fellow academy graduate Tionne, and one year later presided over the Jedi wedding of Luke Skywalker and Mara Jade.

When Master Skywalker initiated a one-on-one teacher–student training program, Solusar took Octa Ramis as his apprentice. Upon her graduation to Knighthood, Jedi Master Solusar returned to the academy with his wife to oversee the newest classes of children.

During the Yuuzhan Vong invasion, Kam Solusar helped project an illusion to hide the location of the jungle moon from the enemy. But soon Solusar was forced to work with Talon Karrde to evacuate the Jedi children just ahead of an attacking Yuuzhan Vong fleet.

NIL SPAAR

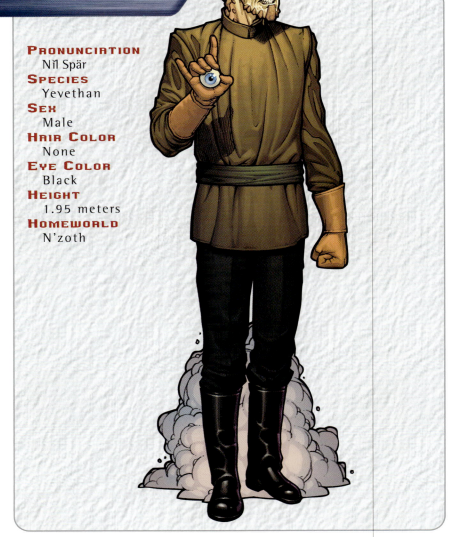

PRONUNCIATION
Nĭl Spär
SPECIES
Yevethan
SEX
Male
HAIR COLOR
None
EYE COLOR
Black
HEIGHT
1.95 meters
HOMEWORLD
N'zoth

Nil Spaar's people, the Yevetha, are an aggressively technological species, in sharp contrast to the antitechnology Yuuzhan Vong. But both embrace fanaticism so extreme it mandates the extermination of all who do not fit their cultural vision.

The Yevetha, discovered only decades ago, inhabit the Koornacht Cluster between the Deep Core and the Unknown Regions. Long convinced they were the galaxy's sole intelligent species, they came to hate the invading Empire for shattering their beliefs and making them slaves. The Imperials built orbital shipyards in Koornacht to service their Black Sword Command "Black Fleet."

Eight months after Endor, Yevethan commandos led by Nil Spaar rebelled against their captors, murdering thousands of Imperials and enslaving the rest. Taking possession of some of the mightiest warships in the galaxy, the Yevetha prepared themselves for the day of purification.

Spaar rose to absolute power by killing Yevethan leader Kiv Truun. As viceroy of all Yevethan worlds—collectively known as the Duskhan League—Spaar whipped his people's fanaticism to a fever pitch. They called him *darama*, meaning "blessed one." Spaar selected the finest females to bear his children and made the Super Star Destroyer *Intimidator*—renamed *Pride of Yevetha*—his personal flagship. Twelve years after Endor, Viceroy Nil Spaar kicked off his plan of conquest with a string of seemingly innocent diplomatic talks with Leia Organa Solo.

Chief of State Organa Solo didn't realize that Spaar could play politics just as effectively as he could wage war. He accused the New Republic of provoking his innocent and isolated people, then used the Black Fleet to obliterate all non-Yevethan colonies inside the Koornacht Cluster's borders.

Leia responded with force, but the New Republic's strongest fleet suffered a stunning defeat at Doornik-319. Spaar then captured Han Solo, beating him bloody in an attempt to intimidate his wife. But Leia refused to surrender to Spaar's evil.

Instead, she declared war on the Duskhan League. As the New Republic Navy prepared for an all-out assault, a Wookiee strike team led by Chewbacca rescued Han Solo from Spaar's Super Star Destroyer.

The New Republic and the Yevetha collided in the devastating Battle of N'zoth, resulting in a tremendous loss of life on both sides. Unfortunately for Spaar, the Imperial prisoners of war aboard the Yevethan warships picked that moment to mutiny against their captors.

As the *Pride of Yevetha* hurtled away from battle, Nil Spaar was forced into an escape pod and ejected into the chaos of hyperspace. He was never heard from again.

Grand Moff Wilhuff Tarkin

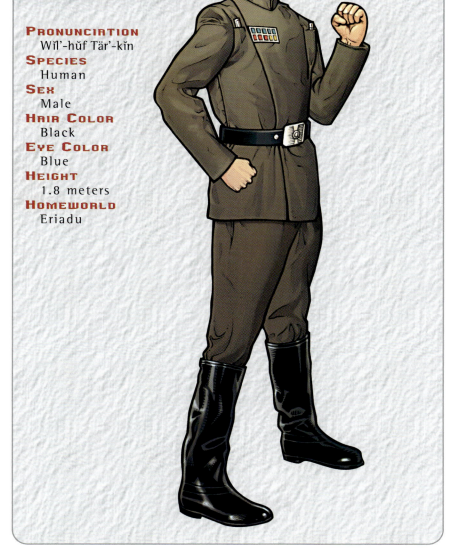

PRONUNCIATION
Wĭl'-hŭf Tär'-kĭn
SPECIES
Human
SEX
Male
HAIR COLOR
Black
EYE COLOR
Blue
HEIGHT
1.8 meters
HOMEWORLD
Eriadu

Among the Omwati, the word *tarkin* has entered their native tongue with a meaning that combines both "butcher" and "demon." Surviving Alderaanians, of course, curse Tarkin's name with unfathomable hatred. By contrast, Tarkin's wife considered him a heroic martyr. And had the Rebels not destroyed the Death Star, Tarkin might have been the ruler of the galaxy.

Even as a youth on prosperous Eriadu, Wilhuff Tarkin had ambition to spare. The Tarkin family boasted of generations of service to the Old Republic, yet they never attained the status enjoyed by the old aristocratic lines. The sting of that insult just made the Tarkins push themselves harder—no one more so than the man who would one day be called Grand Moff.

After graduating from the Imperial Academy, Tarkin—as well as his younger brother Gideon—joined the Republic Outland Regions Security Force. This policing task force patrolled the space around Eriadu and other Rim worlds, to keep commerce safe from pirates. On his occasional trips to Coruscant, Tarkin befriended Raith Sienar, an engineer for Sienar Technologies who was about his age. Tarkin reached the rank of commander before retiring from the Outland Regions Security Force in order to assume a political position on his homeworld.

Family connections helped Tarkin win the office of lieutenant governor of Eriadu. He quickly immersed himself in Eriadu's political and economic spheres, ruling from his ostentatious coastline estate. In order to keep Eriadu's shipbuilding industries supplied with valuable lommite, Tarkin arranged a competition between two Dorvallan mining corporations—Lommite Limited and InterGalactic Ore. The two companies entered a race to deliver their ore to Eriadu, but their barges were sabotaged and crashed into each other. The disaster allowed the Trade Federation to take over Dorvalla's lommite industry.

Approximately half a year before the Battle of Naboo, Lieutenant Governor Tarkin hosted a visit by Supreme Chancellor Valorum at his estate during the Eriadu trade summit. Although many believed Valorum would be the target of assassins, the true targets turned out to be the members of the Trade Federation Directorate, in a hit arranged by Darth Sidious. Tarkin impeded the Republic's investigation of the incident by restricting access to witnesses and allowing key evidence to vanish.

Senator Palpatine's election to the office of Supreme Chancellor represented a major political shift, and Tarkin was bright enough to realize it. He hooked up with powerful and enigmatic figures in the galactic government, and realized that humans—not aliens or superhuman Jedi mystics—would be the torchbearers of the coming New Order. Under instructions from his invisible superiors, Tarkin placed a broken droid near the Jedi Temple, knowing that a mechanically inclined Padawan named Anakin Skywalker would take it in and repair it. The droid acted as Tarkin's eyes and ears, enabling him to see into the secret workings of the Jedi Council. Chancellor Palpatine reactivated Tarkin's commission in the Security Force, and moved him from Eriadu to Coruscant.

Three years after the Battle of Naboo, Tarkin saw an opportunity for advancement if he could acquire one of the legendary "living starships" from the hidden world Zonama Sekot. He looked up his old friend Raith Sienar, and persuaded him to lead a mission to the Outer Rim planet. Tarkin followed, and by the time he arrived at Zonama Sekot with Republic reinforcements, Anakin Skywalker and Obi-Wan Kenobi had made it all but impossible for any to exploit the planet's organic technology. Tarkin briefly met young Anakin, who tried to use a Force chokehold on the older man. To redeem himself from the Zonama Sekot debacle, Tarkin appropriated Raith Sienar's concept for a moon-sized "expeditionary battle planetoid" and presented it to an intrigued Palpatine.

Once Palpatine established his Empire, Tarkin rose rapidly. During a protest against Imperial taxation on Ghorman, Tarkin landed his collection freighter right on top of an angry mob,

crushing and killing hundreds. The Ghorman Massacre, as it became known, spurred Bail Organa and Mon Mothma to discuss open rebellion. It also earned Tarkin a promotion to Moff.

To further his ambitions, Tarkin married a wealthy woman of the Motti lineage on Phelarion, giving him valuable contacts among that influential family. Tarkin did not love the woman, and soon after his marriage he met a brilliant academy cadet on Carida. Her name was Daala, and Tarkin made her both his protégée and his lover.

Five years before the Battle of

Yavin, Tarkin acquired a new pet—a slave named Ackbar from the subjugated planet Mon Calamari. He also received word that his brother Gideon had died in the Erhynradd Mutiny. He accepted Gideon's young daughter Rivoche into his family estate on Eriadu, though he had no way of foreseeing that Rivoche Tarkin would become one of the Rebel Alliance's most effective deep-cover agents.

Moff Tarkin established a refueling outpost on Ryloth, where he recruited a gifted Twi'lek scientist named Tol Sivron. To obtain more such talent, Tarkin established an orbital sphere above the Rim planet Omwat, where he pushed the native children to swallow a force-fed education. Those who failed watched their home cities burned to ash by a Star Destroyer's turbolasers. Dr. Qwi Xux was the program's sole graduate.

Pleased with Moff Tarkin's many successes, Emperor Palpatine made him the first Grand Moff, granting him almost unlimited jurisdiction over Oversector Outer, which was comprised of nearly every square centimeter of the Outer Rim Territories. Tarkin moved back to Eriadu full time to rule over his vast new kingdom.

To augment his team of alien scientists, Tarkin recruited several human designers, including Bevel Lemelisk and Umak Leth. With his personal wealth he financed Maw Installation, a weapons-research think tank hidden in the center of the Maw black hole cluster. The time had finally come to produce Raith Sienar's hypothetical battle station. The Grand Moff believed that such a weapon would epitomize his newly coined Tarkin Doctrine of "rule through fear of force rather than by force itself."

The Maw scientists completed a prototype of Tarkin's Death Star, and Emperor Palpatine approved funding for a finished version. Above the penal planet Despayre in the distant Horuz system, the planet killer slowly took shape. Whenever the construction pace flagged, Darth Vader—the former Jedi boy from Zonama Sekot—arrived to personally motivate any lazy workers.

Tarkin's first act as commander of the Death Star was to destroy the penal planet around which it orbited. Exhilarated by how well the thing worked, Tarkin began plotting long-term strategy with his family associate by marriage, Admiral Motti. The battle station's planet-pulverizing laser seemed even more powerful than the dark arts of Emperor Palpatine. Tarkin couldn't help but imagine what a colossal bargaining chip he would hold should he train the Death Star's superlaser on Coruscant. Perhaps anticipating this kind of treachery, Palpatine sent Darth Vader to the battle station to watch closely over Tarkin's shoulder.

The theft of the Death Star plans did not overly concern Tarkin. He remained convinced of the battle station's invulnerability. When Princess Leia refused to divulge the location of the main Rebel base, Tarkin destroyed the peaceful world of Alderaan on his own initiative, without consulting the Emperor, then moved against the Rebel base on Yavin 4. He refused to heed the warnings of his aide, Chief Bast, who pointed out that the attacking Rebel starfighters had pinpointed a crack in the Death Star's armor. He remained on the overbridge, smugly listening to the firing countdown, and died for his hubris.

In an effort to cover up the Yavin fiasco, Imperial news agencies reported that Tarkin had perished in a shuttle accident at the Tallaan shipyards. Grand Moff Ardus Kaine assumed Tarkin's post as governor of Oversector Outer. After the Emperor's death Kaine turned warlord, turning a chunk of Oversector Outer into the Pentastar Alignment.

More than three years after Tarkin's death, Imperial officers honored his memory by naming an experimental superlaser test bed—essentially a scaled-down Death Star—for the late Grand Moff. Thanks to Rebel saboteurs, the *Tarkin* superweapon met with the same explosive fate as its larger brother.

BOOSTER TERRIK

PRONUNCIATION
Bōōs'-tûr Těr'-ĭk
SPECIES
Human
SEX
Male
HAIR COLOR
Gray
EYE COLOR
Brown (red prosthetic)
HEIGHT
1.86 meters
HOMEWORLD
Corellia

Who could possibly be so brash as to strong-arm the New Republic into giving him an Imperial Star Destroyer? The answer could only be Booster Terrik, the man who turned living large into an art form.

Terrik, Corellian by birth, has been making grand mischief for over fifty years. Early on, he started his own shipping ventures, but quickly drove them into bankruptcy. Deeply in debt to several crime lords, and on the run from bounty hunters, Booster Terrik landed on the Rim planet Borlov in the stolen freighter *Starwayman*.

Llollulion, a Borlovian noble, befriended the human fugitive. In exchange for paying off Terrik's creditors, Llollulion asked Terrik to show him the galaxy. The birdlike Borlovian became the *Starwayman*'s copilot.

When Palpatine declared his Empire, Terrik and Llollulion began smuggling cargo for the resistance. On one of their first runs, the *Victory*-class Star Destroyer *Strikefast* chased them to a nameless planet in the fringes of the Unknown Regions. While Booster hid from the Imperials, the *Strikefast*'s captain encountered the Chiss exile known as Thrawn and brought him back to meet the Emperor. Terrik never realized the menace he had accidentally unleashed on the galaxy.

Soon after, Booster Terrik married and had a daughter, Mirax. As his smuggling business matured, Terrik and Llollulion went their separate ways. While nowhere near the size of Jorj Car'das's operation or the Hutt kajidics, Terrik's business profited from its strong pro-Rebel ties.

Terrik's wife died when Mirax was still a girl, and he had no choice but to raise her on his own, taking Mirax with him on smuggling runs aboard his new ship the *Pulsar Skate*.

Terrik's operations centered on the Corellian sector. He quickly became friends with Jagged and Zena Antilles, who operated the Gus Treta fueling station. Their son Wedge often accompanied Booster and Mirax on out-system missions. Wedge was aboard the *Pulsar Skate* when escaping pirates triggered a fuel explosion aboard the station, killing Jagged and Zena. Terrik gave Wedge one of his Z-95 Headhunters to help him take revenge on his parent's murderers.

Two years before the Battle of Yavin, Terrik's illegal activities in the Corellian system finally caught up with him. CorSec inspector Hal Horn, who'd tangled with Terrik many times before, nailed him on a smuggling charge. Booster Terrik received a five-year sentence to the spice mines of Kessel. Mirax Terrik took over her father's operation, but Jorj Car'das swallowed up most of it. Meanwhile, Booster rotted in the Kessel mines and cursed Hal Horn with every breath. He lost his left eye during his incarceration and had it replaced with a glowing red prosthetic.

Several months after the Battle of Hoth, Booster Terrik returned to society. He gave the *Pulsar Skate* to Mirax. Booster stayed in the smuggling industry, though he maintained a lower profile than before and kept on the move.

Approximately four years after the Battle of Endor, the pilots of Rogue Squadron hired Booster Terrik to assist in the Bacta War against Ysanne Isard. Terrik assumed command of the Rogues' space station headquarters near Yag'Dhul and used his connections with Talon Karrde to obtain hundreds of proton torpedoes and targeting locks. During the final battle against Isard's forces, Terrik pulled off an outrageous bluff, tricking the Star Destroyer *Virulence* into surrendering even though the torpedo magazines on his station were empty. After the battle, Terrik persuaded the New Republic to let him keep the *Virulence*, albeit with most of its weapons stripped. He renamed it the *Errant Venture*.

The *Errant Venture* became a mobile entertainment bazaar with three levels—Black, Blue, and Diamond—catering to the needs of shoppers and smugglers. The expense of maintaining a vessel measuring more than a kilometer and a half long kept Terrik on the brink of financial ruin. He hosted his daughter Mirax aboard his ship whenever possible, despite her marriage to Corran Horn, the son of the man who'd sent him to Kessel.

A year after giving up the vessel, the New Republic tried to nationalize the *Errant Venture* for the fight against Thrawn. Terrik agreed in principle, but insisted that the ship receive a full weapons upgrade, and that he be awarded an admiral's commission. The New Republic Navy respectfully declined.

When Ysanne Isard returned from the grave immediately after the Thrawn crisis, Terrik provided invaluable assistance to New Republic Intelligence by figuring out Isard's "dream ladder"—her step-by-step plan for retaking the Super Star Destroyer *Lusankya*. He also helped Bothan pilot Asyr Sei'lar start a new life after her supposed death in battle. Two years later, Booster Terrik worked with Corran Horn to rescue his daughter after her kidnapping at the hands of pirate leader Leonia Tavira.

During the galaxywide search for the Caamas Document, Terrik's *Errant Venture* became the Imperial Star Destroyer *Tyrannic* as part of a New Republic Intelligence undercover operation. Under the joint command of Terrik and General Garm Bel Iblis, the disguised Star Destroyer attempted to slip past the defenses of the Imperial Ubiqtorate base at Yaga Minor to steal a copy of the document from the Empire's data libraries. The mission failed, but Terrik kept most of the upgrades to his ship. He began painting the *Errant Venture* bright red.

In the wake of the Yuuzhan Vong invasion, Booster Terrik's *Errant Venture* has served as a mobile safehouse for the Jedi children following their evacuation from Yavin 4. Terrik also helped cover the New Republic's flight from Coruscant, and continues to offer assistance wherever he can as the New Republic regroups from its recent setbacks.

BRIA THAREN

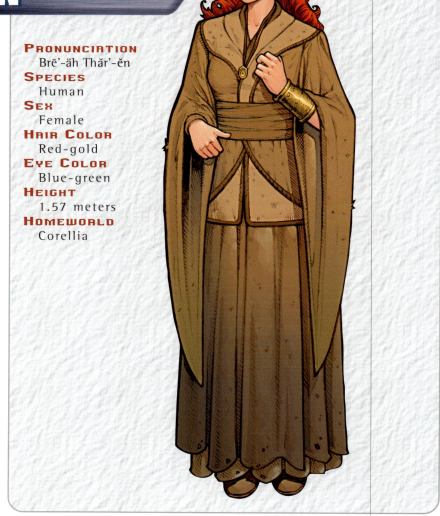

PRONUNCIATION
Brē'-äh Thǎr'-ĕn
SPECIES
Human
SEX
Female
HAIR COLOR
Red-gold
EYE COLOR
Blue-green
HEIGHT
1.57 meters
HOMEWORLD
Corellia

Alliance historians know Bria Tharen as a dedicated soldier of the early Rebellion, but Han Solo, the man who once loved her, can never forget the pain she brought him.

Bria grew up on southern Corellia in a wealthy shipping family made up of her father Renn, her mother Sera, and her older brother Pavik. At an early age her parents arranged for her marriage to Dael Levare, a handsome young man of good breeding, but Bria broke it off. She wanted to attend the University of Coruscant to study archaeology and ancient art.

At seventeen, however, she attended a religious revival and experienced "the Exultation"—a harmonic stimulation of the brain's pleasure centers performed by t'landa Til "priests." Like many others, Bria mistook the sensation for a higher truth. Selling her jewelry to buy passage on a pilgrim ship, she landed on Ylesia and became a slave in the Hutts' spice factories.

Even her name was stripped from her. Now called Pilgrim 921, Tharen clung to her illusions about the Ylesian religion until shown the truth by the Hutts' spice pilot—Han Solo. Just under a year after her arrival, she escaped Ylesia with Solo's help.

The two lovers made it to Coruscant, where Bria abruptly walked out on her rescuer. She was still experiencing Exultation withdrawal and knew she could only beat the addiction on her own. She joined Garm Bel Iblis's Corellian resistance movement and moved rapidly through the ranks. Sometimes she saw Han Solo from afar, but couldn't bear to restart their stalled relationship.

Tharen started her own Rebel attack force, Red Hand Squadron, which she led from the bridge of the *Marauder*-class corvette *Retribution*. Her Rebel superiors were often shocked by Red Hand Squadron's brutality toward slavers of any stripe.

After the signing of the Corellian Treaty—marking the formal establishment of the Rebel Alliance—Bria Tharen orchestrated a plan that would wipe out the hateful Ylesian factories and simultaneously enrich the struggling Alliance. She forged a deal with Jabba the Hutt that enabled Rebel soldiers to join with Nar Shaddaa smugglers in a successful raid on Ylesia. Han Solo and Bria Tharen fought alongside each other for the first time in ten years, their love seemingly rekindled. Which is why it was such a blow when Bria doublecrossed the smugglers, taking all the spice to help fund the Rebel efforts to capture the Death Star plans.

Tharen's Red Hand Squadron received the Death Star schematics on the ground at Toprawa and transmitted them to Princess Leia's orbiting corvette, the *Tantive IV*. Knowing she would be tortured if captured, Bria swallowed a poison capsule and died a martyr.

GRAND ADMIRAL THRAWN

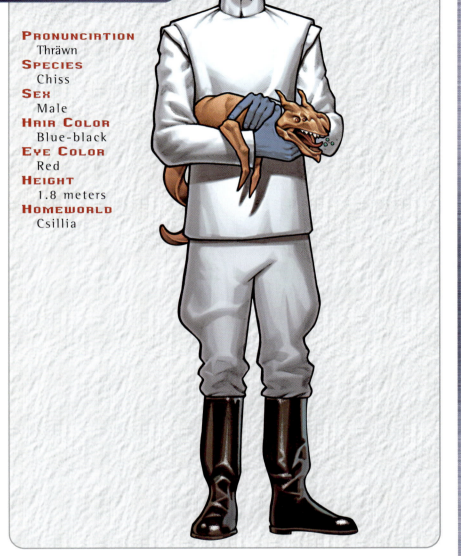

PRONUNCIATION
Thräwn
SPECIES
Chiss
SEX
Male
HAIR COLOR
Blue-black
EYE COLOR
Red
HEIGHT
1.8 meters
HOMEWORLD
Csilla

An outcast from his own people, Mitth'raw'nuruodo possessed the raw skill needed to subjugate the galaxy but was held in check by Emperor Palpatine. Even in death, he had a plan for domination, and it's only through luck that citizens across the galaxy weren't forced to pledge their allegiance to Grand Admiral Thrawn.

Thrawn was a Chiss, a species of blue-skinned, red-eyed humanoids hailing from the Unknown Regions. They are a serious, disciplined people with an impressive military and a large star-spanning empire. Mitth'raw'nuruodo was one of the Chiss's most skilled tacticians, commanding a force of vanguard vessels that patrolled the Empire's outback.

Prior to the Battle of Yavin, Mitth'raw'nuruodo came upon a force of foreign raiders, dispatched by Palpatine to destroy the Jedi mission known as the Outbound Flight Project. Mitth'raw'nuruodo wiped out these invaders, sparing only one—Palpatine's adviser Kinman Doriana, who explained to him the purpose of the mission. Thus convinced that the Jedi were also a threat, Mitth'raw'nuruodo intercepted the Outbound Flight Project vessel and burned it to ash.

The Chiss ruling houses did not agree with Mitth'raw'nuruodo's decision to make a preemptive strike against an unconfirmed enemy. Instead they banished the renegade to a primitive jungle world far in the outer fringes of known Chiss space.

More than a decade passed. Across the galaxy, Palpatine declared himself Emperor. A Star Destroyer under the command of Captain Voss Parck chased the smuggler Booster Terrik into the fringes of the Unknown Regions, coming across Mitth'raw'nuruodo's exile planet. The unarmed alien humiliated the Imperial landing team, using the environment to destroy their landing ships and TIE fighters. Impressed, Captain Parck brought this brilliant alien back with him to the Empire for a personal audience with Palpatine.

The Emperor recognized the potential of this Chiss warrior and knew that Imperial anti-alien policies would keep him from growing too powerful. Known by his shortened core name, Thrawn entered formal Imperial military training.

When he emerged, Thrawn rose rapidly through the ranks. Many Imperial officers who shuddered at serving with an *alien* changed their tune when confronted with Thrawn's genius. By the Battle of Yavin, Thrawn was captain of the Imperial Star Destroyer *Vengeance*. The Emperor's dark-side Inquisitor Jerec often used the *Vengeance*, and

Palpatine trusted Thrawn to keep an eye on the ambitious Force user.

Thrawn had a second duty that took him away from the Empire for long stretches of time. In the Unknown Regions, he mapped great swaths of territory using the Star Destroyer *Admonitor*—ostensibly in service to the Emperor. Thrawn also reestablished contact with his confederates in Chiss space, who flocked to his banner in order to preserve their way of life. The Chiss had been battling many dark threats from the Unknown Regions, and many looked at Thrawn's brand of leadership and saw hope. On Nirauan, in the northern quadrant near the border of Wild Space, Thrawn built a vast information complex—the "Hand of Thrawn" —and made it his unofficial base of operations.

Ten months after Yavin, Captain Thrawn survived an insect infestation among the alien S'krrr. Soon after, the Emperor promoted Thrawn to vice admiral. Some believe that the official promotion was accompanied by a secret promotion to Grand Admiral. Thrawn certainly exhibited the skills, but Palpatine wouldn't accept more than twelve Grand Admirals at one time, and so any such advancement would neccessarily have been off the record.

Shortly before the Battle of Hoth, Thrawn worked with Darth Vader to remove Black Sun lieutenant Zekka Thyne from Corellia. Thrawn dressed as the bounty hunter Jodo Kast to pull off the scheme, tricking CorSec officer Corran Horn into playing a key role in Thyne's capture. By way of thanks, Vader gave Thrawn the authority to call upon his silent legion of Noghri death commandos. Immediately af-

ter, Thrawn planned the Imperial strategy for the Battle of Derra IV, where a Rebel convoy met a fiery end under the guns of Baron Fel.

Following the Battle of Hoth, the Imperial Navy was rocked by two traitors—Admiral Harkov and Grand Admiral Zaarin. Thrawn helped eliminate both. Midway through his campaign, Thrawn officially achieved the rank of Grand Admiral, promoted by Palpatine to replace Zaarin in the circle of twelve. After Zaarin's death, the Emperor sent Thrawn back into the Unknown Regions to continue his mapping mission. In the confusion of the Empire's defeat at Endor, the Rebel Alliance never confirmed the existence of the newest Grand Admiral.

Thrawn returned to his Hand of Thrawn base. He and his followers decimated the Ssi-ruuvi Imperium

and established bulwarks against other, more dire threats. Thrawn kept in touch with the Empire through Ysanne Isard, but didn't trust her. He arranged for many of his former compatriots to join his Imperial/Chiss army, Voss Parck—now an admiral— and Baron Fel among them.

Four years after Endor, following Isard's defeat in the Bacta War, word reached Thrawn that the Empire was on the verge of extinction. With the threats in the Unknown Regions quiet—at least for the moment— Thrawn returned to the Empire.

He came back virtually alone, leaving his Hand of Thrawn forces in the Unknown Regions. The Star Destroyer *Chimaera* became his flagship; Captain Gilad Pellaeon, his second in command. The Imperial Moffs couldn't help but cede control to the Emperor's last Grand Admiral, especially when his genius might restore their lost territory.

Months passed in busy preparation, then Thrawn struck. He was helped in his campaign by three items he obtained from the Emperor's storehouse on Wayland: a cloaking device, a cloning complex, and the mad Jedi clone Joruus C'baoth. C'baoth used his Force powers to coordinate the Imperial armed forces. In exchange, Thrawn tried to kidnap Leia Organa Solo and her unborn twins as C'baoth's "apprentices." The cloaking device proved crucial to the Battle of Sluis Van, in which Thrawn nearly captured a huge New Republic war fleet.

Thrawn began growing clone soldiers by the tens of thousands, using some to crew the Dreadnaughts in his newly acquired *Katana* fleet. Others formed underground "sleeper cells" on planets across the galaxy, as long-term backup should they ever be needed. Many clone pilots were grown from Baron Fel's template; another clone, Major Grodin Tierce, was a one-of-a-kind experiment combining a Royal Guard's reflexes with Thrawn's own tactical sense. Finally, the Grand Admiral sent one Spaarti cloning cylinder back to the Hand of Thrawn and began growing a clone of himself.

Thrawn used cloaked asteroids to blockade Coruscant and scored victory after victory. But amid his triumphs he never realized that Leia Organa Solo had turned his Noghri death commandos against him. In the middle of the Battle of Bilbringi, Thrawn's Noghri bodyguard Rukh stabbed the Grand Admiral through the heart.

Pellaeon eventually succeeded Thrawn as fleet commander, but the Empire shrank to a mere eight sectors in the Outer Rim. As Pellaeon prepared to make peace with the New Republic, Moff Disra and the prototype clone Grodin Tierce hired a talented actor to pose as the late Grand Admiral Thrawn. Most Imperials were desperate to believe their hero had returned, and never questioned Disra's story. Many planets, terrified by the specter of a second round of Thrawn conquests, surrendered without a fight.

Meanwhile, Luke Skywalker and Mara Jade discovered Nirauan and the Hand of Thrawn complex that had been hidden there for so many years. Admiral Parck, Baron Fel, and the Chiss soldiers had been busy over the intervening decade, fighting menaces in the Unknown Regions, but Thrawn had always told them that if he died he would return to them in ten years' time. In light of reports that Grand Admiral Thrawn was leading the Empire, it appeared the prophecy had come true.

Mara and Luke, however, discovered the truth. In a hidden chamber beneath the Hand of Thrawn complex they found Thrawn's clone, fully grown and waiting inside its incubation cylinder. The room flooded when the chamber walls crumbled, and Thrawn's clone died before it could ever be born. At the same time, at Yaga Minor, Moff Disra's ersatz Thrawn was revealed as a con artist named Flim. Disra's scheme fell to pieces. Ten years after his death, Grand Admiral Thrawn's career finally came to a close.

SUPREME CHANCELLOR FINIS VALORUM

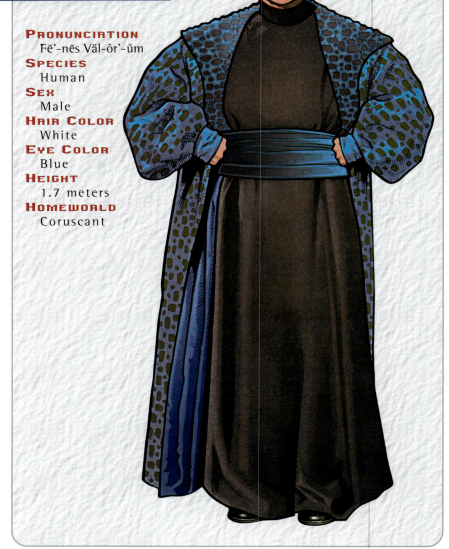

PRONUNCIATION
Fē'-nēs Väl-ôr'-ŭm

SPECIES
Human

SEX
Male

HAIR COLOR
White

EYE COLOR
Blue

HEIGHT
1.7 meters

HOMEWORLD
Coruscant

Tarsus Valorum, Tullius Valorum, Laeca Valorum ... A reading of the Valorum lineage sounds like the induction list for the Hall of Heroes. The Valorums were a renowned political dynasty.

As a young man, Finis Valorum was offered dozens of plum jobs by wealthy family friends, but he chose challenging assignments that would test his character. On Veccacopia, a recently discovered Republic protectorate, Valorum acted as a judge, serving under frontier conditions. Unlike his predecessors in the post, he worked hard to make a difference. When he learned that the native Cacops were hiring stand-ins to serve their sentences—and that his bailiffs couldn't tell the aliens apart—he instituted mandatory retinal scanning. By doing so he broke a corruption ring within Veccacopia's judicial office.

After Veccacopia, Valorum served with Republic police forces as a troop transport driver in the outlying regions. Later he held a post in Chancellor Kalpana's military advisory office. Not until his late thirties did Finis Valorum hold elective office. He switched his residency from Coruscant to Spira and, based in part on his family's reputation and political contacts, was elected Senator of the Lytton sector. Valorum rose quickly through the unseen pecking order that shaped the Republic Senate. He made fleeting friends and lasting enemies.

Valorum's election to the position of Supreme Chancellor less than eight years before the Battle of Naboo should have been a triumph, but it felt shallow and cynical. His enemies thought Valorum would be easy to control, while his allies supported him only because they felt he was the best prospect out of an unremarkable candidate pool. The public knew nothing about Finis other than his famous surname. He seemed remarkably lacking in charisma, and in the Senate lack of charisma was practically a criminal offense. Nevertheless he won a second four-year term in office, but only by the slimmest of margins.

When Valorum failed to turn the tide of apathy and dishonesty that had been eating away at the Republic, what little support he had quickly vanished. He turned to Senator Palpatine, one of his oldest political friends, for advice. Palpatine suggested that he institute a tax on the free trade zones in the Mid and Outer Rims, with a portion of the revenue going back to the Rim worlds for economic development. Valorum hoped the tax would relieve the Republic's fiscal debt, as well as act as a check on the corrupt Trade Federation.

The Trade Federation denounced Valorum's proposal, and Palpatine suggested hosting a summit on Eriadu to let all sides air their concerns. At first the Jedi believed Valorum was the assassination target of the anti–Trade Federation terrorists in the Nebula Front. By the time they learned that the Nebula Front planned to use Valorum's summit to kill the Trade Federation Directorate, it was too late to prevent the deaths of most of the members. Only the Nemoidian representatives survived.

Shortly after the Eriadu summit, a corruption scandal broke in the newsnets. The Chancellor's enemies brought forth accusations that the tax on the free trade zones had been passed, in part, to illegally enrich the Valorum Shipping Company on Eriadu. Valorum's protestations sounded hollow, and no one ever realized that the incriminating evidence had been planted. Suddenly Finis Valorum seemed to invite unflattering comparisons to the legendary Valorums of the past, and the suggestion that he had been elected on family reputation made the corruption charges seem more believable.

As if to spite his critics, Valorum threw himself into his job. He stamped out the Flail terrorist group despite an attempt on his life. He strengthened his ties with the Jedi, whom he had always admired despite a lack of Force sensitivity in his own family bloodline. But then the Trade Federation, goaded into action by Darth Sidious, blockaded Naboo to protest the taxation of the free trade zones. Most Senators blamed *Valorum* for triggering the debacle and lacking the charisma to hold the Republic together.

As the blockade dragged on and his political credibility dwindled, Valorum learned through Jedi Master Adi Gallia that the Trade Federation was planning something more than just a blockade. He secretly dispatched two Jedi ambassadors to defuse the situation, even though such an action required Senate approval.

Valorum gambled his political future to help his friend Senator Palpatine, for it was Palpatine's world that was under siege. The two men were such close associates that Palpatine's personal aide, Kinman Doriana, had become linked to Valorum's own aide, Sei Taria. But Valorum never expected Palpatine's betrayal.

When Naboo's Queen Amidala arrived on Coruscant, Valorum called a special Senate session to allow her to plead her case. He was shocked when she called for his removal from office. The Senate gleefully seized the opportunity to cast him out, and after a quick vote Palpatine assumed the mantle of Supreme Chancellor of the Republic.

GENERAL MAXIMILIAN VEERS

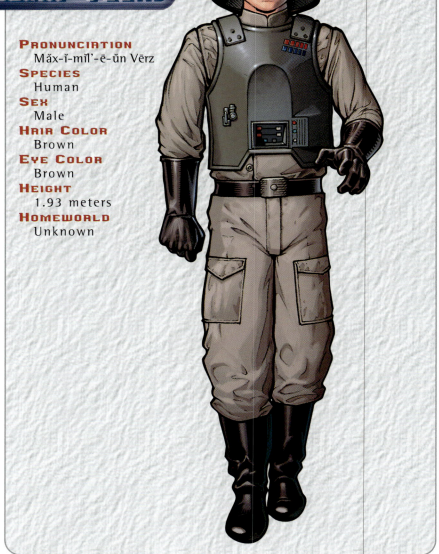

PRONUNCIATION
Măx-ĭ-mĭl'-ē-ŭn Vērz
SPECIES
Human
SEX
Male
HAIR COLOR
Brown
EYE COLOR
Brown
HEIGHT
1.93 meters
HOMEWORLD
Unknown

A soldier's soldier, Maximilian Veers served the Emperor's New Order with spotless snap and polish. The indignity of the post-Palpatine Empire drove him to his grave.

Veers came from a working-class family with few political connections, but with a long history of military service. Upon graduation from the Academy he assumed a junior lieutenant's commission in the Assault Armor Division of the Imperial Army. His first posting came under the command of General Irrv, a man whom Veers considered an idiot. When Irrv attempted negotiations with the savages of Culroon III—and was rewarded with a bloody betrayal—Lieutenant Veers crashed his AT-AT walker through the jungle canopy and rescued the besieged Imperial party. General Irrv was executed on the spot. For heroism under fire, Veers earned a field promotion to major.

Major Veers soon married and had one son, Zevulon. His wife died a few years later during a family vacation. To bury the pain of his sudden loss, Veers committed his every waking hour to the military. He told Zev to honor his mother's memory by becoming a loyal Imperial Youth.

By the time Maximilian Veers reached the rank of colonel, he had earned a posting on Corellia commanding the local Imperial garrison. His peers recognized his outstanding talent, and Veers regularly journeyed offworld to guest-lecture at AT-AT training courses at the Caridan Academy. But the colonel remained outside the aristocratic circles of cronyism that guaranteed rapid advancement. While less gifted officers became generals, Veers's career stagnated.

When Grand Moff Tarkin launched his new Death Star battle station, Veers received the opportunity for the elite advancement he had long craved. Based on their service records, Veers and several other top Carida instructors were told to report to the Death Star for immediate reassignment. Before Veers could do so, the battle station entered the Yavin system and launched into combat against the Rebel Alliance.

Veers was one of only a handful of Imperials who escaped the Death Star's destruction, fleeing in a shuttle that was then shot down by Rebel starfighters. He crashed in the jungles of Yavin 4 and survived on his own for days. Eventually Imperial forces supporting the Yavin blockade rescued him and returned him to the Empire.

The Death Star's destruction vaporized Veers's hopes of promotion. Returned to his garrison posting on Corellia, he did the best he could with unremarkable troops and a hostile populace. Shortly before the Battle of Derra IV, Colonel Veers's soldiers obliterated the fortified estate of Black Sun Lieutenant Zekka Thyne, greatly impressing Admiral Thrawn. On Thrawn's recommendation, Darth Vader reassigned Veers to the Super Star Destroyer *Executor* to replace a general who had "retired" one month prior. Veers's unorthodox promotion went unchallenged.

During the Battle of Hoth, General Veers completely routed an entrenched enemy with minimal Imperial loss of life. One of the casualties, however, was nearly Veers himself, when a snowspeeder rammed into the head of Blizzard One, Veers's command AT-AT. The general managed to throw himself into the neck corridor just before impact, but suffered severe injuries to his legs. Unwilling to accept replacement limbs in a culture that frowned on cyborgs, Veers moved about in a repulsorlift carriage from that day on.

Hailed as a hero for his victory at Hoth, Veers enjoyed his triumph for a few short months until his teenaged son disappeared while serving a young-adult COMPNOR stint. Maximilian Veers would have preferred his son's death to the truth he later learned—that Zevulon had defected to the Rebellion. General Veers tried to put the shame of his son's defection out of his mind. He returned to Lord Vader's service, but his troops were on a planetside mission when the *Executor* was destroyed at Endor.

The Empire's subsequent splintering dismayed Veers. He tried to find a position with a powerful warlord, but this time his close ties to Vader worked *against* him. Many Imperials who had feared Vader now took their revenge on officers such as Veers. During this time it's believed that Grand Admiral Thrawn used Veers as a genetic template for his specialized armies of clone soldiers.

While serving under the resur-rected Emperor Palpatine, Veers lost the motivation that had driven him all his life. Executor Sedriss, who hated Veers but couldn't deny his ability, demoted him to captain and placed him in charge of the reborn Emperor's ground troops. Veers's son Zevulon, now chief gunner aboard the New Republic Star Destroyer *Emancipator*, found himself in direct conflict with his father.

Confined to an armored assault chariot, "Captain" Veers led from the front, suicidally throwing his troops against the enemy in wave after exhausting wave. If he wanted to go out in a blaze of glory, he succeeded. In the Battle of Balmorra during Operation Shadow Hand, Veers led an army of stormtroopers and SD-9 battle droids against the fortified defenses of Balmorra's Governor Beltane. Maximilian Veers met his death under the combined blasterfire of a dozen of Beltane's SD-10s.

VERGERE

Vergere is an enigma, and makes no apologies for it. Her species is unknown and her motives seem utterly unfathomable.

Her people are called the Fosh, though others like her have yet to be found. It is possible the flightless avians were one of the many cultures exterminated by Emperor Palpatine.

Vergere was once a Jedi, and perhaps she still is. The diminutive Fosh served her apprenticeship under Thracia Cho Leem and became a full Jedi Knight many years prior to the Battle of Naboo. Two years after Chancellor Palpatine's election, Jedi Master Mace Windu dispatched Vergere to the distant Gardaji Rift to investigate rumors of alien visitors near the mysterious planet Zonama Sekot.

The aliens proved to be an advance strike force for the Yuuzhan Vong. When the Sekotans refused to surrender the secrets of their organic technology, the Yuuzhan Vong opened fire on them. Only Vergere's promise to depart aboard one of the enemy's extragalactic worldships saved the planet.

PRONUNCIATION
Vûr-jār'
SPECIES
Fosh
SEX
Female
HAIR COLOR
None
EYE COLOR
Black
HEIGHT
1.27 meters
HOMEWORLD
Unknown

The Yuuzhan Vong took a clinical interest in Vergere, but she hid the extent of her Jedi abilities. As the decades passed she became an amusing curiosity—a combination slave and exotic pet.

By the time of the Yuuzhan Vong's invasion, Vergere could be found among the priest caste, serving as a familiar to the priestess Elan. Following the Battle of Ithor, Vergere's mistress allowed herself to be captured by New Republic forces, with her familiar by her side. The Yuuzhan Vong collaborators of the Peace Brigade, not knowing of Elan's undercover mission, recaptured the "defectors" from the New Republic. Han Solo snatched them back, but when the Corellian learned the truth behind their charade, Elan had no choice but to unleash the weapon she'd hoped to use against the Jedi—a lungful of bo'tous spores.

The spores backfired, liquefying Elan's body. Vergere escaped at the last instant, but not before giving Solo a vial of her tears. The strange gift sent Mara Jade Skywalker's Yuuzhan Vong–induced illness into remission.

Vergere made her way back to the Yuuzhan Vong. After convincing the priests of the deception sect that she wasn't a double agent, she became an adviser to Warmaster Tsavong Lah. Executor Nom Anor hated Vergere, and the warmaster—no fan of Anor himself—encouraged the animosity by sending them both on a mission to capture the Solo twins at Myrkr. At first Vergere seemed to protect Jacen Solo; then she surrendered him into enemy custody.

Vergere's philosophy of the Force apparently goes far beyond the limited concept of good versus evil, but whether it has any use in a galaxy rocked by war is a question still left unanswered.

QUINLAN VOS

PRONUNCIATION
Kwĭn'-lŭn Vŏs
SPECIES
Kiffar (near human)
SEX
Male
HAIR COLOR
Black
EYE COLOR
Brown
HEIGHT
1.86 meters
HOMEWORLD
Kiffu

A near human belonging to Clan Vos, Quinlan Vos came from the planet Kiffu. Each Kiffar clan maintained judges called Guardians, and most Guardians possessed the ability to read psychic images simply by handling objects. Vos showed enormous potential in this area, and when his parents were murdered by Anzati killers, Jedi Master Tholme sent the boy to Coruscant to be trained as a Jedi. After Vos became a Jedi Knight, he took the Twi'lek Aayla Secura as his Padawan learner.

Approximately a year into Palpatine's tenure as Supreme Chancellor, Vos and his Padawan uncovered evidence of a new strain of narcotic spice called glitteryll—a synthesis of Rylothean ryll and Kessel glitterstim. When they got too close to the perpetrators, Aalya's clanmate Pol Secura wiped the memories of both Jedi. Aalya was kept on Ryloth as a slave, while Vos was dumped on Nar Shaddaa to die.

Vos awoke on the Smugglers' Moon remembering nothing of his former life as a Jedi. He could still wield the Force, but his conscious lack of Jedi scruples caused him to commit violent acts of vengeance. A Devaronian bounty hunter named Villie helped Vos survive a host of enemies, but only after placing a hefty wager that the Jedi would make it off the moon alive.

On Ryloth, Vos discovered his mind-wiped Padawan serving blankly at the side of Pol Secura. Enraged, Vos tortured the Twi'lek leader with Force lightning until he divulged the name of the mastermind of the glitteryll plot—Republic Senator Chom Frey Kaa. Vos and Villie traveled to Corus-

cant, but Mace Windu stopped Vos before he could murder Senator Kaa.

Shamed by his actions, Quinlan Vos submitted himself to Windu for retraining. Despite their best efforts, the Jedi Knights could not restore his memory. Darth Sidious, meanwhile, lamented Vos's return to the light, but knew the Jedi's time would come.

Soon after Vos's retraining, the Jedi Council sent him on a mission to the interdicted planet Dathomir. Among the native Witches he learned that one of their number, the evil Zalem, had discovered an ancient "Infinity Gate" buried beneath the

planet's surface by a long-vanished civilization. Zalem directed an Infinity Wave to destroy Coruscant, but Vos redirected the stream of energy to wipe out the Gate itself.

On his next mission Quinlan Vos returned to his homeworld. Kiffu's sister world Kiffex, a prison colony, had been overrun by Anzati. Vos teamed up with his former Master Tholme, as well as the Devaronian crook Villie, to thwart the Anzati Dark Jedi Volfe Karkko. At the conclusion of the adventure, his Padawan Aalya agreed to return to the Jedi Order.

WATTO

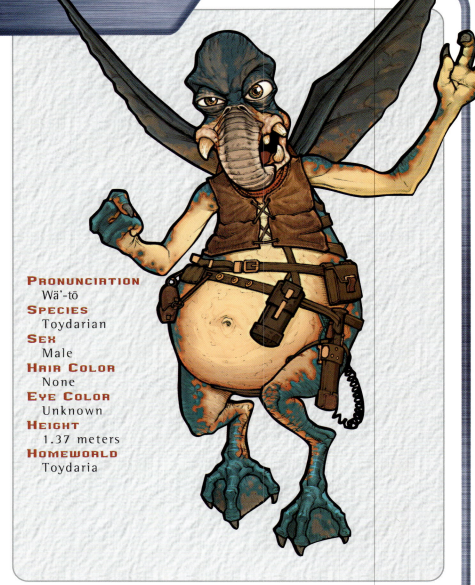

Old Watto is a dirty bird
Hot peggats in his purse
His flippers stink like bantha curd
His breath smells even worse
—Building graffiti on Mos Espa Way,
attributed to one W. Wald

The sight of such graffiti would have enraged Watto the junk dealer, for he despised insolence. But a part of him would have understood the sentiment behind the scrawl. Watto wasn't in the business of winning popularity contests, and he made no apologies for his abrasive personality. If people didn't like it, too bad for them. Life is unfair.

Watto loved to complain. *The suns are too hot, my slaves are too slow, the Jawas are trying to rob me blind.* And he felt that every gripe was justified a thousand times over. He knew he would never be as important a player as Jabba or Gardulla the Hutt, but always claimed it wasn't *his* fault. In Watto's nightmares, two heavy weights kept him from flying to the top of the heap—twin shackles labeled "other people's incompetence" and "my own rotten luck."

Watto's bitterness went back many decades, to his youth on Toydaria. The planet still suffers from cyclical climate changes, bringing about stretches of lean growing seasons approximately once every third decade. Toydarians, who consume huge amounts of high-energy, sugary foods, often saw the famines as opportunities to make war against their neighbors. As a young Toydarian, Watto enlisted in the army of the Ossiki Confederacy, whose soldiers used chemical warfare to poison the food stocks of rival confederacies. Ossiki's

PRONUNCIATION
Wä'-tō
SPECIES
Toydarian
SEX
Male
HAIR COLOR
None
EYE COLOR
Unknown
HEIGHT
1.37 meters
HOMEWORLD
Toydaria

leader stated simply, "If we can't have it, no one can." When the drought ended, so did the war. Watto, however, bore the scars for the rest of his life in the form of a broken left tusk and a lame leg.

Eventually Watto settled on Tatooine, where he drifted among the Jawa clans, learning the secrets of Tatooine's hidden economy and mastering some killer haggling techniques. Like the Jawas, Watto preferred to do business with off-worlders rather than the savvy Mos Espa locals. Newcomers were much easier to con.

Watto retained few personal belongings—he was stingy to a fault, and most of what he owned lay in piles in the junkyard behind his shop. His few major possessions, such as the hard-won slaves Anakin and Shmi Skywalker, were items that brought him status. Sometimes Watto carried a swagger stick or his favorite shisha oil-pipe. Watto had family on Toydaria and elsewhere, but he didn't keep in touch. He feared they would exploit his generosity and hit him up for handouts and favors.

Though Watto was one of the smaller dealers in the Mos Espa merchants' district, his merchandise stock was so eclectic that locals often stopped at his shop first when searching for rare parts. If a customer didn't have anything to barter, Watto insisted on payment in local Tatooine currency. Since the Hutts controlled the money exchanges, converting Republic credits into something spendable was often more trouble than it was worth.

Watto's greatest vice was gambling. His big wins on the Mos Espa Podraces encouraged him to bet even on the simplest things, but he always tried to guarantee that his bets were a sure thing. Watto's "lucky" chance cube was weighted so it would land only on red.

Anakin Skywalker was Watto's favorite slave, and when Qui-Gon Jinn wagered for Anakin's freedom, the Toydarian was certain he would soon own the ship of a very stupid outlander. Of course, Watto lost the Podrace wager, and when Qui-Gon came to claim the boy, the junk dealer felt as if he was losing more than money. "Take him," he said finally, his voice tinged with sadness and regret. Although Watto later hired a pack of thugs to "persuade" Qui-Gon to leave the boy behind, the scam failed.

Even Watto's lucky chance cube was gone—Watto suspected he'd left it lying on the floor of the Podrace hangar after that unlucky toss with the outlander. "Have you seen my chance cube?" he halfheartedly asked everyone who entered his store over the next few months. Despondent and alone, he would spend hours flitting through the streets of Mos Espa, searching aimlessly for his lost luck.

He treated Shmi Skywalker much kindlier after that, too. No longer would he launch into strings of Huttese curses when she made some repair he didn't like. In fact, he suddenly seemed uncomfortable around Shmi, knowing their master–servant relationship had changed, and not realizing what he should do about it. After six years Watto sold Shmi to Cliegg Lars, a moisture farmer out beyond Mos Eisley. He knew Shmi would be happy there. Besides, he told himself, he needed the money.

Ten years after he lost Anakin Skywalker in the Podracing wager, Watto's fortunes had declined and his health had deteriorated. He still owned his junk shop on Mos Espa Way, but he didn't own any slaves at all. Now quite old for a Toydarian, he complained about being on the downside of life and dreamed of wasted opportunities. Into this world Anakin Skywalker returned, all grown up. Watto greeted his former slave warmly and pointed him in the direction of his mother. Seeing Anakin reminded Watto of earlier, happier times, when he had his own private viewing box at the Podrace arena and thousands of credits riding on the outcome.

ZAM WESELL

"Zam Wesell" wasn't her real name; nor was her true form that of a young human female. This bounty hunter had the perfect disguise. As a shapeshifter, she could become anything at all.

Shapeshifters are rare in the galaxy, and Wesell's competitors tried to pin down her species in order to better exploit her weaknesses. Her familiarity with Republic culture implied that she wasn't a Protean or Polydroxol, while her ability to morph into almost any shape eliminated the likelihood that she was a Stennes Shifter. Most identified Wesell as a Shi'ido, which she did nothing to dispute. In truth she was one of the galaxy's few Clawdites. Like all Clawdites, Wesell could assume the form of almost any other species—but her ability to duplicate the features of a specific individual was limited.

This shapeshifter earned fame as a bounty hunter and assassin in the days of the Old Republic. When dealing with clients she wore the guise of the attractive human female Zam Wesell, both to build a reputation and to keep human males off balance. She preferred to hit her targets from afar, with either her long-range sniper rifle or her modified probe droids.

Wesell partnered with the greatest bounty hunter in the Old Republic, Jango Fett, to break into a maximum-security asteroid prison and break *out* the smuggler Bendix Fust. She and Jango then pursued the bounty on the head of the leader of the Bando Gora. Jango admired her skills and kept her on retainer to assist him with larger jobs; in this capacity Zam worked alongside other contract employees such as Aurra Sing and Vana Sage.

PRONUNCIATION
Zăm Wĕs'-ŭl
SPECIES
Clawdite
SEX
Unknown
(female form)
HAIR COLOR
Blond
EYE COLOR
Unknown
HEIGHT
1.68 meters
HOMEWORLD
Unknown

During the unrest caused by Count Dooku's separatist movement, Zam Wesell accepted a job from Jango to assassinate Senator Padmé Amidala of Naboo. She didn't ask from whom the order had originated; all that mattered were the credits.

Wesell used one of her remote probe droids to release crawling kouhuns into Senator Amidala's top-level Coruscant apartment, but the Senator's Jedi guardian, Anakin Skywalker, wiped out the insects. The other Jedi, Obi-Wan Kenobi, hopped atop the droid. Wesell, watching from her speeder, tried to remotely dislodge the hitchhiker and finally blew up the droid. But even this proved ineffective. Kenobi, now accompanied by his Padawan Anakin Skywalker, followed her in a high-speed chase through the traffic lanes.

Wesell hoped to lose them in a lower-level nightclub, but Obi-Wan Kenobi lopped off her right arm with his lightsaber. When Wesell prepared to name Jango Fett as the bounty hunter who'd hired her, Fett struck her with a Kamino saberdart. The dart's toxins raced through her amorphous interior and killed her in seconds.

MACE WINDU

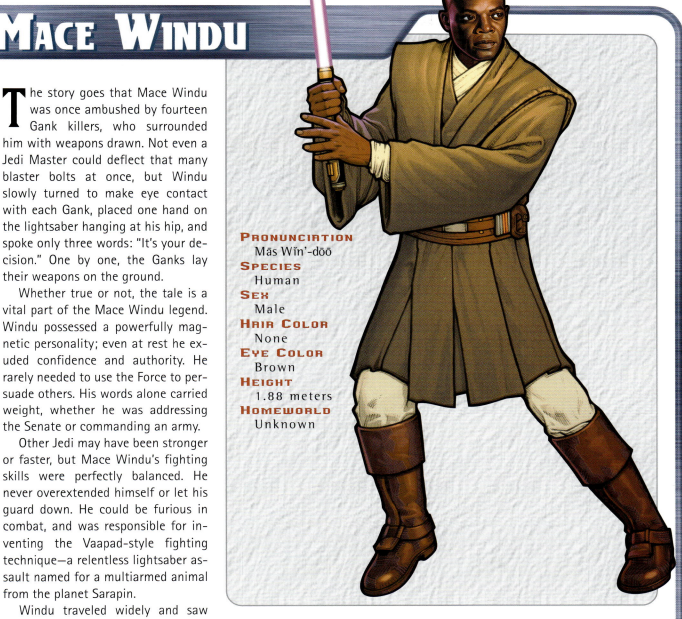

PRONUNCIATION
Mās Wĭn'-dōō

SPECIES
Human

SEX
Male

HAIR COLOR
None

EYE COLOR
Brown

HEIGHT
1.88 meters

HOMEWORLD
Unknown

The story goes that Mace Windu was once ambushed by fourteen Gank killers, who surrounded him with weapons drawn. Not even a Jedi Master could deflect that many blaster bolts at once, but Windu slowly turned to make eye contact with each Gank, placed one hand on the lightsaber hanging at his hip, and spoke only three words: "It's your decision." One by one, the Ganks lay their weapons on the ground.

Whether true or not, the tale is a vital part of the Mace Windu legend. Windu possessed a powerfully magnetic personality; even at rest he exuded confidence and authority. He rarely needed to use the Force to persuade others. His words alone carried weight, whether he was addressing the Senate or commanding an army.

Other Jedi may have been stronger or faster, but Mace Windu's fighting skills were perfectly balanced. He never overextended himself or let his guard down. He could be furious in combat, and was responsible for inventing the Vaapad-style fighting technique—a relentless lightsaber assault named for a multiarmed animal from the planet Sarapin.

Windu traveled widely and saw much as a Padawan, Knight, and Master. Though a member of the Jedi Order since infancy, he spent enough time on the planet of his birth to share his people's talent for raising deadly akk dogs. As a Padawan he served a tour on Wroona, fighting pirates aboard the primitive sailing ship *Temblor*. Later in his career he worked with Republic policing squads to contain the Arkanian Revolution and battled the renegade Arkanian mercenary known as Gorm the Dis-

solver. As a Jedi Master, Windu fought bravely in the Stark Hyperspace Conflict.

Master Windu helped train dozens of younger students within the Jedi Temple on Coruscant. After he rescued the infant Depa Billaba from space pirates, Windu frequently assisted Billaba in her Temple instruction. She, of course, became a great Jedi in her own right, earning a seat on the Council. Windu always expressed pride in his shining pupil.

Forty years old as of the Battle of Naboo, Mace Windu had served on the Jedi Council for more than a decade prior to that event. Despite his relative youth, Windu earned the title of senior representative of the Jedi Council, an honor he shared with Master Yoda. In most situations he acted as the Council's public spokesperson. Windu was also the official liaison between the Jedi and the Supreme Chancellor and he enjoyed a good rapport with Chancellor

Valorum. An effective diplomat, he was often called upon to mediate disputes between warring factions.

Approximately a year before the Naboo incident, Mace Windu received word that the aggressive Yinchorri—a species resistant to Jedi mind manipulation—had started a campaign of conquest. He assembled a team of Jedi, including several members of the Council, and led them to the Yinchorr system. None realized that the Yinchorri attacks had been orchestrated by Darth Sidious. As a result they walked into a deathtrap. Many Jedi died, including Council member Micah Giiett, before Windu's forces vanquished the Yinchorri. Windu recommended Ki-Adi-Mundi for Giiett's Council seat, though it was many months before the vacancy was filled.

Immediately prior to the Battle of Naboo, Chancellor Valorum asked Mace Windu to dispatch Jedi negotiators to Naboo to end the Trade Federation's blockade of that world. Windu sent his old friend Qui-Gon Jinn and Jinn's Padawan Obi-Wan Kenobi. Not long afterward, Qui-Gon returned to the Jedi Council with two startling pieces of news. The Sith were active again, and on distant Tatooine, Jinn had discovered a boy of unparalleled power in the Force.

Windu had long suspected that the balance of the Force was teetering on the edge of a chasm, and that dark Sith magic might plunge it into the abyss. Whether Anakin Skywalker could shore up that balance, who could say? Windu was far more concerned with finding Darth Maul and his elusive Sith counterpart.

Troubled by the growing threat of the dark side, Mace Windu spent long hours alone in meditation in the Jedi Council chamber. During high winds the tower creaked ever so slightly, and the noise was reminiscent of the stretching, groaning rigging of the sailing ship *Temblor*. Relaxed by the rhythmic sound, Windu closed his eyes and concentrated on the will of the Force.

Jedi business prevented him from making a breakthrough in his understanding of Jedi prophecy. Moreover, the nature of the missions convinced him of the dark side's gradual ascendancy. On Malastare, Windu set out to mediate a dispute between two factions and got caught up in a war orchestrated by Lannik terrorists. The terrorists used akk dogs from Windu's homeworld, and this led the Jedi Master to Nar Shaddaa, where he and Depa Billaba shut down an animal-smuggling ring.

Ten years after Naboo, Mace Windu found his hands full with former Jedi Count Dooku and his separatist movement. Windu, Yoda, and leading members of the Senate held frequent meetings with Chancellor Palpatine to discuss how to keep the situation from spiraling out of control. When Obi-Wan Kenobi discovered a mysterious clone army on Kamino, Master Windu decided that the Republic would have to strike against Dooku's forces.

Windu led two hundred Jedi Knights and Masters to Geonosis. Count Dooku counterattacked with his droid battalions and decimated the Jedi. Only the arrival of Master Yoda, at the head of the clone army, turned the tide in favor of the Republic. For his part, Mace Windu faced off against Jango Fett in the Geonosian execution arena, killing the bounty hunter and unwittingly unleashing his son Boba upon the galaxy.

PRINCE XIZOR

PRONUNCIATION
Shē'-zôr
SPECIES
Falleen
SEX
Male
HAIR COLOR
Black
EYE COLOR
Blue
HEIGHT
1.83 meters
HOMEWORLD
Falleen

Xizor, the Dark Prince, was once the third most powerful person in the galaxy, behind Emperor Palpatine and Darth Vader. Like them, Xizor is now dead, a casualty of his own ambition.

Born more than a century before the Battle of Yavin, Xizor never looked a day over thirty, thanks to his Falleen physiology and the army of personal trainers he could easily afford. Xizor was one of that rare species of humanoid reptiles hailing from the planet of the same name, near the Corellian Run. The Falleen possess powerful pheromones that can sway the emotions of other beings, and they exhibit a cruel disdain for non-Falleen.

Xizor was the only son of King Haxim, a provincial ruler on Falleen. Groomed to succeed his father on the throne, he instead pursued an off-world education. Over the decades he traveled the galaxy, establishing a thriving shipping concern, Xizor Transport Systems, and enmeshed himself into the power structure of the crime syndicate known as the Black Sun.

After Darth Maul murdered all of Black Sun's vigos and syndicate leader Alexi Garyn, just prior to the Battle of Naboo, Xizor rose rapidly through the reorganized power structure. When Moff Fliry Vorru of Corellia became an annoyance to Palpatine, Xizor arranged to have him removed from power and imprisoned on Kessel. Approximately seven years before the Battle of Yavin, Xizor became Black Sun's undisputed leader.

But it was a hollow victory for the Dark Prince. Back on his homeworld, two hundred thousand Falleen were exterminated by Darth Vader in an effort to contain a rampaging Imperial bioweapon. Every member of Xizor's family, save his niece Savan, perished in the sterilization. Xizor used Black Sun's resources to erase every record that linked him to the victims, then vowed to exact revenge upon Lord Vader.

Xizor amassed incalculable wealth as head of Black Sun. He purchased a lifelike human replica droid named Guri for nine million credits, and trained her to be his second in command. He spent another fortune on the MandalMotors StarViper *Virago* and the capital warship *Vendetta*, and constructed a luxury skyhook satellite, the *Falleen's Fist*, that remained tethered in a low Coruscant orbit. He also developed an appreciation for beautiful women. No woman who breathed Xizor's pheromones ever resisted his advances.

As the years passed, Xizor put the Besadii Hutt clan in his pocket by helping Durga the Hutt become clan leader, then making him one of Black Sun's nine lieutenants, or vigos. After the Battle of Yavin, many of Xizor's schemes came to a head. He attempted to assume control of the Kuat shipyards by seizing them from their family owner, Kuat of Kuat. Angered, Kuat tried to take down Xizor by creating a false holorecording implicating the Dark Prince in the deaths of Owen and Beru Lars, Luke Skywalker's guardians. Kuat hoped the specious evidence would pit the Rebel Alliance against Black Sun, but he was unable to carry out his scheme.

Xizor also convinced Emperor Palpatine to eliminate the Bounty Hunters' Guild so that he would have the opportunity to create a mercenary force of freelance hunters. Boba Fett, hired to initiate Xizor's stratagem, kicked off the Bounty Hunter Wars. Xizor simultaneously arranged for the overthrow of Kud'ar Mub'at, the arachnid middleman for the bounty hunting industry. Mub'at's offspring Balancesheet, more friendly to Black Sun interests than its parent, murdered Mub'at and accepted Xizor's help in starting a new career.

Xizor's hatred for Darth Vader underscored everything he did. When he learned that Rebel hero Luke Skywalker was actually Vader's *son*, Xizor swore he would take them both down. He arranged for Skywalker's assassination, knowing that such an action would enrage Vader and diminish the Sith Lord's status in Palpatine's court. At the same time, Xizor used his influence with the Emperor to engineer the Rebel Alliance's "capture" of the second Death Star's plans, over Vader's objections.

Leia Organa contacted Black Sun in order to find out who was behind the assassination attempts on Luke, not realizing that Xizor was pulling all the strings. In his castle on Coruscant, Xizor tried to seduce the Princess, but Leia's response was a solid knee to Xizor's groin. Humiliated, the Dark Prince imprisoned her, but she was soon freed by Luke Skywalker and Lando Calrissian. On his way out, Calrissian dropped a thermal detonator down a waste chute, and the castle imploded.

Xizor escaped to the *Falleen's Fist* and ordered his private navy to destroy the fleeing *Millennium Falcon*. The arrival of Darth Vader's *Executor* ironically saved the smuggling ship. Vader had learned of Xizor's attempts to kill his son, and he offered the Dark Prince two minutes to surrender. Xizor refused. With pleasure, Vader destroyed the skyhook and everyone aboard it.

Black Sun crumbled with Xizor's death. His niece Savan attempted to salvage the syndicate, but she was taken into custody by Han Solo, Leia Organa, and Lando Calrissian. Though Black Sun eventually rose again, it did so without the leadership of a Falleen.

YODA

PRONUNCIATION
Yō'-dä
SPECIES
Unknown
SEX
Male
HAIR COLOR
White
EYE COLOR
Greenish
HEIGHT
0.66 meter
HOMEWORLD
Unknown

The highest-ranking Jedi to escape the Purge, Yoda was nine hundred years old at the time of his passing into the Force. He weathered catastrophes; he saw dynasties rise and fall. Yoda looked on as thousands of his students and colleagues died over the centuries. Such is the curse of a long life.

Of course, not every Jedi was fond of Yoda. Preteen students who had not yet been selected as Padawan learners considered him the hardest instructor in the Temple. He was severely conservative, drilling his young charges in mental control and physical exercise. Even the youngest Jedi hopefuls, such as the training class dubbed the "Mighty Bear Clan," received lightsaber training from Yoda. Only upon leaving the Temple did many Jedi students realize just how much they had learned under his tutelage.

Master Yoda believed Jedi traditions existed for a reason. He advocated Jedi training beginning in infancy and sharply criticized reformers such as Djinn Altis who suggested a less rigid approach. He scorned criticisms that the Jedi were "baby snatchers," and in any argument concerning instruction he was sure to bring up the fact that he'd been training Jedi for eight hundred years.

Yoda's long career began approximately a century after Darth Bane sent the Sith Order into hiding. He became a Jedi Master at one hundred years of age, and trained dozens of Padawans to Knighthood in galaxy-spanning adventures. One such Padawan, a tiny Kushiban named Ikrit, trained under Yoda in the Jedi Master's mid-four-hundreds. Many years later, after a period of suspended animation, Ikrit sacrificed his life during the Yuuzhan Vong invasion.

Around Yoda's six hundredth birthday, the Jedi training ship *Chu'unthor* crashed on Dathomir. Although not a member of the Jedi Council at the time, Yoda held so much influence within the Order that he was one of the three Masters dispatched to retrieve the vessel. Though Yoda's first trip to Dathomir only enraged the planet's Force-using Witches, he later returned to negotiate a peaceful settlement. Successes such as the *Chu'unthor* mediation eventually resulted in Yoda's appointment to the Jedi Council.

Centuries passed. Yoda trained Ki-Adi-Mundi to Knighthood, then retired from direct Master–Padawan coaching to take a role as a staff instructor in the Jedi Temple. Yoda specialized in teaching the unifying Force to the youngest Temple students; graduates of his demanding classes included Qu Rahn and Obi-

Wan Kenobi. Yoda kept a small room in the Jedi Temple, constructed with low cozy ceilings and a charcoal-burning fireplace to place him in a meditative state of mind. His few ornamentations included a set of stained-glass windows, which he built by hand.

Easily the oldest member of the Jedi Council—and one of the two senior members, with Mace Windu—Yoda kept a dignified public persona. He opened up only around his peers, a small group consisting of the most distinguished members of the Order. In their company Yoda often dis-

played a mischievous sense of humor and a proclivity for practical jokes, something his students would have found difficult to imagine.

A dozen years before the Battle of Naboo, Yoda nearly died when Xanatos, a former student of Qui-Gon Jinn's, planted a bomb in the Jedi Temple's Room of a Thousand Fountains. Qui-Gon and Obi-Wan thwarted Xanatos's plot, but the attack highlighted Yoda's importance as a symbol for the Jedi Order. After that, the galaxy seemed to grow increasingly restless, in sync with the Republic's decline.

On several occasions Yoda shed blood with his green-bladed lightsaber—only out of necessity, never by choice. He slew many Yinchorri warriors when the reptilian aliens attacked the Jedi Temple. A year later, not long before the Battle of Naboo, Yoda exterminated a squad of Bartokk assassins and foiled their plot to destroy the Corulag academy.

With the Trade Federation's blockade of Naboo, Yoda sensed that great wheels had been set in motion, and tried to divine the future through the unifying Force, a skill for which he had always exhibited a talent. When Qui-Gon Jinn brought nine-year-old Anakin Skywalker before the Jedi Council, Yoda didn't waste time in trying to make the boy feel comfortable. Instead, he asked him penetrating questions about fear and anger. He argued passionately among his colleagues that Anakin was too dangerous to be trained, despite the potential that the boy might be the Chosen One of ancient prophecy. Though Yoda eventually acceded to Qui-Gon's dying request and permitted Anakin's acceptance into the ranks of Padawans, he did so with the gravest of reservations.

At first, Yoda's qualms seemed groundless. Over the next decade Anakin Skywalker became a talented Padawan, if not quite a model student. But Yoda saw signs of the dark side's ascendance, both in the existence of an undiscovered Sith and in his own inability to foresee an assassination attempt on Senator Padmé Amidala. When war could be postponed no longer, General Yoda led a clone army against Dooku's forces on Geonosis, and nearly bested the separatist leader in personal lightsaber combat.

The Clone Wars began, pitting the

Republic's clone soldiers against the droid armies of Dooku and his wealthy corporate backers. Chancellor Palpatine, having been granted emergency powers that allowed him to supersede the Senate, eventually declared himself Emperor. Yoda's worst fears were confirmed when Anakin Skywalker became Darth Vader and committed himself to the dark side as Palpatine's apprentice. Yoda escaped the destruction of the Jedi and fled to Dagobah, counting on the hope that Anakin's twin children were safe in the care of Bail Organa and Owen Lars.

On Dagobah, Yoda built a simple mud hut and meditated on the Force exuded by the bog planet's teeming ecosystem. A few humans—pathetic survivors of an old survey ship—already lived in the swamps, but they didn't cross paths with the Jedi Master. Soon a Dark Jedi from Bpfassh arrived on Dagobah, having commandeered a starship belonging to Jorj Car'das. Yoda defeated the Bpfasshi in a titanic Force battle and healed the injured Car'das, who went on to found a smuggling empire. Years later Car'das returned to Dagobah to demand even more from Yoda. Instead Yoda scolded him for wasting his life, and a shamed Car'das retired to the Kathol sector. Talon Karrde took control of Car'das's operation.

Obi-Wan Kenobi fell in battle with Darth Vader aboard the Death Star, and Yoda felt the shudder in the Force. Soon, he found he could communicate with Obi-Wan's spirit. Yoda and Kenobi talked of Luke Skywalker and the youth's great potential to defeat the evil of Vader. Yoda also considered a contingency plan using Leia Organa, whom he considered the "other hope," should Skywalker fail.

After the Battle of Yavin, Yoda had to turn aside several visitors. The first, Alliance historian Arhul Hextrophon, left Dagobah under a solemn vow not to reveal the Jedi Master's location. Later, the Force-sensitive children Zak and Tash Arranda came to the swamp planet and ran afoul of the survey ship survivors, who had descended into cannibalism. Yoda helped the Arrandas escape and promised them they would one day grow strong in the Force.

Just after the Battle of Hoth, Luke Skywalker journeyed to Dagobah to begin his Jedi training. Though Yoda protested that Luke was by now too old, he knew the son of Anakin Skywalker could be the catalyst by which the balance of light could be restored to the Force. Yoda and Obi-Wan kept the truth of Luke's relationship to Vader a secret, for fear it could lure the young man to the dark side. But Skywalker abandoned his training prematurely, rushing off to face Darth Vader at Cloud City, and barely escaping with his life.

Yoda viewed Luke Skywalker's first confrontation with Vader as a trial by fire. When Skywalker returned to Dagobah, Yoda revealed to him that his training was finished—except for a rematch with Vader, one last showdown between father and son. Yoda knew he had trained his final student. Closing his eyes forever, the Jedi Master joined Obi-Wan Kenobi—and, soon, Anakin Skywalker—in the light of the Force.

WARLORD ZSINJ

PRONUNCIATION
Zĭnj
SPECIES
Human
SEX
Male
HAIR COLOR
Brown (graying)
EYE COLOR
Brown
HEIGHT
1.68 meters
HOMEWORLD
Fondor

Some remember Zsinj as a buffoon; others as a psychopath. Declassified reports from New Republic Intelligence paint a picture of a manipulative genius who considered misdirection the greatest weapon of all.

Given how quickly he went rogue, Zsinj's early career seems incongruous for its diligence. After graduation from the Imperial Naval Academy, Zsinj took command of the *Iron Fist*—an old *Victory*-class Star Destroyer one step away from the scrapyard. Despite his undistinguished posting, Captain Zsinj developed innovative battle tactics and soon earned command of the most prestigious Imperial battleships. The VSD *Iron Fist* eventually became part of Grand Admiral Thrawn's fleet in the Unknown Regions.

Shortly after the Battle of Yavin, Captain Zsinj received word from Emperor Palpatine that the new Imperial prison on Dathomir was too tempting an opportunity for the planet's primitive, Force-wielding Nightsisters. Zsinj bombarded the prison from orbit, destroying every parked shuttle and transport. For his quick thinking in stranding the Nightsisters, the Emperor promoted Zsinj to admiral and gave him the *Brawl*, one of the first four Super Star Destroyers to come out of the Kuat shipyards.

Admiral Zsinj renamed his new ship *Iron Fist* in honor of his first command. Over the next several years he became the de facto ruler of the Quelii sector, a section of the Outer Rim that encompassed the planet Dathomir.

Palpatine's death at Endor splintered the Empire. Zsinj, like the other self-proclaimed Imperial warlords, refused to recognize the authority of Sate Pestage. He cut the Quelii sector off from Imperial authority while coyly sending representatives to the fledgling New Republic. The *Iron Fist* was sufficient to scare off any threats to Zsinj's borders. After Ysanne Isard lost control of Coruscant, Zsinj absorbed many Imperial defectors, and became the most powerful warlord.

Typical of Warlord Zsinj's modus operandi were his "cells" of economic support. Isolated planets—and sometimes just corporations on those planets such as Belthu, Todirium, and Xartun provided ore or transparisteel to fuel Zsinj's war machine. Rarely did one cell know of the existence of any other, maximizing secrecy and therefore Zsinj's degree of control.

Zsinj also created a special military/police squad called the Raptors, who were to his domain what stormtroopers were to Palpatine's. Zsinj's fleet carriers boasted squadrons of TIE Raptors, agile starfighters with four evenly spaced solar panels sticking straight out from their ball cockpits like the fins of hungry narkaa.

Save for his longtime aide, General Melvar, few knew the true Zsinj. He encouraged his enemies to draw mistaken conclusions. The *Iron Fist* featured a false bridge to which he would welcome visitors, then treat them to staged tours of his operation. In the same vein, he created a duplicate of the legendary 181st fighter wing—including a "Baron Fel" played by an actor—to fool enemies and allies alike.

Zsinj also kept many plots running simultaneously. Projects developed by his scientists and engineers included:
• Project Chubar, the genetic manipulation of so-called primitives such as Gamorreans and Ewoks to create superintelligent agents.
• Project Moort, the use of miniature parasite droids to reveal the whereabouts of enemy ships.
• Project Minefield, a massive brainwashing program turning prominent Sullustans, Twi'leks, and other nonhumans into sleeper agents.

Warlord Zsinj arrogantly fought both the New Republic and the post-Isard Empire. In response, a task force under the command of General Han Solo left on an anti-Zsinj campaign just prior to the Bacta War. Zsinj's brutal attacks on New Alderaan and Selaggis's colony moon of Selacron galvanized Solo, who put his best efforts into locating and obliterating the *Iron Fist*. But it was the saboteur-pilots of Wedge Antilles's Wraith Squadron who provided the means to cripple the warlord.

The Wraiths captured Zsinj's corvette, the *Night Caller*, and posed as the ship's standard crew. In the Battle of Ession, Zsinj lost his Star Destroyer the *Implacable* because of the *Night Caller*'s surprise betrayal.

The Wraiths then posed as the Hawk-bat pirates on Halmad, working their way into Zsinj's roster of freelance mercenaries. When the warlord tried to steal a second Super Star Destroyer—the unfinished *Razor's Kiss*—from the stardocks at Kuat, Wraith saboteurs ensured that Zsinj left Kuat empty-handed.

Warlord Zsinj secretly gathered the scraps of the wrecked *Razor's Kiss*, and while his enemies were preoccupied with Project Funeral—a massive assassination campaign utilizing elements of Project Minefield—Zsinj cobbled the wreckage together into a facsimile of the *Iron Fist*. When Solo's forces caught up with him at Selaggis, the warlord hid the *Iron Fist* in the light-absorbing shadow of an orbital nightcloak and jumped the ship to hyperspace. He then blew up the decoy Super Star Destroyer.

General Solo, convinced he'd destroyed the *Iron Fist*, returned to Coruscant. Zsinj limped back to Rancor Base, his ten-kilometer orbital dock above Dathomir.

Solo soon returned to confront Zsinj, albeit unintentionally, during his ill-fated courtship of Leia Organa. Arriving at Dathomir, Solo's *Millennium Falcon* went to ground to avoid the warlord's navy.

Zsinj negotiated with Dathomir's Nightsisters for Solo's head. But Nightsister leader Gethzerion double-crossed him, murdering General Melvar and stealing an armed transport. Gethzerion and her followers made it as far as Dathomir orbit, where Zsinj's Star Destroyers blasted them to bits.

When the Hapan fleet arrived, Zsinj prepared for the fight of his life. His forces battled with stubborn desperation, realizing that their era had reached its end. Warlord Zsinj died when the *Millennium Falcon* fired a pair of concussion missiles into the *Iron Fist*'s bridge.

ZUCKUSS

Hunters and marks alike called him "the Uncanny One." Yet the question remains: if he had such a knack for prognostication, why didn't he stick with the winning side?

A member of the Gand subspecies called "the breathers," Zuckuss left the ammonia mists of his homeworld to seek out employment as a bounty hunter. His family boasted a three-century heritage as Gand findsmen—trackers who use religious rituals to locate their quarry amid the planet's swirling fog. Zuckuss was among the first to practice the trade offworld.

He met with immediate success. The arcane primitivism of the findsman rituals uncovered the whereabouts of hidden targets and even offered glimpses into the future. Zuckuss soon came to the attention of the Hutts, and before long had his pick of jobs from Jabba, Embra, and other representatives of the clans.

Most Gands do not breathe, taking in everything they need through their food. As a rare breathing Gand, Zuckuss wore a cumbersome respirator that supplied him with ammonia-saturated air. More important, the respirator protected him from poisonous oxygen, which could scour his lungs like acid. Zuckuss armed himself with ammonia bombs—toxic to most species—and a snare rifle that could fire a tangle of shockstun spray.

Zuckuss's cosmopolitanism caused him to turn his back on traditional Gand ways. His people habitually refer to themselves in the third person, allowing only those who have done great deeds in the eyes of the community to use the pronoun *I*. Zuckuss rejected community restrictions on his behavior. Sometimes he called

PRONUNCIATION
Zŭk'-ŭs
SPECIES
Gand
SEX
Male
HAIR COLOR
None
EYE COLOR
Silver
HEIGHT
1.5 meters
HOMEWORLD
Gand

himself Zuckuss; often he referred to himself in the first person as evidence of his own achievements. His fellow Gands considered him insane.

Jabba suggested that Zuckuss partner with the mechanical bounty hunter 4-LOM. The droid's cold logic provided a fine counterpunch to the Uncanny One's prescient superstition. Both hunters worked for Embra the Hutt in the search for the Yavin Vassilika, but Zuckuss decided he could achieve greater success as a member of the Bounty Hunters' Guild. Splitting with 4-LOM, he joined the guild shortly after the Battle of Yavin.

Zuckuss's previous record counted for nothing with the other guild members—to them, he was "the new guy." Cradossk, head of the guild, paired Zuckuss with his son Bossk. On one of their first missions together, Zuckuss and Bossk went after accountant Nil Posondum. Rival hunter Boba Fett outsmarted and humiliated them both.

Fett expressed his desire to join the guild, and Cradossk soon accepted him as a full member. Zuckuss foresaw this as an omen of disaster, but soon had other problems to worry about. Cradossk tried to recruit him as his personal spy, and outwardly Zuckuss agreed, but privately he decided to play both sides of the fence.

Promising Cradossk he would help eliminate his ambitious son Bossk, Zuckuss accompanied Bossk, IG-88, Boba Fett, and a mercenary named D'harhan to the planet of the Shell Hutts to claim a bounty. Zuckuss himself didn't lift a finger against Bossk, but he distracted Cradossk long enough for Bossk to bare his fangs and rip out his father's throat.

The death of Cradossk split the guild into two warring factions, which had been Fett's goal all along. Zuckuss stuck with Bossk's Guild Reform Committee and hoped to survive the infighting. Not long after, he and Bossk teamed up with Fett to capture Imperial defector Trhin Voss'on't. Again, Fett outwitted them and claimed the bounty.

Following that fiasco Zuckuss abandoned the remnants of the Bounty Hunters' Guild and hooked up again with 4-LOM. The droid was pleased to continue his personal study of Zuckuss's intuition. By now Zuckuss had attracted admirers back on Gand, and a group of Gand venture capitalists funded Zuckuss's commission of a customized Byblos G-1A transport, which he christened the *Mist Hunter*.

For several years Zuckuss and 4-LOM scored impressive captures, until the day a panicked mark tore the respirator off Zuckuss's face. Reflexively he swallowed several breaths of oxygen, scorching his lungs. Unless he received transplanted lungs, he would die within a month.

To help pay expenses, the hunters captured Imperial Governor Nardix on behalf of the Rebel Alliance, risking the wrath of the Empire. Thus, when they met with Darth Vader aboard the Super Star Destroyer *Executor*, Zuckuss was afraid the Dark Lord would call him out on the Nardix bounty, but Vader let them go in peace.

Their target was the Corellian Han Solo, and Zuckuss and 4-LOM decided the best way to get close to Solo was to infiltrate the Alliance. In the *Mist Hunter* they rescued a transport filled with Rebel soldiers and returned with them safely to the fleet. But instead of betraying the Rebels, Zuckuss decided to join them.

The Rebel medical droids healed his ravaged lungs. Zuckuss and 4-LOM trained with Alliance Special Forces for their first mission—stealing Han Solo's carbonite slab from Boba Fett. To test his cover, Zuckuss accompanied several fellow hunters on a mission for Domina Tagge, then he and 4-LOM posed as their former mercenary selves to recover Solo on the Alliance's behalf.

This mission ended in total failure. Four-LOM, horribly damaged, required a complete rebuild—which changed his personality. Zuckuss began questioning his hasty decision to join the Rebellion, especially now that he had healthy new lungs. Quietly, both he and 4-LOM left Alliance service. They teamed up after Jabba's death to capture the gambler Drawmas Sma'Da, but from that point on they largely worked alone.

As the Rebel Alliance transformed into the New Republic, Zuckuss had ample reason to regret his career decision. Had he only stuck with the Rebels, he could have won a fat government contract, or a powerful military posting. Discouraged, Zuckuss continued freelance bounty hunting in the Outer Rim, though he never regained his former level of success.

APPENDIX: Other Personages of Note

ELEGOS AND RELEQY A'KLA
El'-ĕ-gōs and Rĕ'-lĕ-kĕ Ä'-klä

Elegos and his daughter Releqy, golden-furred Caamasi, were rescued from pirates on Kerilt by Corran Horn. Elegos became Corran's servant, and later helped the Caamasi Remnant on Kerilt relocate to Susevfi. He became a respected New Republic diplomat, helping Leia Organa Solo during the search for the Caamas Document. During the Yuuzhan Vong invasion, Elegos tried to negotiate with Commander Shedao Shai, and died at Shai's hands. Releqy A'Kla currently serves as a Senate liaison.

MAS AMEDDA
Mäs Ä-mē'-dä

A Chagrian from Champala, Mas Amedda became vice chair of the Senate months before Valorum's ouster. His power increased under Palpatine, and he strongly supported the move granting the Chancellor emergency war powers.

ACE AZZAMEEN
Ās Ä'-zä-mēn

This Rebel pilot from a successful shipping family helped the Alliance steal the Imperial shuttle *Tydirium* from an orbital outpost at Zhar just prior to the Battle of Endor.

BLACKHOLE
Blăk-hōl'

A former prophet of the dark side, Blackhole was a mysterious figure who masterminded covert Imperial Intelligence under Ysanne Isard. Behind his holographic illusions he was a frail old man, but his absolute control of information earned him the elite title of Emperor's Hand.

EMPATOJAYOS BRAND
Ĕm-pă-tō-jä'-yōs Brănd

This Jedi Knight survived the Purge and was saved from death by the Ganathans, who gave him a cyborg body and made him their king. Brand became one with the Force on Onderon, taking the reborn Emperor's spirit with him.

ADALRIC BRANDL
Ä-däl'-rĭc Brăn'-dŭl

A stage actor before becoming one of Palpatine's Jedi-hunting Inquisitors, the dignified Adalric Brandl struggled with his dedication to the dark side. He fathered one son, Jaalib.

JORUUS C'BAOTH
Jō-rōōs' Sŭ-bā'-ŏth

An insane clone of the Jedi Master Jorus C'baoth, Joruus assisted Grand Admiral Thrawn in waging war against the New Republic before being killed by Mara Jade on Wayland.

CILGHAL
Sĭl'-gäl

A Jedi Master in Luke Skywalker's new Jedi Order, the Mon Calamari known as Cilghal uses her Force abilities to heal the sick. She was one of Luke's first academy students and earned fame for curing Mon Mothma of a degenerative molecular poison. Tekli, a young female Chadra-Fan, is Cilghal's Jedi apprentice.

GENERAL AIREN CRACKEN
A'-rĕn Krä'-kĕn

On Imperial-held Contruum, Airen Cracken formed "Cracken's Crew" to sabotage the occupation force. After joining the Alliance he used his skills to advise special forces, later becoming a general and New Republic Intelligence director. General Cracken commanded all *official* intelligence operations, as opposed to the secret internal jobs of Admiral Drayson's Alpha Blue. Cracken's son Pash is a respected starfighter pilot.

THE DARK WOMAN
Surrendering her name in service to the Force, "the Dark Woman" trained both Ki-Adi-Mundi and Aurra Sing. Her failure with Aurra made the Dark Woman unpopular with the Jedi Council. Two years after the Battle of Naboo she took over A'Sharad Hett's Jedi training. The Dark Woman died shortly before the Battle of Yavin, when Darth Vader discovered her hiding on a Rim world.

ADMIRAL HIRAM DRAYSON
Hĭ'-räm Drā'-sŭn

Hailing from Chandrila, this colleague of Mon Mothma joined the Alliance navy and rose to become New Republic commander of Coruscant's defensive fleet. Following the defeat of Thrawn, Drayson helped create the top-secret intelligence agency Alpha Blue, which uncovered vital information on Nil Spaar during the Black Fleet Crisis. Drayson retired from service just prior to the Yuuzhan Vong invasion.

HOHASS "RUNT" EKWESH
Hō'-häs Ĕk'-wĕsh

Short in stature for a Thakwaash, Hohass Ekwesh joined the New Republic military after the Battle of Endor. Like all members of his species, he possessed multiple personalities, with each

"mind" exhibiting unique abilities and dispositions. Runt became one of the founding members of Wraith Squadron and fought in the campaign against Warlord Zsinj. He worked as the squadron's physical trainer and kept the Wraiths in good spirits as their unofficial morale officer.

JAGGED FEL
Jäg'-gĕd Fĕl

Son of the legendary Baron Fel, Jagged Fel grew up in the Unknown Regions and rose to command a Chiss household starfighter phalanx named Spike

Squadron. He has grown close to Jaina Solo during the Yuuzhan Vong war.

GALLANDRO
Gä-län'-drō

An orphan and ex-soldier, Gallandro was said to have had the fastest draw in the galaxy. His only real competition as a gunslinger came in the form of Han Solo, who clashed with Gallandro in the years before the Battle of Yavin. Gallandro died on Dellalt when he triggered a treasure vault's defensive laser system. He was survived by his infant daughter Anja, who grew up blaming Han Solo for her father's death.

ZAKARISZ GHENT
Zä-kär'-ĭz Gĕnt

Zakarisz Ghent of Baroli earned a reputation as a legendary computer slicer during his time with Talon Karrde's crew, and as a result he eventually became chief of cryptography for the New Republic.

VILMARH "VILLIE" GRAHRK
Vĭl'-mär "Vĭl'-lē" Grä-rkh

The infamous Devaronian bounty hunter Vilmarh "Villie" Grahrk had no loyalty to anyone or anything except the almighty credit. Prior to the Battle of Naboo, he double- and triple-crossed his employers on Ootoola, and later worked for Darth Sidious against the Jedi Knights on Yinchorr. After Naboo, Villie assisted Quinlan Vos after the Jedi lost his memory, betraying Vos whenever it appeared he could make more money that way. Villie flew a self-aware ship called the *Inferno*.

A'SHARAD HETT
Ä'-shä-räd Hĕt

Son of the great Jedi Sharad Hett, A'Sharad was raised among the Tusken

Raiders of Tatooine, and became the Padawan learner of Ki-Adi-Mundi following his father's death. After A'Sharad accidentally brushed the dark side, the Dark Woman took over his Jedi training.

LORD HOTH
Hŏth

A thousand years in the past, this aged Jedi Master led the Army of Light in epic combat against Darth Bane, Lord Kaan, and the Brotherhood of Darkness on Ruusan.

QUEEN JAMILLIA
Jä-mĭl'-lä

After the conclusion of Queen Amidala's eight-year reign, the young Queen Jamillia assumed the throne. She cannily kept the popular Amidala in the public's eye as Naboo's Senator.

DEXTER JETTSTER
Dĕx'-tûr Jĕt'-stûr

The proprietor of Dex's Diner is a brawny alien with a colorful past. Before opening his restaurant on Coruscant, Jettster worked as an animal hunter, an Outer Rim scout, and a prospector on Subterrel. He had a

KADANN
Kä-dän'

Kadann, a dark side mage and leader of the Prophets of the Dark Side, acted as a kingmaker in the post-Palpatine Empire by proclaiming Trioculus as Imperial leader in opposition to Ysanne Isard. He later named himself Emperor, escaped from the Lost City of the Jedi, and ultimately died in a revenge plot orchestrated by Grand Admiral Makati.

JODO KAST
Jō'-dō Kăst

This bounty hunter, who wore Mandalorian armor and tried to cash in on Boba Fett's reputation, died a year after the Battle of Endor when Fett finally decided to settle the score.

CLIEGG LARS
Klēg Lärs

Father of Owen Lars, this Tatooine moisture farmer purchased Shmi Skywalker's freedom and married her, only to lose his love to a hunting party of Tusken Raiders.

UMAK LETH
Ōō'-mäk Lĕth

This engineer produced dozens of weapons for the reborn Emperor, including World Devastators, tank droids, SD-10 battle droids, shadow droids, and the Galaxy Gun. He died in the explosion of the planet Byss.

ARDEN LYN
Är'-dĕn Lĭn

Born thousands of years ago, this Follower of Palawa battled the ancient Jedi and was forced into a Mortichro-induced Force trance that lasted for millennia. She reawakened at the end of the Jedi Purge, lashing out at the Emperor's Inquisitors and losing an arm in the fight. Palpatine recognized Lyn's talent and made her an Emperor's Hand. She received a prosthetic arm from a war droid and taught the martial art teräs käsi to the Emperor's mages. Lyn turned on her Master just before Endor, but her attempt to kidnap Palpatine for Grand Admiral Zaarin ended in failure.

MANDALORE
Măn'-dä-lôr

Four thousand years ago, the nomadic Mandalorians joined with the fallen Jedi Ulic Qel-Droma to devastate the Republic during the Sith War. The masked warrior known only as Mandalore led his troops in many glorious victories, but suffered defeat at the Battle of Onderon. On Onderon's moon he was devoured by demon beasts, and a new warrior took up the mantle of Mandalore.

BAIL ORGANA
Bāl Ôr-gă'-nä

Viceroy and First Chairman of the Alderaan system, Bail Organa served as one of the Senate's strongest voices for decades. Organa served on the loyalist committee with Senator Padmé Amidala. Following the Clone Wars, he raised Padmé's daughter Leia as his own. Organa signed the Corellian

friendly history with Obi-Wan Kenobi, and as a favor to the Jedi identified a strange weapon as a Kamino saberdart from the water planet of the Kaminoan cloners.

TENEL KA
Tĕ'-nĕl Kä

This Jedi Knight is the daughter of Prince Isolder of Hapes and Teneniel Djo of Dathomir. She studied with the Solo children at the Jedi academy, where she lost the lower half of her right arm in a lightsaber training accident. During the Yuuzhan Vong invasion, Tenel Ka's grandmother Ta'a Chume arranged for Teneniel Djo's death and tried to install a replacement heir. Tenel Ka helped defeat her grandmother, and became the new Queen Mother of Hapes.

LORD KAAN
Kän

Weak-willed leader of the Brotherhood of Darkness, Lord Kaan poisoned his rival Darth Bane but failed to kill him, and ultimately perished in a "thought bomb" explosion on Ruusan.

Treaty which founded the Rebel Alliance, and sent Leia to bring Obi-Wan Kenobi out of retirement. He died when the Death Star destroyed Alderaan.

LIEUTENANT PAGE

Pāj

The son of an Imperial Senator from Corulag, Page defected to the Alliance and fought at Hoth and Endor. Under the New Republic he led the Katarn Commandos, often called simply Page's Commandos.

POGGLE THE LESSER

Pŏg'-ŭl

Poggle reigned as Archduke on Geonosis, where he oversaw the war machines produced by Baktoid Armor Workshop and other manufacturing concerns operated by his people. With his aide Sun Fac, Poggle agreed to build the corporate armies needed by Count Dooku's secessionists, in exchange for lucrative payouts and a favored place in the new galactic order.

DANNI QUEE

Dăn'-nē Kwē

Danni Quee was the first person to see the Yuuzhan Vong invasion force and live. As a researcher at the ExGal-4 outpost on Belkadan, she detected the aliens' entry point into the galaxy. The Yuuzhan Vong captured Danni and imprisoned her in an ice cavern on Helska 4, but she escaped with help from Jacen Solo and joined the New Republic resistance. Two years later, Danni Quee figured out a way to jam the enemy's battle communications.

GENERAL CARLIST RIEEKAN

Kär'-list Rĭ'-kăn

Rieekan witnessed the destruction of his homeworld of Alderaan while inspecting satellites near its sister world Delaya. He vowed to never again allow the Empire the upper hand. General Rieekan commanded Echo Base on Hoth and oversaw its evacuation. Years later he sat on the New Republic High Command and served for two years as Minister of State. During the Yevethan crisis he became New Republic Intelligence director. The Yuuzhan Vong invasion brought him out of retirement to head Coruscant's Planetary Defense Force.

SUPREME OVERLORD SHIMRAA

Shĭm'-rä

Absolute ruler of the Yuuzhan Vong people, Supreme Overlord Shimrra is closer than any mortal to the creator god Yun-Yuuzhan. He proclaimed that, after generations of wandering, a new galaxy awaited the Yuuzhan Vong. Accompanied at all times by his jester Onimi, he has watched from afar as his warriors have cleansed the galaxy of infidels—among them the Jedi—and made it fit for habitation.

BEN SKYWALKER

Bĕn Skĭ'-wälk-ûr

The first child of Luke and Mara Jade Skywalker, this Force-strong infant has already been the target of a Yuuzhan Vong kidnapping plot.

SHMI SKYWALKER

Shmē Skĭ'-wälk-ûr

Shmi spent most of her life as a slave. Captured by pirates at an early age, she was sold and passed among slave owners including Pi-Lippa, Gardulla the Hutt, and Watto. Her son Anakin exhibited a primal connection to the Force, and she suspected the Force may have been involved in his conception. When Anakin left Tatooine to become a Jedi, Watto retained possession of Shmi, and she stayed behind. Cliegg Lars bought her freedom and became her husband. Ten years after Anakin's departure, Tusken Raiders captured Shmi and tortured her. She died after seeing her son one last time.

MAAREK STELE

Mä'-rĕk Stĕl

The Empire conscripted Maarek Stele and trained him as a TIE pilot. His skill with the Force made him a top ace and attracted the attention of the Emperor's Secret Order, also known as the Prophets of the Dark Side. After Stele rescued Palpatine from Grand Admiral Zaarin's attempted coup, he became an Emperor's Hand. He flew with Palpatine's personal TIE escort, the Emperor's Sword, until Endor, after which he joined Baron Fel's 181st fighter wing.

LAMA SU

Lä'-mä Sōō

Prime Minister of Kamino, Lama Su oversaw the creation of the clone army without comprehending the sinister forces behind it all.

VIMA SUNRIDER

Vē'-mä Sŭn'-rīd-ûr

Daughter of Nomi Sunrider, Vima learned the Force, not from her mother but from the disgraced Jedi Ulic Qel-Droma, whom she helped restore to the light.

ORN FREE TAA

Ôrn Frē Tä

This obese, blue-skinned Rutian Twi'lek represented Ryloth in the Republic Senate for more than a decade and was the first to accuse Valorum of corruption. He supported the Military Creation Act to raise an army against Dooku's separatists.

SIRI TACHI
Sē'-rē

The Padawan of Adi Gallia, eleven-year-old Siri worked with thirteen-year-old Obi-Wan Kenobi on several missions during their early Jedi careers. Siri developed a reputation for headstrong independence, but learned to be more cautious after a clash with the notorious bounty hunter Ona Nobis. Nearly fifteen years later, Siri went undercover as a pirate to infiltrate the organization of the infamous slaver known as Krayn.

EMPRESS TETA
Tā'-tä

Five millennia ago, on the eve of the Great Hyperspace War, Empress Teta forcibly conquered the seven worlds of the Koros system in the so-called Unification Wars.

CAPTAIN TYPHO
Tī-fō

Typho, Captain Panaka's nephew, attended many of the same offworld training guilds as his uncle. Captain Typho eventually took over as head of security for Senator Amidala. During the assassination crisis, Captain Typho remained behind on Coruscant with the decoy handmaiden Dormé.

TAHIRI VEILA
Tä-hē'-rē Vay'-luh

Tatooine's Tusken Raiders raised Tahiri Veila after killing her homesteader parents. Luke Skywalker discovered Tahiri's Force potential and brought her to the academy at age eleven. She befriended Anakin Solo, and the two of them freed trapped Massassi spirits from a mystical golden globe. During the Yuuzhan Vong invasion, enemy shapers scarred Tahiri and brainwashed her into thinking she was one of them. Anakin rescued her, and the two grew close until Anakin's death in battle.

VIMA-DA-BODA
Vē'-mä-dä-bō'-dä

Born nearly four millennia after her ancestor Vima Sunrider, the Jedi Vima-Da-Boda lost her daughter to the dark side and nearly lost herself in the madness of despair. She fought the reborn Emperor and in later years instructed at the Jedi academy.

ALEX WINGER
Ă'-lĕx Wĭn'-gûr

Adopted daughter of the Imperial governor of Garos IV, Alex Winger led the underground resistance on her homeworld, and later became a starship captain in the New Republic Navy.

WINTER
Wĭn-tûr

A friend of Leia Organa Solo's from Alderaan, Winter used her perfect memory to aid the Alliance under the code name Targeter. She later married Tycho Celchu.

XANATOS
Zä'-nä-tōs

Years before Qui-Gon Jinn took Obi-Wan Kenobi as his Padawan learner, he trained Xanatos—the wealthy son of the corrupt governor of Telos. Despite Qui-Gon's best efforts, Xanatos exhibited dark-side emotions, and on a mission to Telos the young Padawan betrayed the Jedi and joined forces with his corrupt father. When Qui-Gon was forced to kill the governer, Xanatos swore revenge and disappeared. He earned a fortune as the head of the Offworld Corportation, pouring the profits back into his homeworld and taking control of virtually all activities on Telos. Early in Qui-Gon and Obi-Wan's partnership, Xanatos reemerged from the shadows to sow chaos by sabotaging the Jedi Temple. He died when he intentionally plunged into an acid pool on Telos rather than surrender to his former Jedi master.

NEN YIM
Nĕn Yĭm

Adept Nen Yim is a member of the shaper caste, dedicated to bioengineering all forms of life so they may better serve the Yuuzhan Vong. Her love for science, however, overshadowed her devotion to the strict religious protocols governing shaping. Branded a heretic for the unorthodox experiments she performed on the Jedi known as Tahiri, she was banished to the dying worldship *Baanu Miir* until called by the jester Onimi to serve at the side of Supreme Overlord Shimrra.

GRAND ADMIRAL ZAARIN
Zä'-rĭn

A brilliant tactician and scientist, Grand Admiral Zaarin developed the Empire's TIE defender starfighter. Before the Battle of Endor, Zaarin enlisted Emperor's Hand Arden Lyn in his unsuccessful coup attempt against Palpatine. Zaarin retreated to the Outer Rim, where Grand Admiral Thrawn hunted him down. When Zaarin tried to flee in a corvette equipped with experimental cloak technology, the vessel exploded, and he was killed.

BIBLIOGRAPHY

AC
Ambush at Corellia, volume 1 of The Corellian Trilogy, Roger MacBride Allen, Bantam Books, 1995.

ACHT *Agents of Chaos I: Hero's Trial,* James Luceno, Del Rey Books, 2000.

ACJE
Agents of Chaos II: Jedi Eclipse, James Luceno, Del Rey Books, 2000.

AOTC
Attack of the Clones film, 20th Century Fox, 2002; novelization, R. A. Salvatore, Del Rey Books, 2002.

AS
Assault at Selonia, volume 2 of The Corellian Trilogy, Roger MacBride Allen, Bantam Books, 1995.

ASDBH
Aurra Sing: Dawn of the Bounty Hunters, Ryder Windham and Josh Ling, Chronicle Books, 2000.

ASSDV
Anakin Skywalker: The Story of Darth Vader, Steve Sansweet, Josh Ling, and Daniel Wallace, Chronicle Books, 1998.

BFAD
Boba Fett: Agent of Doom, John Ostrander and Cam Kennedy, Dark Horse Comics, 2000.

BFDLT
Boba Fett: Death, Lies and Treachery, John Wagner and Cam Kennedy, Dark Horse Comics, 1998.

BFEE
Boba Fett: Enemy of the Empire, John Wagner and Ian Gibson, Dark Horse Comics, 1999.

BFTED
Boba Fett: Twin Engines of Destruction, Andy Mangels and John Nadeau, Dark Horse Comics, 1997.

BHAS
The Bounty Hunters: Aurra Sing, Timothy Truman, Dark Horse Comics, 1999.

BHHM
Hard Merchandise, volume 3 of The Bounty Hunter Wars, K. W. Jeter, Bantam Books, 1999.

BHKK
The Bounty Hunters: Kenix Kil, Randy Stradley and Javier Saltares, Dark Horse Comics, 1999.

BHMA
The Mandalorian Armor, volume 1 of The Bounty Hunter Wars, K. W. Jeter, Bantam Books, 1998.

BHSS
Slave Ship, volume 2 of The Bounty Hunter Wars, K. W. Jeter, Bantam Books, 1999.

BHSW
The Bounty Hunters: Scoundrel's Wages, Mark Schultz and Mel Rubi, Dark Horse Comics, 1999.

BP
Balance Point, Kathy Tyers, Del Rey Books, 2000.

BS
Before the Storm, volume 1 of The Black Fleet Crisis, Michael P. Kube-McDowell, Bantam Books, 1996.

BW
The Bacta War, volume 4 of The X-Wing Series, Michael A. Stackpole, Bantam Books, 1997.

CCG
Star Wars customizable card game, Decipher, 1995-2001.

CD
Cloak of Deception, James Luceno, Del Rey Books, 2001.

CE
Crimson Empire, Mike Richardson, Randy Stradley, and Paul Gulacy, Dark Horse Comics, 1998.

CE2
Crimson Empire II: Council of Blood, Mike Richardson, Randy Stradley, and Paul Gulacy, Dark Horse Comics, 1999.

COF
Champions of the Force, volume 3 of The Jedi Academy Trilogy, Kevin J. Anderson, Bantam Books, 1994.

COJ
Children of the Jedi, Barbara Hambly, Bantam Books, 1995.

CPL
The Courtship of Princess Leia, Dave Wolverton, Bantam Books, 1994.

CS
The Crystal Star, Vonda McIntyre, Bantam Books, 1994.

CSSB
Han Solo and the Corporate Sector Sourcebook, Michael Allen Horne, West End Games, 1993.

CSW
Classic Star Wars, issues 1-20, Archie Goodwin & Al Williamson, Dark Horse Comics, 1992-1994.

CSWEA
Classic Star Wars: The Early Adventures, issues 1-9, Russ Manning, Dark Horse Comics, 1997.

CTGD
C-3PO: Tales of the Golden Droid, Daniel Wallace and Josh Ling, Chronicle Books, 1999.

D
Droids, series and specials, Dark Horse Comics, 1994-1995.

DA
Dark Apprentice, volume 2 of The Jedi Academy Trilogy, Kevin J. Anderson, Bantam Books, 1994.

DE
Star Wars: Dark Empire, 6-issue series, Tom Veitch and Cam Kennedy, Dark Horse Comics, 1991–1992.

DE2
Star Wars: Dark Empire II, 6-issue series, Tom Veitch and Cam Kennedy, Dark Horse Comics, 1994–1995.

DESB
Star Wars: Dark Empire Sourcebook, Michael Allen Horne, West End Games, 1993.

DF
Dark Forces PC game, LucasArts, 1995.

DF2
Jedi Knight: Dark Forces II PC game, LucasArts, 1997.

DF2MS
Jedi Knight: Mysteries of the Sith PC game, LucasArts, 1998.

DFJK
Dark Forces: Jedi Knight, William C. Dietz and Dave Dorman, Dark Horse Comics and Boulevard/Putnam, 1998.

DFR
Dark Force Rising, volume 2 of The Thrawn Trilogy, Timothy Zahn, Bantam Spectra Books, 1992.

DFRA
Dark Forces: Rebel Agent, William C. Dietz and Ezra Tucker, Dark Horse Comics and Boulevard/Putnam, 1999.

DFSE
Dark Forces: Soldier for the Empire, William C. Dietz and Dean Williams, Dark Horse Comics and Boulevard/Putnam, 1997.

DHEHC
Dark Horse Extra: Hard Currency, Mike Richardson, Randy Stradley, and Paul Gulacy, Dark Horse Comics, 2000.

DHPA
Dark Horse Presents Annual 1999, "Luke Skywalker's Walkabout," Phil Norwood, Dark Horse Comics, 1999; *Dark Horse Presents* Annual 2000, "Aurra's Song," Dean R. Motter and Isaee Buckminster Owens, Dark Horse Comics, 2000.

DHTCH
Decade of Dark Horse: This Crumb for Hire, Ryder Windham and Allen Nunis, Dark Horse Comics, 1996.

DJ
Dark Journey, Elaine Cunningham, Del Rey Books, 2002.

DMC
Darth Maul, 4-issue series, Ron Marz and Jan Duursema, Dark Horse Comics, 2000.

DMS
Darth Maul: Saboteur, James Luceno, E-book short story, Ballantine Books, 2000.

DMSH
Darth Maul: Shadow Hunter, Michael Reaves, Del Rey Books, 2000.

DS
Darksaber, Kevin J. Anderson, Bantam Books, 1995.

DSTC
Death Star Technical Companion, Bill Slavicsek, West End Games, 1991, 1993.

DTO
Dark Tide I: Onslaught, Michael A. Stackpole, Del Rey Books, 2000.

DTR
Dark Tide II: Ruin, Michael A. Stackpole, Del Rey Books, 2000.

DTV
Droids animated television shows, episodes 1-13, Nelvana, 1985.

EC
Star Wars: The Essential Chronology, Kevin J. Anderson and Daniel Wallace, Del Rey Books, 2000.

EE
Empire's End, 2-issue series, Tom Veitch and Jim Baikie, Dark Horse Comics, 1995.

EGAS
Star Wars: The Essential Guide to Alien Species, Ann Lewis, Del Rey Books, 2001.

EGC
Star Wars: The Essential Guide to Characters, Andy Mangels, Del Rey Books, 1995.

EGV
Star Wars: The Essential Guide to Vehicles and Vessels, Bill Smith, Del Rey Books, 1996.

EIA
Episode I Adventures, 1–13, Ryder Windham and Dave Wolverton, Scholastic, 1999-2000.

EIR
Episode I: Racer, PC and video game, LucasArts, 1999.

EISF
Episode I: Starfighter, PC and video game, LucasArts, 2001.

EITI
Episode I tie-in (compilation of comics one-shots), Mark Shultz et al., Dark Horse Comics, 2000.

ESB, ESBN
The Empire Strikes Back film, 20th Century Fox, 1980; novelization, Donald F. Glut, Del Rey Books, 1980.

ESBR
The Empire Strikes Back, National Public Radio dramatization, Brian Daley, 1983; published by Del Rey Books, 1995.

EVC
Edge of Victory I: Conquest, Greg Keyes, Del Rey Books, 2001.

EVR
Edge of Victory II: Rebirth, Greg Keyes, Del Rey Books, 2001.

FC
Force Commander PC game, LucasArts, 2000.

FP
The Farlander Papers, as reprinted and continued in *X-Wing: The Official Strategy Guide,* Rusel DeMaria, Prima Publishing, 1993.

GDV
The Glove of Darth Vader, Paul and Hollace Davids, Bantam Skylark Books, 1992.

GF
The Gungan Frontier PC game, Lucas Learning, 1999.

GG4
Galaxy Guide 4: Alien Races, Troy Denning, West End Games, 1989.

GG12
Galaxy Guide 12: Aliens, Enemies, and Allies, C. Robert Carey et al., West End Games, 1995.

GOF
Galaxy of Fear books 1–12, John Whitman, Bantam Skylark Books, 1997-1998.

HE
Heir to the Empire, volume 1 of The Thrawn trilogy, Timothy Zahn, Bantam Spectra Books, 1991.

HG
The Hutt Gambit, volume 2 of The Han Solo Trilogy, A. C. Crispin, Bantam Books, 1997.

HLL
Han Solo and the Lost Legacy, Brian Daley, Del Rey Books, 1980.

HSE
Han Solo at Stars' End, Brian Daley, Del Rey Books, 1979.

HSR
Han Solo's Revenge, Brian Daley, Del Rey Books, 1979.

IF
Iron Fist, volume 6 of The X-Wing Series, Aaron Allston, Bantam Books, 1998.

IG
Insider's Guide to Episode I CD-ROM, LucasArts, 1999.

IJ
I, Jedi, Michael A. Stackpole, Bantam Books, 1998.

ISWU
The Illustrated Star Wars Universe, Kevin J. Anderson and Ralph McQuarrie, Bantam Books, 1995.

JA
Jedi Apprentice books 1-15, Dave Wolverton and Jude Watson, Scholastic, 1999-2001.

JAL
Jedi Academy: Leviathan, 4-issue series, Kevin J. Anderson and Dario Carrasco Jr., Dark Horse Comics, 1998.

JASB
The Jedi Academy Sourcebook, Paul Sudlow, West End Games, 1996.

JASE1
Jedi Apprentice: Special Edition #1—Deceptions, Jude Watson, Scholastic, 2001.

JCAW
Jedi Council: Acts of War, Randy Stradley and Christian Della Vecchia, Dark Horse Comics, 2000.

JHAD
Jabba the Hutt: The Art of the Deal, Jim Woodrig and Steve Bissete, Dark Horse Comics, 1998.

JHJT
Jabba the Hutt: The Jabba Tape, John Wagner and Kilian Plunkett, Dark Horse Comics, 1998.

JJAQ
Junior Jedi Knights: Anakin's Quest, Rebecca Moesta, Boulevard Books, 1997.

JJGG
Junior Jedi Knights: The Golden Globe, Nancy Richardson, Boulevard Books, 1995.

JJKB
Junior Jedi Knights: Kenobi's Blade, Rebecca Moesta, Boulevard Books, 1997.

JJLW
Junior Jedi Knights: Lyric's World, Nancy Richardson, Boulevard Books, 1996.

JJP
Junior Jedi Knights: Promises, Nancy Richardson, Boulevard Books, 1996.

JJVF
Junior Jedi Knights: Vader's Fortress, Rebecca Moesta, Boulevard Books, 1997.

JQPT
Jedi Quest: Path to Truth, Jude Watson, Scholastic, 2001.

JS
Jedi Search, volume 1 of The Jedi Academy Trilogy, Kevin J. Anderson, Bantam Books, 1994.

JVS
Jedi vs. Sith, 6-issue series, Darko Macan and Ramon F. Bachs, Dark Horse Comics, 2001.

KT
The Krytos Trap, volume 3 of the X-Wing Series, Michael A. Stackpole, Bantam Books, 1996.

LC
The Last Command, volume 3 of The Thrawn Trilogy, Timothy Zahn, Bantam Spectra Books, 1993.

LCF
Lando Calrissian and the Flamewind of Oseon, L. Neil Smith, Del Rey Books, 1983.

LCJ
The Lost City of the Jedi, Paul and Hollace Davids, Bantam Skylark Books, 1992.

LCM
Lando Calrissian and the Mindharp of Sharu, L. Neil Smith, Del Rey Books, 1983.

LCS
Lando Calrissian and the Starcave of ThonBoka, L. Neil Smith, Del Rey Books, 1983.

LCSB
The Last Command Sourcebook, Eric Trautmann, West End Games, 1994.

MCSW
Star Wars Marvel series, issues 1-107, Marvel Comics, 1977-1986.

MJBEH
Mara Jade: By the Emperor's Hand, Timothy Zahn, Michael Stackpole, and Carlos Ezquerra, Dark Horse Comics, 1998-1999.

MMY
Mission from Mount Yoda, Paul and Hollace Davids, Bantam Skylark Books, 1993.

MTK
Masters of Teräs Käsi video game, LucasArts, 1998.

MTSB
The Movie Trilogy Sourcebook, Greg Farshtey and Bill Smith, West End Games, 1993.

NR
The New Rebellion, Kristine Kathryn Rusch, Bantam Books, 1996.

PDS
Prophets of the Dark Side, Paul and Hollace Davids, Bantam Skylark Books, 1993.

POT
Planet of Twilight, Barbara Hambly, Bantam Books, 1997.

PS
The Paradise Snare, volume 1 of The Han Solo Trilogy, A. C. Crispin, Bantam Books, 1997.

QE
Queen of the Empire, Paul and Hollace Davids, Bantam Spectra Books, 1993.

QOLS
Qui-Gon and Obi-Wan: Last Stand on Ord Mantell, Ryder Windham and Ramon F. Bachs, Dark Horse Comics, 2001.

RD
Rebel Dawn, volume 3 of The Han Solo Trilogy, A. C. Crispin, Del Rey Books, 1998.

RJ, RJN
Return of the Jedi film, 20th Century Fox, 1983; novelization, James Kahn, Del Rey Books, 1983.

RP
Rogue Planet, Greg Bear, Del Rey Books, 2000.

RS
Rogue Squadron, volume 1 of The X-Wing Series, Michael A. Stackpole, Bantam Books, 1996.

RSB
The Rebel Alliance Sourcebook, Paul Murphy, West End Games, 1990.

RSVG
Rogue Squadron PC and video game, LucasArts, 1998.

SA
Starfighters of Adumar, volume 9 of The X-Wing Series, Aaron Allston, Del Rey Books, 1999.

SAC
Showdown at Centerpoint, volume 3 of The Corellian Trilogy, Roger MacBride Allen, Bantam Books, 1995.

SBS
Star by Star, Troy Denning, Del Rey Books, 2001.

SC
Solo Command, volume 7 of The X-Wing Series, Aaron Allston, Del Rey Books, 1999.

SME
Splinter of the Mind's Eye, Alan Dean Foster, Del Rey Books, 1978.

SOL
Shield of Lies, volume 2 of The Black Fleet Crisis, Michael P. Kube-McDowell, Bantam Books, 1996.

SOTE
Shadows of the Empire, Steve Perry, Bantam Books, 1996.

SOTEALB
Shadows of the Empire CD liner notes, Varese Sarabande, 1996.

SOTEE
Shadows of the Empire: Evolution, Steve Perry and Ron Randall, Dark Horse Comics, 1998.

SOTESB
Shadows of the Empire Sourcebook, Peter Schweighofer, West End Games, 1996.

SOTEVG
Shadows of the Empire PC and video game, LucasArts, 1996.

SOTS
Secrets of the Sith, Random House, 2000.

SP
Specter of the Past, volume 1 of The Hand of Thrawn Duology, Timothy Zahn, Del Rey Books, 1998.

SW, SWN
Star Wars: A New Hope film, 20th Century Fox, 1977; novelization, George Lucas, Del Rey Books, 1977.

SWAJ
The Official Star Wars Adventure Journal, issues 1-15, edited by Peter Schweighofer, West End Games, 1994-1997.

SWC
Star Wars: Chewbacca, 4-issue series, Darko Macan et al., Dark Horse Comics, 2000.

SWD
Star Wars Demolition video game, LucasArts, 2000.

SWJDM
Star Wars Journal: Darth Maul, Jude Watson, Scholastic, 2000.

SWJQA
Star Wars Journal: Queen Amidala, Jude Watson, Scholastic, 1999.

SWO
Star Wars ongoing comic series, various creators, Dark Horse Comics, 1998-present.

SWPT
Star Wars: Podracing Tales, published on starwars.com, Ryder Windham and Ken Steacy, Dark Horse Comics, 2000.

SWR
Star Wars National Public Radio dramatization, Brian Daley, 1981; published by Del Rey Books, 1994.

SWSB
Star Wars Sourcebook, Bill Slavicsek and Curtis Smith, West End Games, 1987.

SWT
Star Wars Tales, issues 1-14, various creators, Dark Horse Comics, 1999-2002.

SWU
Star Wars Union, Michael A. Stackpole and Robert Teranishi, Dark Horse Comics, 1999-2000.

SWVQ
Star Wars: Vader's Quest, Darko Macan and Dave Gibbons, Dark Horse Comics, 1999.

SWXS
Star Wars Holiday Special, Lucasfilm, 1978.

TAB
The Truce at Bakura, Kathy Tyers, Bantam Books, 1994.

TABSB
The Truce at Bakura Sourcebook, Kathy Tyers and Eric S. Trautmann, West End Games, 1996.

TAS
The Approaching Storm, Alan Dean Foster, Del Rey Books, 2002.

TBH
Tales of the Bounty Hunters, edited by Kevin J. Anderson, Bantam Books, 1996.

TFNR
Tales from the New Republic, edited by Craig Carey, Bantam Books, 1999.

TFTC
Tales from the Mos Eisley Cantina, edited by Kevin J. Anderson, Bantam Books, 1995.

TFTE
Tales from the Empire, edited by Peter Schweighofer, Bantam Books, 1997.

TGH
The Great Heep, animated television special, Nelvana, 1986.

TJP
Tales from Jabba's Palace, edited by Kevin J. Anderson, Bantam Books, 1995.

TM
Tatooine Manhunt, Bill Smith and Daniel Greenberg, West End Games, 1988.

TOJ
Tales of the Jedi: Knights of the Old Republic, 5-issue series, Tom Veitch, Dark Horse Comics, 1993-1994.

TOJC
Tales of the Jedi Companion, George R. Strayton, West End Games, 1996.

TOJDL
Tales of the Jedi: Dark Lords of the Sith, 12-issue series, Tom Veitch and Kevin J. Anderson, Dark Horse Comics, 1994-1995.

TOJFN
Tales of the Jedi: The Freedon Nadd Uprising, 2-issue series, Tom Veitch et al., Dark Horse Comics, 1994.

TOJFSE
Tales of the Jedi: Fall of the Sith Empire, 5-issue series, Kevin J. Anderson and Dario Carrasco Jr., Dark Horse Comics, 1998.

TOJGA
Tales of the Jedi: The Golden Age of the Sith, 5-issue series, Kevin J. Anderson, Dark Horse Comics, 1996-1997.

TOJR
Tales of the Jedi: Redemption, 4-issue series, Kevin J. Anderson and Chris Gossett, Dark Horse Comics, 1998.

TOJSW
Tales of the Jedi: The Sith War, 6-issue series, Kevin J. Anderson and Dario Carrasco Jr., Dark Horse Comics, 1995-1996.

TPM, TPMN
The Phantom Menace film, 20th Century Fox, 1999; novelization, Terry Brooks, Del Rey Books, 1999.

TPO
The Protocol Offensive, Ryder Windham, Brian Daley, and Igor Kordey, Dark Horse Comics, 1997.

TSC
The Stele Chronicles and its continuation in *TIE Fighter: The Official Strategy Guide,* Rusel DeMaria et al., Prima Publishing, 1994.

TT
Tyrant's Test, volume 3 of The Black Fleet Crisis, Michael P. Kube-McDowell, Bantam Books, 1997.

TTSB
Thrawn Trilogy Sourcebook, compilation by Bill Slavicsek and Eric S. Trautmann, West End Games, 1996.

UYV
Star Wars Underworld: The Yavin Vassilika, 5-issue series, Mike Kennedy and Carlos Meglia, Dark Horse Comics, 2000-2001.

VF
Vision of the Future, volume 2 of the Hand of Thrawn Duology, Timothy Zahn, Bantam Books, 1998.

VP
Vector Prime, R. A. Salvatore, Del Rey Books, 2000.

WEGCTD
Cracken's Threat Dossier, Drew Campbell et al., West End Games, 1997.

WCDS
The Dark Side Sourcebook, Cory Herndon et al., Wizards of the Coast, 2001.

WCSWG
Star Wars Gamer, issues 1-8, Wizards of the Coast, 2000-2002.

WG
Wedge's Gamble, volume 1 of The X-Wing Series, Michael A. Stackpole, Bantam Books, 1996.

WS
Wraith Squadron, volume 5 of The X-Wing Series, Aaron Allston, Bantam Books, 1998.

XW
X-Wing: Rogue Squadron, issues 1-35, Dark Horse Comics, 1995-1998.

XWA
X-Wing Alliance computer game, LucasArts, 1999.

YJK
Heirs of the Force, Shadow Academy, The Lost Ones, Lightsabers, Darkest Knight, Jedi Under Siege, Shards of Alderaan, Diversity Alliance, Delusions of Grandeur, Jedi Bounty, The Emperor's Plague, Return to Ord Mantell, Crisis at Crystal Reef, Trouble on Cloud City, books 1-14 of the Young Jedi Knights Series, Kevin J. Anderson and Rebecca Moesta, Berkley Books, 1995-1998.

ZHR
Zorba the Hutt's Revenge, Paul and Hollace Davids, Bantam Skylark Books, 1993.

Admiral Ackbar
    DA, DS, EC, FP, GG4, SWSB, TT, YJK
Padmé Amidala
    E2, SWJQA, TPM
Nom Anor
    ACJE, ACHT, BP, CE2, SBS, VP
Wedge Antilles
    BW, CE, DA, DE, DTO, EC, EGC, ESB, EVR, IR, KT, MTSB, RJ, RS, RSVG, SA, SW, SWU, TAB, WG, WS, XW
Darth Bane
    EC, JVS, SOTS, TPMN
Jar Jar Binks
    AOTC, EIA, SWT, TPM
Bossk
    ACHT, BHHM, BHMA, BHSS, BHSW, CSW, MA, MCSW, MTSB, SOTE, TBH, UYV
Brakiss
    EC, NR, YJK
Shira Brie
    EC, MCSW
C-3PO
    ACHT, AOTC, BTS, CPL, CTGD, D, DFR, DTV, ESB, NR, RJ, SOTE, SOTEALB, SW, SWC, TAB, TPM, TPO, YJK
Callista
    COJ, DS, POT, SWAJ
Lando Calrissian
    AC, BHSW, BTS, DE, DE2, EC, ESB, EVR, HE, LCF, LCM, LCS, MCSW, NR, POT, RD, RJ, SBS, SOTE, SP, SWAJ, SWT, TAB, TJP, UYV, VP, YJK, ZHR
Gaeriel Captison
    AS, BP, SAC, TAB, TABSB
Tycho Celchu
    BW, DTO, IJ, IR, KT, RS, SA, SWU, WG, XW
Chewbacca
    BTS, CPL, CS, CSW, ESB, HG, HSE, HSL, HSR, MCSW, RD, RJ, SOTE, SW, SWC, SWXS, TAB, TT, VP, YJK
Admiral Daala
    COF, DA, DS, EC, JASB, JS, POT
Jori and Gav Daragon
    TOJFSE, TOJGA
Gavin Darklighter
    BP, BW, DTO, DTR, EVR, IJ, IR, KT, RS, SWU, WG
Dengar
    BHHM, BHMA, BHSS, BHSW, CE2, CSW, DE, DFR, ESB, MTSB, TBH, TJP, YJK

General Jan Dodonna
CSW, DE, EC, IR, KT, MTSB, SW

Count Dooku
AOTC

Droma
ACHT, ACJE, BP

Durga the Hutt
ACJE, DS, HG, RD, SOTE

Kyp Durron
ACJE, BP, COF, DA, DS, EVR, JAL, JASB, JS, TFNR, VP, YJK

4-LOM
BHHM, EGC, ESB, MTSB, SOTE, TBH, UYV

Baron Fel
DTR, HG, VF, XW

Boba Fett
AOTC, BFAD, BFDLT, BFEE, BFTED, BHHM, BHMA, BHSS, CSW, CSWEA, DE, DE2, DF, ESB, GOF, HG, RD, RJ, SOTE, SW, SWXS, TBH, TFNR, TJP, YJK

Jango Fett
AOTC

Borsk Fey'lya
BTS, DTO, HE, IR, DFR, DTR, EVC, LC, SBS, SP, TTSB, VF, VP, XW

Bib Fortuna
MTSB, RJ, SWO, SWSB, TJP, TPM, XW

Rokur Gepta
EC, LCF, LCM, LCS, WCDS

Greedo
MCSW, SOTE, SW, TFTC, TPM, UYV

Nute Gunray
AOTC, CD, DMS, DMSH, EIA, TPM

Corran Horn
BW, DTO, DTR, EVC, EVR, IJ, IR, KT, RS, SBS, SWAJ, SWU, TFTE, WG, XW

IG-88
BHMA, D, DTV, ESB, MCSW, SOTEVG, TBH, TFTC, TM, YJK

Ysanne Isard
BW, EC, IR, KT, MJBEH, RS, TFNR, WG, XW

Prince Isolder
ACJE, CPL, DJ, EGC, WEGCTD, YJK

Jabba the Hutt
CSW, DHTCH, EGC, HG, ISWU, JHAD, JHJT, MCSW, MTSB, RD, RJ, SW, SWD, SWO, TJP, TPM, ZHR

Jedi Council members
AOTC, IG, JA, JCAW, SWO, SWT, TPM

Jedi from the Battle of Geonosis

Jerec
AOTC, CD DF2, DFJK, DFRA, DFSE, EC, GOF, WCDS

Qui-Gon Jinn
AOTC, CD, EIA, JA, JCAW, QOLS, TPM

Kir Kanos
CE, CE2, DHEHC

Talon Karrde
ACJE, BW, DFR, EVC, HE, LC, NR, SP, SWAJ, SWU, TFTE, TFNR, TTSB, VF

Kyle Katarn
DF, DF2, DF2MS, DFJK, DFRA, DFSE, EC

Obi-Wan Kenobi
AOTC, CSW, DHPA, DMSH, EIA, ESB, HE, JA, JASE1, JCAW, JJKB, JQPT, LCJ, MCSW, QOLS, RJ, RP, SME, SW, TAB, TPM

Kueller
EC, NR

Exar Kun
COF, CSW, DA, IJ, JJGG, TOJDL, TOJSW

Warmaster Tsavong Lah
ACHT, ACJE, BP, DJ, DTR, EVC, EVR, SBS

Owen Lars and Beru Whitesun Lars
AOTC, DHPA, MCSW, SW

Bevel Lemelisk
DS, DSTC, EC

Lobot
BTS, EGC, MCSW, MTSB, SOL, SWT, TT, VF, YJK, ZHR

Garik "Face" Loran
IF, SC, WS

General Crix Madine
DF, DS, RJ, RSVG, SWAJ, SWT

Darth Maul
DMC, DMS, DMSH, EIA, SWJDM, TPM, TPMN

Mon Mothma
AC, COF, DE, DESB, FP, JS, LC, MCSW, MTSB, NR, RASB, RJ, SC, SWSB, TTSB, WG, XW

Boss Nass
EIA, GF, TPM, WCSWG

Nien Nunb
EGC, LC, MCSW, MTSB, RJ, SWT, YJK

Nym
EISF, SWT, WCSWG

Ric Olié
AOTC, IG, TPM, WCSWG

Emperor Palpatine
AOTC, CD, DE, DE2, EE, ESB, POT, RJ, SOTE, SWO, TPM, VF, WCSWG

Captain Panaka
IG, TPM, WCSWG

Gilad Pellaeon
DFR, DS, DTR, EC, HE, LC, SP, TTSB, VF

Sate Pestage
CD, DESB, WCSWG, XW

Admiral Firmus Piett
CSW, ESB, MTSB, RJ, SOTESB

Podracer pilots
EIR, IG, SWO, SWPT, TPM, TPMN

Ulic Qel-Droma
TOJ, TOJC, TOJDL, TOJFN, TOJR, TOJSW

R2-D2
AOTC, BTS, CTGD, D, DE, DE2, DTV, ESB, JJGG, MCSW, NR, RJ, SOTE, SW, SWC, TPM, VF, YJK

Dash Rendar
SOTE, SOTEE, SOTESB, SOTEVG, XWA

Naga Sadow
EC, TOJFSE, TOJGA

Thrackan Sal-Solo
AC, ACJE, AS, SAC, WEGCTD

Sebulba
EIA, EIR, IG, SWD, SWO, TPM

Executor Sedriss
DE2, WCDS

Senator Viqi Shesh
ACHT, ACJE, BP, EVR, SBS

Darth Sidious
AOTC, CD, EIA, DMC, DMS, DMSH, SWJDM, TPM

Raith Sienar
EGV, RP

Aurra Sing
ASDBH, BHAS, DHPA, SWD, SWO, TPM

Anakin Skywalker/Darth Vader
AOTC, BFEE, BHMA, CSW, CSWEA, DF, EIA, EITI, ESB, ESBR, GOF, JASE1, JQPT, MCSW, MTSB, RJ, RP, SME, SOTE, SW, SWT, SWVQ, TFTE, TPM, TSC

Luke Skywalker
ACJE, BP, BTS, COF, COJ, CPL, CSW, CSWEA, DA, DE, DE2, DFR, DHPA, DS, DTR, EC, ESB, ESBR, EVC, EVR, FC, FP, HE, JJVF, JS, LC, MCSW, NR, POT, RJ, RSVG, SBS, SME, SOTE, SP,

SW, SWU, SWVQ, TAB, VF, VP, XW, YJK

Mara Jade Skywalker
AC, BP, COF, DF2MS, DFR, DTO, EVR, HE, LC, MJBEH, POT, SP, SWAJ, SWT, SWU, TFNR, TFTE, TJP, TTSB, VF, VP

Anakin Solo
ACHT, ACJE, AS, COF, CS, DE2, DTO, DTR, EE, EVC, EVR, JJAQ, JJGG, JJKB, JJLW, JJP, JJVF, SAC, SBS, VP, YJK

Han Solo
ACHT, ACJE, AS, AC, BP, CPL, CS, CSW, ESB, EVR, HG, HLL, HSE, HSR, JS, LC, MCSW, NR, RD, RJ, PDS, POT, PS, SAC, SBS, SC, SW, SWC, SWR, TAB, TBH, TFTC, TJP, TT, UYV, VF, VP, YJK

Jacen Solo
AC, ACHT, ACJE, AS, BP, COF, CS, DA, DTO, DTR, EVC, EVR, JS, LC, SAC, SBS, SWC, VP, YJK

Jaina Solo
AC, ACHT, ACJE, AS, BP, COF, CS, DA, DJ, DTO, DTR, EVC, EVR, JS, LC, SAC, SBS, SWC, VP, YJK

Leia Organa Solo
ACHT, ACJE, BP, COF, COJ, CPL, CS, CSW, DA, DE, DE2, DFR, DJ, DS, DTO, DTR, EE, ESB, EVR, HE, JS, RJ, LC, MCSW, NR, PDS, POT, SBS, SME, SOTE, SP, SW, SWR, TAB, WG, VF, VP, XW, YJK

Kam Solusar
COF, EC, EVC, EVR, DA, DE2, DS, EE, SWU

Nil Spaar
BTS, SOL, TT

Grand Moff Wihuff Tarkin
CD, CSWEA, DMS, DS, DSTC, JS, MCSW, RP, SW, SWAJ, SWSB, SWR

Booster Terrik
BW, EVC, EVR, IJ, IR, SWAJ, SWU, VF, XW

Bria Tharen
HG, PS, RD

Grand Admiral Thrawn
DFR, EC, GOF, HE, LC, SP, SWAJ, TFNR, TFTE, TSC, TTSB, VF, XW

Supreme Chancellor Finis Valorum
CD, JCAW, QOLS, TPM

General Maximilian Veers
ESB, DE2, DESB, ESBN, FC, MTSB, SWSB, TFTC, TFTE

Vergere
ACHT, CD, EC, EVR, RP, SBS

Quinlan Vos
SWO

Watto
AOTC, EGAS, EIR, EITI, TPM

Zam Wesell
AOTC

Mace Windu
AOTC, CD, EIA, JA, JCAW, SWO, TPM

Prince Xizor
BHHM, BHMA, BHSS, DMC, SOTE, SOTEE, SOTESB, RD, WG, XWA

Yoda
CPL, GOF, AOTC, EIA, ESB, JA, JCAW, JJAQ, RJ, SWO, SWSB. TPM, VF

Warlord Zsinj
CPL, IF, SC, WEGCTD, WS

Zuckuss
BHHM, BHMA, BHSS, CCG, EGAS, MCSW, MTSB, SOTE, TBH, UYV

APPENDIX ENTRIES

Elegos and Releqy A'Kla
DTO, DTR, IJ, VF

Mas Amedda
TPM, AOTC

Ace Azzameen
XWA

Blackhole
CSWEA, WCSWG

Empatojayos Brand
DE2, EE

Adalric Brandl
SWAJ, TFTE

Joruus C'baoth
DFR, HE, LC, TTSB

Cilghal
ACHT, ACJE, COF, DA, DS, EVR

General Airen Cracken
BW, KT, RS, SA, WS

The Dark Woman
SWO, SWT

Admiral Hiram Drayson
BTS, LC, SOL, TT,

Hohass "Runt" Ekwesh
IF, SC, WS

Jagged Fel
BP, DJ, DTR

Gallandro
CSSB, HLL, HSR, YJK

Ghent
BP, DFR, HE, LC, VF

A'Sharad Hett
SWO

Lord Hoth
DFJK, EC, JVS

Queen Jamilla
AOTC

Dexter Jettster
AOTC

Tenel Ka
ACJE, DJ, SBS, YJK

Lord Kaan
DFJK, EC, JVS

Kadann
GDV, LCJ, MMY, PDS, QE, ZHR

Jodo Kast
BFTED, TFTE, TM

Cliegg Lars
AOTC

Umak Leth
DE2, DESB

Arden Lyn
MTK, WCSWG

Mandalore
TOJSW

Bail Organa
AOTC, SWR

Lieutenant Page
IR, TTSB

Poggle the Lesser
AOTC

Danni Quee
DTO, SBS, VP

General Carlist Rieekan
BTS, ESB, MTSB, SBS

Supreme Overlord Shimrra
EVR, SBS

Siri
JA, JQPT

Ben Skywalker
EVR, SBS

Shmi Skywalker
AOTC, TPM

Maarek Stele
EC, TSC

Lama Su
AOTC

Vima Sunrider
TOJ, TOJC, TOJR

Orn Free Taa
TPM, AOTC

Tahiri
> **EVC, EVR, JJAQ, JJGG, JJKB, JJLW, JJP, JJVF**

Empress Teta
> **TOJFSE, TOJGA**

Captain Typho
> **AOTC**

Villie
> **JCAW, SWO, SWT**

Vima-Da-Boda
> **DE, DE2, EE**

Alex Winger
> **SWAJ, VF**

Winter
> **DFR, HE, LC, TTSB, XW**

Nen Yim
> **EVC, EVR**

Grand Admiral Zaarin
> **EC, TSC**

About the Author

Daniel Wallace has been writing in the *Star Wars* universe for years, authoring such books as *Anakin Skywalker: The Story of Darth Vader*, the question set for Parker Brothers' *Star Wars* Trivial Pursuit, and three previous books in DelRey's Essential Guide series: *The Essential Guide to Planets and Moons, The Essential Guide to Droids,* and *The Essential Chronology* (with Kevin J. Anderson). In addition to his published works of short fiction, he is a regular writer for *Star Wars Insider* magazine. With an extensive background in marketing and advertising, he plans mass and one-to-one communications strategies for one of the largest ad agencies. He and his wife live in Detroit, where they are the proud parents of two sons and a daughter.

About the Illustator

For the majority of his life, twenty-seven-year-old Mike Sutfin has been working late into the night scratching images of often bizarre and unworldly subjects onto countless sheets of paper. These works have found a home on collectible card games, role-playing games books and magazines, Sony Playstation and PC video games, comic books, hardcore punk album covers and T-shirts, novels, and several underground 'zines. In his spare time, skateboarding, an ever-growing record collection, and playing drums in his band are frequent distractions. Mike creatively resides in Lake Zurich, Illinois.

The *Star Wars* universe is expanding faster than ever before, and *Star Wars: The New Essential Guide to Characters* has received an exciting face-lift—with completely updated text and more than a hundred brand new, full-color illustrations by extraordinary artist Michael Sutfin.

This all-new *Essential Guide* features detailed profiles of more than one hundred and thirty characters from across the *Star Wars* galaxy, including all of your favorites—such as Luke Skywalker, Han Solo, Princess Leia, Darth Vader, and Mara Jade—as well as, from *Star Wars: Attack of the Clones*:

• JANGO FETT • COUNT DOOKU • ANAKIN SKYWALKER • ZAM WESELL •

And the key players from *Star Wars: The Phantom Menace*:

• QUEEN AMIDALA • QUI-GON JINN • MACE WINDU • DARTH MAUL •

Here is complete, updated coverage of the novels from the incredible New Jedi Order and all of the classic movies, books, comics, TV specials, games, and the rest of the *Star Wars* universe.

This must-have book describes the essential history and personal data for each character—with vital statistics and homeworlds.

MORE CHARACTERS, MORE INFORMATION, BRILLIANT ARTWORK—THE *ESSENTIAL GUIDES* ARE HOTTER THAN EVER!

ISBN 0-345-44900-2

EAN

9 780345 449009

51280